Revolution

There was nothing unusual about Tara Campbell's face and voice blanketing the airwaves of Skye. What was peculiar was the particular *kind* of service to The Republic she was pushing.

"Are you willing to trade your life for freedom?" her vibrantly beautiful and charming, yet solemn, face asked from holovid tanks in living rooms and bedrooms and bars in New Glasgow and Donegal.

"Freedom for your loved ones, freedom for your fellow citizens of Skye, freedom for billions of citizens of The Republic of the Sphere whom you will never even know?" it asked, two stories tall, from cinema screens in New London and Limerick and Sgain Dubh.

"Will you leave your jobs, your families, the safety of your homes and everyday life," her voice asked from radio speakers on fishing trawlers in the North Sea and scientific stations on the southern polar ice cap, "for nothing but a certainty of danger and an extremely high likelihood of death at the hands of a merciless alien invader?

"If so," she told laborers at a sheep station in Otero County at the continent's far end, and in break rooms in the mighty Shipil and Cyclops factories, "then join me in fighting for Skye and Clan Jade Falcon.

"Join me—join the Forlorn Hope!"

MechWarrior: Dark Age

FLIGHT OF THE FALCON

A BATTLETECH® NOVEL

Victor Milán

A ROC BOOK

ROC
Published by New American Library, a division of
Penguin Group (USA) Inc., 375 Hudson Street,
New York, New York 10014, U.S.A.
Penguin Books Ltd, 80 Strand,
London WC2R 0RL, England
Penguin Books Australia Ltd, 250 Camberwell Road,
Camberwell, Victoria 3124, Australia
Penguin Books Canada Ltd, 10 Alcorn Avenue,
Toronto, Ontario, Canada M4V 3B2
Penguin Books (NZ), cnr Airborne and Rosedale Roads,
Albany, Auckland 1310, New Zealand

Penguin Books Ltd, Registered Offices:
80 Strand, London WC2R 0RL, England

First published by Roc, an imprint of New American Library,
a division of Penguin Group (USA) Inc.

First Printing, June 2004
10 9 8 7 6 5 4 3 2 1

Cover design by Ray Lundgren

 REGISTERED TRADEMARK—MARCA REGISTRADA

Printed in the United States of America

PUBLISHER'S NOTE
This is a work of fiction. Names, characters, places, and incidents either are the products of the author's imagination or are used fictitiously, and any resemblance to actual persons, living or dead, business establishments, events, or locales is entirely coincidental.

BOOKS ARE AVAILABLE AT QUANTITY DISCOUNTS WHEN USED TO PROMOTE PRODUCTS OR SERVICES. FOR INFORMATION PLEASE WRITE TO PREMIUM MARKETING DIVISION, PENGUIN GROUP (USA) INC., 375 HUDSON STREET, NEW YORK, NEW YORK 10014.

For the splendiferous Sauer family:
Eric, Jeannie, Frank
and, of course, Michelle.
Just because.

An Enlightened One is an arrow aimed at Hell.

—Japanese proverb

REPUBLIC OF THE SPHERE

PREFECTURES VIII AND IX

AD SECURITAS PER UNITAS · REPUBLIC OF THE SPHERE

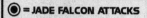

◉ = JADE FALCON ATTACKS

Eason · Freedom · Baxter · New Wessex · Vega · Eltanin
Whittington · ns · Nekkar · Kimball II · Konstance · Kaus B
heston · Chaffee · Izar · Marfik · Komephoros · Kessel · Kau
Zebeneschamali · Ryde · Kau · Ka
Carnwath · La Blon · Alrakis
Glengarry · Unukalhai · Dromini VI · Mod
Gladius · Kochab · Alphecca · Skondia · Sabik · Lar
Seginus · Skye · Zebebelgenubi · Atria · Ko
Laiaka · Alkalurops · Dyev
Alkaid · Syrma · Nusakan · Lyons · Imbros III
Carsphairn · Galatea · Summer · Asta
Vindemiatrix · Alcor · Mizar · Menkent · Dieron
Cor Caroli · Zollikofen · Muphrid · Yorii · Altair
Gacrux · Alioth · Lipton · Thorin · New Earth · Rigil Kentan
Zaniah · Milton · Chara · Alula Australis · Sirius · Terra · Keid
Shiloh · Alchiba · Zavijava · Graham IV · Procyon
Phecda · Denebola · Oliver · New Ho
Wing · Wyatt · Zosma
Alhena · Callison · Marcus · Pollux · Liberty · Epsil
nelle · Chertan · Dubhe · Castor · New Ho
Kalidasa · Devil's Rock

Prefecture IX
Prefecture VIII

Maximum Jump approx 30 LY. For nav purposes use 9 PARSECS (29.34 LY).

40 PARSECS OR 130.4 LIGHT YEARS

8 PARSECS

Coreward · Spinward · Anti-spinward · Rimward

THE INNER SPHERE

REPUBLIC TERRITORY

PREFECTURES OF THE REPUBLIC

IX · I · II · VIII · X · III · VII · IV · VI · V

©3134 ComStar Cartographic Corps.

PART ONE

Maskirovka

"A means of securing the combat operations and daily activity of forces; a complex of measures designed to mislead the enemy as to the presence and disposition of forces and various military objects, their condition, combat readiness and operations and also the plans of the commander."

—*Soviet Military Encyclopaedia*, Terra, 1978

=== 1 ===

**Lyran Commonwealth Chartered JumpShip Faust
von Himmel
Approaching Zenith Jump Point outbound
Summit
Lyran Commonwealth
4 March 3134**

"*Three hundred minutes to jump.*"

As the automated warning rang through the bridge of the
Lyran Commonwealth-chartered merchant JumpShip *Faust
von Himmel,* the tall, almost spectrally lean black captain
turned and nodded to his short, square executive officer.

"Give the order to begin securing for transition, *Herr*
Sánchez. Alert all DropShips to prepare to depart Summit
system in five hours."

"*Jawohl, Kapitän* Grünblum!" The exec gave him a salute like an ax blow, then turned to relay the command to
the helmsman sitting at his station. His square-cut beard,
white as the first snow of winter on the captain's homeworld of Ludwigshafen, wagged emphatically to the rhythm
of his words.

The captain smiled behind his own neat beard, in which

he had recently, to his chagrin, found a single gray hair. In the thirty-second century such repetition of orders, to a crewwoman clearly in earshot and regarding a procedure the computers would handle by themselves unless a human intervened, might have seemed a quaint relic.

To an amateur.

Early on in his twenty-three proud years wearing the midnight black of the Lyran Commonwealth Merchant Marine, Bernhard Grünblum had learned to take nothing of space for granted. It had been crucial to his earning his Master and Commander rating after a nearly unprecedented eight years. It had also enabled him to captain the *Faust*, her crew—including his wife and three children, although the children were too young to take up shipboard duties yet—and the DropShips they carried like a mother opossum, safely through hundreds of jumps across the Inner Sphere in the five years since he had taken command. Redundant, yes; quaint, never.

Because space had a hundred thousand ways to kill you; and even though humankind had largely turned its back on galactic exploration, one thing humans kept discovering was brand-new ways to die in the long, cold night among the stars.

Nor had spacefarers merely the mischances and caprices of the universe to fear. Man's most dangerous threats, as ever, came from other men. Even though he and all his crew had grown up during the era of relative peace imposed upon the Inner Sphere by the will of Devlin Stone and The Republic he had called into being at the core of human-settled space, they still knew what it was to be menaced by human sharks.

And now that interregnum of relative order and safety had ended. War had returned to human space, and with it, all its attendant evils.

The void's chill seemed to seep into the brightly lit bridge, even as the bridge hummed around him like a finely tuned machine. Of all things he knew, *Kapitän* Grünblum most hated *disorder*. And while the hand of House Steiner—strong and alone, undiluted by a mad attempt to share power with the Davions, as in his grandfather's day— so far held firm within the Lyran Commonwealth, dark days had been seen already.

He feared his children would see worse.

He shook his head as if to clear it. *Ach so, Berni, why cloud your mind with unpleasant thoughts? The cosmos lies before us, waiting. You have all that any man could desire: a fine ship, prosperous trade routes, and of course Kimiko and our children, Winfried and Tamiko and Taro. Taro, eldest son and pride of a loving father's heart, soon to be old enough to leave the* Faust *for his own midshipman cruise. . . .*

Klaxon blare filled the bridge with a pounding pulse of noise. Grünblum scowled.

"What is it?" he demanded of Leutnant Liu, who had the helm.

Her report was icily professional as always. "Infrared detectors have picked up turbulence indicating an imminent emergence at the jump point, Captain." And then the merest shadow flicked across that carven-ivory countenance. "Several emergences, sir."

"Ensign Kohl, bring up video from the sail-mounted cameras on the main viewing screen, if you please."

"Jawohl, Herr Kapitän!"

The sensor station duty officer plied his keyboard. He was a youngster just out of the Merchant Marine Academy on Tharkad. This was his first cruise as a fully commissioned officer of the merchant fleet, although he had put in his time as a middie, of course.

The giant screen that dominated the bridge's forward bulkhead lit with stars. To Grünblum's eye it was a reassuring sight; he was as familiar with the constellations lying beyond the Summit jump point as with his own cabin.

A new star appeared. It brightened perceptibly. A JumpShip deploying her kilometer-wide sail to recharge her Kearny-Fuchida drive capacitors for the next jump of her route. Nothing unusual or sinister there.

However: "We're getting continual preemergence thermal releases, Captain," Ensign Kohl said. "A half dozen signatures or more."

Grünblum frowned. In his long career, happenstance multiple emergences were rare. He could recall only one or at most two circumstances in which he had observed more than one vessel appearing at a jump point at nearly the same instant, or even within hours of one another, even before the collapse of the HPG network and the attendant depression of trade as planets turned their attention inward. Unless the JumpShips were traveling together in a fleet. And even though the Lyran economy, characteristically, had begun to rebound more strongly than any other Inner Sphere power's, why should more than one merchant JumpShip appear here now?

He hated surprises. The unexpected was disorderly.

"Bring up the visual gain, Ensign, if you please."

Other novas blossomed: one, two, several, a miniature constellation of sails reflecting the light of Summit's far-away primary. Then all were eclipsed as the bridge computer enlarged the first sail's image.

"Himmel Herr Gott sei dank!" the white-bearded exec exclaimed, and crossed himself.

"A *Nightlord*," Ensign Kohl breathed reverently. "The largest of all Clan WarShips. I never dared hope to see one!"

"The Clans?" somebody repeated with a stutter of dread.

Captain Grünblum stared, stunned wordless. He himself had no idea whether the youth's identification was correct. The Inner Sphere possessed few WarShips at all, and no Clan WarShip had been seen in the Sphere since the early days of the Invasion eighty years before. Yet this JumpShip was unmistakably a ship of war, fantastically huge and bristling with heavy-weapons hardpoints. Upon the inner surface of her sail glowed the bird-of-prey and katana emblem that in all the universe of Man meant one thing and one thing only. Clan Jade Falcon had come to Summit, bringing a full-blown fleet of war.

Jade Falcon Naval Reserve Battleship **Emerald Talon**
Summit Jump Point orbit
4 March 3134

"It was an aberration that allowed two sibkin to win Bloodnames," the giant man said in a voice like shifting boulders, as comrades helped him shed a tunic that bore the insignia of a screaming jade falcon with a naked katana clutched in her claws, set against a blue-shadowed planet. "I intend to rectify that error now, Aleksandr so-called Hazen."

The man on the opposite surface from the nearly naked mountain of bone and muscle, like him standing with the flexible magnetic soles of ship slippers binding him to the empty cargo bay's bulkhead, would, in comparison to a normal human, be considered extremely tall and imposingly muscled. His physique was well displayed in the brief trunks, which were all he wore. His skin was olive, tanned rich brown, his hair a shaggy hank of raven's-wing black, so coarse that it stood off his forehead of its own accord. His face was broad-jawed and handsome as a trivid actor's.

He smiled.

"You are a brave warrior, Star Captain Lopata," he said, addressing the monster as if it were the huge man who stood at blatant disadvantage. "I salute your courage and your dedication to upholding the traditions of Clan Jade Falcon. Yet you display erroneous beliefs concerning the duties incumbent on a Trueborn warrior. It now becomes my solemn duty to instruct you."

The Circle of Equals, a few Bloodnamed mingled among the other warriors, kept the chiseled-in-stone impassivity their ceremonial task required. But the Elemental's supporters, like him officers of the elite Turkina Keshik, scowled and murmured hotly to one another at the smaller man's astonishing impudence—though in fact he far outranked a Star Captain. The less numerous contingent backing the commander of Turkina's Beak, the green Zeta Galaxy, hid smiles behind their fists. All except for a red-bearded man even larger than Aleks Hazen's opponent—his guffaw made the metal hull ring like crystal.

Thinking himself mocked, the Elemental Star Captain bellowed like a wounded ghost bear and launched himself into the air. Halfway to his opponent he wrapped himself into a giant ball, prepared to turn and land on his own magnetic-slippered feet.

A smile still faintly visible on his lips, Aleks stood waiting.

Three meters away the Elemental starfished open his limbs. Having noted the slight ripple of tension among the great muscles of his bare back, Aleks was already moving, gathering himself and springing away at an angle.

Lopata landed with a thud that seemed to the onlookers to reverberate through the great starship's whole fabric.

The bay was a cube with rounded corners and one rounded surface: the WarShip's hull itself. Its cavernous depths seemed to suck up light despite additional floods brought in for the duel. Aleks landed agilely on all fours at an angle above his opponent, light as a spider.

"Flee all you want, little man," Lopata said. "Disgrace yourself like the *chalcas* you are. In the end I will do the Falcon the great service of crushing you."

He launched himself. Aleks awaited him, crouched and grinning. Before the hurtling giant reached him, he leapt again.

"Your knowledge of tactics is flawed, my friend," Aleks said, standing at an angle to the Elemental with hands on hips as the giant raised himself. He had come within a hair of scattering some of his own supporters—thus breaking the sacred Circle and forfeiting the trial.

That was Aleks Hazen, who loved to ride the razor's edge.

"As is your appreciation of the meaning of our class. Not merely our lives but our holy quest and the honor of our Clan depend upon our techs. To bully them is foolish—and unworthy of a warrior, who exists to serve those weaker than he, not the other way around."

"Lecture me, will you?" With startling speed Lopata crouched and shot himself at the normal-sized man like a bolt.

Aleks stood unmoving. Time seemed to stretch as the Elemental unfolded his huge limbs to catch him, bear him down and crush him. Aleks' warriors shouted for him to *do something*.

Beyond the last instant, or so it seemed, he did. He stepped aside, grabbing the wrist behind a vast outstretched right hand with both of his. And yanked.

Had he done no more, Lopata would have struck the hull like a flesh meteor, crushing his skull or breaking his monstrous neck. It would have been an acceptable outcome—heroic, even, for a mere MechWarrior facing the apparently impossible odds of bare-handed battle with a mighty Elemental.

But Aleks tucked the arm into his own chest, partially arresting the giant's momentum.

It was not an untrammeled act of mercy. Lopata bellowed as his shoulder was wrenched from its socket. Then the WarShip hit him slam in the back.

The Elemental's agonized cry ended in a voiceless gust as all breath was driven from his body. He bounced, floated up again, stunned and inert. Aleks reeled him in, encircled his neck with an arm that looked like a child's against it and choked out the Star Captain.

He stood up, stepped back and touched a finger to his brow. "I salute you, Star Captain," he told the sleeping giant. "Perhaps in future you will treat my technicians with the respect due those without whom the mightiest warrior would be but a mud man waving sticks at the moon. If not—"

He shrugged his own not-inconsiderable shoulders. Then as his seconds gathered about him like an asteroid swarm drawn to a giant planet, he threw back his head and laughed, as for the sheer joy of living.

He was Aleksandr Hazen, Bloodnamed, and he was a hero.

2

"There is no question possible, Galaxy Commander," Star Admiral Dolphus Binetti said, gazing up into the holographic display of space near the emergence point which floated in the middle of the *Emerald Talon*'s semicircular bridge. "The merchantman could not miss us if he were blind and his sensor crew drunk."

Binetti was a short man, pompous and somewhat stocky, with a black spade-shaped beard around a jaw that remained firm in outline, despite his paunch. Age and declining fitness should have made him unlikely to maintain either high rank or Bloodname, which were generally held as they were won: by combat. But even before decades of enforced peace and, worse, contact with the soft races of the Inner Sphere had brought decadence to Clan Jade Falcon—so he and his hearer both believed—the Clans had realized there were roles even for warriors in which a decline in physical prowess, or indeed its absence to begin with, could not be allowed to trump knowledge and skill. Piloting a BattleMech or an aerospace fighter was not a job for an uneducated clod, but it paled beside the technical knowledge required to run a starship, much less a battlegroup. Binetti would lose his place when his command skills declined, not when someone wrestled him out of it.

Not that his guest was inclined to criticize on that basis. He himself would have fallen by the wayside long ago, had he been forced to rely purely upon his prowess in personal combat to maintain his own exalted place in his Clan. Given decadence, why not enjoy it? And anyway, whatever he had done to ensure his own survival, career and literal, had kept the Falcon from being robbed of one of her most able and dedicated servants.

As Khan Jana Pryde, ruler of Clan Jade Falcon, herself said often, "Traditions are worth respecting only if they further our cause."

Binetti's companion smiled and banished such mostly pleasant reveries from the cathedral of his mind. "Let him look, then, Star Admiral," said Galaxy Commander Beckett Malthus, leader of the proud Turkina Keshik—and of the expeditionary force as a whole. "There is no way to stop him."

"We could interdict," Binetti rapped. "Blast him from space."

"The Khan has commanded the *Talon* be used only to awe, not to fight," Malthus reminded him.

Binetti snapped up a hand in irritation. "Loose our fighters, then. They could use the blooding."

"We could," Malthus agreed, nodding and smiling gravely. "But to what end? The plan, remember, is to avoid conflict with our unwitting Lyran hosts if at all possible."

"Best way to do that is to keep them in the dark," the admiral said.

Malthus shrugged. He was a man of imposing height and breadth of shoulder, not unusual for a MechWarrior. He had a not insignificant bulge about the middle, which was unusual; but it was hidden by the artful drape of the robe-like garment he wore, green trimmed with black—the Jade Falcon colors.

Of course, such artifice was itself none too common within the Clans.

Topping all he possessed a great rounded square of head on which russet hair retreated between temple and crown, leaving a wide arrow-shaped salient down his broad forehead, and a wide, square jaw fringed with beard. To the extent the Clans, which tended to select against age, had any such thing, he fit perfectly the archetype of an elder statesman who remained, however, a prime MechWarrior. Which was why Khan Jana Pryde had flouted tradition and decreed to him the coveted command of Turkina Keshik, lead formation of the entire Falcon Touman, and hence the great *desant* into the heart of decadence in the Inner Sphere, instead of leaving the outcome to a bidding Trial.

That, or Bec Malthus had come out second-best in a game of intrigue, a game in which he held himself past master among Clan Jade Falcon—but that thought did not bear thinking.

"They will inevitably learn, my friend," he murmured sonorously. "Indeed, they may know already. Someone might have observed us on one of our previous jumps through Steiner space, without us observing them in turn."

"That is so," Binetti acknowledged, only somewhat stiffly. Disagreements were best handled circumspectly, lest they turn into open dispute—in which case the party who came out second best would be compelled by Clan custom to claim the "right" of *surkai*, the rite of forgiveness for being divisive. Khan Jana Pryde had specifically enjoined her warriors from intramural dueling, common among the Clans and incessant among Falcons. So desperate was their undertaking that literally no one could be spared.

Which made the fight currently taking place in one of the WarShip's bays that much more remarkable. Neither Binetti nor Malthus *officially* knew of the combat trial taking place between a Star Captain and a Galaxy Commander, even though it was being carried out with full Clan ceremony.

"The success of our *desant* is of course all," Malthus intoned. "And however much it might cut against our warrior grain, old friend, all depends upon avoiding conflict as long as possible. For even given the superiority of our Clan ways and our Clan warriors—and Jade Falcon's warriors are supreme without question in all of human space—those truths notwithstanding, our mission is so supremely ambitious, so daring, that we must seek every advantage as zealously as a Sea Fox merchant-captain grubbing after the last possible penny of profit."

Binetti nodded his square head almost dolorously. "What you say is true, Bec Malthus," he said. "But I burn to *act*. And I am not the only one: already my Naval Reserve warriors grow restive. Patience has not often been reckoned high among the Falcons' virtues."

"How well I know," Malthus said. He still marveled at the sheer sententiousness of his fellow ranking Clansmen, and not just cement heads like the Admiral. "Yet sacrifice *has* been so reckoned, and so we must sacrifice immediate gratification of our longing for the hot blood of action, no matter how strong that demand."

"I suppose," Binetti said grudgingly.

"In any event, emissaries of Khan Jana Pryde should shortly make official representation to the Archon to announce our mission, avow peaceful intent toward the Lyran Commonwealth, and demand our passage not be contested upon pain of war."

"Speaking of actions with little precedent in our Clan," Binetti said, "I do not know, friend, if I can truthfully say that I hope the emissaries succeed in mollifying the Steiners, but I will admit I have little faith that they will."

Malthus smiled. "We shall see ourselves, in the fullness of time. In the meantime, we are agreed, are we not, that we shall not contest or molest this little merchantman fleeing us so incontinently?"

"We are, Galaxy Commander," said Dolphus Binetti. He pushed a brief snort through his broad short nose. "Bid well and done."

"That was stupid," the giant said, grinning all over his red-bearded face as he enfolded Aleks Hazen in his tree trunk–sized arms.

"I am grateful as always for your unflagging support, Magnus," said Aleks, his voice muffled by the Elemental's slablike pectoral muscle.

"Not so," a voice said from behind Aleks. He disengaged from the giant and turned.

The voice belonged, as well he knew, to a small, compactly built, strikingly beautiful woman with a meter-long white-blond braid tossed over the shoulder of an almost all-black Jade Falcon field uniform.

"It was good for discipline," she said in a voice crisp and cool as a springtime wind on Sudeten. "We must allow those who support us to see that we support them, inferior though they be."

Having availed themselves of the opportunity to pop his shoulder back into its socket, tech-class medics bundled the fallen and still unconscious Star Captain from the hold. The spectators had begun to filter out. The red-bearded Elemental tossed a clean white towel at Aleks. "Some of us have duties to tend to. I'll see you later, Galaxy Commander." He tipped a finger off one bushy eyebrow to the small woman and walked away with the customary ponderous grace of his specialized breed.

Aleks looked down at the compact woman. "For all that your own uniform is not quite regulation," he said. "I understand you are a stickler for discipline, Galaxy Commander Malvina Hazen. Forgive me if I wonder whether you would have the same attitude had I undertaken to so instruct one of your Gyrfalcons?"

Her laugh was musical, and despite her rigid military bearing neither forced nor strained. "Of course I would! Has it been *that* long since we were sibkin, Aleksandr dear?"

Malvina sat up in bed with the covers bunched any old way around her breasts. A pink-tipped pointy one poked out regardless.

"Why did you not?" she asked, not looking at him.

"Why did I not what?" asked Aleks. He lay beside her with his hands laced behind his head. His white teeth gleamed faintly in the light of a dimmed lamp beside the bed in his austere courtesy quarters aboard the flagship.

"Why did you not bid for command of the Gyrfalcons? The real prize, Turkina Keshik, lay beyond both our grasps—we knew going in that Khan Jana Pryde had earmarked it for old Bec Malthus. But you might have won the right to command the Delta Galaxy—rather than picking the Zetas, green and still suffering the taint of long-ago *dezgra*."

She lay down beside him and drew the nails of her right

hand down his muscular, nearly hairless chest. Many female Clan warriors wore their nails square-cut short. Malvina Hazen wore hers long, enameled white, with stars in silver on them that were visible only in the proper light.

She was as fanatical a supporter of Jade Falcon tradition, and the Crusader cause, as Aleks himself. That did not mean that she was orthodox.

"We might have had a lovely battle, you and I," she almost purred.

He uttered a short laugh. "Why fight? I got what I wanted."

She sat bolt upright and glared at him with a flash of genuine anger in her ice blue eyes. "Don't play coy with me, Aleksandr!" She dropped her voice low. "Do you not recall how I held you at night, in our sibko barracks, when you wept at the harshness of our lives?"

"I do not forget." His grin never faltered. "I never forget, Malvina. You know."

She frowned. Her anger softened and flowed into perplexity. "Do you scorn the Delta Galaxy, then?"

"Not in the slightest, sister dear. I merely wanted the challenge."

"Challenge." A hunch of her bare snow-white shoulder added the question mark.

He nodded. "The Gyrs are a fine Galaxy, veteran and eager as their totem birds; they will win great glory for themselves and the Jade Falcon with a fire-eating *ristar* such as yourself to lead them. Many are the songs you shall inspire together, and long will they be sung. Turkina's Beak—" He shrugged his great, muscled shoulders. "Turning them into a Galaxy as splendid as any in our history— that will be a feat which wins me remembrance in a different kind of song."

She said nothing about his implicit assumption that he could reform the notably incorrigible Zeta Galaxy into a top-grade formation. She doubted it no more than did he.

"Besides," he added, "you would have won anyway. You always beat me, back in the sibko." The word meant *sibling cohort*. It referred to a brood of Clan children, genetic siblings, decanted simultaneously from the canisters in which they had been conceived and grown to viable infants.

"Not *always*," she said. "Not hand-to-hand."

"Nooo," he said, drawing out the word. "Not after I grew to half again your size." And he laughed.

She shook her head. "You must laugh more than any Clan warrior in history. Certainly among Jade Falcons."

"Ah, no, Malvina dear, I fear I cannot claim that honor even among our own Bloodnamed. That belongs to my chief of Elementals, Star Colonel Magnus Icaza."

"I do not place him."

"The red-beard, huge even for an Elemental. He stood me second in my Trial of Honor this day-cycle."

She made a thoughtful noise. "I expected to see that change. The readiness of your laughter. After all the years."

He laughed again. "If I could keep laughing through what we went through as children," he said, "I can laugh through anything."

She turned sharply to look at him, although her expression was as mild as her chiseled features would permit. "You find fault with our system, then?"

He shrugged his shoulders. "In our case it seems to have worked, certainly. Let us say, rather, I regret the necessity of treating children so."

For a moment he lay staring at the overhead, vaguely visible in the butter-colored light. She turned her head and regarded him, her triangular face unreadable in the dimness—and probably also in full sunlight.

"Look at us," she murmured. "Two playmates, once. And now the Eyes of the Falcon."

He made an amused noise, half back-of-the-throat laugh, half muted snort. "They call us worse things as well."

It was unusual for two of three unit commanders within a Clan force to bear the same Bloodname. What was truly rare, perhaps unprecedented, was that Aleks and Malvina were sibkin: members of the same sibko.

Among the Clans sexual liaisons among sibkin were not considered remarkable and were not discouraged, since both males and females received long-term contraceptive implants while still infants. Reproduction among the warrior classes was conducted in vitro according to scientifically planned breeding programs, not left to accidents of sweaty biology. Perhaps because of their extreme closeness—and the fact that they were the sole two of their sibko to survive to maturity, in large part because of that bond—Malvina and Aleksandr had long referred to one another as brother and sister. Terms which for virtually all other Clanners carried emotional weight only in reference to comradeship, not relationship.

"Let them talk," Malvina said, giving her head a defiant toss that made her braid slither across a bare shoulder. "We fought for our names and won them."

Bloodnames were rare, much rarer than in the days of the Clans' first onslaught against the Inner Sphere. Originally Nicholas Kerensky decreed that each Bloodname—the surname of a man or woman who had helped him found the Clans—could be borne by only twenty-five warriors. Then, along with persuading the Clans to draw down their stores of weapons, especially BattleMechs, Devlin Stone, founder of The Republic of the Sphere, told them they were so correct about the holy exclusivity of a warrior's role that they should actually reduce the percentage of their total populations who were born into the warrior caste. In order to prevent Name bearers from becoming a disproportionately large part of their thus-depleted warrior classes, diluting the sacred purity of the Bloodname concept, most Clans had Reaved themselves, ruthlessly reducing the number of holders of each Bloodname in brutal Trials. They then left the Bloodcount reduced, and Bloodnames consequently much harder to come by. Or keep.

That Aleks had shortly followed Malvina in winning the Hazen Bloodname, each in their first Trial, had been considered a scandal in some quarters. Though each sibko was descended from a particular Bloodname's originator, and its members entitled to compete for that Name, it seldom happened that two sibkin succeeded. And Hazen was a name of special reverence: it sprang from Elizabeth Hazen, keeper of Turkina herself, the Jade Falcon who gave the Clan her name.

"And I killed none of my opponents in the Trials," Aleks said, "whereas you left none alive."

She refused to be baited. Instead she smiled dazzlingly. "Of course."

"The official line," said Aleks, "as concocted behind the scenes by none other than our esteemed *desant* commander Bec Malthus, is that our shared triumph proves the superiority of the Clan breeding scheme—as perfected by Jade Falcon, of course." He chuckled. "Of course, within Clan Jade Falcon, if you say 'behind the scenes,' you have just *said* Bec Malthus."

She frowned, drew a knee up under her chin. "Does that not bother you, then, that overall command has devolved upon a known intriguer?"

"Perhaps that is what we need."

She looked at him with something near outrage. "But was it not to avoid such corruptions that Aleksandr Kerensky led us out of the Inner Sphere in the first place, centuries ago?"

He shrugged. "Indeed. And all honor to the Kerenskys and their vision. Yet whether we like it or not, change has been forced on us—was forced on us decades before our sibko was ever turned out of its artificial wombs. Even before Bec Malthus was born. Besides—"

He sat up. "This whole *desant* upon which we've staked the future of the Clan—of all humanity—is nothing but a grand deception, is it not? And you and I are the ones who dreamed it up."

She nodded judiciously. "That is true," she said and smiled.

"Which is why it cannot fail." She reached for him again.

3

Skilled Workers' Housing Bloc
Madlock, Shionoha
Draconis Combine
4 March 3134

"**T**ake him down!" the police *chu-sa* in the swept-tail helmet barked. Bulky in black assault armor highlighted in the weird gleam of orangish sunlight filtering through amber waves of smog, his Friendly Persuaders special tactical squad approached the mid-level skilled-workers' housing with their machine-pistols pushed out before them like insect proboscises.

Because their quarry was a responsible member of a skilled craft—computer network administration—he was privileged to live in his very own one-bedroom apartment, in a two-story bloc of a mere dozen. Granted, itself only one of dozens of such blocs lined up like domino ramparts in the residential district of Madlock, on the planet Shionoha, a world positioned near the tip of an arrowhead of space between the Lyran Commonwealth and The Republic. Yet privilege it was.

And here was how the dog repaid the Dragon's generosity:

a subtle virus that had infected the navigation system of the JumpShip *Dan-no-Ura,* stationed in planetary orbit for servicing, which would have caused it to attempt spontaneously to abort transition from hyperspace at the conclusion of its next jump. The police colonel did not understand the ramifications of it; they were the bailiwick of the pointy-head mob, who themselves disagreed on the precise outcome, so he gathered. Apparently, it would either cause the great ship to tear itself apart, or simply maroon it eternally in hyperspace. In either case depriving the Dragon of itself, its DropShips, and the thousands of Sons of the Dragon and their expensive equipment the great ship carried. Internal audit by the Internal Security Force of the system planetside had led right to this man: one Jinro Noguchi.

The *chu-sa,* who was himself in denial over the number of *gaijin* in his own family woodpile, shook his head to think of the perfidy of one whose roots lay in the Land Where the Sun Is Born. One might expect such behavior from those who sprang from lesser breeds. But a true *nihonjin?*

Thus he had not hesitated to give the order to use whatever force was necessary to apprehend the traitor. Even if it meant annihilating the apartment bloc and all its occupants. It was their Confucian duty to scout assiduously for signs of deviance in their neighbors and report them to the appropriate authorities, anyway. Any damage collaterally visited upon them by the *chu-sa*'s tactics was nothing more than due deserts. Indeed, it was possible some of them were guilty of more than simple negligence of civic duty: the miscreant's personal computer had contained an extensive list of coconspirators within the technical division, encrypted but using a logarithm ISF had quickly cracked.

The corruption ran deep and wide. The entirety of planetary computer services would have to be exhaustively screened if not purged. It would take months or years.

And the invasion preparing to stage from here into Prefecture I of The Republic of the Sphere would have to be indefinitely postponed.

Moving in brief rushes, half the team covered with their weapons while the others darted toward the door of the second-floor unit. Frightened faces appeared in windows, oval or dark, then vanished as the cohort of men in body armor with candy-striped greaves and armpieces surrounding the *chu-sa* swung their automatic shotguns to bear on them. To discourage snipers, of course, in case the rot had spread further than even the security forces feared. But mainly because it was not *appropriate* that mere civilians should gawk at the actions of the Civilian Guidance Corps as if they were some action-entertainment holovid. The *chu-sa* knew in his well-developed *hara*—the center of him, what the vulgar would call a potbelly—that it was allowing citizens who, however skilled, were still but lowly workers to give themselves airs that had caused all this trouble.

He was more than a Friendly Persuader. That went without saying: sealing a security breach of such magnitude was far too crucial to be left to a mere flatfoot civilian cop, however exalted his rank. The *chu-sa* was himself an officer of the Internal Security Force, nominally undercover.

In the wake of the Blakist Jihad's devastation, some worlds had bonded together for mutual defense in de facto prefectures, quite without regard for their Great House allegiances. Shionoha had formed such an alliance, scandalously with Rasalhague Dominion traitors and Lyran planets. Launching an invasion of The Republic from here would go far toward purging that taint: it could not happen too quickly, so far as the *chu-sa* was concerned.

The squad reached the target apartment. The men arrayed themselves on both sides of the door and the window to its left, several crouching down and duck-walking below the level of the sill to avoid being glimpsed through drawn but flimsy white curtains, or casting betraying shadows. The *chu-i* in charge of the tac assault team gestured peremptorily with a Nambu handgun gripped in a black-gloved hand. His *gun-sho*—sergeant—shook out a meter-long pentaglycerine X-charge, peeled away the plastic strips from the adhesive on its inner surface and pressed it carefully and quietly against the door. The lieutenant looked down at his colonel.

The *chu-sa* drew his katana, raised it over his head and hacked down. Instantly two men standing nearby fired stubby grenade launchers at the apartment window. As they smashed through and exploded with the dazzling flash and deafening report of stun grenades, the *chu-i* by the door touched off his door knocker with a sharp crack of shaped-charge detonation.

The *chu-i* and *gunsho* pivoted swiftly around the suddenly vacant doorjamb and into the apartment. The rest of the squad vanished inside by twos, spreading out within to secure the premises. The *chu-sa* smiled. The traitor would never escape.

A yellow-white flash within the apartment froze the expression on his face like a blast of liquid nitrogen. The last two men into the unit were flash-silhouetted for an instant. Then they were hurtling back out, one over the metal railing, one *through* it, propelled and engulfed by a rapidly expanding front of white smoke and vivid orange fire, visibly coming apart like insects plucked apart by a giant's fingers.

The *chu-sa*'s retinue made love to the pavement. The *chu-sa* himself stood upright, sword angled down, staring in dumb incomprehension as the *chu-i*'s severed arm, still clutching its Nambu, bounced on the gummy black surface within two meters of him. Its ragged stump bled not blood but smutty gray smoke.

Several blocks away, a man on a motorcycle glanced over his shoulder to see, through extreme-angled wraparound sunglasses, a globe of black smoke roll up into Madlock's dingy afternoon sky. Given the frequency of power outages—the Dracs blamed the HPG breakdown, implausibly—and the age-old Japanese propensity, transmitted like some kind of virus to the Combine's subject races, for using indoor charcoal grills for heat and cooking when better sources of power were unavailable, fire was a fairly common event. Even if House Kurita did successfully discourage too much use of structural rice paper in Combine buildings.

But this was clearly a hot-and-fast blaze, not some kicked-over *kotatsu* lighting off a *shoji*-screen room divider. The man on the Mitsu-Gurevich café racer braked, put a leathered leg down and let the big bike slide through a quarter rotation to a halt as pedestrians and bicyclists scattered and cursed him.

There were no candy-striped civilian cops in sight. Traffic was light; the change of the sixteen-hour shift was far away. The rider looked again, moved his glasses down his nose to give himself a better view. He was a medium-sized man, his build difficult to determine under his padded gray-and-khaki jacket. He had spiky straw-colored hair, rather fine if unremarkable features, and green Asian eyes.

He hoped none of his erstwhile neighbors had been harmed. Before fleeing his apartment he'd set a device that should have triggered a fire alarm—directly, since the smoke detectors were sporadically maintained at best, like so many things in the Draconis Combine—fifteen minutes ago.

As fervently he hoped his little surprise had paid off the accounts of a few of House Kurita's paid leg-breakers. Mostly low-level, granted, but it was the grunt-class Friendly Persuaders who did most harm to the ordinary folk who suffered beneath their sullen gaze. The true professional torturers of the ISF did not deign to waste their attentions upon the downtrodden and everyday.

He smiled a not altogether pleasant smile. More than likely the last thing the first candy-stripe thug into his small cell of a bedroom had seen on this world was a single playing card: the Knave of Hearts. Naturally, he had picked it up—

Triggering multiple charges of pentaglycerine secreted throughout the small apartment along with plastic containers of gasoline siphoned from official internal combustion engine land-vehicles.

The card itself was unlikely to survive the conflagration currently sending a quite satisfactory pillar of jet-black smoke to join the general aerial crud and corruption. If it did, it might be overlooked in the ham-handed search of the rubble—the officials in charge of the investigation being far, far more interested in finding someone, anyone, besides themselves to saddle with blame for the debacle than in actually getting to the bottom of what had happened. And if it survived, and were turned up, its significance might be missed, depending on whether it was civilian cops or sorely overextended ISF operatives who came across it.

The man on the big Drac bike was an artist. His medium was chaos.

He hated all external authority and government. It was the ruling passion of his life. Even that government which he served—judging it the least of available evils, including the swaddling totalitarian nanny-state of The Republic, now collapsing inward on itself in the wake of the HPG shutdown.

For their part, his superiors were inclined to overlook his

little foibles, even though members of their service were supposed to be fanatically loyal to their House. Themselves professionals in the art of chaos, they knew they had a Mozart in their midst.

It might be a security risk to leave the calling card; yet the man on the bike would escape the planet and Kurita space, or he would not, and the leaving of the card would likely have no bearing. And most important, his mission was accomplished: his neat framing of a sizable portion of the competent computer techs on Shionoha would derail the Dracs' invasion plans for months. Why precisely his masters should care if the Kuritans invaded The Republic, the operator had no need to know. His surmise—not that he greatly cared—was that they didn't want the Combine getting too big for its *hakama*.

And if the ISF should, at some point, realize the significance of the card, and that it was not a hoax, that their military had been infiltrated and victimized by the Knave of Hearts, the legendary—or was it imaginary?—LOKI operative: that would increase their paranoia and insecurity and long-term disorder, and further serve the passions of the man behind that name, and House Steiner, whom he served reluctantly and yet to the fullest extent of his extraordinary gifts.

An old man in a conical rice-straw hat, with a scraggly graying blond mustache and a white duck in a bamboo cage on one slumped shoulder, stood near the tail of the stranger's bike berating him loudly in low-caste Japanese.

The Knave of Hearts smiled to him, nodded and, with a snarl of his big V-twin engine and a squeal of road-grabbing wide-track tires, was on his way.

Hotel Savonarola
Florence, Southern Europa, Terra
Prefecture X
The Republic of the Sphere
4 March 3134

Tara Campbell, Countess and Prefect of Northwind, threw herself on her belly on the hotel bed.

"The cliché 'bird in a golden cage' comes to mind," she said. She picked up the remote control and clicked on the holovid.

As if to validate her fatalistic mood, her own head and shoulders appeared: spiky white-blond hair, hazel eyes, snub-nosed cover-girl features, big silver hoops in her ears and an off-the-shoulders top that looked like a white T-shirt that had had the collar and upper parts of the shoulders torn out. It had been 'grammed from above and in front of her.

"*The glamorous Countess Northwind was seen last night at Formio's, Florence's hottest night spot, taking a break from a grueling round of meetings with the Exarch concerning the current crisis within The Republic—*"

"They also serve who hang out in the rear with the gear and look good on the propaganda tri-dees," said her aide, Captain Tara Bishop, coming into the room behind her. She was a larger woman than the Countess, which wasn't saying much, not truly tall but strong and trim. With a shock of hair between dark blond and brown and dark green eyes, she was plain by comparison to the other Tara, but only by comparison.

She stopped dead when she saw her boss' image. "Hoo, you were pretty décolleté there, TC."

In the months since she had been assigned as the Countess' aide, between the first and second Battles of Northwind against Anastasia Kerensky and her Steel Wolves, she had proven herself an infallibly efficient and indispensable assistant, as well as a fierce and fearless MechWarrior. Especially in the weeks since they had defeated the Steel Wolves on the wintry Russian steppes, she had also become a close friend and confidante to her Countess.

"Shot from that angle, sure," Tara Campbell said grimly. "They might as well have just dropped the pickup down the front of my top while they were at it."

"Don't let them hear you say that."

Tara Campbell muted the sound but left the three-dimensional video display live: she was hoping against hope they might show actual *news* that might cast light upon the situation in the crisis-racked Republic. Hyperpulse generator comms to several planets near Terra had been restored, and JumpShips entered Sol system every day, from Republican worlds, the Great House domains, even the Clan Occupation Zones—although, ominously, the last category had been few of late. Not that any Clanners were particularly welcome since the Steel Wolves had invaded.

"You'd think," she said, rolling onto her back, "that I'd earned the right to do something real, TB. Something *substantial*."

Captain Bishop folded herself into a chair at a table by the window and plucked an apple from the basket of fresh fruit the hotel provided its important guest every day.

"You don't consider a show-the-flag and reassure-the-taxpayers tour a major contribution to the war effort?" she asked.

Tara produced a most un-Countess-like snort through her dainty nose.

"You made one crucial career mistake, TC," TB said, biting into the fruit. She waved it in the air. "You were publicly right when a big important man was just as publicly wrong."

Having seen their homeworld, Northwind in Prefecture III, devastated by Anastasia Kerensky and her renegade Steel Wolves—with help, impossibly, from a turncoat Paladin of The Republic of the Sphere—the two young woman warriors had arrived on Terra with such of the Countess' surviving forces as could be quickly scrambled into a relief force. The beautiful, bad and entirely mad Anastasia Kerensky was obsessed, Tara Campbell knew, with the dream of succeeding where all the Clans' previous efforts had failed: the conquest of Terra.

Once on Terra, the Northwinders found themselves virtually under arrest, suspected of *collaboration* with the Steel Wolves—and Paladin Ezekiel Crow, Northwind's betrayer, with a mortal lock on the ear of Exarch Damien Redburn.

Paladin Jonah Levin had helped Tara expose the truth: that Crow was a serial traitor, not just on Northwind but as the famed Betrayer of Liao, who sold that world to a brutal massacre by Capellan Confederation invaders in 3111. Barely in time, the Northwinders had been rehabilitated to play the key role in turning back the Steel Wolf invasion.

Longtime media darling Tara Campbell became a more-hyped heroine than ever before: the Savior of Terra, she was labeled on all the newscasts. She protested, loudly, sincerely and truthfully, that she was only one among many who had saved the planet; naturally, she was ignored. And Exarch Damien Redburn had to smile and nod approvingly as the Terran media piled acclaim upon the diminutive young woman he had publicly dismissed as a hysterical weakling.

It was not something the proud ruler of an interstellar superpower enjoyed.

"I know I stepped on the Exarch's cape," she said now, sitting up and clasping her knees. "But we're supposed to be The Republic's fire brigade. Why doesn't he send us to fight the Capellans?" The bulk of her Northwind troops was still on Terra, though in more comfortable billets than the frigid internment camp-cum-bivouac outside Belgorod they had been confined to upon their initial arrival.

Her aide frowned. "It may be that the Exarch fears you might just be too successful. You're already walking away the single-most popular human being in The Republic, if not the whole Inner Sphere. Maybe he's afraid you'll get some Roman notions about the best solution to the current cascade o' crises."

"Then he's a bigger ass than I thought he was!" Tara flared. "Serving The Republic is my whole *life*. I've never done anything else—never wanted anything else. It's not power—it's principles: the ideals of Devlin Stone."

"Strange how having a lot of power seems to change a person's perspective. I'm just a poor little soldier girl, but I have a feeling Exarch Redburn is pretty suspicious of professions of idealism."

"But it's *true*. What do I have to do to prove myself?"

Seeing the gleam of moisture in her boss' hazel eyes, the captain decided to lighten the mood. "Face it, TC: you do look good on recruiting posters. For women, you're an inspiring role model: Countess Tara, fearless lady warrior who still has keen fashion sense. For the men, well——"

The Countess said a vulgar word. "I was a poster girl as a *child*, TB. I'm an adult, I'm thirty years old. I've fought battles. I've *won* battles. Besides——" She shook her head. "My people are scattered across a dozen planets. Fighting now. Some will die today. Maybe right now, as we speak. And my place is with them. Not *shopping*."

4

Alone in his dark cabin with his dark thoughts, Bec Malthus sipped cognac.

By now the Jade Falcon trade factors upon Tharkad would have delivered their ultimatum to House Steiner: *hands off or else!* He did not doubt the manner of it would be gauche and brutal. *We are a gauche and brutal people, by and large.*

It was not a judgment on his part, but a sober assessment of fact, and not at all condemnatory in his mind. The thing upon which he prided himself most, the one thing which in his mind justified and redeemed the entirety of his existence and his acts by means of the service he rendered his Clan, was his capacity for total, ruthless objectivity.

He took another mouthful, almost daintily, rolled it about on his tongue, savoring the smoky piquancy. Although by the standards of the soft and self-indulgent Inner

Sphere, he knew, he would be held something of a prude, by Clan precepts he was a raging hedonist. He concealed most of his pleasures from the scrutiny of his fellows as scrupulously as he did his political machinations. Yet the one weakness he permitted to be seen was his love of fine food and drink.

He might have justified his indulgences to himself by observing that, after all, none served the Falcon better now, and few had ever served Her as well, as he. He didn't bother. Frankly, he did not give a pinch of Turkina's holy poop for such nonsense. He felt neither guilt nor shame; what he hid, he hid because others' awareness of it could cause them to act in ways adverse to his interests.

His table was a tame enough vice, indeed, a somewhat reassuring one, inasmuch as it was known and unlikely to bring harm or discredit upon the Falcon or her get. The Clan rhetoric, particularly Jade Falcon rhetoric, about iron will and self-denial contained, as he well knew, an element of willful self-deception. Few adults of the warrior class failed of having at least one vice—as defined by the Spartan Clan ethos, that was; to Spheroids, it was the Clans' self-defined *virtues* that were terrifying.

He smiled. *And now I and a pair of warrior children lead an army of naïfs to liberate people whose closest approach to a unifying passion is a desire* not *to be subjected to the harsh will of the Clans.*

When they planned this initiative months ago on Sudeten, the two Hazen ristars had given it a curious name: *desant*. In Russian, the native language of Nicholas Kerensky, Founder of the Clans, it meant what it sounded like in English, *descent*. But in the ancient Soviet military art from before the age of space flight, it had another meaning. It referred to a drop of air-mobile troops—generally a very daring one, striking at key targets deep in enemy territory.

Both Aleks and Malvina were keen students of military history. That itself represented a departure from pure Clan tradition and was one of the Inner Sphere encroachments that Bec Malthus at once resented and embraced. For the Clans had been designed to spite the past. By forgetting about it.

That had failed. Ever objective, Malthus would acknowledge that, at least to himself.

He smiled, sipped. *In order to preserve Jade Falcon ways,* he thought, *I am willing to destroy them.* He held up the goblet to the dim ocher shine of a potted-down lamp beside his chair, in a toast to himself. That in itself was true to the spirit of rough-and-tumble Clan ways.

Yet there was another word from the same lexicon that applied to this mission equally well. More specifically, to that of the emissaries on Tharkad. That word was *maskirovka*. While it had been appropriated by House Liao for its intelligence service, neither of the hotblooded young ristars was reluctant to reclaim its use per the original meaning.

The word meant *masquerade*. It had been used by the Soviets to signify a ruse concocted to cover intelligence or military operations.

The *desant* meant to see the Steel Wolves eradicated, no doubt about it. Every Jade Falcon did. And every woman and man of the expeditionary force down through the techs to the lowliest laborers burned with the desire to be part of that holy extermination.

But it was not the real objective.

That was: to conquer a bridgehead in the Inner Sphere, centered upon the world of Skye, the capital of Prefecture IX. And if they could win and hold that bridgehead convincingly enough, the full strength of Clan Jade Falcon might, Khan Jana Pryde willing, eventually join them in one great final Crusade to liberate Terra and all of the decadent Republic.

5

Jade Falcon Naval Reserve Battleship **Emerald Talon**
Jump Point
Crevedia
25 March 3134

"We cannot do it!" burst Aleks, starting from his chair in Malthus' elegant stateroom. He jumped up with such force that the rubberized magnets on his boot soles broke contact with the carpet and he floated to the overhead, and was compelled to push himself back down to the deck with his hand like a planetlubber. He had been thoroughly trained and seasoned in microgravity maneuvering long before this mission began. And he, like the rest, had had little enough to do *but* practice it.

His brief flight was a clear sign of his agitation.

Sprawled in another plush red chair, Malvina tilted a twisted grin toward her sibkin. "Here you were always the amenable one, Aleks," she reminded him.

He shook his shaggy head as if shedding water from his square-cut bangs. "We must not do this thing. It would be a disaster!"

Malthus' eyelids were at half-mast, as if he were drowsy. "What do you mean?" he asked mildly. It was a mildness few Clanners would recognize as dangerous.

"To raid Porrima," Aleks said, "would disrupt our schedule."

"The schedule is flexible," said Malthus. "It is ten days' round trip from jump point to planet. Allowing one day for the raid, or even two, will not add unacceptably to our time loading; we cannot depart the system within one hundred sixty-four hours of our arrival in any event, owing to the necessity to recharge our star drive. Four or five more days will not compromise our ultimate victory."

Aleks paced the cabin, careful not to break loose again, his long legs taking him the length of the available space in two strides each way. "We risk rousing opposition— warning our foes to prepare for our arrival. Do we wish to discard the *maskirovka* completely?"

"After our arrival at Chaffee," Malthus said with something resembling humor in his voice, "few will harbor any doubt as to our true intentions. To be sure, the purpose of our *maskirovka* was to forestall any significant attempt by the Steiners to halt us. Yet always we have had the odds on our side. The ultimatum that our people delivered upon Tharkad will likely have caused the Lyrans to equivocate, in accordance with their essentially mercantile nature; there was a reason Jade Falcon took so many worlds from them when first the Clans returned to the Inner Sphere some eighty-five years ago.

"Even should they decide to try and intercept us, the message lag caused by the collapse of the HPG network would make that problematic at best; after all, it is not as if they know our itinerary. And finally, we know through intelligence gathered by our own Watch that House Steiner prepares a major initiative of their own against the disordered remnants of the Free Worlds League, and have no desire to disrupt their own preparations chasing phantoms."

"All this is true, Galaxy Commander," Aleks said. "Yet once we perform a hostile act, the chance exists that JumpShips will carry word before us to our target systems. We have yet two jumps before we reach our first objective, to Edesich and Whittington. The locals might attack us as we recharge."

Seated behind the small polished mahogany desk in the richly paneled stateroom, Malthus turned his heavy face toward Malvina. "Let them try," she said, laughing. "Old Dolphus Binetti would kiss them before he vaporized them with his main batteries for giving him his shot at glory. Even if Galaxy Commander Malthus will not let his War-Ship go weapons-free, DropShips and aerospace fighters would give the Spheroids short shrift."

"We should not overlook that Porrima is the personal holding of the Archon Melissa Steiner herself," Aleks said. "Merchants though they are, the Lyrans will not take such an insult lightly."

"They will never catch us up," his sibkin said. "Once we have our foothold in the Inner Sphere, let them *try* to dislodge us!" She laughed like a child at the thought.

Aleks' normally dark face was ashen and tense. "What honor is there, then, in falling upon an unsuspecting world?"

"What honor is there in attacking Chaffee, come to that?" Malvina asked.

"It serves a direct military end," he said. "Therefore it serves the overriding interests of Clan Jade Falcon—and all humanity, ultimately."

Malthus rose languidly from behind his desk. "As does a raid upon Porrima," he said. "Our warriors grow impatient. They need the taste of hot blood in their mouths. We have already seen one death result from an attack prompted by a chance remark in the corridors of this ship. That incident was a certain harbinger of what we can expect a great deal more of, and soon, if we cannot slake our war birds' appetites for action!"

Aleks' broad shoulders slumped and he looked down at the crimson carpet. "A repetition would be disastrous for morale," he acknowledged.

"At last, my fine young ristar shows evidence of his famed clarity of thought!" Malthus said. "You are widely esteemed as a military genius, boy, as well as a true Jade Falcon warrior—both of you are. Indeed, I myself so represented you to Khan Jana Pryde. Yet in this matter you display no more wit than a street-sweeping laborer!"

It was a risky thing to say to any Clanner, much less a Jade Falcon. But Bec Malthus knew his man.

He always did.

Aleks sighed and stared down at his big, strong hands as if doubting their utility. "There is something to what you say, Galaxy Commander."

"It is not softness of the head which troubles you," Malvina said, "but softness of the heart."

He brought his head up sharp, and when his dark eyes fixed upon her there was something of the Falcon in their gaze.

"It is your silly sympathy for the bellycrawlers," she said. "You scruple to risk spilling any of their precious blood, though only the very best of them is worth more than the lowest Falcon laborer."

"You easily dismiss these 'bellycrawlers,'" Aleks said, "yet billions of them dwell under Jade Falcon control in the Occupation Zone."

"At least they are *under* control, not living and rutting like beasts of the fields." She tossed her head, making her snow-colored bangs bounce on her forehead and her heavy braid slither on her shoulder like a restive serpent. "And perhaps if *I* were Khan they would be under better control still."

Aleks goggled, looked from Malvina to Malthus and quickly back again. Plain on his face was concern that his beloved sibling should voice such sedition in the presence of a man far and not always well-famed as the pure creature of Khan Jana Pryde.

"Do not let your own heart's hot blood betray *your* head, Galaxy Commander Malvina Hazen," Malthus said blandly, showing no reaction to the woman's shocking words. "The Inner Sphere has its true warriors; it was not Wolf perfidy and cowardice alone that stymied our first Crusade. And the distance between us and them has diminished, do not forget, in the years since we agreed to our Devil's bargain."

The last came out tinged with bitterness. *Devil's bargain* had been gaining currency of late among the radical traditionalists of the Crusader faction, referring to the modus vivendi the Falcons, even of the homeworlds, had agreed to with The Republic of the Sphere. It was itself a play upon a rare Clan play on words: those same fervent traditionalists had taken to calling The Republic's vanished founder *the Devil in Stone*.

Malvina made a circular gesture with her hand, as if deferring to her superior without conceding his point.

"Our mission is to protect the people of the Inner Sphere," Aleks said, calmly and quietly now. "Even from themselves. Such was the Founder's vision."

"Yet they *are* inferior—with all respect, Beckett Malthus, allowing them the odd hypothetical hero. The fact remains that as warriors, man and woman, they cannot touch us. I know you are no *chalcas*, Aleksandr, entirely the opposite, in fact. Why then this soft spot for Freebirths, whose lives are as chaotic and undisciplined as their breeding habits?"

"Precisely because of what you say, Malvina," he answered gently. "Yes: we Clanners are superior. As we warriors are superior to our laborers and techs. And with that superiority comes a burden: *responsibility*. The Founder, Nicholas Kerensky, decreed the one when he set about to build the other."

"All this to the side," Malthus said, overriding Malvina, whose sculpture-perfect face had started to crease with anger, "we can all agree without hesitation that Turkina's interests outweigh those of the people of Porrima—and that if we do not find some way to bleed our internal pressures fast, they will rupture us like a faulty fuel cell. *Quiaff?*"

"*Aff,*" said Malvina, lightly, as if nothing said previously were of any consequence to her.

Aleks hesitated. "*Aff,*" he said at length.

Malthus smiled and nodded heartily. "Excellent. Now as to the raid itself—"

"I bid my first Cluster," Malvina piped up promptly.

"*Neg,*" Malthus said, still smiling, but forcefully. "Devoted as we all are to our traditions, *batchall* has been honored as much in the breach as in the observance since long before any of us was born, among the Falcons no less than any other Clan. This is a matter not of bidding but of necessity of war—and it behooves us all to remember that Khan Jana Pryde herself instructed us most explicitly that the success of our mission took precedence over any imaginable consideration."

"So I suppose you'll be leading the raid—" the woman began, sulky now, almost petulant.

"*Neg,*" Malthus said again. "Young Aleksandr shall carry out the raid upon Porrima. With his entire Zeta Galaxy."

She snapped upright in her chair, risking a brief embarrassing flight of her own, staring at him in open disbelief. "But I thought—"

"Yes, but perhaps no more clearly than your sibkin but a moment ago," Malthus said. "Your Gyrs are battle tested. Their skills and fervor are second only to my own Turkina Keshik—and perhaps the rest of the Turkina Galaxy—in all of Clan space. Which of course means all of human space. What need have they, therefore, to learn what it is like to wet their claws in the blood of prey? They *know*."

"But—" She scowled and her small mouth grimaced in confusion. "Our warriors, yours and mine, it is they who most need the release only battle can give, *quiaff*?"

"Aff," said Malthus. "Yet they are Clan warriors, Jade Falcon warriors, and they know discipline and their duty. They must settle this time for *vicarious* battle. It must suffice them that the great *desant* in which they are privileged to take part is striking a blow against the foe. They will participate by remaining with the JumpShips at Porrima's proximity point, and celebrating Turkina's Beak's success upon that Galaxy's return. They also serve who only sit and wait; we shall remind them of that, you and I. And of their duty."

Malvina's ice blue eyes were wide. "If you say so, Galaxy Commander," she said softly.

"I do. I know the sons and daughters of Turkina, what makes them go, and what makes them come. It is the great study of my life. Now go, the both of you. Aleksandr has plans to write. And it is not too early for you, Malvina Hazen, to begin preparing your Deltas for their role as enthusiastic spectators—no matter in how little esteem they hold the Zetas now."

Both the young ristars, the unique sibkin set, were subdued. Malthus considered that in itself a minor triumph. Malvina slipped almost furtively from Malthus' stateroom. Aleks hung back, seeming abashed.

"Well?" Malthus demanded with one eyebrow arched—an expression which had cost him hours of practice before a mirror, in his youth, and repaid his investment many times over in the years intervening—looking up from several moments' apparent study of the display screen inset at an angle in his desktop. "Have you further business with me, Galaxy Commander?"

"I claim my right to *surkai*," the taller, younger man said. "I would undergo the Trial of Forgiveness."

"Fast for twenty-four hours."

Aleks drew his head up and blinked his eyes once in surprise. The "right" of *surkai* was the penalty a Clan warrior paid for pressing an issue and losing. The price exacted for having opposed one's will to that of the Clan could be highly arduous or even literally agonizing punishment. No Clan was inclined to give out second-place prizes in any endeavor.

The penalty Malthus had named was almost insulting.

"But, Galaxy Commander—"

Malthus looked sternly at him. "Grow up, Aleksandr," he said. "We are embarked upon a mission to rekindle the holy flame of the Crusade, without interference from the cowardly Wolves who have diluted and denatured the blood of Kerensky. And without having to share the glory with any other Clan. Do you not feel that is more important than your ego, or if you would call it that, your honor? I cannot afford to have you wasting time and energy being tortured.

"Now go, and plan, and think only of ultimate victory!"

6

The first that residents of Allison City knew of the drastic change in their lives was when two Points of aerospace fighters from Trinary Echo of the Third Falcon Velites streaked over their city at hypersonic speed, shattering the glass from most every window. While the citizens were still dusting broken glass fragments off themselves the four fighters came back, much slower this time, to destroy an entire company of VTOLs parked in a yard by the wall on the west side of town.

Three new stars appeared high in the overcast sky, grew quickly to novas, then to suns, and finally crosses of blue drive fire. Two came down east of the city, on the mud flats of the Equanica River. The third descended directly into the huge spaceport outside the high city walls, blasting with its formidable armament anything that moved or looked remotely threatening, including a hapless electronic mule dragging a series of baggage carts to a DropShip out of The Republic of the Sphere, and the control tower itself, which exploded into fragments from the single kiss of a PPC.

Three Demon wheeled medium tanks of the Lyran Commonwealth Armed Forces, stationed at the spaceport more as a convenient place to park them than for any military considerations, bravely ventured forth with all weapons blazing. One flashed into incandescence under the attack of a *Jagatai* aerospace fighter, which had stooped like a falcon from the swarm of five fighters orbiting the descending DropShip. The underwing-mounted extended-range particle guns attacking the thin upper armor probably made the arrival of a volley of twenty long-range missiles overkill.

The DropShip itself, *Red Dragon,* met the other two tanks with a glittering ruby volley of pulse laser fire. The large and medium weapons' beams, precise and relentless as the needles of an industrial sewing machine, sieved both Demons in a matter of seconds. One managed to rake two glowing slashes across the rounded underhull of the descending craft with its turret-mounted lasers, achieving little more than to scour away the char of rapid descent through atmosphere, leaving two shiny streaks of hull metal virtually undamaged. The other tank did not accomplish that much, but staggered, sagged on pierced and melting tires and severed suspensions. Its turret rose into the air on a geyser of hellish red fire, slipped to the side, and fell with a ringing clang on the pavement.

It was Aleks Hazen's intention to give maximum battle experience to his ground forces rather than his fighters and DropShips. But everyone in his Galaxy fought under orders to protect the landing ships at all costs. All the resources the expeditionary force possessed were none too great for the awesome task confronting it. Combat DropShips, like other military assets, had been reduced in number throughout the Inner Sphere through the intercession of Devlin Stone. The invaders could not rely on replacing the vital craft from *isorla,* the Clan term for plunder.

Allison starport's day-to-day defense was in the charge of a company of local militia, infantry armed primarily with slug-throwing assault rifles and armored with battle-dress blouses. Few even wore helmets, affecting instead jaunty teal berets or olive drab boonie hats. At any one time, one platoon was deployed in active patrols around the perimeter and among the ships and structures, one was on standby in the central terminal structure, and one stood down in the attached barracks. In practice that meant that most of the platoon in the terminal was asleep, many of the one officially in barracks away on leave.

Once upon a time the port had boasted substantial defenses: missile pits, great lasers and particle-beam cannon. These had been disassembled decades before in the Inner Sphere-wide euphoria over The Republic's swords-into-plowshares policy. To maintain such pre-Republic defenses, it was generally held, if not frequently put into words, was tantamount to inviting the bad old times back.

So the heavy defensive weaponry was long gone. And the bad times came back in trumps: a trey of stars, three Jade Falcon DropShips riding sunfire.

Of the troops on foot and vehicle patrol around the port, some simply hid, or scaled the fence and ran away across the fields to hide in the transient suburbs which sprang up nearby during the sixty-two-year calm spells between bouts of catastrophic weather. The rest, most of them, turned to meet the invaders.

Even before the *Union C*–class vessel had settled its forty-seven hundred tons on its landing jacks on the pavement and the last flames had quit flickering above the blast-pit rim, sally ports opened and the bulky man-shapes of Elementals in Clan battle armor suits sailed out on the impulses of their jump jets. They fanned out around the vessel as muzzle flashes sparked from militiamen lying in the grass around the apron or crouching beside parked service vehicles. A few laser rifles stabbed ruby beams toward the leaping squat figures on the ship.

A point of aerospace fighters streaked past low and subsonic to the north of the main terminal. Flame blossomed as they strafed and rocketed the barracks.

The Elementals struck ground twenty meters or so beyond the ovoid DropShip's splayed landing jacks, bounded into the air again. Ramps had descended to the pavement. BattleMechs now began to clump down behind them, a dozen, more.

At sight of the metal behemoths, some vaguely manlike, some not at all, many more of the militia threw down their weapons and fled. Everybody knew what 'Mechs were—the tri-vid adventures were full of them. Which was the problem: they were terrifying potencies, monsters from another age. Most people of The Republic of the Sphere had never seen more than one or two in person in all their lives. Now, confronted with what to them was a stupefying profusion of the giant killing machines, many simply panicked.

The Elementals descended toward the ragged lines of prone riflemen. Liquid flame gushed from the arms of their armor. The militia troops became torches, to rise and run screaming, leaving footsteps of flame dying slowly behind them in the dew-moist morning grass.

Other power-armored giants unleashed rockets from launchers rising to either side of their heads like grotesque shoulder padding. The heavy short-range missiles shattered stacked cargo crates and the bodies of troops firing from their shelter. One cargo mule rose several meters in the air upon a speed-growing stalk of smoke flowered scarlet in flame, then toppled back to the pavement.

From a fen outside the perimeter wire a huge flock of waterfowl rose into the sky on two-meter wingspans. They streamed away from the port like a cloud of white crosses.

With the BattleMechs laying down a base of fire the Elementals moved onward, pursuing fleeing foes or rooting them out from among the buildings nearest the ship. Vehicles and unpowered infantry were streaming down the ramps now, spreading out in turn to secure the vast facility.

The battle for the spaceport was over. Only the killing went on.

"We cannot do that!"

"The word *cannot* is not in the Clan Jade Falcon lexicon, Star Captain Mason," Aleks said affably into the boom microphone of his neurohelmet. He sat in the cockpit of his fifty-five-ton *Gyrfalcon* BattleMech clad only in shorts over his coolsock. He was totally relaxed. His reservations, strategic as well as moral, about the assault remained in full effect. He had pushed them totally from his consciousness, and was now aware of nothing except happy anticipation of doing what he had literally been bred, raised and trained his whole life to do.

"Besides," he continued to the officer commanding his

DropShip, descending toward the outskirts of Allison City with atmosphere pounding and shrieking at the hull as if in protest of this violation, "we obviously can. The place I told you to land lies beneath us; we are dropping toward it. All we need do is allow things to take their natural course."

"But it is swamp," the captain protested. "I would not dare even hot-drop you and your 'Mechs into such terrain, Galaxy Commander!"

By *hot-drop* he meant dropping the jump-capable 'Mechs of Aleks' command, which was most of them, from his craft while it remained airborne. He was bold to speak in such a manner. Almost any other Galaxy Commander would have relieved him of command by now and called him out into the bargain. Malvina would probably have popped out of her cockpit, clambered up to the bridge, and put the captain's brains all over his own bridge viewscreen with her sidearm. The thought made Aleks smile.

He himself felt no rancor toward Star Captain Mason. Although he had not fought with Mason before—only Magnus Icaza and Folke Jorgensson had accompanied him to Zeta Galaxy—he was satisfied that Mason was a competent, courageous officer. His concern was how best to use his ship in the Falcon's service, not craven personal safety.

"I test the mettle of my pilots as much as my MechWarriors," Aleks said. "You have landing jacks, Star Captain, *quiaff?*"

"Aff."

"Use them. Put us down where I have said. Hold us level with jets and gyros while we debark. If you start to sink after, blast free and fly away and land where you please. Only get us off first!"

"But, Galaxy Commander! If we topple we could all be killed, our equipment lost!"

Aleks laughed. "We all die sometime, Star Captain. If I am wrong I shall pay the price. Now show me that as a true Falcon's son you know how to fly—or how to die. *Quiaff?*"

Since Porrima was the direct holding of the Archon, ruler of the Lyran Commonwealth, both jump points were watched by remote observation outposts. When the Jade Falcon fleet appeared at the zenith point it curtly informed the station of its ostensible purpose in entering the system: the *maskirovka*. The station's commander protested the intrusion briskly.

Given that it was an unarmed space station with a complement of about twenty confronting a sizable fleet including armed JumpShips, DropShips and a full-on battleship, the sheer bravado of the stationmaster's reply favorably impressed the Clanners from Star Admiral Dolphus Binetti down. It probably saved the station crew's lives.

Shortly after emergence, one of the JumpShips launched a shuttle and a Star of ten aerospace fighters. An underofficer on the *Emerald Talon* broadcast a "courtesy" call to the station to inform them that this was a training exercise, of no concern to the Porrima authorities nor the station occupants, and, of course, to threaten prompt retribution if the station interfered in any way. Which it palpably could not, thus showcasing Clan Jade Falcon concepts both of courtesy and humor.

In the course of juking through space, spilling bundles of radar-reflecting aluminum-coated plastic chaff in hopes of evading its pursuers, the shuttle dodged within a hundred meters of the station. The flyby evoked a storm of complaint from the station, which this time was met with bland obduracy, as if Falcon Clanners understood neither English nor German.

Between their excitement at the reckless near-miss and the war fleet's infuriating nonresponse, and a good deal of internal commentary on high-handed Clan arrogance, no one heard a thing as ten small rubberized magnets clamped themselves to the hull near the main airlock. Nor did they hear the lock's outer hatch open and close, nor hear it cycle.

Their first warning was the slight pressure change as the inner hatch opened. And then it was much too late. The station's unarmed crew—nominally military, but in fact LCAF technicians who had no weapons nor even instruction in their use beyond a gesture in that direction during basic training—found themselves facing five figures, four gigantic in armor and one dwarfed by them in a standard EVA pressure suit. They also faced three microlasers swapped with flamers—a daft weapon in enclosed quarters—in the arms of three contemporary suits of Clan battle armor, an old-style suit's small laser, and one pulse-laser pistol gripped in a spacesuit-gauntleted hand.

"I am Galaxy Commander Aleksandr Hazen of Clan Jade Falcon," the smallest figure, who still loomed over all the observation post's crew, said in a pleasant and cheerful baritone voice. "You are now my captives."

And so they were. In part because of the courage shown by their initial challenge, no Falcon challenged Aleks' mandate that the crew be kept safe under lock down and then released unharmed when the Clanners had no further use for their silence.

After the initial excited reports of the Jade Falcon emergence, all further beamcasts from the station indicated that nothing whatever of interest occurred.

Somehow they omitted to mention when half a dozen DropShips detached themselves from JumpShips and headed for the ecliptic at a one-gee standard burn.

"No opposition, Aleks," Star Colonel Magnus Icaza's voice said into Aleks' earpiece. "I am disappointed in these Porrimans."

The giant stood in his Elemental battle armor beside the *Gyrfalcon's* right foot on the low, marshy bank of the river. It was the classic armor with head and torso one immovable egg-shaped piece, not the current mark with a helmet that could swivel like a tank turret. When monster Magnus had passed his Elemental Trial of Position on Winfield in the Jade Falcon Occupation Zone, it was determined that none of the modern armor in the armory fit him. The techs had to pull an old outfit out of storage.

"Hmm," Aleks said, smiling. "I think they will oblige us right enough."

He called his fifty-five-ton BattleMech "White Lily," after the personal insignia painted on the front of its left shoulder: a lily gripped in a steel-gauntleted fist. He swiveled the machine's torso right to point toward a black column of smoke unspooling into the sky from the superhighway, several kilometers south, which led into the walled city. It put behind him the looming egg-shaped mass of the DropShip, which had sunk in almost to the flared Venturi nozzles of the drives in the soft bank. Star Captain

Mason had put the ship down without further demur and with exquisite skill.

For his part, Aleks had already forgotten the man's reluctance. What was this misbegotten raid for, if not to give his men and women the chance to show what they were really made of?

"Our friends in the First Mixed Cluster report some brisk resistance," Aleks said. He had taken the unorthodox step of combining his Eyrie and Solahma Clusters and then splitting them into mixed formations. The second he had dispatched north to raid the great Heimdal mining complex on Steinerheim, the supercontinent sprawled across the planet's north pole.

Eyries consisted of youngsters who had yet to prove themselves in battle. The Solahma comprised older warriors who had lost Trials of Position and were deemed no longer fit for front-line service. He felt the youngsters—who as, basically, adolescents were reckless even by Jade Falcon standards—could use the tempering the veterans could provide. And the older warriors might benefit from exposure to youthful eagerness and energy. He had tried similar expedients successfully before, and hoped it would help his green Galaxy with its legacy of disgrace stand up to its first immersion in the combat cauldron.

"The defenders have deployed heavy anti-armor weapons in reasonably good hasty positions," reported Star Captain Folke Jorgensson, approaching in his *Black Hawk*. Clan Jade Falcon maintained none of the fifty-ton 'Mechs in its BattleMech park. The Ghost Bear *abtakha* had taken the machine from Clan Wolf even as he himself had earlier been taken from them. "That's one of our precious few Mars assault vehicles you see burning down there; apparently the Porrimans have mastered the concepts of ambush and rear-aspect shots at heavy armor."

Aleks' brow creased briefly. The boxy one-hundred-ton Mars with its massive armor and bristle of heavy weaponry had made up much of the mass of the blow the Mixed Cluster was hurling down the blacktop toward the city's now-sealed stressed-cement floodgates. Most of the Third Falcon Velites' BattleMechs and all their own armor, landed from Aleks' DropShip, were striking south overland to take the highway defenders in the flank.

"They wanted us blooded," he said in a clouded voice. "Now blooded we are."

Magnus Icaza clanged his suit's right arm, the one mounted with a manipulator claw, on the bulging armored housing protecting the right-ankle actuator of Aleks' *Gyrfalcon*. "We'll make it up with *isorla* and more, Aleks, lad."

"If they have any booty worth the taking—" Jorgensson began.

Magnus Icaza snorted thunderously. "We need no Ghost Bear gloom here, Folke Jorgensson."

"—or if any survives the taking, my overly sanguine Elemental friend." Aleks had long learned he could trust the two to banter almost ceaselessly without one ever going for the other's throat. Magnus, outsized since birth, had enjoyed a situation opposite to runt Aleksandr's sibko experience: he had been so huge even other Elementals were reluctant to tangle with him. Folke, a perfectionist, shared Aleks' keen hatred of waste. Nor did he feel, having won his freedom, his BattleMech, and his right to use the Bloodname he had already won in blood in his birth-Clan, that he had anything more to prove. Seven Falcons decanted had taken Jorgensson's reticence for cowardice since Aleks had severed the last of his bondsman's cords. Two had actually survived, though one was so badly injured that he had been forced to retire to a Solahma unit and had found an honorable death against Periphery pirates.

Aleks set off straight toward the city, leading a Star of five jump-capable 'Mechs and a Star of twenty-five Elementals—five Points of five warriors each. Shortly they came on a great cement-lined gouge in the earth: a flood-control ditch, meant to channel the catastrophic floods which occurred every sixty-two years away from the city's walls. Aleks' DropShip had mapped the channel complex from space; a display of it glowed in the cockpit before him. A path in red led to a point hard beneath the walls themselves.

He led his scratch Binary right into the channel. A trickle of oil-sheened water meandered along its wide bottom. The channel provided his strike force a high-speed route, allowing the machines to move at near the top pace of the slowest BattleMech. It also gave excellent concealment from observation. The channels were twelve meters deep, as required to contain the violent floods of storm season; the BattleMechs could march unseen. To avoid having them leap into view like killer locusts, the Elementals rode clinging to the BattleMechs like baby opossums.

Aleks hoped that by gaining a swift, decisive advantage he could persuade the poor children of Allison City to surrender before he had to kill too many of them.

They reached the nearest approach of the channel to the city walls. Not built as defenses, at least against human threats, the walls here rose almost sheer twenty meters above ground level. Overhead observation on descent had confirmed what Aleks learned from the world's entry in the Fleet database: that the walls were thirty meters thick at the base, sloping along the backside to ten meters' width at the top.

A leap from the bottom of the flood-control ditch brought him to the lip between it and the wall. With neither command nor checking to see if the others followed he gathered his 'Mech and jumped to the top of the wall. As he did, he extended the metal wings built onto the back of his hawk-headed BattleMech; they served no purpose but to strike fear in foes and make the statement that Clan Jade Falcon had come. Aleks liked their theatrical touch himself.

A half kilometer to his right rose the control housings for the massive floodgates that blocked the road into Allison City. The leading elements of his mixed Cluster had already battled within a few hundred meters of the gates along the eight-lane highway and the ground to both sides. They had successfully forced passage of the long bridge over the Equanica River and now fought to cross the second bridge, across the flood channel from which Aleks and his strike force had just emerged.

White smoke tentacles reached out toward Aleks' BattleMech.

7

Allison City
Porrima
3 April 3134

Aleks looked down into the city. A mixed force of armor and unarmored infantry approached the gate from within, supported by a gigantic M1 Marksman tank and a *Ryoken II* BattleMech.

He grinned. A favorite among the Wolves, the seventy-five-ton 'Mech was an old friend. It was a very serious machine, as for that matter was the ninety-five-ton tank. Golden Age of Peace or not, the Archon had provided her suzerainty some real firepower.

" 'Mech's mine," he said over the Binary command channel, and jumped. "Take down the rest. Try not to damage the gatehouses."

The rocket barrage, fired from both tank and BattleMech, smashed down where the *Gyrfalcon* had briefly stood, sending out great geysers of grayish dirt from the wall's berm backslope and slabs of cement flying from its top. He shot back with the Ultra autocannon in his 'Mech's arms. His *Gyrfalcon* bled heat beautifully; he could run and jump and shoot all day so long as he was judicious in firing his two large extended-range lasers, also arm-mounted.

"Unidentified Porriman *Ryoken II* pilot," he broadcast on what, during their descent, had been identified as a general armed-forces channel. "I am Galaxy Commander Aleksandr Hazen of Clan Jade Falcon. I challenge you to single combat."

A burst of light autocannon fire raked across his 'Mech's chest armor, rocking it back. The heads-up indicators showed no damage done.

"I am Leutnant Colonel Rähne von Kleist of the Eighth Lyran Guards," a woman's voice answered. "You have come a long way to die, Galaxy Commander."

Aleks roared laughter. Although Allison City had a population of over two million, according to his latest information—updated regularly by Jade Falcon merchants plying the Inner Sphere, and generally quite reliable—unless the Lyrans had a wholly unlooked-for troop concentration on hand, it stood no chance of successfully resisting the Clan assault force disgorged from the three DropShips the Leutnant Colonel, like everyone else across half the southern continent, had seen descend through the thin overcast this morning.

"You have the spirit of a Clanner," he told her. "Let us see if you fight as well as you talk."

He lit on the roof edge of a square, solid-looking warehouse across the street which ran along the inside of the wall. As he expected, it began to crumble as soon as the machine's enormous weight came down on it. He bent the *Gyr*'s legs and jumped again, letting his jets carry it deeper into the city. A hellstorm of long-range missiles pulverized the whole southern side of the warehouse in a sparkle of white flashes, raising a great cloud of cement dust. One rocket exploded against the armor plating of his right upper leg, cracking a plate. The medium BattleMech swayed alarmingly, but gyros and his own light touch on the controls held it, kept it from crashing to the ground.

Instead he landed under power in the street in front of the warehouse. Most of the immediate district seemed to be light industrial. The parking lots were mostly bare; either the invaders had beat the morning shift or the civilians had evacuated.

*   *   *

Elementals bounced in crisscrossing patterns like fleas on a dog. Thin pink lines stabbed through dust and smoke as infantry lasers flashed at them. The Marksman tank was concentrating on Folke Jorgensson's *Black Hawk,* firing its Gauss rifle and medium missile launchers and clearly trying to close within range of its powerful and plentiful Streak SRMs. Jorgensson darted his *Hawk* up the inner slope of the seawall and back down to the broad street as fleetly as a light 'Mech, twisting its torso to shoot back with the two large lasers mounted in the 'Mech's body.

The *Black Hawk* staggered as a solid hit from the big Gauss rifle slammed into it, locking up the shoulder actuator for its right arm. At the same time, a threat warning shrilled in the erstwhile Ghost Bear's ears: the tank was trying to lock him up with its Streak guidance system. Firing his own heavy-missile volley from his immobilized right arm, Jorgensson jumped straight up and then veered for the top of the wall.

The Marksman lost its lock. A lucky hit from Jorgensson's snap shot smashed the Streak quad rack on the left hand side of the turret. A moment later Magnus Icaza's old-style Elemental battle armor landed on the tank's front glácis to the right of the main gun.

The four Bulldog miniguns mounted in two pairs atop the turret blasted him. They chipped the fierce green visage, yellow beak, and buff belly of Turkina, Elizabeth Hazen's own Jade Falcon, enameled on the armor's front, began gouging streaks in the durable plate itself. But their impacts failed to dislodge the one-ton suit as Icaza grabbed the barrel of the Lord's Thunder Gauss rifle with the armor's right manipulator and bent it upward.

Frantically the Marksman gunner let go with the two sextuple SRM launchers mounted to either side of the now-defunct main weapon in hopes of blasting its tormentor free. But Icaza had already bent his legs and, squatting, wedged himself beneath the useless Gauss-cannon barrel outside both launchers' arcs of fire. He plunged the manipulator down, tore away the heavy hatch over the driver's position, and discharged the small laser in his left arm down into the tank. Steam boiled up around him as the energy beam flash-boiled the bodily fluids of the hapless driver within.

Aleks raced toward the broad highway running from the great floodgates. Explosions ripped street and structures as the Lyran armor fired desperately at racing Falcon 'Mechs and Elementals. The impacts of the *Gyrfalcon*'s feet buckled pavement and jarred up into Aleks' tailbone. He scarcely noted the punishment, as he barely noticed the heat building in the cockpit. He was inured; this had been his home from an early age. It had been the first environment totally under his control—the first over which he had any degree of control whatever.

Past the end of the warehouse, a Demon wheeled tank was burning in the middle of the highway. The *Ryoken II* appeared at the corner, silhouetted against the beacon-like yellow flame. Its two twenty-millimeter autocannon chattered from its torso.

Not even Clan Jade Falcon's most proficient MechWarrior—which Aleks was, after Malvina—had reflexes faster than cannon shells. But Aleks had a seasoned fighter's cunning; he anticipated both the *Ryoken II*'s appearance at just that spot and its pilot's response to seeing him. He had already triggered his jump jets when von Kleist triggered her guns.

One burst raked the inside of the *Gyr*'s left thigh. Aleks' display lit red: he processed the information without conscious thought: *grazing hit, armor penetrated, a few sensors lost but no function.*

A beat after firing her autocannon the Porriman volleyed her shoulder-mounted LRMs. But she had been aiming for Aleks on the ground; the rockets drew a twisting skein of smoke trails beneath and around his 'Mech's legs without any striking him. As he soared over the enemy 'Mech he kicked the cockpit at the front of its fuselage—it was built more like an aircraft with arms and legs than a human. In years past, the Clans had generally disdained physical 'Mech combat. That was beginning to change; though some still adhered to the unwritten code against physical attacks, Aleks was not one of them.

Von Kleist's reflexes were surprisingly fast for an Inner

Sphere warrior. She managed to slip the blow's brunt by thrusting hard with her left leg, even though that and the glancing kick threatened to topple her. Instead, she slammed into the façade of the building across from the warehouse. Cement cast to look like cut-stone block exploded in powder and shards—and the *Ryoken II* bounced right back onto its raptor-clawed feet.

But Aleks, using his jets and the rebounding energy of his own kick, had spun while still airborne. He touched down behind the Lyran BattleMech, so close he could almost reach his machine's arms out and touch his foe. Von Kleist spun her 'Mech's "fuselage" without moving its feet in a desperate attempt to bring weapons to bear.

Aleks triggered both large lasers, sending his own heat soaring. Dazzling ruby beams converged on the *Ryoken II*'s right-leg actuator.

Blue dazzle arced like a cutting torch as the tough aligned-crystal-steel armor and the myomer pseudo-muscle beneath flashed into vapor. The 'Mech's right leg blew off in a shower of sparks and fragments. So violent was the reaction that the fifteen-missile launch box mounted on its right shoulder blew open; half the ready missiles' propellant lit off in a crackling series of sympathetic explosions.

The brutal noise reverberated between the industrial building-fronts, muted by Aleks' cockpit, which computer-filtered out potentially damaging levels or frequencies of sound. He could still clearly hear shrieks behind him as Lyran infantrymen were set ablaze by Elemental flamers or dismembered by their powerful claws. He felt a stab, not of triumph, but of sympathy: *these are brave men and women to face BattleMechs and battle armor unarmored, with nothing more than small arms and a few support weapons.* They died bravely, but hard.

But flesh and mere human will could take only so much. Especially when the whole supporting armored column was now shattered and ablaze.

"Aleks," Magnus Icaza's voice said in his ear, as his heat indicator retreated back through orange, "it is done. The last have thrown down their weapons and fled. The gate controls were secured without loss to either side: the crews saw reason."

And no dishonor, to Aleks' mind: the crews were techs,

not warriors. Not all Clanners felt the same. Yet to him, expecting techs and laborers to fight like warriors itself bordered on *chalcas*.

"All units Zeta Command Binary cease fire," Aleks directed at once. "Do not pursue, fire only if fired upon." Then on a restricted channel: "What is the butcher's bill, Magnus?"

The Elemental chuckled. "No damage done to man or machine," he said, "that a little time in the shop won't set right. Your pet Ghost Bear got his 'Mech's arm pinned solid for him. And my armor needs a new coat of paint."

"Well done," Aleks said to his whole Binary. "Now open the gates."

Aleksandr the conqueror strode tree-shaded streets he had made his. Although the raid sent to seize the planetary governor, Countess Orianna Steiner, had failed, the city administrator and the southern continent's governor had yielded to Aleks' radioed demand when he had the floodgates thrown open. Indeed, it was the first communication he had accepted from them, since his fear was they would roll over too soon. Now that he desired their capitulation, and quickly, he had sweetened the pot by promising they had no intention of staying, and would be off-planet and headed out-system before another sunrise.

The defenders who still hung on with admirable, if doomed, tenacity between the walls and the attackers approaching from outside had gratefully obeyed their commanders' orders to lay down their arms. They had also obeyed their conqueror's orders, relayed through the loudspeakers of his fighting machines, to disperse into the surrounding suburbs and countryside. Aleks desired neither gratuitous slaughter nor to be burdened with prisoners for the few hours he intended to remain upon Porrima. Broadcasting that anything, human or vehicle, armed or not, spotted moving within five hundred meters of the forces outside the walls would be instantly destroyed had the desired effect of moving along the surrendered troops.

He had made a token pass through downtown, mainly to impress upon the local authorities that they were to cooperate entirely with the team of scientists and high-level and specialist technicians who would choose the Falcons' *isorla*, or plunder. It would consist of low-mass and -volume items, primarily data, although technology of sufficient novelty or interest would also be taken. Gone were the days when any Clan enjoyed a decisive technological edge over the Inner Sphere; the top scientists worried out loud that the Clans might be in some ways falling behind, though Jade Falcon kept better abreast than most of technological developments in the Sphere by means of their large and active merchant class. Especially here in affluent, forward-thinking Steinerspace—most especially on a world of such emotional, if not enormous strategic or economic, import to the Commonwealth's ruling house—the raiders might well find lore or artifacts new to Turkina's brood.

Now Aleks toured a pleasant subdivision outside the walls, not a kilometer from the Archon Katrina Spaceport. Curious to see for himself how the Spheroids lived.

A mixed security detachment of Eyrie and Solahma infantry trotted warily behind and to either side of him. A BattleMech stood on the suburb's edge. It was a light machine, an *Eyrie*, only thirty-five tons, but its alien appearance with flamboyant wings deployed was overawing to Inner Sphere civilians whose sole experience of 'Mechs had been on tri-vid or the odd Archon's birthday parades; and the advanced tactical missiles and lasers packed into its arms and torso provided enough authentic menace to squelch any thought of resistance. And had it not, Aleks' own *Gyrfalcon,* parked up the street, lent the *Eyrie* all the authority it needed.

An Elemental Point also accompanied him, leaping on their jump jets to maximize their own visibility to the apprehensive faces peering out windows. One battlesuit was a classic Toad, its snarling, wings-spread portrait of Turkina badly chipped, with bright streaks of metal exposed by Bulldog minigun bullets.

The streets were deserted. The day was hot and humid; the air redolent of peculiar odors: cooking oils and indigenous spices, diesel exhaust, the smell of summer-lush foliage, itself unfamiliar yet somehow unmistakable; a faint hint of decaying fish from the mud flats. And the smell, just tainting the somewhat sluggish breeze, of burning. Buildings. Machines. Oil. *People. That* smell, Aleks knew, would linger for days in air and hair and clothes. And longer in the people's memory.

Though his mouth smiled, it was primarily out of habit, despite his triumph.

No trace of devastation showed here. Devastation had been kept to a minimum. Yet Aleks' spirit was troubled.

Is not the object of our Crusade to free the people of the Inner Sphere from their incompetent and barbarous overlords, and deliver them from the horrors of civil war and disorder? he kept asking himself. *Yet we have not brought the blessings of rational Clan life and all-important order to Porrima: all we brought is destruction, controlled or not; and that is all we shall leave behind us.*

If successful, the *desant* might pave the way for Porrima's eventual liberation by his Clan's Touman. *But still—*

He shrugged his wide shoulders. Which were bare: he wore his cooling vest, his coolsock, trunks, short boots, a synthetic-mesh belt supporting a holstered pulse-laser pistol, and nothing else, having climbed straight down from the Lily's cockpit. He was not the sort to brood or plague himself with his thoughts, albeit for reasons different than most Jade Falcons, even in the throes of the systemic slump following the adrenaline jag of battle.

We are destined by the Founder's will to save these people. Yet in the process we are compelled to frighten, displace, injure and sometimes kill them. That is simple reality. Such is our burden as Clan warriors.

He headed toward a hoverbus kiosk that was plastered with bright placards, set diagonally across from a refueling point for civilian ICE vehicles, currently deserted. It had a cement bench well-shaded by maroon-leafed trees with widespread branches springing out like parasols from about seven meters up straight, grainy-barked boles.

As he walked, he waved at the battle armor with the chipped enamel, which never strayed far. "Hoy, Magnus. Trust your troops to keep me safe and join me; you've not been out of that can all day."

He wore a headset with boom mike. He didn't bother activating it, but let the Elemental Star Colonel's external pickups convey his words. The bulky suit descended toward him on small blue flames.

"Refreshments," Aleks told the Eyrie warrior in charge of the infantry detail. He nodded toward the fuel stop. "Inside you should find a machine dispensing cold beverages. Bring some for me and the Star Colonel, then distribute them to your people."

The young woman bobbed her helmeted head and barked earnest orders to her troops. Aleks smiled, pleased with his knowledge of alien culture.

An older trooper with his full-head helmet tipped back on his close-cropped graying hair came over bearing two cans. The gaudy printing on their thin-gauge metal skins was already glazed with condensation. They had been secured by the simple expedient of one of Magnus' Elementals grounding, walking through the security-reinforced front door—without the formality of opening it first, far less bothering to unlock it—and wrenching the door off the dispensing machine.

Alex took both cans with a nod of thanks. He sat down on the shaded bench, placed one can beside him, popped the opener, and drank, savoring the coolness and crisp alien sweetness. A breeze ruffled his hair with thick fingers.

Magnus stood in the middle of the intersection as the traffic-control lamps cycled disregarded from green to amber to red above the domed top of his suit. The Star Colonel's cheery nature did nothing to vitiate a much-seasoned warrior's wariness. Temporarily mollified by the scene's slumbering tranquility he lumbered over to plant the armor's broad foot-pods in the shade near his leader's bench.

He popped the seal with a hiss of equalizing air pressure. "Why do we loiter here, small Aleksandr? What *isorla* do you think to find?"

Aleks laughed. "Knowledge. Understanding of the people we have come to help."

Grinning, the red-bearded giant shook his head. His carapace's breastplate had swung open, revealing his head and powerful torso down to the trunks which, with his coolsock, constituted his sole garments. Notwithstanding their girth, his fingers were deft as they unfastened various sensors from his skin.

Then he stiffened and thrust his arms back into the arms of his battle armor. His suit was powered down: a metric ton of inert mass, it was almost impossible for even the strongest of Elementals to budge it by muscle power alone.

Magnus Icaza was among the strongest of Elementals. He made the powered-down suit lunge forward three meters at running speed for a normal human. The manipulator-tipped right arm swung, striking Aleks in the center of the chest, knocking him over the back of the bench.

It was as if a black explosion went off behind Aleks' sternum. The air was smashed from his lungs by the impact of the massive armored club. As he toppled he saw a line of dirty white smoke streaking toward him from the alley just north of the fuel stop.

It was a short-range missile fired from a man-portable launcher. It struck Magnus Icaza at the left side of his chest, right at the edge of his open armor shell, and detonated with a white flash that momentarily blinded Aleks.

Falling behind the cement bench saved the Galaxy Commander from flame and fragments. Overpressure withheld air from his empty lungs. The other Elementals of Aleks' escort let go all six of their own shoulder-mounted SRMs at once toward the point from which the shot had come, while the unpowered infantry added a crackling volley from their Gauss rifles. The whole brick side of a dry cleaners collapsed onto the Porriman missile crew.

A Solahma infantryman knelt above Aleks, concern on his face. Aleks waved him away, clambered to his feet as briskly as he could. He had cracked the back of his head hard on the ground and trying to breathe felt like daggers through his chest where his friend had struck him with the arm of his suit.

When Aleks knelt in turn over Magnus Icaza, his friend still lived. Somehow. The one remaining blue eye opened and recognized Aleks, the scorched and shredded lips smiled; and the one lung still extant, fully exposed in the seared and excavated cavern of rib cage, provided air for the Elemental to speak.

"Have a . . . care, my friend," he croaked. "It is not the fighting that kills you, but the downtime. . . ."

Pink froth bubbled from his lips. He died.

Aleks rose. A single tear cut a track through dust and cinders on a cheek that was frozen like a slab of fired clay.

"Let them learn what befalls those who treacherously murder a warrior of Clan Jade Falcon," he said in a voice like a raven's croak. "Destroy the district. Leave no building intact, nor anything living within."

PART TWO

Desant

". . . (1) *n.* Descent; *esp.,* an airmobile landing operation, generally to attack strategic targets deep in an enemy's rear areas. *Russ.* From Soviet Military Art, Terra. *Archaic.*"

—*New Avalon Institute of Science Unabridged Dictionary of the English Language,* Edition CCCV, New Avalon, Federated Suns, 3032

8

Central Government Complex
Geneva, Terra
Prefecture X
The Republic of the Sphere
3 April 3134

The hush between the briefing room's powder blue walls was almost palpable as Tara Campbell, Countess Northwind and Prefect of Prefecture III, and her aide-de-camp, Captain Tara Bishop, were solemnly ushered within by an aide. Exarch Damien Redburn did not rise from his central position on the far side of the long, truncated-oval table.

The ruler of The Republic of the Sphere and successor to Devlin Stone nodded his narrow, brown-haired head. "Countess Campbell," he said, "it is good of you to come on such short notice."

"The Secretary's message indicated it was a matter of grave concern to The Republic," Tara Campbell said. The Countess' gaze did not quiver by a micron from his, but she could feel the pressure of her aide's eyes like heat upon her cheek. The lack of any discernible quantum of irony in Redburn's voice only emphasized the seriousness of the matter that had caused the two to be summoned here. Because, in truth, the Countess Northwind and the Exarch, duly elected ruler of The Republic to which she had sworn her life to serve, cordially detested one another.

The two women settled themselves into seats across the table from the Exarch. Various other high officials were present. They acknowledged the women from Northwind with muted mutters of greeting.

Exarch Redburn placed his hands interlaced on the table before him. "At 0533 this morning, local time, we received a communication from our HPG net. It came within the scope of our restored coverage at Imbros III in Prefecture I. Prior to that, the information was carried via a virtual command circuit—passed on from JumpShips entering systems to the next ship jumping out in the direction of the Core."

He looked to the end of the table at an aide with the flashes of Republic Military Intelligence on her tunic. "Major Kiyosaki, if you will provide particulars."

"Yes, Exarch." The woman rose. Her hair hung across her forehead in a coppery bang. Her eyes were almond shaped and dark.

"Some weeks ago a Clan Sea Fox merchant JumpShip was preparing to depart from the zenith point of Kandersteg, in the Lyran Commonwealth, not far from the Jade Falcon Occupation Zone. Just before it jumped for New Exford, it detected a transmission from the observation station located at the system's apex proximity point. It was a panicky broadcast, intended for planetary authorities. It included video images."

The room darkened. The space behind Major Kiyosaki evidently contained a large tri-vid set, because that end of the room abruptly filled with stars. The viewpoint dove dizzily toward a central cluster of light-points seeming brighter than the rest. Unlike the stars, these grew in apparent size, became disks.

"JumpShip light sails," Captain Bishop murmured. Then, in surprise: "A good half dozen of them!"

As she said this Tara Campbell's eyes began to resolve the image painted on the sunward surface. She knew it before she could make out any detail, just by general outline. "Jade Falcon?" she asked in wonder.

As if there was any other possibility, she chided herself at once. Her stomach, which had begun to feel as if it was sinking through some extraspatial dimension at the mention of the words *Jade Falcon Occupation Zone* went into full reentry free fall.

"A Jade Falcon fleet," the Major intoned, "apparently out of the Falcon Zone. Yet that was not the most unsettling thing."

The circular sails continued to grow. Then the stars swam as the display centered upon one particular sail. It expanded until the JumpShip itself, tiny by comparison, appeared like a seed pod, attached to the sail by invisible cords.

"But that can't be—" Tara Campbell said.

Kiyosaki nodded. "A WarShip."

Tara shook her head, not in refutation of the intel major's words, but in denial of what her eyes were telling her. "Not just a WarShip, but a battleship," she said. "I've seen them in books. An actual *battleship.*"

"*Nightlord* class, we believe," the Exarch said, so as not to be excluded.

"Yes, sir," Major Kiyosaki said. "From its outline our archivists have tentatively identified it as the Jade Falcon Naval Reserve *Emerald Talon.* It took part in the invasion of 3049. After the Smoke Jaguars' genocidal bombardment from orbit of the city of Edo on Turtle Bay produced a surge of revulsion among the Clanners themselves, Clan Wolf took the lead in ostentatiously bidding away all naval assets in all future actions. The other Clans had to follow suit or lose face. All WarShips were recalled to the home worlds. The *Talon* went with them."

"And now she's back," Tara Campbell said. The fingers of her right hand played a quick arpeggio on the table. She frowned. "The Falcons are invading the Commonwealth, then?"

The virtual model of the battleship behind Kiyosaki was replaced by a stylized star map of the outward reaches of Steinerspace, where they fetched up against the Falcon zone. "As you can see, Countess Northwind, the fleet would have had to have made one jump into the Lyran Commonwealth already, via Graceland, to reach Kandersteg. A JumpShip arriving at the nadir jump point from

Graceland shortly before the Jade Falcon emergence brought no mention of any Clan attack. Apparently the Falcons escaped detection in the Graceland system altogether."

Tara's diplomatic-corps upbringing allowed her to mask her surprise. Kandersteg certainly seemed to be receiving a substantial amount of JumpShip traffic despite the HPG collapse. Her own home on Northwind seldom saw JumpShips these days.

"Countess," Captain Bishop said in a low voice.

"Speak up, Captain," Tara Campbell said.

"In the past, whenever the Clans have come to call, they've killed people and broken things at every step along the way. Does that accord with what your archivists have to say, Major, ma'am?"

"It does."

"So it certainly appears that whatever they're up to, the Falcons aren't invading Steinerspace. Or at least they're sure not going about it in their classic manner."

Tara Campbell's eyes narrowed as she studied the star map. "But they brought a battleship—not to mention that many JumpShips—for *something*. How did this tidbit happen to fall into our command circuit?"

"Apparently the Sea Foxes hastily recalculated their jump and went to Grunwald instead," the Exarch said, "heading for the Inner Sphere. They passed the data along to a Lyran trader at Arcturus, in Wolf territory."

Tara felt the skin contract on her face as if the room's carefully conditioned air had suddenly become dry as the lunar surface. She did not like or trust any Clanner. *Dislike* and *distrust* were paltry euphemisms for the feelings she harbored for the Wolves.

"The Wolves trade with everybody," said General Cordesman, who sat to the Exarch's left. "Everyone does, and has for generations. Including the Falcons."

"Even had Clan Wolf learned somehow of the message the Sea Foxes carried," Major Kiyosaki said, "we believe it unlikely they would have tried to prevent it reaching The Republic of the Sphere. It's a tossup as to who hates the Falcons more, the Wolves or the Foxes."

"Why did the Sea Foxes assume the Falcons were headed for The Republic?" Captain Bishop asked, not bothering to petition for the floor this time. "For that matter, why do we? A line drawn from Graceland through Kandersteg heads them right into the middle of the Commonwealth."

"But, just as you pointed out," Tara said, "their behavior is inconsistent with an invasion of Steinerspace. It's as if—"

She turned to the Exarch. "—as if they don't want to be slowed down on their way to their real goal. And what target would they want badly enough to commit so large a portion of their total military resources, so deep in the Commonwealth?"

Redburn looked around the table. "A decapitation strike at Tharkad?" Cordesman suggested. He had a heavy, deeply lined face and bristling eyebrows. "Perhaps they feel they can conquer the Commonwealth by destroying the Archon and her government at a stroke."

"They haven't learned from their mistakes if they think that," Captain Bishop said. "I know the Clans disdain any history but their own, but even they have to've noticed that taking out Inner Sphere leaders doesn't stop their subjects from fighting Clan conquest tooth and nail. The Clanners can be mighty thick-headed at times, but few of them are actually stupid. Ahh. General. Sir."

Everybody had turned to stare at the junior officer with the temerity to speak right out among so many stars and important civilians.

"They're headed here," Tara Campbell said quietly but firmly across the silence.

Redburn sat a moment, gazing at her with eyes sunk deep in his skull. He glanced at the high-ranking officers who flanked him. "We dare not operate on any other assumption," he said in a voice as papery as a dried corn husk.

Tara turned back to the display. The circuits in her head were working madly. "They won't come near to following the path the Foxes took," she said, "because for the Falcons to take a WarShip into Wolf space would mean instant, all-out war between them. Raids're one thing; a battleship is quite another."

She paused, then shook her head. *What a bother! To have to think of people who hate Clan Wolf as much as I do as enemies!*

Aloud, she went on: "So, if we stipulate that their target

is The Republic—and I agree with you, Exarch"—with effort, she forbore from adding, *for once*, out loud, anyway— "that we dare not assume anything else—they will probably enter our territory in Prefecture IX."

"Which, Countess Northwind," the Exarch said, flattening his palms on the table before him, "is why I have decided to dispatch you at once to Skye, the Prefectural capital, to begin organizing a defense against a possible invasion of The Republic of the Sphere. Which honesty compels me to warn you will be a most desperate undertaking indeed."

She stared at him. It was as if the air had solidified within the column of her throat.

"What about the Triarii Protectors IX?" she asked. "The Principes Guards and Hastati Sentinels?"

"It is this *peace*," Cordesman said, not bothering to conceal leaden distaste. "The golden age: the universal drawdown of forces, the pressure from the Senate and the civilians to keep spending less and less on the military."

He sighed. He did not acknowledge either the Exarch's look of mild alarm or Tara's narrow-eyed anger at his criticism of policies which sprang from Devlin Stone himself.

"In sum, Countess, the three Republican regular combined-arms regiments charged with defending Prefecture IX are paper tigers—as they were even before the HPG went down and Jasek Kelswa-Steiner seduced the lion's share of their remnants into his Stormhammer regiment, gutting Skye's militia into the bargain. Aside from whatever planetary forces may remain, Prefecture IX lies open to the Falcon fleet."

9

The Forest Primeval
Near New London, Skye
Prefecture IX
The Republic of the Sphere
30 April 3134

Overhead a virago screeched outrage at the intrusion. Much occupied by his thoughts, Duke Gregory Kelswa-Steiner, Governor of Skye and Lord Governor of Prefecture IX (and only the second to hold both titles), continued to ride, oblivious to the possibility the jaylike local bird-analogue might dislodge a hard, baby fist–sized seed pod from the lofty branches and drop it with remarkable accuracy on his head. He almost wished it would; it would give him a chance to vent some of the anger simmering within him by blasting the creature with the pulse-laser pistol in its flapped holster on the belt of his leather riding breeches.

His horse Iago's dark chestnut coat was sheened with sweat and the beast breathed hard despite the morning's early-autumn cool. The animal was a gelding. The Duke was a man's man, a qualified MechWarrior who had fought in The Republic's armed forces against the first Capellan invasion before resuming civilian life, and secure enough in that fact not to burden himself with an uncut stallion.

Which occurred to him in a most unflattering way in his almost-ritual daily thinking about his son, Jasek, and possible omissions he had made in the boy's upbringing.

Duke Gregory should have been a man at peace: a big, fit, middle-aged man in robust health, with most of his hair, and that seal brown going to distinguished silver at the temples. A crisp morning ride in beautiful woods outside the Prefectural capital of New London, with mountains close enough on one hand to break into view at times above the trees to the north, and Thames Bay close enough on the other to smell salt-sea breeze as well as sun-warmed leaves. The great trees were upon the cusp of turning, and late-season field insects sang sawing yet melodious tunes without awareness of the impending arrival of first frost to still their voices.

His domain enjoyed relative peace and order, unlike the Prefectures on the other side of The Republic, wracked by rebellion and factional warfare, or even Terra itself, which had suffered invasion by the Steel Wolves some months before—a poignant thing for the Duke, as for most Skyians, since Clan Wolf had played a key role in freeing Skye of the brutal violence of the Blakist Jihad decades before. It was part of his collective memory, as it had happened before his birth. Skye shared no boundaries with any Clan zone. Its only neighbor not of The Republic was the Lyran Commonwealth, of which Skye itself had once been part; and House Steiner still maintained, at least publicly, its cautious bourgeois approval of The Republic, and disavowed any interest in reclaiming the territory it had ceded to Devlin Stone. The Draconis Combine, an ancient enemy, lay dangerously near, it was true, as did the perilously disordered fragments of the Free Worlds League. Yet planet and Prefecture generally prospered.

He had, Duke Gregory knew, fortuitous placement between the core Prefecture X and the trade-minded Commonwealth to thank in large part for that fact, as for the relative rapidity with which Skye had recovered from the Jihad. Interstellar traffic had dropped sharply in the wake of the HPG collapse. Yet it had also rebounded, if not to pre-collapse levels. Without question, trade was facilitated by faster-than-light communications, yet it did not depend upon them. The nations of pre–space flight Terra had enjoyed substantial, even global trade long before they possessed means of communicating faster than a good ship could sail with favorable winds.

They had also seized, held and administered empires. That latter thought was not so comforting.

Which was only tangentially why the Duke scowled as he rode through the beautiful morning.

The main reason was none other than his son and, as soon as he got around to it, erstwhile heir: the Landgrave Jasek Kelswa-Steiner.

The problem was, the boy longed to be a hero. Which would not have been so bad. Except he had the stuff for it.

The Lord Governor bore no animosity toward the Lyrans nor their ruling family, House Steiner; best not, inasmuch as he had not found the latter half of his surname in a box of breakfast food.

Yet he was two things, and these deeply: a Skye patriot, glad in his heart that his home planet and most of the former Skye Protectorate had at last gained independence after centuries in the grasp of the iron Steiner fist. More even than that, he was a patriot of The Republic of the Sphere, and believed in it and in the transcendent vision of its vanished founder Devlin Stone.

Though no one had invaded Skye yet, nor seemed likely to anytime soon, all was not placid perfection. Below the surface tensions bubbled. And boiled over with increasing frequency into disputes, demonstrations, and of late even communal violence.

Most of the population felt as he did, though generally less fervently with regard to The Republic. But some among the English speakers, primarily of Scottish or Irish descent, longed for a time before the Steiners ruled Skye, when the planet was seat of its own vest-pocket empire, the Protectorate. These felt they had exchanged a foreign master on Tharkad for another on Terra. They viewed The Republic's diminished influence as a result of the HPG loss as an opportunity to seek true independence. If not more; a prospect the Duke knew annoyed and worried other planets of Skye's erstwhile dominion.

On the other hand, an extremely vocal minority among

the German speakers cried out for reannexation by the Lyran Commonwealth: *Anschluss.* The planet's most visible, and audible, agitator for resorption under Steiner rule was Arminius Herrmann. *Freiherr* von Herrmann, as he had recently if dubiously taken to styling himself, was the tall, stout, choleric scion of the family which owned controlling interest in Skye's, and indeed the Prefecture's, largest media corporation, Herrmanns AG.

Herrmann was a bumptious buffoon, a ripe target for caricature by media rivals—who were cheerfully aware of the fact, and egged on besides by Arminius' propensity to fly into trumpeting rages whenever someone landed a particularly barbed lampoon. Indeed, Duke Gregory believed the man's very name indicated a certain softness of the head had set into the Herrmann clan at least a generation back: *Don't the imbeciles realize "Arminius" and "Herrmann" are the same bloody name?*

Yet Herrmann possessed an uncomfortable degree of influence by virtue of his media control. His wealth and prominence gave him a substantial buffer, especially in a Republic dedicated to liberal principles of freedom of speech. He had never quite *crossed* the line into open sedition, although if it had been demarked with chalk, he'd have more than a few yellow stripes on his trousers.

And speaking of crossing the line . . . there was Landgrave Jasek.

The boy had been a dutiful lad, strong and smart and brave, as befit the heir to a noble house. The Duke had never seen reason to curb his love of the history, and most particularly lurid tri-vids and books recounting the glories, of the Lyran Commonwealth. That was part of the heritage of Skye—and his own birthright. All to the good.

Yet the romantic yarns had produced unhealthy effects on the boy. He had come to identify more with the Commonwealth than The Republic. His father, preoccupied with concerns of state—running a planet and a Prefecture was not an easy or uncomplicated job, even in what now seemed the lost Golden Age before the blackout—had seen no danger signs. Indeed, he had been proud when Jasek followed his own example, took military service and qualified as a MechWarrior, rising to command The Republic Skye Militia, distinguishing himself fighting raiders from the chaotic Marik-Stewart Commonwealth and *ronin* strikes out of the Combine.

Then came the blackout. Like most people with any vision past the ends of their noses, Duke Gregory felt foreboding: for the HPG net was the glue that held together the hard-won civilization represented by The Republic. He took solace in the fact that even though their numbers were continually pared by budget cuts, well-trained, well-seasoned troops under command of his son—his own son, heir to his name and title and estates—stood on hand in case the chaos came.

As it came to other planets, other Prefectures. Yet when young Jasek heard tales from JumpShip captains of what Duke Aaron Sandoval and Katana Tormark and others had done—the whole grim cavalcade of treason and opportunism—he took their actions in turning against The Republic they had sworn to serve as a clarion call.

Jasek had called together those soldiers of the sadly diminished regular regiments, the Hastati Sentinels, the Trirarii Protectors, and the Principes Guards IX, as well as his own Militia, who like him favored the Lyran Commonwealth over The Republic of the Sphere, or whose devotion to their beloved battle leader transcended their own sworn loyalty to The Republic. They acclaimed him their commander. He then declared for House Steiner and fled Skye literally steps ahead of an arrest-squad of his father's police under orders to bring the heir back at all costs, alive—or not.

It was as if the guts had been scooped out of Duke Gregory's defenses. And, when he thought about it—as he did now, as he did daily, if not hourly—of Duke Gregory himself.

The betrayal that rankled most of course was of him.

The young fool! thought Duke Gregory, taking his horse in a low jump over a fallen bole and resisting the temptation to vent his fury on the beast's flanks with his spurs. *He not only turns on the man who fathered and raised him, and The Republic which it was his family's—and his own—privilege to serve. He prates on about his love for Skye and her lost glory—and then when the skies darken and storms threaten our horizons, he abandons us and leaves us all but helpless!*

For the Duke was not deceived. Already the evil had struck at Terra herself. Despite apparent peace and prosperity—indeed, very much because of the latter—Prefecture IX and Skye herself would not remain untouched. Could not.

He raged inwardly as well against his kinsmen and women in Lyra. After the fact, his counterintelligence service had identified several likely Lohengrin operators among the Militia troops who lifted with the Landgrave. Duke Gregory had not failed to exact a measure of revenge: two more Lohengrins and a suspected Loki agent had been identified, and quietly eliminated on his personal orders.

Obviously House Steiner felt it served their ends that young Jasek should wrest a powerful weapon from The Republic's hands and place it in theirs. For the sake of strengthening themselves rather than weakening The Republic, the Archon's government had assured Duke Gregory in an unofficial official communiqué delivered under the rose. The cynical, expertly political side of him was even inclined to believe that, although his office in the Planetary Governor's New Glasgow seat had required extensive remodeling after he received the note.

Yet even if the armored fist of Steiner disdained to pluck the ripe and newly undefended fruit of Prefecture IX, Duke Gregory Kelswa-Steiner knew someone would accept the invitation.

Thanks to the faithless brat. Bastard in fact if not in law— and the one good thing about his mother's premature death is that she did not live to see that fact made manifest.

He stuck a dagger in my back. Such blades can cut in both directions.

It could happen. It had been known to happen—in the greatest of Houses. There was a dark strain in the Kelswa blood, the Duke was aware. House Steiner itself had not been free of internecine violence. . . .

There was much to be said for . . . extrajudicial . . . handling of his son's treason. The Republic itself would strenuously disapprove such action. Should they chance to become aware of it. The universe had always been a place where deadly mishaps occurred as if by chance, and all the moreso since the HPG collapse. Removing his all-too-capable heir might well prove a signal service to The Republic: the current forbearance of Jasek by reason of apathy of House Steiner toward The Republic and the former Lyran holdings therein could change at the whim of the Archon, and the whims of princes were notoriously mercurial.

Or the reigning Archon could change—the whims of Fate being more infamously mercurial still.

I could, I could so . . . The Duke's thoughts trended toward a dark place. Yet there was that within him which bid him *pull back, pull back.* . . .

The personal communicator hung at his belt, as if to counterbalance the laser pistol, buzzed for attention like an amplified insect. He became aware that he had all unthinking urged his horse into a full gallop, a reckless pace to set among the thick but widely spaced trunks of the forest giants rearing sixty meters and more above his head, with sometimes fallen limbs to cause a stumble. His horse's flanks were even darker than usual with sweat and his nostrils distended. The Duke reined in to a walk, patting the beast on the neck and cooing apologetically as it bobbed its head and blew. He felt chagrin: it was not the Duke's way to use any creature so, without consideration.

Overhead a tilt-rotor scout VTOL, scrupulously unseen, maintained a watch on the Duke via forward-looking infrared and televisions with telescope lenses. It conveyed the Duke's approximate location and vector to the lance of hoverbike troops maintaining a loose moving perimeter about him—while staying themselves out of eye- and earshot—and the lance of attack VTOL keeping similarly discreet watch from somewhere above the treetops. Before the HPG collapse he would never have countenanced such a thing. Now, with civil unrest on the rise and shadowy menaces moving, unseen, in a universe grown dark with the end of instantaneous interstellar communications, he still did not welcome such nursemaiding. Hence the bodyguards' extreme diligence to avoid actually making their presence manifest to their charge. He would still not have accepted it, certainly not ordered it, had his chief minister not insisted.

Ah, Solvaig, he thought with a certain guarded warmth—which was generally the only kind of warmth he allowed himself to feel, especially since. . . . *How lost would I and Skye be without you?*

At last he stripped the riding glove from his hand and took out the communicator, which had maintained its ungentle insistence all along. "Yes?" he said in a clipped tone that served to reinforce what the party at the other end must well have known: *this better be important.*

"Your Grace," said the professionally anonymous voice. "We have just received a double communication from the zenith proximity point. A JumpShip has emerged, outbound from Terra; we have word of its arrival from our observation station, as well as a communication from the vessel herself."

Duke Gregory's brows beetled. He had wonderful brows for the gesture: as he had grown older they had become bushier, shot with fierce, longer black strands. Now the shorter hairs were brushed with gray as was his beard, leading to a most striking effect.

"What does the JumpShip captain say?"

"She brings with her Tara Campbell, Countess of Northwind and Prefect of Prefecture III, your Grace. The Countess herself transmitted a coded signal containing the appropriate courtesies. She has also informed us that she, her staff, and elements of her Highlander regiments are inbound for Skye with an estimated arrival time of forty-seven hours, and in The Republic's name begs leave to be allowed to make planetfall at the New London spaceport soonest."

Now the Duke's splendid brows rose. *The Exarch's pet poster girl herself sees fit to grace my world with her presence,* he thought. *On some business she dares not even entrust to Prefectural-level encryption.*

She was sending an unmistakably clear message, however: the transit time from Skye's jump points to planetary orbit was four days, relatively trivial as such things went; Alkaid in Duke Gregory's own Prefecture had a transit time of 124 days. The Countess' projected arrival indicated her DropShip was burning insystem at two gees, the maximum acceleration considered safe and twice the normal. That she would subject self, staff, troops, and the DropShip crew to the brutal discomfort of two full days at twice normal weight to shave a trifling two days off her transit time spoke volumes.

It also, he thought with an amused quirk of his bearded lips, indicated her intentions were pacific toward the planet of Skye. So taxing was it on the human system to sustain higher-than-standard gees that it was a rare and rash commander who used them on an invasion drop. Two days of their hearts pumping blood against twice the normal resistance would leave the ship's occupants as drained as if they had run multiple marathons, even if all they did was lie on couches, which unless they were fools *was* what they were doing.

"Return the appropriate acknowledgment and permissions," he commanded. "Add that I am most eager to receive the Countess so soon as she may have recovered from the rigors of her journey."

The subtext of the tri-vids would seem to be justified, he thought with certain scorn. *Fluff-headed glamour girl! She'll no doubt be more than two days recovering abed, mere slip that she is.*

He gazed around him at the glory of the trees and their gilt-edged leaves in the golden-yellow glow of the Sol-like sun, then sighed, filling the lungs in his substantial chest with a last free draught of autumn air like the finest vintage wine. He had an intimation that this was his last unencumbered breath of wild air for a long time. If he once again smelled the smell of woods before the year's turning, he suspected, it would be in the field—and not on maneuvers.

"There is a clearing some three hundred meters to the northwest of my position," he said, and spoke coordinates from the map-display on the datapad strapped to his thick, hairy wrist. It kept track of his position by a combination of inertial tracking and analysis of known patterns of geomagnetism; it would not do, in today's unsettled environment, to have the Duke of Skye constantly broadcasting his location to anyone with the nominal equipment and only slightly less nominal know-how required to crack the satellite positioning system. "Order a cargo VTOL to pick up me and my horse. I return to the Prefectural compound at once."

"Sir?" the voice said. "Might I remind your Grace that the Countess is not due for another—"

"You have," he said crisply but not harshly. He had no desire to surround himself with toadies, preferring forthright subordinates who exercised initiative. It did not guarantee them immunity from outbursts of his famous temper; but no one had actually suffered harm to career, much less person, from the competent discharge of duty. Indeed, no few had benefited from ducal repentance of hasty words, although it was not the Lord Governor's way to apologize in words.

Now, strangely, the blackness of his prior mood had lifted. He was faced with a puzzle. And while it would undoubtedly complicate the Duke's life still further, something about it quickened his hunter's blood.

"Whatever tidings the Countess is bringing us, I suspect two days will be no more than enough to prepare to hear them," he told his communicator. "The Duke out."

He snapped the small device shut and reholstered it. Then he leaned forward to slap the neck of his horse, now halted and stretching to crop maroon bunch grass, and murmur a few endearments.

He would make quickly for the clearing and his rendezvous with the VTOL; the aircraft was standing by in New London a few minutes' flight time away against just such contingencies.

But first he would visit a stream he knew nearby to let Iago drink of cold waters, down from the mountains already capped with snow. It was the least he could do, for having pushed the animal so.

10

Jade Falcon Naval Reserve Battleship Emerald
  Talon
Jump Point
Whittington
Lyran Commonwealth
30 April 3134

Malvina Hazen launched herself toward her brother in a
blinding-fast spring. A slim twenty-centimeter leaf of razor-
honed Endo steel glinted in her hand.

Aleks' dark mass of hair formed a flash halo about his
head as he pivoted right. The dagger missed his cheek by
a centimeter. His big left hand swept out, seemed no more
than to brush his sister's back.

She flew forward. But tucking chin to clavicle she turned
uncontrolled flight into a half-roll, ending with the bare
soles of her feet planted against the grav-deck exercise
compartment's padded bulkhead.

Instantly she sprang away, turning in midair to come
down in a crouch facing Aleks, her dagger held reversed,
blade flat along her slim pallid forearm. "Why did you not
cut me?" she demanded. "You had clear opportunity."

He laughed and shrugged his massive shoulders. "Time enough."

She straightened, scowling ferociously. It just made him laugh again. "You always look like an angry child when you scrunch your face like that."

Her expression mellowed as she walked toward him. She wore white trunks and a sports halter. He made do with trunks alone. Jade Falcon regulations for live-blade knife practice specified goggles and belly-protectors: attrition to their extreme-Darwinian customs was severe enough without every realistic practice session ending in the death or long-term incapacitation for duty of one or more warriors.

As was not at all unusual for them, both sibkin ignored the regulation. Such hardly pertained to Galaxy Commanders, or were even intended to. And besides, they'd ignored the regulations they disliked all their lives—and answered each and every one of the frequent challenges arising therefrom on the duelling grounds.

Upon which, famously, Aleks had never allowed a foe to die. Nor Malvina, one to live.

In this, in practice, they knew themselves well-matched. Why rob themselves of the benefits of practicing all-out, with real danger to hone the edge? Each felt that if she or he could not prevent themselves suffering serious harm, they so deserved to suffer.

"Or is this more of your damned *compassion*?" she demanded, voice husky with scorn. "If so, then look well and see how false it is, now and always: if you do not go all out against me, how can I practice for the real thing?"

She was near him now, touch range. And flowed forward like a striking snake, blade licking out to lash across his belly and side.

Steel sang upon steel. His own blade was a mere ten centimeters long, with a broad single-edged right-triangular blade. It was actually his back-up; when in the field, even in the cockpit of White Lily, he bore a thirty-centimeter blade, clipped and sharpened halfway down the back from the point, as much short sword or machete as fighting dagger: a classic Bowie. It weighed a full kilogram—a brutal mass for knife to be wielded by a normal human. While he could wield the monster *almost* as fast as he could his bare fist, he believed that speed beat all in a knife fight.

And in any event, he claimed, his Bowie was such a potent weapon there was hardly any *point* to practicing with it.

Like her he held his knife tip-downward from his hand. He barely had to pivot his arm at the elbow to block her strike. At the same time, grinning like a handsome gargoyle, he turned about his body's center line and took his sister with a pistoning palm-heel strike on the sternum, between her small but full breasts.

She flew backward all the way to the wall. The long ice-white queue in which she wore her hair slapped the padding a beat after her body did, with as loud a sound.

He knew better than to snag her braid, did Aleks. She left it loose by design—as a lure to the unwary. Like all her muscles, those of her neck were like a BattleMech's myomer bundles, and she was agile as an interstellar gymnast; anybody thinking to break her neck or otherwise control her only found themselves stuck to her, to their severe if not fatal dismay. It was a particularly poor move in a knife fight, since her riposte when her hair was grabbed was to reel herself in close and stab like a snake striking: about a dozen shots to the softest available target. Even with her holdout knife—pretty much the same her sibkin used—she could unstitch somebody's guts in about the time it took them to gasp in horrified surprise.

"It is natural to take pity upon such a tiny little girl as you," Aleks said. "Even one so tricky."

She laughed. *"Surat."*

She pushed herself away from the wall and advanced again, this time stalking like a killer cat, keeping all her inconsequential weight upon her planted foot while extending the other, not transferring any until the leading sole laid flat on the floor before her. She circled toward his left, away from his stubby blade.

"You think to anger me," she said. "Good tactics, brother dear—so long as you forget all the practice we both have had in swallowing our rage!"

She darted to her right, his left. He lunged forward with speed scarcely less blinding than hers for all he outmassed her cleanly two to one. His arm streaked toward her face in what was more than anything a straight punch—but aimed to lay open her cheek with the blade trailing from his huge dark fist.

Her own move had been a feint. As he committed himself to his charge she turned and simply jumped *at* him. Her left arm extended, elbow slightly bent, fingers of her open hand extended to touch an imaginary plane extended from her body's center line; the outside of her arm struck the inside of his knife arm just above the elbow, too far for a wrist roll to cut her with his short weapon. At the same time she wrapped both legs about his narrow waist, kissed him quickly on the lips, and sliced his cheek above the high prominent bone with a quick, vicious cut.

At once Malvina launched herself into a back flip. It would land her outside reach of a retaliatory strike, and him with his weight still on his heels, to keep himself from falling backwards when she struck him.

But her sibkin's neuromusculature was as Clan-bred as her own, his training as brutally Clan-intensive. Even off-balance he managed to lash out. The tip of his blade flicked lightly across the swell of her left buttock, slicing silvery synthel fabric and white skin.

She landed on her bare feet, harder than intended, staggered back several steps to regain her own balance. "Damn you!" she yelped. "That *stung*."

He laughed. "You will remember me when next you sit in the cockpit of the Black Rose," he said. Which would be for the invasion of Chaffee, after the jump for which their fleets now recharged using their solar sails, here in Whittington system. In a matter of days the *desant* would at last land in force upon its first true objective.

Malvina circled to Aleks' left again, weaving her hands before her with her fighting blade laid against the inside of her slim white forearm. The pulse in her wrist made the blade jump just at the edge of visibility.

Aleks gave the weapon no more than a cursory glance. Malvina's sinuous motions intended to render it difficult for her opponent to calculate a way past her defenses, or know when or from what angle she would launch a strike. It was also meant literally to hypnotize a foe; if an opponent made the mistake of watching her hands too long, especially her knife hand, she would program him, with surprising quickness, to anticipate her patterns even though they appeared random. Then she would strike from an unforeseen angle.

It was a killer technique—again, literally. Aleks had seen it work in duels. To prevent it working on *him*—since he knew from bitter experience that foreknowledge would not protect him if he allowed himself to watch her hands—he kept his eyes in soft focus, intent upon her shoulders. They were a far better indicator of imminent action anyway, though Malvina was expert at avoiding telegraphing of any sort.

"I am glad you showed some spirit," she said, smiling. "I had begun to fear your famous compassion was getting the better of you."

His brown eyes narrowed slightly and his nostrils flared. That was a cheap shot. Aleks had shed more tears after Porrima than the single one he allowed himself in the doomed suburb where Magnus died. Not even he, renowned, feared, admired as he was, dared weep openly in front of Clanners. Except Malvina, holding his head to her breast in bed in her quarters aboard her own flag JumpShip *Black Dalliance*. In her arms he let go entirely of his iron self-control and the tears flowed like waterfalls. Not for the first time; but for the first time in years.

He also knew, quite well, she was trying to provoke him. An angry fighter makes mistakes. All combat at all levels of scale, from interstellar wars to tête-à-tête duels such as this one, hinged ultimately on who made the fewer, or less telling, mistakes. And no fighting more than knife fighting, where the slightest cut, like the slice on his cheek or the one he had given his sibkin on her backside, would given enough time bleed a combatant to the point of fatal weakness.

So he laughed. It was his most effective defense against the world.

Annoyed, or seeming so, she essayed a cut for his left forearm. The knife fighter's mortal sin, each knew, was obsessing on the kill shot: there are very few knife strokes that will *instantly* incapacitate a foe. Each had witnessed many fights in which a combatant had been mortally wounded by an enemy to whom she had already dealt her own deathblow.

Steel rang again as Aleks blocked effortlessly with his knife. "You think I took pity on you, then?"

It was her turn to frown. And then laugh, like a silver

bell. "I know how much you loved the tales of knights, of Europe and Japan, when we were children in the sibko together," she said. "The lore of medieval chivalry and *bushido* still clog your head—even though both were largely made up of whole cloth in the nineteenth century."

He would only laugh. "Whenever they were invented, those tales speak to me," he acknowledged. He was circling to keep facing her, taking advantage of his far longer stride to force her to move more quickly to make sure it was not she who was outflanked. His own hands he kept extended toward the plane of his center line, left hand high and open, knife hand at about navel level and very slightly refused.

"They fit so wonderfully well with the Kerenskys' vision: of a warrior's duty to care for and shield the weak. Which is, after all, the engine that drives this great Crusade of ours: to save the childlike peoples of the Inner Sphere from themselves, and their leaders' selfishness and venality. Do not the tales of knightly chivalry and *samurai* honor accord better with our ways than the Mongols you were so taken by?"

Again they exchanged a flurry of cuts. The clash of blades was tinkling music. Neither was marked again.

"The Mongols triumphed against great odds," she said. She herself seemed to be fighting from downhill; his strength and, of much greater importance, reach were far greater than hers. To have a chance of victory, therefore, she had to either snipe from outside, slice him well and bleed him until his reactions slowed, or get inside his long arms.

Aleks' mention of *Mongols* had double impact: a faction had arisen in recent years among Jade Falcon's warriors that called itself by that name. They contended, heretically, that had Nicholas been perfect, as Clan lore held, the Clans would have conquered Terra eighty-two years ago. Since the Founder borrowed so much from the Mongol hordes of old Terra, the movement demanded that the other aspects of Mongol warfare should be adopted: total conquest by any means, however harsh or "dishonorable"—all in the service, yet, of the Founder's dream.

In the years since their last parting the sibkin's paths had diverged in more than just spatial dimensions. Malvina was herself the Mongols' leading proponent, had attained ristar status despite it, as had Aleksandr despite his contrary compassion. She was their focal point among the Falcons, but also within those Clans who yet considered their Inner Sphere territories to be Occupation Zones; Hell's Horses and even Clan Wolf, ancient enemy, whom she claimed to detest more than any.

The sibkin had, with a resumption of that effortless nonverbal communication they had developed so long ago as frightened children alone against their sibko and the universe, simply mooted such issues when they came together under the eyes of Bec Malthus and Khan Jana Pryde to plot Clan Jade Falcon's return to the Inner Sphere. But Aleks understood a conflict of their visions approached as fast as the first for-real planetary assault. And he at least did not look forward to that confrontation.

"Yet so effective were their tactics, their foes came to hugely exaggerate their numbers in their own minds," Malvina said. She kept her tone steady, conversational. She breathed normally. As did he.

Malvina Hazen did not lack advantages of her own. Although Aleksandr possessed astounding speed for a man his size, she was as much faster than he as he was stronger.

And then—except in unarmed combat, where the disparity in strength and size was simply too great for her to overcome with any regularity—he had never beaten her.

"Their situation was not so different from what we face," she said. "Overwhelming odds: a vastness to conquer; rich, teeming, powerful nations to defeat. The Founder did not scruple to borrow terms from the Mongols, *Touman* and even *Khan*. Should we, Turkina's brood, designed for ferocity, be too nice to learn from their methods and so risk throwing away our holy cause?"

As she spoke they dueled, a duet of lightning slashes and open-handed blocks and blows. An outsider would have thought it rehearsed. It was—but only in the sense that these two were both masters of the form of combat, and had spent hundreds of hours squaring off against one another in just this way.

Aleks' big brow furrowed, and his eyes seemed to focus into the distance, past the padding affixed to the bulkhead for three meters, over his sister's moon-pale shoulder. "Yet we must not be so entranced, even by victory, that we be-

tray our reason for fighting, our very purpose for existence
as warriors—"

They had had this debate often before.

Which was why she drew it out now. Hoping his mind
would follow. . . .

As he spoke she reversed knife in hand and thrust for
his groin. He danced back, turning his right hip to back her
blade, which parried hers in a cool counterclockwise arc.
He caught her with sufficient force that his strength told
then, knocking her knife hand well past his buttocks. He
followed through, up and over in a backhand reverse slash
at her cheek with savage speed.

She had already dropped, turning, using the momentum
his parry's violence imparted. She laid her free hand on the
mat to pivot and came around full circle to slam the heel
of her straightened left leg against the inside of his planted
right ankle. Its full force delivered normal to his line of
balance, the sweep scythed the leg right out from under
him. He fell.

And Malvina bestrode him in the mount position, him
on his back, her butt on his belly, her strong legs clamped
about his hips. The needle-sharp tip of her long, widening-
tapering blade depressed the skin of his Adam's apple, ever
so slightly. She leaned forward with both palms stacked on
the pommel, and smiled.

"And so I win again," she said. A droplet of sweat fell
from her well-sheened forehead to his lips. He licked it
away. "And so I always will. It is good that you are the
one thing in the cosmos I love, brother dear!"

She laughed, threw away her knife—and before he could
react had leaned forward again, pinning his wrists with her
small fists, and crushed her mouth to his.

After a moment he let go his own knife, and laughed
into her mouth, and returned the kiss with equal fervor.

11

Tara Campbell, Countess of Northwind and General commanding the three Highlander regiments, had been favorably impressed by the "honor guard" sent to meet her and her retinue as they debarked their DropShip *Parris Mac-Bride.* The air was lightly brushed with chill despite a vigorous late-morning sun and the heat still radiating from the funnel-shaped cement blast pit. They appeared most businesslike, altogether professional and turned out for action rather than ceremony.

Her lifelong diplomatic training to always guard her reactions served her just as well as her equally lengthy study of the martial arts in not flinching when a half-brick, thrown from the crowd jostling just beyond the vibrowire perimeter, bounced off the clear polycarbonate dome of the hovercar.

"Bloody heathen," murmured Command Master Sergeant Angus McCorkle, senior noncommissioned officer of the Countess' own First Kearny Regiment, from his seat in front of Tara—with its back to the car's outside, and hence to the angry mob of protesters. He sat upright, every crease in his utilities razor sharp, his black skin taut as a drum. If spending two days under doubled weight had taken the toll on him it had on Tara, he showed no sign of it. And he, she thought jealously, did not even have discreet makeup to fall back on.

"This does not seem a propitious sign," said Tara's aide, who sat beside her at the rear of the passenger compartment. She was pale and there were circles under her eyes—but those eyes were alert, as was her posture, despite the way her body was crying almost audibly for rest. Captain Tara Bishop had been a combat MechWarrior long before she became a REMF with a cushy billet. She knew from long experience how to stay sharp in a threat zone despite bone-deep weariness.

"I apologize for this part of your reception, Countess," said the earnest and almost painfully handsome young captain who led the reception party. Like the rest of the escort, he was dressed in urban-camouflage battle dress; his sole concession to ceremony was that he wore the powder blue beret of The Republic Skye Militia with the insignia of the Ducal Guard. Neither he nor any man or woman of his security detail wore any visible rank badges. Tara approved that too: Sar'nt McCorkle would have called them "sniper aim-points." She was sure that despite his wearing soft cover, the hovercraft's driver, her own head concealed by a boxy helmet, had a second lid for him tucked away out of sight up in the driver's pit.

It also took all Tara's tungsten-carbide self-discipline to keep her changeable eyes—at the moment pale blue—from focusing obsessively on the tattoo on the shaven side of his head beneath his beret: the snarling wolf's head affected by many a full-fledged warrior of Clan Wolf.

She made herself look away, out at the mob. There seemed a thousand of them, pressing as close to the wire as they could without getting a good jolt. The ones right across the perimeter waved signs written mostly in Commonwealth German. Yet the bunch ahead, across the high-

way that led away from the spaceport gate into the
Prefectural capital itself, brandished English placards.

"I wonder if *Teufelscheiss* means what I think it does,"
she murmured.

McCorkle frowned. His moustached face seemed by hue
and apparent hardness to have been carved from a chunk
of ebony. "If I knew, I'd not be tellin' ye, lass," he rumbled
in a rare appearance of the thick Northwinder brogue to
which he had been raised.

He fixed young Guard Captain Martin with a glare that
had reduced a good many higher-ranking officers to quiv-
ering protoplasm. "What d'ye mean, letting this lot greet
the Countess so?"

Captain Martin looked distressed—not an expression
Tara expected to see on a Clan face. "We uphold the law
that guarantees free speech, Master Sergeant," he said.
"We, at least, are still loyal to The Republic."

The Master Sergeant's eyes blazed red. Literally, as the
capillaries within became engorged. It was a very, very bad
sign: it meant that McCorkle, whose own self-control could
put to shame Tara Campbell's, was on the very brink of
killing rage. No matter how composed he looked, two days'
high gee had told on him, too. "And what might you be
meaning by that?" he demanded.

Tara leaned forward to touch his arm. "Peace, Top," she
said. "Don't you see he's talking about troubles in his own
house; not ours?"

"It is true, Master Sergeant," Martin said. His gray eyes
were haunted-hollow and the skin of his tanned, healthy
face had gone slack and slightly ashen. "I meant no
offense."

McCorkle drew a deep breath, nodded. His eyes began
to clear.

Tara leaned back, hiding her own sigh. *And so my life
has gone, these last few years,* she thought with a bitterness
that surprised her. *My arrival sparks a riot, and my first
semiofficial act on Skye is to defend a Wolf.*

She had studied the world's current state as extensively
as she could during the nine days' voyage to the Terran
jump point and the much shorter high-gee hop from this
system's. She knew the shame of Skye's military to which

Captain Martin had obliquely referred. As she knew that Skye had received a substantial number of Wolf Clanners during Devlin Stone's resettlement program. Feeling a certain resentful pressure from Skyians, these were known to cleave strongly to The Republic, as a buffer against the locals. But he was still *Clan.*

"I will apologize for leaping at conclusions," McCorkle husked. "I'll not ask you to go against your stiff-necked Clan pride."

"Thank you. But no apology is necessary: your instinct was to defend your honor, as any warrior's would be. Yet please understand: I am of The Republic of the Sphere, and of Skye; and then I am a Clansman."

The young officer spoke with unmistakable quiet pride—itself not particularly Clanlike. Yet loathing crawled within her for all things Clan—and for none more than the Wolf. It was the Steel Wolves who had twice attacked her home world, had forced her to destroy her own ancestral castle to keep it from falling into their hands, who had burned and flattened Tara itself with widespread butchery of civilians who had not been able to flee the fighting. The Steel Wolves whom she and her Highlanders had turned back from Terra itself scarce months before, by the skin of their teeth.

Like this soft spoken and oh-so-good-looking young man, the Steel Wolves had proclaimed themselves loyal citizens of The Republic, not so very long ago.

But be fair, she reproved herself sternly. *He's already had one chance to turn his coat, and passed it by—no doubt at great cost to himself.*

"They're protesting against The Republic, though," Tara Bishop said, jerking her head toward the shouting mob.

Captain Martin nodded. "They desire reunion with the Commonwealth. Your presence particularly excites them because they feel the Exarch underscores their subservience to The Republic, by here sending The Republic's most famous hero."

Something in the cadence and placement of the words made Tara look at him with a stirring of amusement. She had finally realized that, although he spoke English with a cosmopolitan accent little different from her own, his own birth tongue was almost certainly German.

"At least they hate you for the right reasons, Countess," Tara Bishop murmured.

McCorkle gave her a Look. He had seen her in action in her *Pack Hunter*, as he had seen their commander in her signature *Hatchetman*. He knew it was as great a mistake to downcheck Bishop for her attractiveness and often flippant manner as it was to underestimate the Countess herself, as so many did, because of her own cover-girl looks and pixy size. Yet he sometimes had a problem remembering that when Captain Bishop cracked too wise.

Tara could not help recalling that the one prior time she had seen the bloody-eyed death look of McCorkle's ancient Terran ancestors, now thankfully faded, come into his eyes was when he looked upon what Anastasia Kerensky had made of Tara-the-city.

The gates slid open as the hovercar approached. As if that were a signal, the crowd on the highway's far side broke through the thin cordon of militiamen armed with truncheons and clear curved shields and lunged out onto the pavement. But not, it seemed, to block the car's path. Rather to fall upon the pro-Steiner mob, who obligingly broke free of their own restraining line and charged to meet them in a fist, boot and sign-swinging melee.

"Okay," Tara Bishop said, "I'm confused."

"For once I agree with you, Captain," McCorkle said. "A bad omen, doubtless."

Martin was speaking softly for the benefit of the commo set clipped to his right ear. He trembled perilously on the edge of a smile.

"What's this about, Captain Martin?" Tara asked.

He snapped his expression back to a milspec mask before turning it toward her. "These are rival anti-Republicans, Countess," he said.

"Why are they dusting it up with the Steiner fans?" Bishop asked.

"They are remnants of the Free Skye movement that fought for freedom from the Commonwealth, Captain Tara Bishop. These folk are angry because they feel they have exchanged one foreign master for another. They wish us shut of The Republic, but have no desire to be again subjugated by House Steiner."

With a whine of turbines that was clearly audible through

the hovercar's polycarbonate dome along with the crowd noise, which was swelling enthusiastically in response to the brawl, a squad of Guard hoverbikes zipped through the opening gates. Tara Campbell gasped. It looked as if the armored and helmeted riders meant to drive full speed right into the battling mob.

Instead they turned at the last instant, banking their rides, whipping them about, and racing their engines. Great blasts of air spilled out from under their flexible skirts.

The hoverbikes were comparatively small and light—but their blowers would push them, their riders, and their weaponry along at fifty-four klicks an hour. The force of their wind sent rioters tumbling across the blacktop. The hoverbikes began to perform what Tara recognized as a *caracole*, like sixteenth century cavalry: advancing, turning, blasting air, moving toward the rear to let the riders behind them have their turn.

Martin spoke another sotto voce command. A burly six-wheeled, forty-five-ton Ranger infantry fighting vehicle with Ducal Guard flashes rolled out the gate. With the fight blown out of them along with whatever dignity they may have been clinging to, the erstwhile brawlers parted before it, scampering back to their respective mobs. The riot-equipped militia troopies sealed the line behind them, and Martin's driver steered their own hovercar adroitly out the gates.

"Very professionally done, Captain," Tara Campbell made herself say as the little convoy gathered steam toward the skyscrapers of downtown New London. "Please pass my compliments to your people."

He nodded. "I will, Countess Tara Campbell. Thank you."

He went back to scanning the green hills, now blessedly devoid of demonstrators, rolling by to either side of the road as he passed on Tara's compliments via his commo headset.

Casually and discreetly, attracting the attention of neither man, Tara Bishop took hold of her commander's hand and gave it a quick squeeze.

Tara Campbell was tempted to flare at her aide. To tell her she was an adult, that she did not need such childish reassurance.

But she didn't. Instead she flashed her a quick and vulnerable smile, and mouthed the word, *thanks*.

12

Northern Hemisphere
Chaffee
Lyran Commonwealth
15 May 3134

Chaffee was easy.

Just the way the Jade Falcon Watch said it would be. The merchants had muttered veiled warnings, but these were disregarded.

Chaffee was easy.

For the first twenty-four hours.

It was a not particularly appealing world, hot and relatively dry, orbiting too close for comfort to its white sun. Although possessing some valuable minerals and metal ores, Chaffee had no particular industry; its half-billion population was sufficiently occupied eking out a living from agriculture and keeping at bay the amazingly diverse and contentious fauna. Safaris to hunt the various horrors, from hectare-sized swarms of tiny acid beetles to pack-predating aliosaurs, had been the major source of off-planet income. Like Northwind in the Republic, the hyperpulse implosion had meant economic depression since it basically put an end to casual interstellar tourism.

The inhabitants of Chaffee endured. They were used to privation simply by dint of getting up every morning.

The system did retain one feature of marked interest to outsiders. It was a highly convenient jumping-off point for far richer precincts—including Prefecture IX of The Republic of the Sphere.

It had changed hands repeatedly during both the Federated Commonwealth's breakup and the Word of Blake Jihad. The contending forces had no interest in *staying* in the system, and less in straying down to the high-gravity surface of Chaffee itself. They fought, died and passed on, leaving small mark on either the world or its scattered, self-reliant inhabitants.

But Chaffee's luck had played out.

The Jade Falcon *desant* required a solid foothold in the Inner Sphere. Chaffee's location made it an excellent prospective base, not just for the invasion of the Prefecture beyond the frontier and the eventual taking of Skye, but for the fervently hoped-for follow-up: a great Crusade by the Jade Falcon *Touman,* to reclaim sacred Terra and liberate humankind in Kerensky's holy name.

Poor, uncomfortable and sparsely settled as it was, Chaffee was anticipated to be relatively easy to seize and likewise to hold. Life was hard on Chaffee. Surely its people could readily see the benefits of adopting Clan ways—and providing fresh Clanners, in time, as well as immediate resupply.

So it was that Chaffee was chosen as the point at which the *maskirovka* was stripped away, and the *desant* began in lethal earnest.

Chaffee's proximity point lay an inconvenient twenty-four days out at a standard one-gee acceleration. Jade Falcon merchants had obtained coordinates for a pirate point only five days out. Overruling the objection of his sibkin subordinates, Bec Malthus declined to make use of it.

The problem with pirate points, aside from finding them in the first place, was that if you tried jumping to them, you didn't always come out where you intended to. Or maybe at all; whether the vessels that over the centuries had been lost on known pirate-point jumps came out in some other galaxy, some other time, or never anywhere, was a matter of heated debate today among the tiny minority of the scientific-minded who still paid attention to such issues. The Supreme Commander was unwilling to risk having his entire fleet, on whose wings rode all Turkina's hopes, jump out of Whittington never to be seen again by human eyes. Two later jumps would require the use of pirate points by virtue of totally unsustainable flight times from the proximity points; but these would involve only portions of the expeditionary force, not its entirety.

Instead, the invaders adopted the expedient of accelerated boosting: three hours at two gravities, three hours at one, then back to two and so on. Although less enervating than the approach Countess Tara had made to their final objective unbeknownst to them, it was a grinding regimen even for Clanners. But vastly less taxing than a straight two-gee shot would be. And the DropShips' orbit was calculated so that the final twenty-four hours would be at a benign one gee, allowing the warriors to recover.

And besides, Chaffee would be a walkover.

Once more Bec Malthus called for no bidding. Nor did the invaders bother broadcasting a formal challenge to the planetary authorities. With no observation station at either jump point, nor pesky telescopes pointed out normal to the plane ecliptic, Chaffee like Porrima received no advance warning of its peril until drive flames burned nova in its skies, some fourteen days after the fleet emerged into the system.

A Cluster from each Galaxy was committed to the assault alongside Turkina Keshik. Chaffee's eastern hemisphere was dominated by a supercontinent named Addisonia, mountainous, and in its northern latitudes temperate and well-forested. Almost all the planet's cities, such as they were, were located along its northeastern seacoasts. Aleks, leading his second Cluster, and Malvina, leading her first, attacked the two next-largest population centers, cities of eighty-five thousand and fifty thousand, respectively. For the Keshik, itself actually the Turkina Galaxy's First Cluster, substantially reinforced for the invasion, and for himself, Beckett Malthus claimed the honor of seizing the capital city of McCauliffe on Addisonia's northeastern peninsula, with its population of just over a million and the planet's lone spaceport.

Changes in the Falcon military, ultimately mandated by economic and political pressures brought about by the Military Materiel Redemption Program, colloquially known as the BattleMech Buyback, of the cursed Devlin Stone, had been reflected in the Keshik's structure. Two new nominal Trinaries had been added years back: Foxtrot, granted the nickname Turkina Lightning and consisting of three Stars of VTOLs, and Gamma, primarily armored vehicles, known semiofficially as Turkina's Hammer and in-unit as the Gamma Hammas. The slurred pronunciation was affected to display the unanswerable superiority of anyone serving in the Keshik, hand-picked as they had been by Khan Jana Pryde—somewhat defensively, of course, since true old-school Invasion-era Falcons would have sneered at mere armored fighting vehicles being included in the Keshik.

They would have molted on the spot at what had been done specifically for the *desant*: Khan Jana Pryde had decreed two further Trinaries, an Eyrie and even more heretical, a Solahma—and worst of all, in both cases *mechanized infantry*. She had convened an assembly of every Keshik warrior to announce her mandate. Since everyone in Turkina Keshik served at the Khan's pleasure—granted, that could be said of virtually everyone of any import in all Clan Jade Falcon, except perhaps the Loremaster, whose position was supposed to be above politics—she could issue such a fiat. And make it stick: "Any warrior," she declared, "who believes his or her honor fatally impugned by serving alongside your new comrades has my permission to accept reassignment elsewhere."

Her tone had suggested, quite strongly, that anyone who did so object would find herself instantly reassigned to the *dezgra* Zeta Galaxy, plying a wrench with a nice new caste tattoo on her shoulder.

"And anyone," she had added, lowering her voice, while the female Jade Falcon perched on her shoulder spread its wings in response to a hand-signal, "who harbors reservations about serving with your new comrades of the Turkina Keshik, and acts upon those reservations, shall be cast forth from the nest of Clan Jade Falcon as unworthy and without honor."

A couple of Bec Malthus' creatures in the Keshik—the man himself stood behind his Khan's right shoulder, beaming heartily, a place he had spent her whole public career—had cried out, "*Seyla!*" pretty smartly at this. It was gilding the lily.

Pretty much everyone in the Clan who doubted that Khan Jana Pryde was capable of doing *exactly* what she said she would was already dead.

Expecting no serious opposition and eager to blood his Keshik, Malthus dropped his *Overlord C*–class command DropShip, the *Bec de Corbin,* carrying his 'Mech force and most of his armor, alongside the *Union C*–class vessel *Caracara* with his VTOLs and infantry, directly onto McAuliffe's small spaceport. He let loose a wing of his aerospace Trinary, the Turkina Fighters, to fly around and blow things up.

It was unnecessary. The small contingent of clerks, customs officials, civilian cops, and technicians on hand fled into the gray dusk at the first sign of attack. The port was deserted by the time the jacks of the two landing craft settled above the blast pits.

Malthus had sent out a Star of his Trinary Delta Elementals with a few machine-gun-armed Nacon armored scout hovercraft to secure the terminal buildings and the hulk of an ancient Inner Sphere *Union* DropShip that had been blasted off its jacks during some prior conflict and subsequently dragged off the apron by prime movers and dumped. Presumably, it had fallen during the wars of the last century's latter half, but by its decrepit state and the port's general air of lassitude and decay it might have lain there since the Star League fell. The Falcons encountered no opposition. Indeed, they encountered no one at all: even the commissary staff had run off into the enclosing fields of low, olive-green ground cover.

Facing no aerial opposition whatever, the canny Galaxy Commander called back his Echo Wing One fighters and grounded them on the apron near the offloading DropShips. No point exposing such rare and precious assets to a lucky shot by a surface-based missile or energy-weapon battery. Instead, Malthus played the game precisely by the relatively new Jade Falcon combined-arms warfare book, leading with vehicles, Elementals and a few light 'Mechs, then transport-mounted infantry, mostly Eyrie fledglings, following all up with heavier armor and BattleMechs. His Solahma warriors secured the spaceport and perimeter and dug in; Malthus was not radical enough to emulate Aleks' mixed-force experiment, though he recognized it had performed well in limited action.

The city's defense force consisted of a few light vehicles, a medium tank or two, and a gaggle of light infantry, mainly civilian cops ostensibly stiffened by planetary militia. It mounted a brisk resistance from a strip mall on the city's outskirts, which itself mostly appeared as derelict as the rusted-out *Union*. Although they blew up an infantry-hauling hovertruck looted from the port and inflicted a few casualties on the lightly armored Falcon foot soldiers, they collapsed quickly under the attentions of a single Alpha Trinary *Eyrie* and a medium Bellona hovertank. Perhaps their initial hardihood sprang from the fact they had no idea what they were getting into—and indeed no idea of just who their assailants *were*, although upon grounding Malthus had broadcast an imperious order for the planetary government to surrender.

Several Donar assault helicopters rocketed the mall, and then their lasers and Elemental flamers torched the wreckage. Underlit by lurid orange flames, the invaders advanced through the now-purple evening gloom as the blue-white pinprick of the sun dropped out of sight behind the mountains to the west.

They encountered sporadic resistance when they entered the city proper. They responded with appropriate enthusiasm.

Not having a military tradition to speak of, the planetary government promptly surrendered.

Aleks' forces at the seaport of Lazenby, and Malvina's assault against the inland city of Hamilton on the Yeoh River, both encountered somewhat more determined resistance. They dealt with it briskly, the Turkina's Beak warriors, proven at Porrima, no less professionally than the

Gyrs. In both cities some resistance actually continued after the world's noble ruler, Duke Oswald Sorrentino, broadcast his surrender to Clan Jade Falcon. Aleks crushed his with a judicious use of overwhelming force, Malvina with carnosaur exuberance.

By the time full night descended upon McCauliffe, the supercontinent's easternmost city by virtue of its location at the end of its large peninsula, the Falcons were in possession of the world's three population centers of note, largely intact, and having incurred only nominal losses themselves.

It was not an overly glorious victory, perhaps. But complete.

Or so it seemed.

13

McCauliffe City
Chaffee
Northern Hemisphere
15 May 3134

At about 1000 hours on the first day of Chaffee's existence as a fiefdom of Clan Jade Falcon, a small group of armed men overpowered civilian security elements at Siegfuhr Airport on the eastern side of McCauliffe, north of the harbor and on the city's far side from the spaceport. They proceeded to commandeer a Planetlifter Air Transport heavy-lift VSTOL and take off.

Though after the HPG failure interstellar traffic making planetfall on Chaffee had fallen from slight to virtually none, the world had a lot of airports. With a widely scattered populace and a not particularly impressive road network, air travel made a lot of sense even when not an outright necessity. The lucrative offworld hunting trade had served the planet well in this regard, providing sufficient offworld exchange to make air transport affordable, so that few and miserable were the settlements that did not boast at least one VTOL or fixed-wing aircraft, and many families possessed their own.

Off-planet replacement parts were not easy to come by, nor cheap—but relatively poor as it was, Chaffee *was* a world, complete, with five hundred million occupants. Who by the very fact of surviving upon the arid, high-gee planet with its contentious wildlife, at the very least sprang from highly resourceful stock. Chaffee had abundant metal deposits, even if large-scale mining had never come to the planet, largely because of its hostile environment (and in later years because of environmental laws enacted to preserve it in relatively pristine hostility). Chaffeeans made their own replacement parts, even if they had to use their own manual mills, lathes and welding rigs in homestead workshops.

The big, jet-powered Planetlifter was fully refueled but only partially loaded with cargo. At Malthus' order, all civilian air traffic had been grounded immediately upon Sorrentino's surrender. The backwoods folk enthusiastically ignored the ban, but it was observed scrupulously in the three major cities—under Falcon guns. Later, when things settled, aerospace fighters would fan out on patrol across the whole globe, assisted by DropShips in orbit, to teach the refractory what the Clan expected by way of obedience.

The invaders depended, as they would for the foreseeable future, upon Chaffee law enforcement and its tiny militia to enforce their writ across the planet's broad surface. Local authorities were obliged to cooperate by terms of their ruler's lawful surrender. It was possible, however, that the security contingent at Siegfuhr did not resist their assailants as valiantly as they might have.

Scientists and technicians attached to Turkina Keshik manned the main atmospheric and traffic control station at the spaceport. They spotted the unauthorized takeoff on their radar and promptly ordered the aircraft to return to the airport. The command was ignored.

Initially.

Since the vehicle's own transponder identified it clearly as an unarmed and unarmored civilian transport, and no Falcon sensor saw anything discordant, the controllers were not particularly exercised. They took for granted it was intent on escape to the supercontinent's mountainous interior. Rather than scrambling the aerospace fighters and combat VTOLs waiting at the spaceport to respond to threats, they passed the word along the chain of command. It was all they could do: the warriors would respond to a warning of danger from good lower-caste Clanners and true, but never to orders.

The hijacked aircraft was, after all, just a big cargo plane; lumbering, with poor maneuverability, easily spotted by radar or, in today's clear skies, the naked eye, and broadcasting its location to all the world. Whenever a fighter rose up to knock it down would be ample time.

The tower was more preoccupied with the launch of *Caracara,* carrying *isorla* of captured fighting vehicles, and more eagerly awaited, fresh water and food to the orbiting craft. It also carried fourteen Clan troops wounded during the brief assault on McCauliffe. It was scheduled to return with a Supernova Trinary of Solahma infantry to serve as garrison troops. Its ports had been sealed and takeoff alarms begun to blare even as the hijacked Planetlifter took off and tucked in its landing gear.

Under the thrust of its two huge turbines, the partially laden lifter climbed quickly to an altitude of three thousand meters. Then, instead of fleeing to the mountains marching in ever-higher ranks along the peninsula's spine to the west, it banked steeply and headed east, back over the city.

The *Union* DropShip's engines shot blue-white fire into the shallow blast pit. The ovoid vessel rose on columns of brilliance into a muddy, pale burgundy sky.

Approaching from the west, the big VSTOL dropped its nose. Its turbines whined at maximum throttle as it dove toward the lifting DropShip.

The *Caracara*'s formidable weapons were fully crewed. But no one expected trouble, not even when the ship's own radars picked up the Planetlifter. It was a civilian aircraft. The planet had surrendered. And these were *bellycrawlers*.

Finally, a ruby volley rippled from the medium pulse lasers that happened to bear on the diving airplane. Its starboard wing was stitched off at the root.

It made no difference. Trailing a hundred-meter plume of yellow fire, the seventy-five tons of aircraft and cargo smashed into the *Caracara*'s rounded upper surface at eight hundred kilometers an hour.

Pale flame and black smoke unfurled across half a klick of cerulean sky. Despite its mass and velocity, despite breaching the DropShip's armor and inundating compartments and gangways aft of the bridge with blazing jet fuel, the suicide plane failed to cripple the tough assault craft.

It did, however, tumble it off its drive-thrust columns, dramatically enough that gyros and Clan-rapid work with attitude jets by Binetti's naval crew still failed to prevent catastrophic return to the blast pit.

The resultant explosions rocked *Bec de Corbin* on her landing jacks, destroyed seven of her weapons emplacements, and lit the whole side facing the wreck with burning fuel. The combustion did no additional damage to the armored DropShip, designed to resist high-speed atmospheric re-entry temperatures.

The blast and spreading inferno did envelop an Elemental, five Solahma infantry, and an unknown number of indigenous civilian laborers pressed into service unloading supplies from the *Bec*, as well as the supplies themselves. Three VTOLs were kicked across the blacktop by the dynamic overpressure; one smashed into the central administrative structure. All three were destroyed by fire, as were many spaceport service vehicles. Two aerospace fighters were damaged by blast and splashed with liquid fire, but rapid action by stood-down pilots and groundcrew technicians saved them.

As for the passengers and crew inboard the *Caracara,* it was fervently hoped among their comrades that none survived the shock and explosion of crashing into the pit. Nothing but fused lumps remained of them or the cargo when the inferno was finally beaten down.

In white fury, Malthus ordered Duke Oswald—across a table from whom he sat negotiating administration of the captured world when word of the disaster reached him—executed with his family on planetwide tri-vid. It was a standard technique from the unwritten Clan handbook on pacification of conquered worlds, and far from unknown among the Great Houses of the Inner Sphere. It was also a blood-rare exhibition of emotion for Beckett Malthus.

The response was not what the handbook said it would

be. Either the planetaries were roused to vengeful fury at the murder of their noble rulers; or they thought good riddance. Or possibly both. What they were not was *chastened*.

Within two hours a truck bomb shattered civilian police headquarters in Lazenby. Shortly after that, reports of casualties from sniping began to filter in.

Lacking a military tradition to speak of, Chaffee had quickly folded under assault from two complete Galaxies and a reinforced Cluster.

Lacking a military tradition to speak of, Chaffee's widely scattered residents did not feel bound by any surrender socalled "authorities" claimed to make in their names.

The aliosaur would have been a fearful sight, even to a mighty Jade Falcon MechWarrior, had it not been piteous. The darkness did not hide its grievous injuries: missing its hook-taloned right forelimb, scaly hide charred and blistered. It limped, dragging a stump of tail along the cinderstrewn ground, drawing a line of blood behind it that glowed black in the corpse-blue shine of the gibbous moon Grissom.

Its intent upon approaching the tall, unarmored man who stood with his heavy black hair blowing in the stinking breeze was unguessable.

With a firecracker crackling, a spray of pulse-laser bolts caught it in the back, pale yet brilliant pink in the darkness. The creature squalled, threw its head back, and collapsed. Its single remaining eye fixed reproachfully on Aleksandr Hazen as it slowly glazed.

"Did you ever meet anything you did not kill?" he asked the small, slim, night-clad figure who approached from behind the ruined beast, reholstering its sidearm.

"There is you, my brother," Malvina Hazen said with a sweet, angular smile. Cinders and fragments of charred wood beams crunched beneath her soles.

He waved a hand at the blackness, greater than the night, that stretched out along the ground for kilometers to all sides of them. "This is all that remains of Hamilton. One stone scarcely stands upon another. Not one thing remains alive—now."

Malvina paused to push over a heat-glazed stub of brick

wall, perhaps a meter long and half that high, with a boot's armored toe. "Unforgivable sloppiness on my people's part," she said, "unacceptable in a Gyrfalcon. I expressly directed that *no* stone be left upon another. And that hapless raptor, which I presume wandered into town scavenging for food and got caught in the overkill, had best be the only multicellular organism left living, or all my field officers from Star Commander up will soon be exercising their rights of *surkai!*"

"This was deliberate?" Aleks asked. A hot ember flake from one of an uncountable number of fires still guttering low in the devastation lit on his cheek to cling and sting like an acid beetle. He made no acknowledgment, neither flinched nor moved to brush it off.

"It takes a lot of work to utterly level a city, complete with fifty thousand inhabitants," Malvina said. "How do you imagine it might have been done by accident?"

He lowered his head and shook it as if it weighed a hundred kilos. "Why?"

Malvina's head was encased in a somewhat bulbous Jade Falcon field helmet; neither was dressed for the cockpit of a 'Mech. In the moonlight her expression of puzzlement was unmistakable. And at least seemingly authentic.

"To end resistance, of course," she said, hauteur and sarcasm gone from her voice. "To stop the killing."

He waved his hands about him. All was a black plain as far as the eye could see, to the mountains on one side and the sea upon the other. "The whole city is *gone*. Scrubbed from the face of Chaffee. The river scummed over with ash and grime and . . . and the grease of melted bodies for ten kilometers downstream! How could you *do* that?"

She shrugged. "It took but a day to accomplish. But my command DropShip *White Reaper* added its firepower, which expedited things considerably. We might have used orbital strike, but I would have had to trouble the Supreme Commander for clearance."

She smiled again. "Besides, my people needed the practice."

"That is not what I meant," he said hoarsely.

"I know that. I was only seeking to save you embarrassment. As you may remember, I have long shielded my brother, the only companion of my childhood, from harm. And now when there is none in the universe who can touch him, I seek to save him from the only one who can."

She reached up to touch his cheek with gauntleted fingertips. "Yourself."

His hand snapped up as if to smash hers away. At the last millisecond it slowed. The great hand that enfolded her slim wrist and removed her touch from his leather-brown cheek did so as if she were spun of gossamer.

She ripped it free, whirled from him, stormed away three paces. The brief black cape of her not-quite-regulation dress uniform fluttered about her shoulders.

"Do you care nothing for our people?" she snapped. "Our warriors struck down from coward's cover? Let me tell you of these Freebirths. Within the cities most of them carry arms, even technicians and laborers—not that these bellycrawling mongrels make such distinction."

At the uttering of the word "bellycrawler" Aleks' lower left eyelid twitched. He said nothing.

"Outside the cities they *all* have firearms—and all know how to use them. And not just small arms. The Zeus heavy rifle is considered suitable to be left with minor children when parents are compelled to leave them unattended at their homesteads. The parents carry super-powerful laser rifles in their vehicles for defense against the larger local beasts. And for hunting or protection from some of the local fauna, nothing less than portable short-range missile launchers or even particle-projector cannon are required."

Aleks nodded reluctant concurrence. "I understand. I have lost three Elementals in the last two days, all sniped from over two kilometers' distance. Not even our ballistic radars can pick us out the snipers—who run away as soon as they see their targets fall through their scopes."

She turned to face him. She seemed in control of herself again; her voice was almost light. Almost taunting. "And you have taken retribution."

He grimaced, shrugged. Nodded slowly. "We must. We cannot permit the people of a conquered world to defy us. Especially when all our plans hinge upon pacifying Chaffee and using it as a base."

"To liberate the Inner Sphere," she said. "Precisely."

She drew near him again. He did not draw back, but

neither did he show sign of softening. "Do you not care about your precious belly—precious Spheroids? The ones we are on Crusade to save from their venal leaders—and themselves?" she asked.

He turned away. "These folk are masterless even for *stravag*," she said to his wedge-shaped back. The word was a term of abuse for Freeborn. "They have no honor."

"Perhaps they have much honor," Aleks said. "While they strike from ambush like cowards, even as you say, the ones we catch fight until death. The ones we capture commit suicide—or contrive escape."

She faced him again. Her eyes glittered like silver coins in the moonlight. "Those whose honor is only for themselves have no true honor," she said. "But you make my case, Aleksandr. They will not honor their leaders' surrender. They refuse to surrender themselves. What can we do but to hunt them down one by one and kill them, then?"

He spread his great hands in a gesture of helplessness. Something caught Malvina's eye; she half-turned.

A skull, discolored, partially charred, with blackened wisps of tissue clinging to it, but its smooth dome gleaming with organic oils. A small skull. A child's skull.

"We can show them what resistance will cost, not just them, but their loved ones," she asked, "with one single punishment so terrible"—she stepped forward and crushed the tiny skull beneath her bootheel—"that it will be felt in the most remote corners of this burdensome world."

His upper lip had peeled back from white teeth. "This is where your Mongol-worship leads."

She took off her helmet, unpinned her hair, shook it free in a cascade like moonlight itself that fell past her shoulders. "This is where the path of true compassion leads. I submit, brother dear, that I have saved lives by what I have done here. Theirs as well as ours."

The face he turned to her was twisted like a rag. "Is this what is demanded of a warrior, a protector of the lesser and the weak?" he asked, in a voice as if an Elemental's manipulator were crushing his throat, and flapped a hand like broken wing. "Is this *honor*?"

"Victory for Clan Jade Falcon," she said, "is honor." And walked away.

14

Sanglamore Military Academy
New London
Skye
The Republic of the Sphere
2 May 3134

"**R**eally, Countess," Chief Minister Augustus Solvaig said, "I believe we know how to conduct our own business here on Skye, thank you."

Tara Campbell felt her cheeks flush hot. She sensed her aide, the other Tara, going tense at her side, and channeled the energy of embarrassment and anger into willing the captain into silence. The small and balding minister with red muttonchop sideburns covering most of his round red cheeks like fuzzy symmetrical birthmarks did not just accidentally happen to be sitting at the strong beringed right hand of Duke Gregory Kelswa-Steiner.

Tara was past any career considerations of her own: she had laid her life on the line for The Republic time and again. If The Republic—or its rulers—found it impossible to cooperate with her she could always go back to Northwind and serve her ideals by strengthening her home world.

Captain Tara Bishop served at Tara Campbell's discretion, no one else's. So long as she did as well as she always had, her job was secure, notwithstanding her vivid if sometimes spiky personality.

Yet Tara still cared desperately about The Republic and what it stood for. She knew it lay in dire danger, and that the danger would come through Prefecture IX, if not Skye itself. While she could not be cashiered, Duke Gregory could have her shipped off his planet and out of his Prefecture if he found her—or even her aide—difficult to get along with. So could Prefect Della Brown and Planetary Legate Stanford Eckard, likewise in attendance.

"Mr. Chief Minister," Eckard said. His voice was dry, but it was the aridity of bloodlessness, not irony. "I fear you do Countess Campbell an injustice. I did not hear her criticize, but rather try to call to our attention the potential seriousness of the situation. In that at least, I concur."

Glancing aside at Captain Bishop, Tara saw her aide's compressed lips curve in the shorthand of a smile. She felt the Legate was sticking up for her boss.

More experienced in such matters, Tara Campbell suspected his support was far less substantial than Bishop presumed. Indeed, she had a hunch it amounted to little more than a career military man—a military *bureaucrat*, like his superior Brown, but a lifer nonetheless—reflexively defending a fellow professional against civilian impugnation. A tall, narrow Asian man with salt-and-pepper hair wisped up on top, he looked more elderly than his dossier made him. He impressed Tara as being one of those people who, attitudinally, entered middle-age at about the same time they exited puberty.

Solvaig glanced at his own master, who sat silent. That surprised Tara: an expression so thunderous should have been rattling the leaded-glass windows in the long, narrow chamber in the Gothic pile of the once-noted Sanglamore Military Academy in a suburb of New London. *Does the Duke always look like that,* Tara Campbell wondered, *or only when I'm around?*

"Really, her intent is irrelevant, your Grace," the Chief Minister said in a petulant whine. "I would submit that we have more pressing concerns than fantasies of some latter-day Clan Crusade against the Inner Sphere. Really, we might as well dread the renascence of the Mongol Horde, if we are going to summon phantoms of the past with which to frighten ourselves."

He shook his head. "The domestic pressures upon our world are real and pressing—as I would have thought the Countess herself might have noticed upon her arrival yesterday."

"Oh, I noticed quite well, Mr. Minister," she said, trying to keep her tone light to defuse the man's overt hostility or at least the mood it was creating. "I've seldom encountered a more enthusiastic reception."

Solvaig's red face went scarlet to the wings of his receding hairline. "And what is that supposed to mean? Are you saying that we cannot control our citizenry?"

Tara stared at him, unable to feign diplomatic indifference. *Did I really make that big a botch of defusing tension,* she wondered, *or is he just out of his mind?*

Duke Gregory Kelswa-Steiner turned to look at his minister. His craggy face softened slightly. "Go easy, my friend. I agree with our . . . esteemed guest that there exists sufficient evidence of threat to Prefecture IX and to Skye itself to cause concern. The Exarch himself endorses the intelligence, after all. And indeed, my greatest fear has been that some enemy might seek to take advantage of our weakened condition."

"Yes, your Grace," Solvaig murmured, subsiding. The crescent-slit eyes through which he regarded Tara showed no sign of friendliness.

"Please forgive Minister Solvaig, Countess," the Duke said. "He cares deeply about our world. Sometimes the intensity of his feelings get the better of him. It seldom clouds his judgment, however."

His brows drew closer together again. "I hope you will understand that I regard this potential threat as primarily an affair of Prefecture IX, and Skye."

"Surely your Grace agrees The Republic has a vital interest in defending its territories?"

He glared at her a moment. His eyes were gray, currently an icy pale.

I faced the Wolf Bitch Anastasia Kerensky in her Ryoken II *without flinching, and defeated a rogue Paladin of the*

Sphere 'Mech to 'Mech, she thought. *I'm damned if I'll quail for a mere Duke.*

"Surely the Exarch understands we are competent to handle the situation," Della Brown put in with a trace of asperity.

"No doubt he does, Prefect," Tara said. She thought it no good sign the Prefect—a Republican official answering directly to Geneva—should side with the local governor in a jurisdictional dispute. Worse was that she or anyone thought there should *be* a jurisdictional dispute.

Then again, Tara thought, unable to prevent herself feeling bitterness she was too proud to show, *it's not as if Redburn sent me out with any official standing. I might as well be a mercenary like One-Eyed Jack Farrell—or just another highborn meddler.* "This is not about command or control. I was sent to offer any and all assistance I was able to."

"Without troops, what help have you to give?" Solvaig sneered openly.

"The troops are coming," she said. It was true she and her staff had been bundled into space before even the Highlander company which had remained on Terra could be mustered aboard DropShips. They would follow as soon as possible, as would the troops who had returned months before to Northwind. But the majority of her Highlanders were strewn across two Prefectures fighting fires. How many of them could reach Skye before the threat materialized, as she knew in her bone marrow it would?

Duke Gregory glared at her a moment longer. Then he sighed volcanically.

"I am in no position to stand on pride," he said. He laced his fingers and put his big hands on the table before him. "Suppose you tell us what hope you do propose to tender us, Countess."

"Countess Campbell."

The corridor was narrow and, despite the broad daylight outside the dressed stone walls, dim. It gave her a pang of nostalgia for her own Castle Northwind, in which she had spent so much of her childhood, and which she had ordered destroyed to prevent it falling into the hands of the Steel Wolves. Sanglamore Academy had enjoyed a storied career turning out top-rate military professionals for the Federation of Skye, the Lyran Commonwealth, and the short-lived Federated Commonwealth. Like military establishments everywhere after the rise of Stone and his Republic, the Academy, which had already suffered severe losses to its faculty in the FedCom explosion and the subsequent Jihad, had gradually faded to a wisp of its former self, with whole wings mothballed for a generation. In the new Golden Age a *military academy* seemed a barbaric throwback.

Tara stopped and turned around. Her aide stood poised at her side like a watchdog. "Yes, Prefect Brown?"

"A word with you, if I may."

"Certainly," Tara said.

The Prefect came up with them. She loomed over the tiny Countess: a handsome woman in middle age, light-skinned black, with a cap of coiled dark red hair dusted with gray and large amber eyes. She had clearly once been willowy, possibly athletic; but from the spread of hips and thighs it was obvious she had spent most of her recent career piloting a desk rather than a BattleMech.

She looked meaningfully at Tara Bishop.

The captain looked back, smiling tightly, refusing to budge from her superior's side. The Prefect focused her out.

"I must suggest you keep a tighter rein on your emotions, Countess Campbell," the Prefect said in a tone somewhere between reproof and condescension. "You risk acting in an unprofessional manner when you allow yourself to be drawn into arguments with influential civilians."

"You mean Minister Solvaig?"

"I do."

Tara Campbell felt her aide stiffen. Despite the fact that her eyes stung at the patent unfairness of the Prefect's reproach, she touched Tara Bishop covertly on the arm, signaling restraint.

"I appreciate your concern, Prefect Brown," she said. "Should that concern extend to wondering whether the publicity that tends to accompany me goes to my head, I can only request that you please accept my assurance that it does not.

"Moreover"—she allowed steel to touch her voice—"I beg to remind the Prefect that despite my appearance I am *not* a child, not even an adolescent; and that I am, in fact, myself the Prefect of Prefecture III, and not some actress engaged to play the role."

The big liquid eyes blinked twice rapidly. "Northwind is a long way from here, Countess," she said huffily.

"Let us all hope it's not too far for my soldiers to get here before the Falcons do."

With a grim "Good day," Prefect Brown strode off down the hall on her long legs. Tara Campbell stared after her with a gaze like icicles.

"Well," she said, when she and the other Tara had the corridor to themselves, "I'd say I handled that pretty badly."

"You didn't punch her," TB said brightly. "If you made a mistake, ma'am, I'd say it was not letting *me* do it."

15

Jade Falcon Naval Reserve Battleship **Emerald Talon**
Jump Point
Chaffee
Lyran Commonwealth
20 May 3134

"**N**estlings of Turkina," Beckett Malthus' voice intoned in the darkness, "attend me."

It was the briefing theater inboard the *Emerald Talon*. The auditorium, like half a bowl, was full of expeditionary force officers. Malthus stood at a podium with Aleksandr and Malvina Hazen seated flanking him. They were all but unseen in the dark: all eyes were fixed above and behind them, upon the holovid tank displaying a giant map of Prefectures VIII and IX of The Republic of the Sphere and the Lyran Commonwealth frontier, in which Chaffee was highlighted, a glowing green orb bigger and brighter than the rest.

"The time has come," the Supreme Commander said, "to drop all pretense. The *maskirovka* has served its purpose. Now the time has come for the Jade Falcon to swoop in a mighty *desant*."

Shrill falcon screams pierced the dark, and cries of *"Seyla!"*

"In the first wave, Zeta Galaxy shall jump first to Lai-aka." A red line descended from Chaffee and to the left, away from Terra and into Prefecture VIII. It touched a star which glowed yellow. "From that staging point, Turkina's Beak shall have the honor of striking Alkaid."

The line took a short jog down and right to a star that suddenly expanded into a red giant, as if going nova. The Zeta contingent cheered lustily. The Turkina Keshik offi-cers looked bored and restive, and the Gyrs openly hostile, at the scantling Zetas being named first.

"The Gyrfalcon Galaxy"—the Deltas uttered falcon screams—"jumping through Zebeneschamali and Carnwath systems, shall strike at Ryde." A white line zigzagged to the right.

"Finally," Malthus said, as a third, green line radiated a short distance down and right from Chaffee, "the Tur-kina Keshik will seize and hold the world of Glengarry." The Keshik officers maintained an aloof silence, as if to signify to their rivals and inferiors—to be redundant—that they were professionals, and had done this sort of thing before.

"In the second phase, the Keshik will consolidate its hold upon Glengarry and begin its reconstruction according to the Founder's precepts, as has commenced on Chaffee. Zeta Galaxy will take Summer." The red line looped be-neath and past Skye, through Alcor and Mizar, then hooked up and right, almost to the border of Prefecture X, The Republic's core.

The white line forked like lightning. One line stabbed almost straight down, through a system called Unukalahi, and then to a system right next door to Skye, virtually on a line between it and Terra. The other white line thrust a short jump up and right.

"The Gyrfalcons will split at Ryde. One element will take Zebebelgenubi, near our final objective. The other will strike at Kimball II."

He paused. The cheering, which had devolved into a

lusty exchange of insults between the Gyrs and the Zetas, dwindled to silence.

"And then," Malthus said, "ten weeks from this very day, we rendezvous in Skye system. The Falcon shall spread her wings above Skye itself as all three forces converge. Skye shall fall. The road to Terra will lie open before us, and then Khan Jana Pryde will not withhold the Jade Falcon *Touman*. They will surely join us in our triumph. Our ancient Crusade will be victorious at last: General Kerensky shall have truly returned home!"

"*Seyla!*" the Falcon's brood thundered in a voice of one.

"I knew I would find you here."

The tall, broad-shouldered shape brooding over the railing that overlooked a shuttle deck, which was a cavern of darkness whose floor was grown with little mushrooms of light between dark, gleaming masses, looked up and around.

She saw the flash of his teeth in the dimness of the gallery, the darkness of his face. "I am surprised you would seek me out."

The command council following the *kurultai* had quickly curdled into rancor. Malvina pressed her case for harsh action: Chaffee had been subdued by her destruction of Hamilton. It could provide their model for conquest: *applied frightfulness*. The Mongol way.

Her sibkin had argued that conquest by terror was repugnant to Clan ways. That while harsh measures might be necessary in response to extreme provocation, the Falcons could not rely on them too greatly without overturning what they stood for, what they had returned to the Inner Sphere for: to free and safeguard the people there, not destroy them.

Sentiment clearly ran against him. The officers of Beckett Malthus' Turkina Keshik had supported Malvina almost as enthusiastically as her own Gyrs. Only among his own commanders had Aleks found support; and even some of them seemed dubious.

Despite the fact the consensus was going away from Aleks, Bec Malthus ordained compromise: each Galaxy Commander might conduct his and her campaign as they wished; and when the fleets rejoined, at the zenith jump point four days out from Skye orbit, they would see what had been seen.

Pale face and silver hair appeared to float in air, vaguely agleam as if from within. The rest of her was cloaked in deep-space black with token green, itself scarcely other than black. The difference could not be seen in the dim amber footlights.

"It seems a waft of the air of home blows through," he said, his voice a gentle rumble, "banishing for a moment the smell of hot metal, lubricants and ozone."

"The soap with which I washed my hair and body," she answered artlessly. "Made of Sudeten herbs. Home, if you would call it that."

His smile was crooked. "We Clanners," he said. "We dote upon nature, even though we ourselves are but little products of it. We so love to retreat into it during training and brief respites from duty. And to smuggle its smells and sometimes stolen scenery into the steel wombs into which we were born from glass ones."

She was close enough that he could see the arch of her brow. "You find fault with our Clan ways?"

"I am amused by some of them, right enough." He turned back to the rail, folded his big arms onto it, leaned there gazing out across the hangar deck. Above and beyond the shuttles being made ready for departure to the other JumpShips in the fleet, two great oblongs of starfield shone, silver upon black, one on either side of the central launch-lock. So arrogant had Clan Snow Raven been in their technology and might that they built huge crystal viewports on the battleship's hangar deck, as if the shuttles were mettlesome steeds and needed to be able to see the starry realm to which they would soon or late return. In times when danger impended, armor shutters heavy as a *Broadsword*-class DropShip descended before each like closing eyelids.

"Our ways have changed since the first return to the Inner Sphere. Some out of need, others . . . just changed. Some changes were for the best. Others I would see made right again. And others are not yet made, that need to be."

She stood close beside him. She seemed clenched, and at

the same time aglow with something like fury. It was as if she had something to say but could not.

He turned and looked at her in wonder. There were few things she could not do, if she chose.

"You have right," she said at last. "But we might differ as to what should be changed, and how."

"It is true."

He turned, reached a broad square hand to her. It stopped midair. It seemed as if some sort of membrane, invisible, insensible to touch, but real nevertheless, had descended between them.

His eyes met hers. He dropped the hand.

"Change comes," he said. "Changes greater than any of us expect."

"Not greater than I expect."

"We shall change the Inner Sphere as drastically as did our predecessors of the First Crusade, win or lose," he said. "What upheavals will the Inner Sphere inflict on us—win or lose?"

"Exalt us," she said. "Or destroy us. Better that than slide deeper into decadence."

She laughed. It was brittle music, like tiny icicles shattering in a cold Sudeten dawn.

"You disappoint me, brother," she said. "I had come here hoping you might give me answers. Instead all you have in your mouth is more questions."

She turned from him. "What answers we find, we shall find in action. And so our ways part. For now."

New London Spaceport
Skye
15 May 3134

Though the day was warm, especially here with the primary sun—so much like Terra's own Sol—bouncing its heat off the blacktop of the spaceport into the faces of Tara and her escorts, the breezes blowing down from the Sanglamore Mountains west of New London were bladed with chill. They carried the scent of great splayed leaves turning all gold and tan and russet and orange, and the smell of the rich black soil they sprang from, and from heights greater still lordly evergreens twice taller than any 'Mech.

"Here she comes!" the shout went up from the troops around them. A point of blue-white brilliance had appeared above, burning laser-like through the white horsetails of clouds brushed across a sky as achingly blue as Northwind's own. The powerful defensive emplacements, which like the ones guarding New Glasgow's spaceport boasted powerful weapons remounted from DropShips as well as conventional anti-aircraft armaments, moved automatically to track its descent.

"About bloody time," said Command Master Sergeant Angus McCorkle, standing a respectful distance behind his commander and her taller, brown-haired aide. He wore full Northwind regimentals, including a kilt and sash of the blue and black Campbell tartan, though he wore a tartan-banded cap instead of a bearskin-covered helmet. The two Taras wore conventional dress uniform, khaki with trousers. Although neither tradition nor regulation forbade a woman of the Highlanders wearing the kilt, and although she was in fact *the* Campbell, with better claim upon the sett—the traditional plaid pattern—than any, Countess Tara seldom wore it. She had enough trouble overcoming her pretty-girl image without appearing at solemn public functions wearing what was in reality a short skirt. *Especially* on a day as breezy as today.

And far less regimental, she reflected. *Although it would almost be worth it, to hear that fat fool Herrmann howl.*

With a roar of drive jets the DropShip *Blue Bayou* settled toward the designated blast pit. It lay well away from the spaceport's main buildings, beyond any number of invitingly vacant landing spots. Tara suspected the remote location was another half-subtle dig from her hosts. It did sport a boggy fen of tall, feather-headed grasses gone gray in the long summer heat across the wire to discourage the protesters who still dogged Tara's steps.

There seemed no guile behind the smile of Lieutenant Colonel Brigid Hanratty, commander of the planet's largest remaining military formation as well as today's escorts and security detail—no more Ducal Guards for Tara. Hanratty was a big, rawboned woman with a face like a prizefighter and a great mass of curly, metallic red hair bound, unlikely enough, into pigtails. Despite the fact she looked like the cliché image of an Irish washerwoman, she had shown herself, in the few days Tara had been liaising with her, to be at the least a competent officer with a solid grasp of military matters.

She also professed a high regard for Tara Campbell's military accomplishments, from Sadalbari onward. Far from resenting the petite and beautiful Countess, she seemed vastly tickled that such a redoubtable battle leader should appear to her in the guise of what she termed a "wee porcelain doll." So hearty were her expressions of admiration that Tara had not even felt the usual stab of resentment—champion martial artist that she was, as well as much-bloodied MechWarrior and proven battlefield commander—that being referred to as a "porcelain doll" normally inflicted.

Hanratty seemed legitimately delighted to have Tara Campbell on Skye and working with her, under whatever plan. *Well, she's the only one,* Tara thought as the ship's landing jacks extended and it settled onto the ferrocrete rim of the pit with a vast roaring and grinding.

That statement was not altogether true. The Skye mass media were as adulatory as the media on Terra had been—except for those owned by the powerful Herrmanns AG, who portrayed her as a demon incarnate. Yet her official reception had little warmed: Planetary Legate Eckard was so introverted as to be a cipher, Prefect Brown was aloof and disapproving, Minister Solvaig openly hostile. In general the Duke himself seemed to find her as welcome as a cold sore; yet he had shown no reticence about intervening in her behalf, either at the first unfortunate meeting with Prefecture officials or subsequently when Tara had been reluctantly compelled to call instances of bureaucratic obstruction and noncooperation, quite frequent at first, to his attention. It was as if he was torn between resentment and relief at her presence—and blamed her for both.

Whatever the case, she knew full well she could not be running incessantly to the Lord Governor for help. Not without sacrificing any credibility and authority she might have, not to mention that self-esteem which she was only now becoming able to permit herself to feel.

Seeming to read her mind, as she had more and more in

the weeks since the victory on Terra, Tara Bishop leaned her mouth close to the smaller woman's ear and murmured, "At least we'll have some *troops* now. That should get us treated a little more seriously."

Tara nodded.

With a hiss of equalizing atmospheric pressure, the main locks opened and flower-petaled into ramps. "Sar'nt Major!" rapped Hanratty. Her own top kick, an immense, square, slab-faced man named McDougall who looked remarkably like an ancient North American Plains Indian warrior from Terra and wore a uniform with kilt and sash of a plaid unknown to Tara, barked orders. The regimental band of the Seventh Skye Militia enthusiastically if not expertly began skirling out "The Campbells Are Coming," which they had also played for Tara on her first visit to the regiment's cantonment outside New London several days before. It seemed that Hanratty's easy grin tightened a bit at that, and her eyes narrowed. Then she relaxed again as if accepting something inevitable.

Tara's eyes, a cool green today, flicked up and aside to her aide. A corner of the taller woman's mouth quirked up. "I'd rather fight Nasty Kerensky in her *Ryoken II* naked with a sidearm on the steppes in September," Captain Bishop muttered, "than listen to bad bagpipes."

"Are there any other kind?" grumbled McCorkle. His own Northwind-Scot upbringing did not extend to an appreciation for the culture's traditional music.

Led by their commander, Colonel Robert Ballantrae, riding in a *Cougar* BattleMech taken as spoils from the Steel Wolves on the Belgorod plain, Tara's Highlanders stepped and drove forth into the bright sunlight in smart style. They formed a column of infantry with shouldered arms, flanked by armored vehicles and with the *Cougar* striding in the fore, and marched toward their waiting commander, her immediate entourage, and the militia platoon behind. The band finished off their tune, mercifully, only to begin another: a lively, driving air that they played with such panache as to almost make up for their lack of skill.

Tara found herself nodding her spike-haired head in time. "What's that tune, Colonel? It sounds familiar."

Hanratty's homely face split into a gap-toothed grin. "That's the 'Garryowen,' marm," she said. "We've our unit nickname from it. And might I ask that you call me Brigid, if the Countess pleases; I forget I'm no longer a major, the rank's that new."

The Seventh's commander had gone with Jasek and his followers—and a sigh of relief, if scuttlebutt were to be credited. He was a hard-core, Lyran-loving hardass. Whereas the Seventh's grunts were overwhelmingly Anglophones.

Tara nodded to the woman's request. "If you'll call me Tara," she said.

"But how the devil will you know which one I mean?"

"Tone of voice," Tara Bishop said. "We're used to it; we'll know. Or just call me TB, ma'am."

The colonel shrugged.

With a final stomp of broad metal feet that rang on the pavement and rattled Tara's teeth, Ballantrae brought the *Cougar* to a halt ten meters from his Countess. He raised the 'Mech's right arm in the stiff-armed Highlander salute.

"Countess Campbell, ma'am!" boomed from the 'Mech's loudspeakers. "Colonel Robert Ballantrae and Task Force Bruce reporting as ordered, *ma'am*!"

TF Bruce was a scratch company of First Kearnies and Fusiliers, with nearly an equal number of Republican Guard newbies recruited on Terra after the Steel Wolves' defeat. Tara wondered how glad the latter would be to be restored to the presence of Master Sergeant McCorkle, who had been the bane of their existence until crash-dispatched with his Countess and her aide and a bare-bones staff to Skye to begin shoring the defenses remaining after the defection of Jasek Kelswa-Steiner.

She returned the Highlander Colonel's salute smartly. "Welcome to Skye. The strength of our arms is The Republic's!"

The Highlanders gave back the slogan with the enthusiasm of men and women who had fought to make it real.

Behind her back, though, Tara thought she heard snickers from the assembled Seventh troopers.

It did not betide particularly well. But it was small surprise. The Seventh Skye Militia was not only the planet Skye's largest intact military formation. It was also legendarily the largest collection of sad sacks and screw-ups in the planetary armed forces. And a hotbed of Free Skye subversion, to boot.

=== 16 ===

Alkaid
Prefecture VIII
The Republic of the Sphere
14 June 3134

The rotary-wing VTOL seemed to stumble in air as a double-speed burst from the Ultra autocannon in the left arm of Aleksandr Hazen's *Gyrfalcon* caught it full in the nose. Its fuselage vanished into a comet of yellow flame that continued to streak against the merciless white desert sky trailing black flame, its rotor still spinning above it, until a plane-topped column of wind-graven sandstone halted its careen.

"The defenders of Alkaid are brave," he said over his general frequency channel. "But we outmatch them."

This time he had issued a batchall. And more: it had been accepted.

Reviewing Alkaid's history, reports from Jade Falcon intelligence and intercepts of radio traffic from the surface on their seven-day transit from the pirate point whose coordinates had been provided by Jade Falcon merchants, Aleks and his analysts had calculated their strategy carefully. Alkaid possessed a small but proficient defense force. More to the point, it possessed a history of successful guerrilla resistance against the brutal fanatics of the Blakist Jihad, who had seized the spaceports and beaten down its conventional defenders.

Aleks wanted no rerun of Chaffee. Nor did he believe the *desant* could afford it—nor the grand long-term plans he had had such a hand in shaping. It was imperative to subdue Alkaid as expeditiously and yet as completely as possible. Aleks faced a fight for a far more populous world after this one, as well as a tight timetable leading to the three-pronged attack on Skye itself. And his Clan needed Alkaid for a base and more. Unlike Chaffee, Alkaid, also hot, also dry and even higher-gravity, possessed strategically significant resources in the form of vast chemical extraction and processing operations. All qualms or compassion aside, the Jade Falcon plan required Alkaid be subdued with minimal disruption, either of the physical plant or the workers who made it run.

With a full Galaxy at his command, Aleks could have seized the world in a coup de main, simply dropping ships to seize the spaceports at the industrial center of Moravska Ostrava and the planetary capital Verstigrad in the far north, and Nobadi on the southern supercontinent of Inahalia. Such an expedient would have put the bulk of Alkaid's slightly more than one hundred million population under his guns.

Aleks instead chose a plan he deemed less liable to produce unnecessary destruction. Even before his DropShip fleet shaped Alkaid orbit, he was blanketing the planet with a challenge to Governor Chandler Neville and Legate Renee Zollern to block his entrance to Moravska Ostrava from a landing spot forty kilometers into the desert with a militia battalion, which he promised would enjoy at least a two-to-one numerical advantage over the attackers. He assured the authorities—for the consumption of the populace, to whom the powerful communications gear inboard *Red Heart* helpfully beamed the whole negotiation—that he had no intent of disrupting Alkaid's normal way of life or imposing Clan values. All he asked was submission, with all resistance ceased, should he win the battle.

The local authorities went for his deal. They weren't

eager to get smashed flat by the preponderant force Aleks could bring to bear. The cost of losing would be tolerable. And the local militia might actually win—the old overwhelming Clan superiority was history, whereas the old overbearing Clan arrogance was not. Who knew; the invaders might just bid themselves into bringing too small a force.

As it happened, Aleks himself won the enthusiastic bidding for the honor of carrying out the attack, with his tender of but a single Trinary—armor, Elementals and conventional infantry, stiffened by three 'Mechs and two points of VTOLs. That bettered the deal he had offered the local authorities.

It also raised the possibility that the defenders' hopes for Clan overconfidence might be borne out.

"Galaxy Commander," said a voice in his ear. *"This is Red Eye One. We have visual contact."* Aleks' kicker back was that he had selected only hovercraft for his vehicles, for their superior mobility over the uncertain Alkaid terrain.

"They lead with Scimitars and hoverbikes. They appear to deploy only all-ground-effect vehicles, even as we do."

"Well done, Warrior Till," Aleks said to his scout.

He laughed. *This will be a battle of maneuver,* he thought. *Just as I intended. The Alkaidians mean to take advantage of their knowledge of local terrain; against that I oppose our proficiency.* That the Turkina's Beak Galaxy had never heretofore been notorious for its proficiency did not dampen his eagerness to join battle. Instead, *challenge* whetted his appetite.

"Second Star Points One and Two, skirmish forward," he commanded. "MechWarrior Nina, join them in your *Eyrie.* Engage them, hurt them, pop smoke and withdraw at speed." All according to the plan he had sketched to his troops in advance.

"But, Galaxy Commander," Nina responded, *"it would be dishonor to flee."*

"One of two things now happens," Aleks said levelly. "You will carry out your orders as a Falcon Clanswoman. Or you will swap 'Mechs with me, you will provide firesupport in my *Gyrfalcon* and I shall carry out your orders in your machine."

"But, sir—"

"Never shall it be said Aleksandr Hazen ordered a subordinate to do something he dared not do. Now do as your honor bids, MechWarrior. But choose within the next ten seconds."

The light 'Mech instantly broke into a ground-eating run after the red-dust rooster tails raised by the light hovercraft, which had plunged instantly ahead as if to shame the high and mighty MechWarrior.

"Galaxy Commander, I obey!" Nina's voice said.

"Well done." With purpose but without hurry he deployed the rest of his forces. His infantry dug into a semicircle, twenty-five trooper Points widely spaced, bowed toward the enemy. His Elementals, useless at range but horribly effective close up, he grounded behind them. His remaining vehicles he kept back in defilade with a *Spirit* 'Mech and the Lily, except for his pair of speedy little Nacons, which he split to patrol the red wastes to either side of his main force. The sun, a blinding bluish pinpoint above their left shoulders, would shine full into the enemy's eyes. It was a potent defensive formation—and surprisingly static for a commander bent on mobile warfare.

Aleks was a man who loved surprises. Especially when he did the surprising.

"All static units to air-defense mode," he directed at last. "VTOLs, give their flyers as much to worry about that isn't us as possible."

His four helicopters put snouts down and spurted toward the onrushing enemy, now visible as columns of dust. Aleks saw the Alkaidian VTOLs on radar and magnetic-anomaly detector—some of them. The enemy craft were making maximal use of the terrain, hugging the ground, following saw-backed ridge lines, masking themselves behind the numerous tall, flat-topped ventifact columns. The high iron content of the rocks played hell with the MADs, a phenomenon Aleks had encountered before.

It worried him not at all. His Donar assault helos were fast and potent, each built around an extended-range long laser that gave them lengthy reach; and no matter how shaky their morale and state of readiness had been when he took command of Turkina's Beak, his jocks were still purpose-bred Clan aerospace warriors, as superior in their perceptions and reaction time to standard Spheroids as were their MechWarrior kindred. And they were as skillful as intensive hands-on Clan schooling could make them, keen for action from many hours of simulator combat during the endless weeks of waiting for the fleet's stardrives to recharge.

Reports rattled in his earpiece as his skirmishing detachment engaged the oncoming Republic Alkaid Militia. He had sent forward two twenty-ton Fox armored cars carried away as booty from Porrima, an Asshur armed with a single-volley Streak SRM launcher and a pair of extended-range medium lasers, a forty-five-ton Bellona for punch, and MechWarrior Nina's *Eyrie*. He listened to their quick falcon-screams of triumph as his eyes scanned skies of pale blue, alternating with his instruments, keeping a wary eye for intruding VTOLs.

His eye caught a flicker to the left edge of his windscreen. A Crow scout helo had popped up from behind a ridge just half a klick from his defensive line behind low hills and clumps of red boulders. Before he could respond, Mech-Warrior Mordechai had fired the large laser in his 'Mech's left arm. The chopper flared ruby, then banked and swooped down out of sight with smoke pouring black from it like blood into water.

Two more VTOLs streaked toward them from the direction of the growing, multiplex dust cloud. Aleks noted symbols on his display indicating they were two of his own Donars. He hoped his people would check their own sensors and hold fire. *This as much as battle itself will indicate whether I am succeeding with these warriors*, he thought, *whether I have begun to instill discipline and, more important, pride where before there was but* dezgra.

His Trinary refrained from firing up their own air. A black smoke ball rolled up the sky in the wake of his VTOLs, which banked to his left with a swarm of enemy ships after them like angry hornets. Green and red lasers stabbed at the Jade Falcon helos but missed.

With satisfaction Aleks noted that MechWarrior Mordechai had shifted to a secondary firing position and crouched back down so that his machine was mostly behind cover. He hoped the Alkaidians had been too preoccupied to note the origin of the shot that wounded their VTOL, but it did not matter hugely. The locals already knew—roughly—where his troops were. All lay in the details.

A white smokescreen wall sprang up from the desert. His skirmishers came flying back through it. All were functional, though the Bellona had a blown-out missile launcher box trailing a thin gray streamer of smoke.

The first of the enemy craft hove into view in pursuit, two Fox armored cars closely followed by a lance of Scimitars: sleek machines painted mottled tan and gray, bristling with armaments, sliding over the rocky desert soil with sinister ease. The Jade Falcon craft split to pass to either side of their hull-down comrades.

The lead pack of pursuers all chased the bunch to Aleks' left. The rest of the Alkaidians began to appear on Aleks' MAD, behind the smoke.

Despite Aleksandr Hazen's unremitting efforts over the weeks to instill his Turkina's Beak warriors with their namesake's headlong zeal, now they, at his order, *contained* that zeal, withheld their fire. It was a most un-Clanlike discipline, but it too was part of war—Aleks Hazen's way.

"All long-range units choose targets and prepare to engage," he commanded. Then: "Weapons free."

Heavy lasers and PPCs drew scarlet and blue-white lines between dug-in Jade Falcons and attacking Alkaidians. The giant autocannon of an SM1 tank destroyer thudded from Aleks' right, so near he could feel the vibration through his cockpit thrust falcon-like from the *Gyr*'s upper torso. White trails of long-range missiles sprouted from the Falcon positions and grew toward the onrushing hovercraft like shoots.

White flashes and black smoke balls appeared among the Alkaidians. A Fox disintegrated into a rolling ruin tumble. Aleks' target, a fifty-ton JES tactical missile carrier, veered away from a laser and autocannon volley belching smoke from its left-hand SRM launcher. It disappeared behind some irregularity of the red ground Aleks could not see.

What he could see, even without White Lily's vision enhancements, was the Alkaidian infantry hastily dismounting. Some rode in poorly armored personnel carriers, others clung to the backs of combat hovercraft like baby scorpions to their mother. Neither offered much shelter against the metal storm the Jade Falcons now unleashed upon them.

Aleks smiled and nodded. Infantry was always a concern, although Clan MechWarriors all too often dismissed them as mere residue, even today. They carried support weapons heavy enough to be dangerous, and could swarm and capture vehicles or even an unwarily piloted BattleMech. Now, though, they were afoot, hence slow—and meat for his Elementals when it was time to let their leashes slip.

Although they had lost over half a dozen vehicles in the first surprise volley—and destroyed no Clan machines in return, Aleks' display told him—the Alkaidian forces carried on undaunted with their plan: swarming around both flanks of Aleks' surprisingly dug-in Trinary. Even forcing their infantry to dismount probably did not disrupt their tactics: they would want a force out front to pin Aleks' troops in place, or flanking would mean little.

"MechWarrior Mordechai," Aleks directed, "attack as ordered."

With red sand cascading from its flanks, Mordechai's *Spirit* erupted from cover, weapons flaming. At the same time the waiting Falcon hovercraft rose up amidst hurricanes of swirling dust to lunge at the flankers to their left in a smashing attack. MechWarrior Nina's *Eyrie* joined them, as planned.

With his infantry out front, in good cover with overlapping fields of fire should the Alkaidian foot seek to advance, Aleks was left to handle the right-hand flanking force with the aid of his squat-armored Elementals.

It was not an even fight. Nor a long one.

Ryde
Prefecture VIII
The Republic of the Sphere
24 June 3134

Malvina Hazen descended upon Ryde like a plague from ancient prophecy.

Although the voyage from the jump points was only eleven days, that was too much for the impatient Galaxy Commander, who took the risk of employing a pirate point five days out—and like her sibkin won her gamble. Upon arriving in-system and before launching her DropShips, Malvina convened her officers in the briefing amphitheater inboard her flag JumpShip, *La Vie en Rose*, captured from the Davion contingent of the then-Federated Commonwealth in the last century and renamed; Malvina had insisted upon restoring its original name, and as a ristar got her wish, especially since Khan Jana Pryde could not care less what they called their ships so long as they *won*.

Naked, Malvina stood before her subcommanders. She held her slender white arms above her head, cut them with her great-bladed fighting knife—carefully, so as to avoid damage to muscle, nerve and tendon—and let the blood stream over her silver pale hair, down her face, to spatter her breasts and shoulders and run in twining networks down her flat domed belly.

In a ringing voice she promised: so it would be with all who stood in the path of the Falcons' return to the Inner Sphere. She would bathe in their blood.

Her Gyrfalcons screamed themselves hoarse in an orgy of approbation.

She broadcast the ceremony live to Ryde, so they could see in full tridee what Fate had in store for them.

In the glare of a bright but distant yellow-white sun, her DropShips descended through thin, sulfurous atmosphere to land at strategic locations on the world's three continents. She herself led her First Falcon Striker Cluster in a drop on the vital Water Pure complex, which provided drinkable water to the cold, dry world's populace and lay near the capital Heaven's Gate on the southerly continent Kale. Her command ship came down inside the wire, its landing jacks digging deep into the pavement of its parking lot, vehicles and cement melted into a bubbling cauldron by its drive jets.

Her Gyrs sprang forth ready for battle. Ryde's defenders did not disappoint her. Most of the strongpoints erected during the Succession Wars, when the chemical-rich planet had changed hands frequently between Houses Steiner and Kurita, had been stripped of armament and allowed to fall into desuetude after The Republic's rise. The fort near the water-purification plant had not. It was not the prize an invader would seek the planet *for*—but it was unmistakably key to possession of the planet itself. The peace of The Republic notwithstanding, the Ryde authorities had kept the plant carefully guarded.

The Republic Ryde Militia strongpoint lay near the facility but several kilometers outside its confines, sprawled on a yellow plain not far from the capital. By dropping audaciously into the facility itself Malvina put the militia in the position of having to invade its own industrial complex to dislodge the Falcons. However, the Corridan IV-based Water Pure Industries, wealthy and powerful, owed both wealth and power—especially on Ryde itself—in no small part to this very plant. It maintained a large and comprehensively trained security detachment of its own, equipped with VTOLs, armored vehicles, armored infantry equipped with Gnome power suits based upon the older Elemental design, and even a *Hatchetman* BattleMech; WPI gave protecting its precious plant precedence over Devlin Stone's desire to eliminate 'Mechs from private hands. As reliant as anyone else on the planet upon the steady stream of purified water flowing from the facility, successions of Governors had done nothing to pressure the corporation into scrapping the machine.

While Gyrfalcon aerospace fighters drew networks of white contrail against mauve sky, dueling in the stratosphere with Ryde fighters, Malvina herself burst forth from the landing ship's bay in her huge, hawk-headed *Shrike*, ornamental wings extended, followed by an Elemental swarm. Ten 'Mechs emerged after hers. A Star of five immediately set off to the south to counter any thrusts by the Defense Force regulars. The rest, supported by the Elementals in their super-sized power armor, strode off at once into the Cubist jungle of pipes and giant tanks after their commander, leaving the Galaxy's vehicles, VTOLs, and unpowered infantry to sort themselves out.

It was not that Malvina disdained the combined-arms paradigm dominant in modern war; like her brother she had earned ristar status and Galaxy command by successfully leading troops in battle as well as by her sheer prowess as a MechWarrior—and her force-of-nature ferocity. Battles were not won without understanding how to fight vehicles and infantry in concert with BattleMechs; and battles she had won. What made her plunge right in was her sheer bloodlust, her desire for the hunt, especially in the wake of the frustrations of Chaffee. She had gone to extremes to instill the same *yarak*—the bird of prey's eagerness for the hunt—in her Gyrfalcons.

Now she unhooded them and let them fly.

Although a range of jagged mountains, source of the plant's raw material, stood near, the morning was warm. Ryde's sun stood high in the sky. It was already hot in Malvina's cockpit as she settled her 'Mech down just beyond a hash of white-gleaming pipes two meters through.

Gunfire flashed in her peripheral vision. Heat-blooms of chemical propellant ballooned in her IR display. A fire team of WPI security troops was engaging her with conventional projectile rifles. And somewhat more: she felt a tiny shudder ripple through Black Rose's ninety-five tons of mass as the shaped charge warhead of a light anti-armor rocket spent itself on the armored housing of her left hip actuator.

A subconscious glance at her internal status displays confirmed what she already knew: the rocket had left a hot spot and dug a slight crater in the armor.

She laughed as she destroyed the unarmored infantry with a burst of flechette rounds from the heavy autocannon twinned in the *Shrike*'s left arm.

Around her men and women hunted others, killed, died. The shrieks of unarmored infantry soldiers caught by Elemental flamers shrilled in her audio pickups like the cries of startled seabirds—on a world that had seas, and birds. Explosions boomed and crackled and cannon cracked on all sides.

Not all the dying was being done by one side. A Point of Elementals leapt into the sky like giant fleas to attack a group of light armored vehicles with their short-range missile launchers. A Crow scout chopper appeared abruptly from behind a huge, yellow-painted tank as if falling up. Its lasers flared scarlet, tumbling two giant warriors from the sky. A third power suit exploded as first its right-hand launcher and then its flamer fuel were ignited by the beam's hot kiss. The other two Elementals ducked for safety behind a spatter of missiles that missed. Then a PPC bolt from somewhere behind Malvina blew the VTOL into a black cloud raining yellow fire.

In her ears rang the raptor cries of her MechWarriors outside the plant striking south. The planetary militia, fore-warned, had reacted to her landing with exemplary quickness. It was killing them. With their own vehicles, in-fantry clinging to armored backs and flanks, trailing after, the five Gyrfalcon BattleMechs charged at full speed through the defenders' advancing armor, slashing, slaying, more like diamond sharks ripping through shoals of ice cod in the chill, inhospitable waters of Strana Mechty than Jade Falcons stooping on prey.

The metal tangle all around made gibberish of Malvina's magnetic anomaly detector. She didn't know the *Hatchet-man* was there until it suddenly lunged from behind a three-story cinder-block pumping station. Its huge depleted ura-nium hatchet, the size of a house wall, swung toward her cockpit in a desperate all-or-nothing shot for the one target that might permit the forty-five-ton 'Mech to take down her twice-as-heavy and more behemoth.

But Galaxy Commander Malvina Hazen had senses keen and reflexes quick even for a Clan MechWarrior. Although she could read the display strip beneath the low, wide wind-screen that compressed the whole three-sixty view around her machine as readily as her natural vision, it was her peripheral sight that showed the heavy blade flashing in the glare of the distant primary. She folded her 'Mech's right knee, pivoting clockwise in a flash.

Just missing the *Shrike*'s head, the great blade smashed into the extended-range medium laser set in Black Rose's left shoulder. White smoke gouted from it like arterial spray. Malvina's board lit with red lights and warnings shrilled. It had been a good stroke, a vicious one.

But not enough. Far from that.

She swung her machine's torso back the other way. The hatchet had sunk deep into the *Shrike*'s torso and stuck fast. The Rydian jock managed to wrench it free, and then the two autocannon that made up Black Rose's left arm blasted the codpiece-like armored housing protecting the *Hatchetman*'s groin area and slammed it back into the pump house. The wall cracked and sagged.

With commendable speed, the *Hatchetman* pushed off from the crumpled wall with its elbows and jumped straight up. Malvina followed. The humanoid 'Mech with the odd

Parasaurolophus-like head, with its long back-sweeping crest, could climb away from her spiky monster; even wizard Clan design could only do so much with a ninety-five-ton machine.

But the lighter 'Mech had not gotten that great a literal jump on Malvina—Clan reflexes again. The pilot aimed another hatchet blow at Malvina's cockpit. Laughing, with gentle pressure on the attitude jet controls, Malvina pirouetted the vast machine out of its path.

The massive weapon's momentum almost toppled the *Hatchetman* off its drive columns. The pilot managed to keep it upright and airborne, just barely.

Until with a blast from her 100mm autocannon Malvina blew off one of the Spheroid 'Mech's Luxor 2/Q jets.

The *Hatchetman* fell to the sulfurous hardpan with such force that displaced air rocked the hovering *Shrike*. The Rose had excellent thermal efficiency, but heat rose quickly in the cockpit, coating Malvina's near-naked body in instant sweat. The stink of sulfur pressed like thumbs at her nostrils, infiltrating through the cockpit seal or perhaps gaskets aft in the fuselage—she would have words with her tech crew on returning to the ship.

It was time to come down. An unfamiliar voice spoke in her ear across the general frequency she left open in case the locals found something to say to her.

"Terms," it said. A woman's voice.

"As if," Malvina replied. Her taloned right foot came down on the front of the *Hatchetman*'s sloped head, eliciting a sharp scream, quickly cut off.

With the Water Pure plant secured, the Ryde planetary government capitulated, even as fighting continued at other Jade Falcon landing sites across the planet. Malvina was almost disappointed. Yet with limited numbers and less time—both needed careful husbanding, for the crowning glory at Skye—she could not afford the luxury of a campaign of any length. She had places to be and people to kill. There had been no choice but to go for the planetary jugular.

Unlike Chaffee's, Ryde's defenders were professionals, thoroughly conventional. When they surrendered it was likely they considered it binding. Yet despite their unconditional surrender, Malvina wanted to ensure that there would be no repetition of the guerrilla campaign that had caused such difficulties on the Lyran world.

Of a global population of almost 680 million, Malvina's Gyrfalcons quickly rounded up sixty-eight thousand at random and herded them into confinement areas improvised from sports venues and factory parking areas near the Clusters' landing sites. Then with local media broadcasting the scene on tridee under threat of Elemental flamers, they proceeded to decimate the captives: making them count down, having every tenth one step forward, driving that tenth portion together and then killing them with machine gun and laser fire—men, women, children.

Evolution had come to Ryde, Clan style. Or at least that version practiced by Malvina Hazen and her Mongol faction.

═══ 17 ═══

Skye
Prefecture VIII
The Republic of the Sphere
25 June 3134

An Elemental sat weeping on a rock when Captain Tara Bishop came into the Seventh Skye Militia cantonment beneath a glory of endless blue autumn skies brushed with white wings of cloud.

Tara B managed not to gape. Instead, she cocked an eyebrow at Master Sergeant Angus McCorkle, who stood awaiting her nearby, just inside the gate with the neatly carved and painted wood sign bearing the legend, "Welcome to the Home of the Garryowen" arched over it. His hands were clasped behind his back, and there was a studied lack of expression on his rugged black face. He was the one bearing the day-by-day brunt of trying to whip the remaining local main-force unit into shape. It had so far not been a happy task, even for as crusty an old top kick as McCorkle.

"What?" she asked.

"Lieutenant Padraig took offense at something one of our young gentlefolk said," McCorkle said. "Captain."

"Young gentlefolk" was what the senior noncoms in the regular Highlander regiments, the First Kearny and the Fusiliers, termed officers, mostly lieutenants junior grade, who had enlisted shortly before the first Steel Wolf invasion of Northwind and won quick commissions via plain attrition. While they had displayed outstanding courage, or at least a strong survival streak, to win their promotions, not all were as polished as even a man like McCorkle might prefer: imminent danger had forced Countess Campbell to take what she could get, including half-unlettered backwoodsfolk. Hence the habit of ironically reminding sundry that they were all gentlemen and ladies by order of The Republic's Senate.

The air was full of the smell of ripening grain and wood smoke. Off toward the mountains a cloud of migratory birds wheeled, sojourning south before the gathering winter. The flyers were dark against the brilliant blue sky.

First Lieutenant Anders Monsen appeared beside Tara Bishop. He was the usual training liaison between the Highlanders and the Seventh. He greeted her warmly, but his boyish face showed deep consternation. "The problem bein'," he said in his thick Skye Irish brogue, "that one of your snot—that is, a lieutenant junior grade used the term 'motherless' quite prominently in poor Paddy's hearing."

Tara shut her eyes.

The Clans were, to say the least, not popular with the Highlanders—nor any Northwinders, from Countess Tara on down. "Motherless," a reference to Trueborn Clanners' in vitro birth, had become a common epithet among soldiers who had seen their home worlds raped and Terra itself defiled by the Steel Wolves. That it had quickly devolved into a general term of abuse, no longer reserved for Clansfolk alone, did not exactly help.

Thanks to Devlin Stone's voluntary resettlement program, a number of ethnic Clanners dwelt on Skye. Some held to the Canister; others had completely assimilated, still others practiced natural reproduction yet strictly among their own nominal caste, and termed themselves "Purebloods" in defiance of the classic Clan stigmatization of

Freebirths. They were overrepresented in the Republic Skye Militia—including Trueborn warriors who were, so the Duke's counterintelligence services assured them, unswervingly loyal to Skye and The Republic: Ghost Bears, Nova Cats, even a few Wolves and Falcons.

Whatever else he was, the sobbing man was pure Elemental. On hearing his officer speak he raised a great tear-stained face. "I *had* a mither," he said plaintively—in an Irish brogue which, to Tara's near-horror, was every bit as marked as Monsen's. "An' it's not even a year since she joined the saints."

"Don't tell me he's Catholic," Tara said, before she could stop herself.

"What else might he be, and him a good Bogtrotter?" Monsen asked, perhaps a bit too ingenuously. "You should meet our Padre, Captain Seamus. Two hundred fifty centimeters of faith and fury is he; and wasn't he free-fighting champion of all Skye when he was just a tad of a seminarian at St. Angela's? A *largish* tad, I grant you that, now."

What's worse, Tara thought, *is I don't think he's pulling my leg.* She turned to McCorkle.

"First Lieutenant Monsen informs me that Lieutenant Padraig is a very valorous man." He hesitated only momentarily before speaking the last word. "He served with distinction in combat with the Hastati Protectors IX."

"It's only that he's a sensitive nature to him," Monsen said. "Sure, he did his stint, won his medals, and home he came to Skye to help till the family farm in County Loguire."

Only by dint of superhuman effort did Tara restrain herself from blurting, *Hitched to a plow?* She *hoped* his mother had been Elemental as well as his father. If not . . . she shuddered discreetly.

"And now he's taken up arms again, in defense of the soil in which his blessed mother's bones rest," Monsen said.

Tara went to stand before the sobbing giant. "Lieutenant Padraig," she said crisply, "I am Captain Tara Bishop of the First Kearny Highlanders Regiment. I'm also aide-de-camp to Countess Tara Campbell. In the Countess' name, in the name of the Northwind Highlanders, in the name of The Republic of the Sphere, and on my own behalf, I would like to offer my sincerest apologies for any distress our officer's thoughtless remark caused you. I am sure that officer meant nothing by it."

If only because I damned well hope none of our ninety-day wonders is stupid enough to piss off a full-blooded Elemental in the wild, bottle-baby or not!

Padraig nodded and dropped his enormous hands. "That's mighty big of ye, Cap'n," he said to the woman a third his size without apparent irony.

"My honor, warrior." *I'm double-damned,* she thought fiercely, *if I'll condone trying to impose censorship on our hot-blooded girls and boys. Yet—heart and minds!—we can't go wounding the sensibilities of loyal soldiers of The Republic with racial slurs, of all bloody things.*

But it was not her decision to make. And then, despite her regard for her commander and the deep personal friendship that had sprung up between them, she grinned from ear to ear at the realization that she could pitch this particular hot potato right into her namesake's deceptively dainty hands. *A terrible thing to do to a friend. Ah, but duty's a harsh taskmistress. . . .*

She left the lugubrious giant to Monsen's puppy-dog ministrations and joined McCorkle walking down a company street between tents and plywood shacks. No litter was visible, but the place had a slipshod air. Disreputable, somehow. A few loungers watched them warily. The rest, it seemed, were off somewhere. *Hopefully improving their skills,* Tara thought.

"How's it going, Master Sergeant?" A light breeze kicked dust along the street past their boots, and tugged playfully at the cuffs of their trousers.

He hesitated. That itself spoke volumes. He was a man who had been raised since puphood to the doctrine that a wrong decision *right now* is light years better than a "correct" decision too late. And as senior noncom with nearly three decades of service—he was older than he looked— he had no fear of any officer, even one of far more exalted rank than Tara Bishop herself, nor for that matter of the Countess herself. He would have stood up to Exarch Redburn without a second thought: in a fighting army *no one* outranked a good NCO.

He was not a man, in short, accustomed to choosing his words. Nonetheless he did so now.

"Unevenly," was what he chose.

She cocked an eyebrow at him. She had gotten over being intimidated by the man, for all that he seemed an animated obsidian statue. After showing a certain initial reserve, he had come to treat her with pure professional correctness. It meant he respected her. Master Sergeant McCorkle was not a man who suffered fools gladly. Indeed, neither she nor anyone she had talked to was aware of any evidence he suffered them at all.

"Meaning what exactly, Top?"

"They're as undisciplined a collection of barroom sweepings and gaolbirds as ever a sun of any color has risen on," he said, his own brogue coming on more thickly than usual with the intensity of his feeling. "If I drop one for twenty, he gives me twenty more for the Old Sod. They think of us as a passel of Republican busybodies with asses so tight—begging the Captain's pardon—that we might as well be Lyrans ourselves. I think we've shown them we're a bit more than parade-ground Janes and Johnnies. But they're wild as mountain cats, all the same."

"Will they fight?"

That graven image face, it seemed to her, threatened to crack a smile. "If the JFs come here I think they'll fight like demons."

"But will they fight *with* us? Or on their own hook?"

"There's the rub, Captain Bishop," McCorkle said.

They reached a parade ground. The flags of The Republic and Skye snapped on a flagpole across it, over the regimental headquarters. On a separate staff snapped a blue flag with a black horse head, and the words "Seventh Skye Militia" above and "For Garryowen In Glory" below.

"Who the blight," Tara asked in a quiet voice, "is Garry Owen, anyway, Master Sergeant?"

"Damned if I know, Captain," he said.

The speaker horns mounted above the HQ buildings began to emit a rising-falling banshee wail. At the same time Tara's personal communicator chimed for attention. She snatched it from her belt carrier.

"Bishop here," she said, as men and women began to tumble out of barracks around them.

"This is Major Sinclair at Sanglamore." He was a Highlander staff officer who had come in with Ballantrae and

the first group of regulars from Terra. *"Get back here at once. Have Shugrue assign you an escort."* Major Lars Shugrue was the Seventh's adjutant, on whom Tara had been on the point of paying a courtesy call before observing a training exercise supervised by McCorkle and the other training staff seconded from the Highlanders.

"Affirmative on the quick return, Major, negative on the escort." She was mildly annoyed. Sinclair was not a combat type, but neither was he usually officious. "I'm a big girl now."

"No doubt," came back dryly. *"But the Countess wants you to get an escort anyway."*

"Yes, sir. May I ask what the matter is? Have the Falcons arrived?"

"Yes, you may ask; no they have not. And I'll waste no more time talking when you should be moving, Captain!"

"Yes, sir." She hesitated. "Should I bring Master Sergeant McCorkle along as well?"

"Negative, Captain. But have him gather his cadre together somewhere secure. Discreetly. Just in case. Now, move."

She lowered the communicator and stared briefly at McCorkle. He shrugged.

"We're mushrooms, ma'am," he said. "Just SOP."

A frozen-faced Skye staff lieutenant ushered Tara Bishop into the briefing room in the rectory of the erstwhile Sanglamore Academy.

Duke Gregory Kelswa-Steiner was there, as were Prefect Della Brown and Planetary Legate Stanford Eckard, dressed in severe black trimmed with gray. Chief Minister Solvaig, whom the captain had privately described to her Countess and friend as having eyes like the crescent-moon marks you might make with your thumbnails in spoiled cheese, was not in evidence, to her pleased surprise.

Tara C. sat, not across from the others, but at the end of the table, side-on to the door; she had grown too wary to sit with her back to an entrance. It was a change Tara Bishop approved even though she regretted the need. The Countess' smile was brief, sincere and strained.

"Glad to see you made it intact, Captain."

Tara Bishop shrugged. "We had no trouble at all, ma'am.

If anything the streets were deserted even for this time of a work day." Her Garryowen escort, uncharacteristically silent and grim, had brought her on the quickest route from their bivouac outside town to the former military school on its bluff overlooking a thickly wooded suburb also known as Sanglamore.

"There is rioting, Captain Bishop." To her surprise it was the Duke himself who answered. As much to her surprise, both he and Eckard had risen to her entrance. She was so junior as to merit any notice whatsoever solely because of the fact she was chief aide-de-camp to Tara Campbell, who despite her nominal disparity in title to the Duke of Skye was in fact full peer to both Kelswa-Steiner and Prefect Brown, superior to Eckard. As Prefect of III, Tara Campbell held a rank approximating field marshal, far too heavy in grade for command of her de facto division. Then the captain realized it was old-fashioned gallantry that made the men rise, deference to a lady entering a room.

"Certain elements of the populace have panicked at the latest news," the Duke said, resuming his seat. Tara Bishop sat too. "From your account, the disorder does not appear yet to have spread to the suburbs, or at least the western ones. Chief Minister Solvaig must be succeeding in containing it."

Tara Bishop clamped her lips on the question she wanted to ask. Sometimes she remembered she was just a captain.

"A few hours ago, a Republican merchant JumpShip entered the system," Tara Campbell explained. "Her captain broadcast a warning: the Jade Falcons have invaded Chaffee, just across the frontier in Steiner space."

"They conquered it, Captain Bishop," Eckard intoned. His pale face looked more tightly pinched than usual. "With, it would appear, exemplary brutality."

Tara Bishop gasped. She was no cherry; she had been a combat MechWarrior long before getting slugged as aide to the Countess, nor had she stopped driving her *Pack Hunter* 'Mech into harm's way since receiving that assignment. She had seen the elephant—not to mention the Wolf. She knew that war is misery and pain *hurts*.

But to hear that a Jade Falcon war fleet had once again invaded the Inner Sphere was like having some kind of childhood nightmare, at once fanciful and terrifyingly visceral, come true: as if the Duke and his Legate had just told her a dragon had just landed in New Glasgow and begun laying waste the central business district.

"Impossible!" It burst out before she could stop it. Its banality appalled her. Especially since, of course, it wasn't.

"My reaction was the same, Captain," Prefect Brown said. "But impossible or not, it's true. We received a massive data dump, complete with tridee documentation of the destruction of an entire city by the Falcons."

"These aren't wannabes like the Spirit Cats," Tara Campbell said. Despite her rigorous lifelong training in diplomacy the bitterness was clear in her voice: but then again, she wasn't bitter on her own account. "Or our old friends the Steel Wolves." As far as Republican intelligence had been able to discern since her explosion onto the scene a little over a year before, Anastasia Kerensky, Canister-born on the world Arc-Royal in the Commonwealth, was the only real Wolf in her pack.

"These aren't Republican citizens gone renegade," the Countess continued. "They're the genuine article, straight from Sudeten itself. Just as the Sea Fox reports suggested."

Tara Bishop frowned. "But, Countess, the riots—"

"The initial broadcast was made in the clear," Tara Campbell said. "The merchie captain was spooked. And I don't blame her. She entered Chaffee system within hours after the Falcon invasion fleet jumped out to parts as yet unknown. There was still a JF JumpShip in-system, but by sheer chance orbiting at the zenith proximity point, whereas the merchant entered at the nadir. Although the planet was pretty thoroughly under the heel of a Falcon Cluster—"

"And not just any Cluster," Della Brown broke in, "but the Turkina Keshik itself."

Tara Bishop's eyes widened. She didn't know a lot about what went on in the blessedly distant Jade Falcon Occupation Zone, but she did know quite a bit about the military history of the Inner Sphere. Turkina Keshik, the first Cluster of the elite Jade Falcon Galaxy, was the Khan's own guard, leading formation of the whole Falcon *Touman*.

"—certain elements on the surface caught the merchant's broadcast greeting and responded with an account of what had happened, and was still going on," the Countess continued, showing no resentment of the interruption. "The merchie captain sat out the recharge, no doubt sweating blood every millisecond, then jumped here quick as she could."

"Unfortunately," Duke Gregory said, and his heavy handsome face was pale with the effort of containing his rage, "someone else heard her initial transmission to Skye. And that someone spread the word to the whole planet: Clan Jade Falcon has seized and ravaged a world right across the border in the Commonwealth—and their course seems to point them *here*."

18

Wolf Moon (Backside of Ivanov, moon of La Blon)
Prefecture IX
The Republic of the Sphere
27 June 3134

In slow motion, the woman dropped toward the commissary floor. The new third eye in the center of her forehead wept a single long red tear up into the air. The shot that placed it there had quit echoing in the confines of the pressure chamber, but its aftereffects still rang in the ears of the Steel Wolf officers standing before their overturned chairs.

Anastasia Kerensky had already returned her right-hand weapon, a Lyran-issue M&M Service automatic, to its holster. She was a woman of arresting beauty, with a cloud of midnight-black hair floating about her head in the low gravity and highlighted red by the overhead illumination. Folding her arms in a gesture of deliberate contempt, she faced the others of her restive pack.

"Who else thinks I'm not fit to lead the Steel Wolves today?" Her use of the contraction cracked *challenge* like a glove across the face.

Eyes asmolder with sullen anger, the half dozen officers, Bloodnamed MechWarriors all, turned away. Star Captain Kimiko Fetladral finally reached repose on the mat covering the decking of the prefab pressure structure. Her own Nakjama laser pistol landed beyond the tips of her lifeless, outstretched fingers with a soft thud. Ignoring her late challenger, Anastasia sat down, picked up her bowl of soup, raised its pressure-valve to her full lips.

It froze just shy of them. Her blue eyes looked across the covered bowl into the almost white-blue eyes of Ian Murchison. Although as a mere tech he would not normally be suffered to sup with warriors, the grizzled Northwinder was Anastasia Kerensky's personal medic, as he had been when he was her bondsman. She still insisted on keeping him with her most times.

"What?" she demanded. "You told me to exert myself less."

Murchison frowned. It was not usually a prudent thing for a member of a lesser caste to disapprove of a warrior's actions, much less one who also happened to command more than a Galaxy of Clan warriors. But Murchison had never been prudent: though he had started out not just as a Spheroid but as a lifelong civilian as well—contract medico on Balfour-Douglas Petrochemicals Offshore Drilling Station #47 off Northwind's Oilfields Coast, captured along with it in a covert action led by Anastasia herself—he had the balls of a Wolf MechWarrior, and not just one of these Steel Wolf posers, either. Which was why he still had his life, his status as adoptee into Clan Wolf, and, yes, his balls.

For her part, keeping him around seemed an uncharacteristically sentimental gesture for the Wolf Bitch. It was no such thing. He was a skilled medic—and the only living soul in the Steel Wolves she trusted to tend her when she was weakened or incapacitated. Which seemed to be happening a lot lately.

"I won't counsel you to be more prudent," he husked in his gravelly voice. "I'm too old to waste the breath. But I will remind you that bullet wounds—not to even mention lasers—are a bit harder to recover from than knife cuts."

He had even less use for the Clan prejudice against contractions than Anastasia: he had not asked to become a Wolf. Neither had he demurred when Anastasia cut his final bond cord and conferred Clan status upon him. Not that he had much choice—and brave or not he was not a total fool.

Not a fool of any stripe or species. Which was also why Anastasia kept him alive, and at her side.

Slowly the others righted their chairs and sat back down. Hot gazes began to drift back toward her. She paid them no attention, though she was fully aware of each angry glare.

They were nothing new. Ever since the initial setback on Northwind, she had faced challenges from subordinates. Even once the holdouts from the days when Kal Radick, whom she had challenged and killed in unaugmented combat, led the Steel Wolves had been weeded out, through combat or by failed challenges of their own, plenty had stepped forward to try to wrest command from her.

And now, in the wake of the disastrous invasion of sacred Terra, which ended in defeat and disgrace after Anastasia's physical incapacitation—itself in large part a result of her incomplete recovery from having her belly laid open in a knife duel with the last of the Kal Radick bitter-enders, Star Colonel Marks—the challenges came almost weekly. Even if they all had the same depressingly predictable outcome: the same one that Star Captain Kimiko Fetladral's had produced.

Because right over the restive Steel Wolves' heads hung the rich pleasure planet of La Blon, so ingenuous in its happy hedonism that it believed the horrors of war would never touch it. Indeed they had not, for centuries; even the Word of Blake Jihadists had spared it. Literally beneath the renegades' feet, on the planet-facing far side of the tidelocked satellite that the locals called Ivanov but which its secret inhabitants named Wolf Moon, lay the prosperous city of Overlook Point, with a big automated spaceport five hundred kilometers away. All were ripe and ready as staked lambs.

Yet Anastasia forbade her raiders to pluck those prizes. She understood too well, as her unruly subordinates would have had they the brains to be *fit* to command, that to take any of those morsels would bring the final retribution of The Republic of the Sphere slamming down like a rogue planet upon their heads.

The Republic was decadent; the Steel Wolves' defeat

upon Terra had been a narrow thing. Yet The Republic was huge and The Republic was mighty, mightier than Anastasia herself had given it credit for being. And it was angry now. She and her Steel Wolves were outlaws, hated by trillions. The next time Republican forces caught up with them would be the last.

Anastasia could hardly have cared less about the Steel Wolves save as means to her own ambitions—which were only banked, far from extinguished. As far as she was concerned, her followers were sheer ersatz, Spheroids themselves, for all they aped Clan ways. But she was not quite ready to yield her own personal adventure, *life,* to her nemesis: plucky, platinum-haired Tara Campbell, the "pretty little Countess" as Anastasia called her, whom, over the course of their many meetings on the field of war, the Wolf Bitch had grown secretly to like almost as much as she hated.

Her personal communicator buzzed for attention. She flipped it open and held it to her ear. It was one of her electronic intelligence officers in the central pressure-dome, monitoring communications between La Blon and the lively space traffic, both intrasystem and a surprising profusion of interstellar visitors. La Blon was no backwater like Northwind, and even the vanishment of the HPG net had scarcely scratched its trade. Which perversely made it a better place to hide: it was easy for Steel Wolf craft to blend in with all the rest.

Her medico watched with keen eyes as she listened. The others' attention was more furtive but no less intent.

She snapped her communicator shut and snorted a laugh. "A trader in from Steiner space has caused a sensation with some surprising news," she announced to the room as a whole, although she was looking at Murchison.

The other Wolves stopped talking and eating and turned to look at her. Although they knew their leader had passed herself off as a Spheroid on more than one occasion—some quite recent—none of them suspected she would bore them with trivia. Which, to them all, mere gossip about Spheroid doings was by definition.

"It seems that there's a fleet crossing the Lyran Commonwealth," the commander said. "A war fleet. Out of the Jade Falcon Occupation Zone."

If the room had been silent a moment before, now it became a vacuum. The warriors stared at their alpha bitch as if trying to draw the rest from her with the suction of their eyes.

"It seems the turd-birds gave an ultimatum to the Archon herself—they have balls if not brains, I give them that. They blithely violate Steiner space, and they demand the Squareheads do not interfere with them, upon pain of war."

"Crossing Steiner space?" demanded the recently elevated Star Colonel Aretha Vickers. Her voice was crumpled like wastepaper, relic of a forearm blow to the throat during her sibko days. She had disdained surgical correction. "To do what?"

Anastasia rose and smiled. "Why, to carry out a Trial of Annihilation," she said.

"Against whom?" demanded Star Captain Maynar Carns.

"Against us," Anastasia said, "of course."

Sanglamore Academy
New London
Skye
28 June 3134

"Excuse me, please," a man's deep voice said from the break-room door.

Tara Campbell's head snapped up. She blinked. She realized her chin had been trending down toward her clavicle, into the open collar of the man's white shirt she wore. She had taken to wearing masculine dress when liable to be seen, to counteract the Skyean perception of her as, candidly, a bimbo.

The initial panic over the Chaffee horror had subsided quickly, once people realized no Clan invasion fleet followed hard upon the heels of that news. Still mysterious was why the reaction should have been so vehement—and so immediate. Duke Gregory's thaw toward Tara had proven temporary; he was again as frostily remote and his staff as stiffly uncooperative as before. It did not appear he blamed Tara for the situation in any way, but his anger had boiled over again. He was mad at the universe.

Tara's aide had jumped up and turned to face the door. Her attitude bespoke protectiveness, like a dog guarding her mistress. "Can I help you, sir?" she asked with a diplomacy that made the Countess proud—and which the young captain's ready-to-rumble body language eloquently belied.

The man smiled, half-shy, bobbed his head, and entered. "I apologize for intruding. I'm looking for Countess Tara Campbell."

So is half the planet. Although Tara Bishop did not say it, Tara Campbell heard it through the mists of her drowsiness, too slowly dissipating from behind her eyes. Some wanted to interview her, others to marry her, and a sizable majority to ride her offworld on a rail—if anything so nice. . . .

"I'm sorry, sir." Tara Bishop was shaking her head, giving her protestation the lie again. "The Countess is extremely busy now. You'll have to get in touch with her staff and make an appointment."

Tara C. got a better look at the man past her friend, who was now in full Valkyrie mode, ready to slay dragons. The Countess had a vague memory, just before the man's voice intruded, of her aide's voice asking if she were all right? TB had been nagging her to sleep more, to rest more, and Tara knew she was right. But it was hard to tear her mind away, sometimes, from a threat that, although this world was not hers, seemed to dwarf the menace the Steel Wolves had posed to Northwind.

The intruder smiled. He was a plain man, Asian looking, dark eyes on a bit of a bias, a head of slightly receding dark hair. He had a medium height and build, although the cut of his subdued business garb suggested an attempt to hide some softening around the middle. On the whole he looked not much different from anyone who might happen to stand next to him in any city on any world of The Republic. Until he smiled.

"I have important business with the Countess," he said apologetically.

Tara Bishop started to go into attack mode. Despite herself Tara was intrigued. "At ease, TB," she said lightly. "He's gotten this far, so he's either resourceful or determined. What is your business, exactly, Mr. . . . ?"

"Laveau. Paul Laveau." He blinked and grinned a little wider. "I'm a spy."

Both women stared. Tara Bishop's left hand began to stray behind her back—toward the hideout laser pistol riding beneath her battle-dress blouse, behind her left hip.

The intruder laughed. "I hope I didn't alarm you." He raised his left hand from his side, deliberately, just slowly enough so the women—and his attention seemed for the moment centered upon the captain—could see his hand was cupped, not holding a weapon.

He revealed in his palm a badge displaying the seal of The Republic of the Sphere and his likeness. "I'm on your side."

Captain Bishop stepped forward to peer at the badge. " 'Systems and resource auditor,' " she read, raising her head to study him with new scrutiny. " 'Office of the *Exarch*'?"

"Real spies aren't usually very glamorous," he admitted. "I'm what you might call a forensic accountant."

"You've come to check our *books*?" Tara Campbell demanded.

"In the midst of a Clan invasion?" asked Tara B. She took the badge holder from him, studied it, then unceremoniously tossed it to Tara Campbell, who fielded it as if the move was the most natural thing in the world and peered at it herself, brow furrowing so that her snub nose tipped up slightly.

Paul Laveau grinned again. It seemed a natural expression for him. Not precisely what she would expect of an accountant, even one who appeared to include a cloak and maybe even a dagger among the tools of his trade.

"What better time to ensure that The Republic of the Sphere's resources are being properly employed, Countess? Don't worry; you are not the object of my investigation."

"Who is?" Tara Bishop asked with characteristic bluntness.

The Asian eyes appraised her calmly. "Captain Bishop— I hope I've not made a terrific gaffe and got your name wrong?"

"I'm Captain Tara Bishop."

He nodded. "Captain Bishop, that information is confidential and need-to-know—apologies for the security mumbo-jumbo.

"However"—he looked at Tara Campbell—"I *can* tell you that my mission concerns events that preceded our learning about the Falcon war fleet, as well as your presence on Skye. Not much real mystery there."

"I see," Tara Campbell said. She did: *Jasek's defection with the heart and spine of the Republican Skye Militia.*

Without preamble she flipped the badge holder at him. He fumbled it, dropped it, picked it up grinning apologetically. TB's stern face cracked in a smile.

But she wasn't ready to let go. "Look, Mr. Systems and Resource Auditor Laveau—"

"Paul, please. Or if you must, Mr. Laveau. The rest is too awful to say aloud."

"Paul. All respect, but aren't you a little light in the pay grade for a job this big?"

Paul shrugged. "Of course you're right, Captain," he said. "An investigation of such magnitude would normally be handled by a Knight of the Sphere. But as I'm sure you already suspect, The Republic has a good many more emergencies on its hands right now than it has Knights to attend them. I was what was available; the next planet to tumble into crisis is liable to get a stockroom clerk."

"What exactly is the nature of your business with the Countess?" Tara Bishop demanded. "I have a need to know *that,* I think you'll concede."

"Your manner suggests I damned well better, Captain," he said. "Good for you. A person needs loyal friends, as a public person requires zealous assistants. The answer: simply, I have come to ask a favor of your boss."

"A favor?" Tara Bishop echoed.

"Ask," said Tara Campbell. "I've got to warn you, Exarch's combat accountant or not, there's not much I can spare you."

"Your kind cooperation is all I need. I am unfamiliar with Skye. For that matter, I don't know anything *truly* about you: I am not so encumbered with a bureaucrat's soul as to believe a dossier can tell me anything truly vital about anything so complex as a world—much less a person."

Tara Bishop whistled admiringly. "The Republic diplomatic corps took a major hit when you opted for chartered accountancy, Mr. Laveau. You could preach pacifism on Sudeten with a delivery like that."

Laveau laughed delightedly. "You truly think so? My great-grandmother always tells me I'm too glib for my own good. I am most appreciative, Captain Tara Bishop, although I think you do me too much credit. The truth is, a field accountant needs quite an array of talents, many of them unlooked for." .

"Since you've done your homework you know I'm a bit preoccupied here," Tara said. "But I can spare you a little time, I suppose. Your work's important to The Republic too."

"Far from the same level as yours, Countess. Still—might I take up a fraction more of your time now, please?"

Tara sighed, considered. "Why not? Shall we sit down?"

"Why not ride?" he asked.

"Ride?"

He nodded enthusiastically. "There are excellent riding stables not far from this gloomy pile, with most appealing bridle paths through the woods. If the brochures are to be trusted, of course, although the evidence of my eyes tends to bear them out. You do ride, Countess, and well, as you do everything you turn your hand to; I trust the mass media that far at least."

She shook her head. The short pelt of platinum hair, not currently spiked, shifted as to a breeze. "I don't know—"

All this time Tara Bishop had been studying Paul Laveau with a penetrating eye.

"She accepts," she said abruptly.

"But—" Tara started.

"Go." Her aide made shooing motions.

"My duty—"

Tara Bishop snorted. "Your *duty* is to take better damned *care* of yourself! There's only so much you can do, you need to rely more on your staff, and you won't do anyone a bloody *bit* of good if you've fatigued yourself into a coma or psychosis when the Falcons finally blow into town. The best thing you can do for Skye right now is get some fresh air, exercise, and then about fourteen hours' sleep. *Ma'am.*"

She braced to attention and fixed her eyes above the top

of the break room door. "You can now bust me back to private and assign me to waste-burning detail in perpetuity for rank insubordination, Countess Campbell, ma'am."

Tara was shaking her head. Laughing. But tears glittered in her eyes.

"I had no idea you felt so strongly, Tara," she said. "I hardly know how to respond."

Paul Laveau cleared his throat discreetly. "Might I be allowed to suggest: with humble pride at inspiring such devotion in a warrior the caliber of our Captain Bishop? And also, by accepting my invitation, of course."

And he turned his side to her and offered his crooked elbow.

To her entire amazement, Tara Campbell slipped her arm through his, and allowed him to squire her out the door.

19

Chaffee
Lyran Commonwealth
The Republic of the Sphere
1 July 3134

With the shortest distance to travel and only one combat objective before the climactic confrontation on Skye, Galaxy Commander Beckett Malthus and his Turkina Keshik spent several weeks solidifying the Clan's grip on Chaffee before advancing to their intermediate destination, Glengarry.

It was a grindingly frustrating time for Bec Malthus. Malvina Hazen's destruction of the city of Hamilton had put an end to organized resistance to Clan occupation on the planet. Yet the majority of the planet's widely scattered citizenry continued simply to ignore the Jade Falcon writ—as, the invaders' collaborators reluctantly revealed, it had ignored the indigenous government. The settlers were far too dispersed to be rounded up by the few Falcons Malthus had at his disposal. Raids by VTOL-borne commandos tended to turn up empty homesteads. But they did lose troops, to snipers and booby traps.

Malthus responded by rounding up more civilians in the cities and executing them publicly in retribution. But the hinterlanders, it developed, were none too fond of city folk. The net result was increased unrest, uncooperation and sabotage in the cities themselves.

Meanwhile, the fractious minded discovered that while direct attacks on Clanners or Clan assets brought immediate smashing vengeance—no matter how seldom it managed to land on actual perpetrators—native collaborators, including the civilian police and military, bound by the surrender terms to serve the Falcons, offered far more available targets. Neither Malthus nor his subcommanders was going to burn scarce Expedition resources because some local cop with a hastily manufactured cloth falcon-and-katana brassard wrapped around his arm got his brains splashed on some alley wall, or a bush ranger or ten got smoked in a back-country ambush.

Attempts to set up native-run centers in the back country for Chaffeeans to turn in their now-proscribed personal arms produced nearly one hundred percent casualties among the staff sent to run them inside three days. When indigenous rank-and-file enforcers simply refused to accept the duty, Malthus had to back down—unless he wanted to try policing the whole planet with the handful of Solahma retreads he could afford to leave behind as occupiers. Forcing the quisling commander of planetary police to actually announce the climbdown, and then sending her to the wall, made Malthus feel somewhat better, but produced no discernible improvement in either civilian compliance or law-enforcement morale.

Nor would any conceivable hostage-and-retribution scheme render Chaffee's indigenous wildlife any more submissive. Creatures prowled forest and shore that could peel an Elemental power-armor suit like a can of processed meat product—and treat the occupant accordingly.

In sum, everything on Chaffee hated the Falcons.

It was with undiluted, if not exactly public, relief that Malthus lifted his DropShips from the surface per the invasion schedule, leaving a Solahma garrison under the command of a *dezgra* Star Colonel with a handful of vehicles, mostly loot of Porrima, to keep the peace and introduce Chaffee to the enlightened Clan way of life.

*   *   *

Malthus was intrigued by the Mongol doctrines espoused, and put into horrific effect upon Chaffee, by the wild, mercurial Malvina Hazen. Even though he understood, as even her sibkin—whose intelligence and acumen Malthus had never made the mistake of underestimating—failed to, that at the root of her unorthodox methods lay blackest heresy.

Despite Malvina Hazen's far-from-secret stance as focal point of the Mongol movement, just a few words from Malthus—words already chosen—would still see her broken from Galaxy Commander and condemned by a Trial of Abjuration. Or worse, no matter her accomplishments. Which made him well pleased with his subordinate and protégé.

For Beckett Malthus loved none so well as those with strings for him to hold. Even if they themselves did not know they had them.

20

Sanglamore Military Academy
New London
Skye
2 July 3134

Rotating a finger's breadth above the table in the darkened briefing room, the holovid bust seemed fully as substantial as meat and cloth and hair: a broad head with long reddish hair sweeping back from a widow's peak almost to the collar of a black and green tunic. Russet beard fringed a broad jaw; the long upper lip was shaved clean. The eyes were sleepy looking slits in which murky green could be glimpsed, like concealed pools. The nose was broad. Something about the image radiated a sense of the certitude of power.

"Galaxy Commander Beckett Malthus, now Supreme Commander of the Jade Falcon expeditionary force," the woman said. She was tall and rangy, with a knife scar down the right side of her long, unhandsome face, slanted blue eyes flanking an oft-broken nose. Her graying blond hair was shaved to a scalp lock. In the dimness, the badges on her spacer's jumpsuit, of a senior member of the merchant caste on one side and of Clan Sea Fox on the other, were vague circular blurs.

Tara Campbell's eyes kept straying from the holographic image of the Jade Falcon commander to the actual Clanswoman. Her emotions were a roil.

"How is it you come to know all this, Master Merchant Senna?" asked Planetary Legate Eckard. The very emotional desiccation of his words robbed them of any taste of challenge.

"We trade in the Jade Falcon OZ," the woman said bluntly. "We don't like them; they don't like us." Like many Sea Fox merchants, she showed no compunction about using contractions. Yet Tara was chillingly aware that she was *alien,* poured from a bottle in lieu of birth like the most fanatically mystic Nova Cat or rabid Wolf.

And while her manner was one of rough camaraderie, the Countess also knew that could be no more than a trade-convenient pose: she dare not assume that this woman or any Clanner's agenda was the same as hers, far less The Republic's. Yet one thing she did rely upon: Clan Sea Fox hated the Falcons—trade rivals as well as blood enemies—as bitterly as she herself detested Anastasia Kerensky and her Steel Wolves.

One side of the Clanswoman's mouth quirked up. "But they can't afford to *not* trade with us, any more than we can afford to not trade with them. You know how it goes: everybody trades with everybody. Or did until the HPG went out."

She shrugged wide shoulders. "Sense tells us we should trade now more than ever, all of us, since JumpShips are the only thing now that pass between most stars any faster than light. But leave that. The point is, we don't have to love the Falcons to trade with them, nor the other way 'round. And even among Clanners, *trade* means *talk.*"

"What ought we know about this Malthus, Master Merchant?" It was easy for Tara to keep her voice genial: all it took was a lifetime's schooling and practice in the rigors of diplomacy, and the exercise of a will which enabled a tiny slip of feminine body to make itself an interstellar unarmed-combat champion. Not much at all.

Those strange slanted eyes appraised her for a long moment before the Clanswoman spoke. "He's a snake. A conniver and contriver."

. "They have those in the Jade Falcons?" asked Colonel Robert Ballantrae with both surprise and a sneer. "Outside the merchant caste, of course."

"Go easy, Robert," Tara murmured.

The knife-damaged face showed no reaction. It struck Tara that this woman was probably little less skilled at her own brand of diplomacy than Tara herself. She tried to imagine what that would cost a Clanswoman bred. Even among the Sea Foxes, who honored merchants scarcely less than warriors—if indeed, they recognized such a distinction.

Outside experts, self-proclaimed, debated that latter point. Although they were the most ubiquitous of the true Clanners—the wild true breed, not Republicans of Clan descent—in the Inner Sphere, the Foxes were in many ways the least known. Where most Clans were notable for their braggadocio, they were extremely private, holding their daily lives and culture as closely as their treasure.

"They have connivers everywhere—even in the Spheroid military," Master Merchant Senna said. Tara Campbell braced herself to hear her say, *even among the Paladins of The Republic*. The media had trumpeted her own disgrace by traitor Paladin Ezekiel Crow throughout The Republic; there was no way a Sea Fox more than a jump inside a Prefecture, as Skye was, could fail to know of it. Nor was it egotism that assured Tara Campbell this woman knew everything about her which was publicly known, and probably a good deal besides. Sea Fox merchants undertook their caste calling with the same zeal with which other Clans' warriors attacked theirs, but with considerably more foresight and preparation.

"The key to Beckett Malthus, and the threat that you face, is that Malthus is brilliant, versatile and entirely sociopathic, by Clan or normal human standards."

Tara looked around at her companions: her aide Tara Bishop at her side, Colonel Ballantrae nearby, Legate Eckard and Prefect Della Brown, each also with an aide. Duke Gregory took the Sea Fox woman and her intelligence seriously, even if he had declined to attend in person.

"He is old for a Clan warrior," the woman said, "in his

fifties—he was born in 3081, the year Devlin Stone proclaimed The Republic. His right arm has been prosthetic since he won his Bloodname: he's always disdained regeneration. He remains a formidable MechWarrior."

She chuckled. "Which is *not* why he is the most feared being in Clan Jade Falcon, not excepting Khan Jana Pryde."

She paused and sipped from a mug. It was coffee poured by a Sanglamore cadet pressed into service as an aide; she had fortified it with a shot of something from a silver flask of her own which, by a waft of scent, Tara judged to be brandy.

"He has fought few Trials in his time," she said, leaning a forearm on the table. "You see, a very long time ago, not long after he won the Malthus Bloodname, a prominent MechWarrior set about destroying him. He did not immediately call Malthus out, but preferred to belittle him, hoping to provoke the one-armed young warrior to challenge him.

"Instead, through a series of events no one could quite piece together after the fact—and after the fact, perhaps, no one particularly wanted to—Malthus' rival found himself subjected to a Trial of Annihilation. He was killed, and his whole genotype purged."

Tara glanced at her aide. Tara Bishop was nodding. Clan warriors, especially those of proud Jade Falcon, feared little, least of all death. But such were Bec Malthus' gifts that he found something they *did* fear.

"Now a Trial of Annihilation is far too potent a weapon for frequent use, although that first luckless warrior isn't Beckett Malthus' only rival to suffer it. His enemies, let us say, have a way of ending up *dezgra*—disgraced. Make no mistake, he's capable of fighting when he has to—and winning. It's just been quite a spell since he *had* to."

"Intrigue doesn't come naturally to Clanners," Prefect Brown said musingly.

"Nicholas Kerensky tried to breed it out of his bottle babies," Tara Bishop said. "So now that the Falcons have a master manipulator among their warrior caste, nobody can deal with him. I guess that's what you call the law of unintended consequences."

Prefect Brown looked at her sharply. She still had not softened to Tara Campbell, and patently believed officers as junior as Bishop should be seen and not heard. And not much seen.

"Quite astute, young lady," Stanford Eckard said. Tara Campbell made herself refrain from glancing at him. Was he, then, starting to accept her?

"There is one," Senna said. "Khan Jana Pryde. He has been her left-hand man throughout her rise to Khanship of the Falcons. She knows the colors of his soul, you can bet your final stone."

"Which may be why she chose him to command the invasion force," Tara Campbell said. "I wonder that he never acted to seize the Khanship himself."

Master Merchant Senna smiled her crooked smile. "One thing Bec Malthus is not is mad, Countess. He's an altogether functional sociopath—like your playmate Anastasia Kerensky." Tara stiffened; she felt the other Tara's touch brief and light upon her arm where the others could not see.

"Unlike the Wolf-bitch," continued Senna, who had not glanced at Tara Campbell in naming her nemesis, "his sociopathy enables him to become something even rarer, especially among the Clans: a man capable of total objectivity. One of the things his terribly clear vision has shown him is that anything one can be seen to possess is potential *isorla* to every other warrior. He decided early on, therefore, that his ambition would be far better served by being the power behind the throne than the occupant thereof. Instrumental as he was in Jana Pryde's rise to the Khanate, he successfully convinced her that he posed no threat to her position."

"But now she suspects he's outlived his usefulness?" Tara Campbell asked.

Senna shrugged. "We understand the Clan mind as, candidly, few other Clanners do. But our analysts aren't psychic. Let us say the Khan has decided he'd best serve Turkina, and her, a hundred light years from the Clan Occupation Zone."

Robert Ballantrae shifted in his chair. A big bluff Northwind Highlander of the old style, he had little more love for fancy talk than he did for Clanners. "So this madman's the main threat to our peace here in the Inner Sphere?"

Tara Campbell noted he did not say, *The Republic*; during the second fight for Northwind the Colonel had made it clear that his primary loyalty was to Northwind itself, and if The Republic would not protect his home world, then it could go hang. Fortunately, his loyalty to planet was inextricably intertwined with loyalty to the person of that planet's hereditary ruler: Countess Tara Campbell. He would serve The Republic of the Sphere as zealously as did Tara despite his skepticism, because he would serve his Countess as loyally as her own right hand.

Senna laughed softly through the dark. "No, Colonel. Not at all. He's neither main nor maddest."

She touched a control surface on the remote she held. The image of Bec Malthus was replaced by that of a woman: strikingly beautiful, with skin like snow, eyes like winter sky, and hair like a frozen waterfall.

"Galaxy Commander Malvina Hazen, commanding the Delta or Gyrfalcon Galaxy. The White Virgin, the Ice-Bitch, the Butcher of Wotan. Since leaving her sibko, she has never left an opponent who faced her in single combat alive—not enemies on the field of battle, nor fellow Falcons in Trials. The leading ristar of Clan Jade Falcon, its foremost MechWarrior and battle commander. Excepting only one. It is said you can see a furnace of fanaticism and fury burning through her pale skin, although I wonder if that's just the light of madness."

"She murdered Hamilton." Tara Campbell almost spat the words. She saw no need for diplomatic evasion here.

Senna nodded slowly. "She did. And whether you believe me or not, Countess, I despise the deed as heartily as you. No matter: she has done as much before, and worse. A few years back, laborers mutinied on Wotan against the incompetent administration of a MechWarrior who had caused a famine claiming a thousand lives. That MechWarrior was later broken by the Clan Council, and died Solahma under command of Malvina herself. In spite of that, then–Star Captain Malvina, not yet Bloodnamed, exterminated the population of an entire bloc. Five thousand workers. Children, women, men. By way of example, you see."

Silence filled the room like sickly fog.

"She is even smaller than you, Countess Campbell," Senna said. "The confrontation between you will be epic despite your physical statures."

"I'm flattered," Tara said dryly. And yet she knew the compliment was real. Clan warriors disdained to lie, and facile trader stereotypes notwithstanding, the Sea Fox merchants did no less.

"However," the tall woman went on, "I do not deem her your greatest threat either."

"Good Lord," murmured Tara Bishop. "What's worse than *that*?"

Another figure appeared in her place: the broad shoulders, muscular neck and head of a man with brown skin, an unruly hank of coarse black hair, big cheekbones, a lantern jaw and a straight nose. The wide mouth and brown eyes smiled. To Tara Campbell, adept at reading people's expressions, the smile seemed one of genuine joy.

She wondered what, in the grim and violent world of the Clans, he found to be so happy about.

"*He's* more dangerous?" Tara Bishop burst out. "He looks like the big brother every girl wished she had. Well, maybe not *brother*, since he looks like a holovid star. . . ."

Senna smiled. "Interesting you should say that, Captain. These two are a rarity: sibkin—brother and sister—who have both won Bloodnames. The first in Clan Jade Falcon that we know of since Aiden and Marthe Pryde—and we know all, we Sea Foxes. Every word of every Clan's Remembrance; the contents of records other Clans don't even know they keep. That is our business, ultimately: to know."

She gestured. "Galaxy Commander Aleksandr Hazen. He is Malvina Hazen's sibkin. Fraternal twin, to all intents and purposes—especially inasmuch as they are the only members of their sibling cohort to survive to win warrior status."

"How do the genetics of *that* work out?" Prefect Della Brown wondered aloud.

"Recessives for fair skin, hair, and eyes in the gene-stock," Merchant Senna answered. "Sibkin can be even more diverse in appearance. These two couple; there are even rumors that emotional attachment has evolved."

Ballantrae squinted at her. "What does that mean?"

"They have long been lovers, it is said."

"That's unnatural!" Ballantrae exclaimed.

"Of course it is," the Sea Fox woman said equably. "There is nothing natural about our Clan society, least of all our mode of reproduction. Though we profess great affinity with nature, we meddle with it in every particular of our own lives. That's another reason we and the Dracs feel such affinity for one another."

Tara Campbell leaned forward. "So *this* is a greater threat than the bloodthirsty little blonde vampire? He must be a happy lunatic."

"Your judgment for once is clouded, Tara Campbell," the master merchant replied. "Aleks Hazen is entirely sane, although by Clan standards stranger than Malvina. Even as Malvina has never spared a foe faced in a duel, so he has never slain one. He is famed—or notorious—for his mercy and compassion."

"How does he manage to keep his head on his shoulders among such a bloodthirsty lot?" Ballantrae burst out.

"Nobody is good enough to separate the one from the other, Colonel. He has fought Elementals unaugmented—barehanded—and won. As a MechWarrior, only one can touch him: Malvina, whom it is said he has never beaten. As a field commander he may be her better."

"You say he's the worst threat?" Tara Bishop said. "Why, if mass murder isn't to his taste?"

"For precisely that reason, young Captain. Tell her, Countess: teach your fledgling. She shows great promise, but still lacks full wisdom."

"Malvina's methods inspire anger and hatred," Tara said slowly, as her aide looked death beams at the master merchant. "They fill the survivors with desire for revenge. A chivalrous foe such as Aleks doesn't give even those he conquers much to hate."

The merchant nodded. Then laughed.

"Lucky for you that he is a freak. The reason the Crusaders lost the first invasion, and lost it so disastrously, was that they had no *history*. The Founders thought to start anew, to create the New Kerensky Man. And so the Crusaders lost because they knew nothing of human interaction except that peculiar hothouse-grown variety we enjoy in the Clans; and so they knew nothing of strategy. But Aleks Hazen knows his history."

She drank again and smiled. "We might have seduced you within three generations with our marvelous toys, we Sea Foxes. It wasn't just our killing tech that was superior to yours. But the warriors had their way, as is ever the case except in our own Clan; and we Foxes have always been despised in the Grand Council; when there was a Grand Council."

The master merchant lowered eyes to her mug and lapsed into a reverie much at odds with her previous loquacity. With her unwilling knowledge of Clan lore, Tara Campbell realized, as the others seemed not to, that there had not been a Grand Council in decades. Nor was Senna likely to ever see one herself.

"Why are you helping us?" Tara Bishop asked.

Senna paused with her mug just short of her scarred lips. Her eyes had gone a deeper turquoise again: there was no danger there, only appraisal.

"The simple, obvious answer—that we hate Turkina's brood—is true. But it's so small a piece of the truth as to be a lie, if nothing more were said. We are Kerensky's children, woman warrior. No less than the Wolves—nor the Falcons. We represent the Founder's hedge against the possibility his vision was wrong: an alternative strategy to eternal war for dubious peace. No less than our more bloodthirsty brethren do we feel we have a mission to save humanity from itself."

She shrugged, drank again. "Ironically, it is not so different from the vision of Devlin Stone, which your Countess there serves with such famed devotion. Our agenda is our own, our plans our own; I give nothing away in telling you that, because I credit you with sufficient intelligence to take it for granted."

Carefully, she set the mug down on the table before her, as if it was spun from fine glass. "Clan Jade Falcon poses a threat to all humanity. Not just your precious Republic, whose time is past—pardon if I give offense, Countess; but you have paid me for the truth. We Sea Foxes honor our bargains, always.

"Malthus is a devil, yet by himself he is nothing, for he needs a long shadow in which to hide to work his mischief. But Malvina and Aleksandr Hazen together create a *taiji*, dark and light, the ancient symbol of unity in duality, the endless interplay of opposites. Together they are awesome, and may yet prove unstoppable. Yet individually they may pose even greater threats. For each is an elemental force—

not Elemental in our Clan sense, but in the classic meaning: a force of Nature Herself."

"Mystic nonsense," Ballantrae rasped. It was almost a spit. "Countess, we might as well have brought Kev Rosse himself here, to spin us some daft Spirit Cat vision out of mushrooms and drug smoke!"

Ignoring the Colonel's outburst, Master Merchant Senna looked Tara Campbell deep in the eyes as she spoke. "Let me give you one final counsel: kill both if you can, but under no circumstances slay one and leave the other living. Or even the Blake Jihad will seem a trifle.

"For by himself Aleksandr will bring you a smiling slavery from which humankind will not escape for a thousand years. While Malvina untempered by her brother's true compassion will create such devastation that in a thousand years our descendants will still be gibbering and eating each other in the ruins of it."

21

Summer
Prefecture VIII
The Republic of the Sphere
14 July 3134

Aleks hit Summer, three jumps from Alkaid.

Summer hit back.

It was a hot, hard-luck world with a population just under a billion. Its ozone layer was decaying and its old capital, Curitiba, had been nuked by Blakists during the Jihad. The planet's primary industrial infrastructure on the northern continent Lestrade had likewise been shattered. The war depopulated Summer; some residents returned afterwards, their ranks augmented by the Resettlement Act of 3082.

Despite its negatives, Summer was a plum objective, being a major source for JumpShip parts, oil and radioactives. The planetary capital and major city of Mount Breighton was defended by a formidable defense force, including several BattleMechs and numerous Industrials.

Aleks dispatched his other three regular Clusters to various strategic targets on the northern polar continent of Aberdale, where both the population and the renascent industrial production centered. He personally led his Third Falcon Velites, augmented by his command Star and some Solahma and Eyries, into the assault on the capital.

His batchall challenge having been declined with blunt defiance by Legate Carlos Adler, Aleks dropped his DropShip in some rolling hills between sprawling Mount Breighton and the Summer InterStellar Components complex, crown jewel of Summerite industry, which had resumed production of JumpShip parts less than ten years before. A substantial thunderstorm buffeted *Red Heart* as it descended toward the surface.

"It rains upon the defenders as well as ourselves," he observed from the cockpit of White Lily, his *Gyrfalcon*, strapped in its bay with blastaway bolts. His waiting warriors responded with a chorus of piping falcon cries.

How different they sound than when I took command, he thought, exulting. *They are true Falcons now, and know it.*

Yet today would be their greatest test to date, because a full division, three militia regiments, defended the capital and its environs, according to intelligence garnered by the ever-vigilant Jade Falcon merchants. Aleks was outnumbered roughly nine to one. Granted, the defenders were for the most part sheer cannon fodder, weekend warriors with hunting rifles: it was still long odds for his Zetas.

But keen tactician Aleks had no intention of fighting them all at once. Indeed, as usual, he reasoned if he could win a rapid enough and smashing enough initial battle he would not even have to defeat them in detail: the planetary government would capitulate. Especially since, as was also his custom, his shuttles in orbit blanketed the globe with promises of good treatment and minimal disruption of daily life, corroborated by testimonials recorded by numerous Alkaidians, clearly bemused that he had honored such promises to *them*.

Lightning stabbed the great armored egg as it burst through the water-heavy, blue-gray bellies of the clouds; in essence a giant Faraday cage that rendered neutral nature's power, the ship suffered no harm. A country mall catering both to workers at the JumpShip parts plant and other residents of the city lay beneath, nestled among hills covered with Summer's characteristic purple scrub. Fifteen minutes before, two points of Aleks' fighters had overflown the mall faster than sound to produce a sonic boom and get the attention of shoppers and employees, then streaked back low in a finger-four formation, subsonic, dropping leaflets telling people to get out *now*. Aleks had convinced his mettlesome pilots that this was a marvelous game and not a menial task demeaning to true warriors. When it was done, they streaked away to join their mates in combat air patrol keeping planetary defense VTOLs away from the drop zone.

Their work was well done: the highways leading from the mall were clogged with fleeing cars. The parking lot, which had not been overfull since this was an early workday afternoon, had largely emptied. Those motorists still stalled in traffic waiting to get out had their attention quickly drawn to the small constellation of blue-white drive stars descending upon them, and fled on foot with commendable alacrity. No one was injured, although numerous vehicles turned molten in puffs of igniting ICE fuel as the *Heart* sank her landing jacks three meters into blacktop.

Aleks had achieved the situation military history had taught him was optimum: strategic offensive and tactical defensive. While the balance shifted occasionally with the ebb and flow of doctrine and technology, that was the rest state. He quickly threw out pickets of fast scouts, vehicles and something new, hoverbikes liberated from Alkaid. His Eyrie youngsters loved those. The scouts formed a circling mobile perimeter, augmented by infantry observation posts with powerful sensor gear, to watch for counterattacks as Aleks unshipped his warriors and machines and readied them for action. VTOLs quickly rose to cover them.

The aircraft reported a regiment on the move from Mount Breighton. The militia had tracked the DropShip's descent on radar and begun mounting their response before it made planetfall. Meanwhile, Aleks lost a Donar scout VTOL to an air-defense battery, learning that the somewhat smaller force protecting the JumpShip parts plant and the organic security was alert and angry but apparently digging in, making no moves to sally and confront the invaders.

Aleks' lean, hard gut told him that would not last, was indeed likely a ruse—but he didn't care. He had the trust of his Galaxy now, and they his. He would rely on them to carry out his commands as crisply as the veterans of Delta or the elite Turkina Keshik—indeed better, because unlike the "superior" units the once-*dezgra* Zetas had grown accustomed to subordinating their individual lust for glory to the tactical needs of their Galaxy; and the will of their charismatic commander.

Leaving his circle of pickets out, reinforcing those to the southwest to cut the likely axis of any advance from the Summer InterStellar Components factory plex, Aleks marched the rest of his Cluster rapidly northeast to meet the defenders speeding down an eight-lane superhighway toward them. Per his custom, he left a tactical command post in the now-abandoned mall, under the powerful armament of *Red Heart,* in command of an injured MechWarrior.

Aleks' force quickly dug in under defilade of low hills flanking the highway. A bridge crossed a creek, now a roaring flood that had already escaped its banks, half a kay in front of his main line of resistance. Hoverbike-borne sappers wired it for destruction, just in case, but he left it intact for now, with his personal coded signal the only thing that would drop the span: he wanted to invite the defenders in at full speed, not slow them down.

And so they came. Having been alerted by a jump-point observatory to the Jade Falcon emergence, they had made good use of the short three days intervening, even loading big, slow BattleMechs, including Legate Carlos Adler's personal *Centurion* and a *Legionnaire,* fifty tons each, onto flatbed haulers for rapid transport to contest the expected invasion wherever it touched down.

As Summerite scouts clashed with Falcon pickets, the clouds opened up. The air between clouds and hills became a flickering pixilated ocean, pierced by angry red-tinged lightning. As battles went, it was epic, and many valiant deeds were done—and many men and women on both sides were mangled, crushed, burned, died weeping and rolling in tangles of their own intestines or crying for their mothers. But it was not particularly remarkable: another installment of humanity's perpetual war with itself.

Though cliché anciently claims no battle plan survives first contact with the enemy, the fight developed much as Aleks anticipated it. With cover and stable firing platforms on his side, his Falcon Assault Guards levied thoroughly professional slaughter on the advancing Summerites: men, vehicles and even 'Mechs. Concentrated fire forced the militia infantry to dismount well outside their effective battle range. Grimly determined, the armored fighting vehicles, BattleMechs and IndustrialMechs forged on.

Aleks did face one threat none of the *desant's* Galaxies had encountered before now: heavy artillery firing over the horizon. Bombardment by Arrow missiles and Thumper and Sniper tube artillery from self-propelled launchers blasted his hasty positions within half a minute of their opening fire, shredding dozens of infantry and even some Elementals in full power armor, several vehicles, including a Sekhmet assault vehicle, and two hovertanks, a fifty-ton Epona Pursuit tank and a forty-five-ton Bellona. A direct hit by an Arrow IV volley blew to pieces an *Eyrie,* vaporizing MechWarrior Nina, who had been so reluctant to incur dishonor on Alkaid by withdrawing.

Surprised by the speed and effectiveness of the enemy arty, Aleks nonetheless had the best counter already in hand: *counterattack*. He led his Falcons in a charge as the distant artillery churned the muddy soil of their now-vacant positions.

Drawn out in front of their infantry, the Summerite vehicles and 'Mechs had lost their support. With the non-powered infantry riding on the backs of hovercraft and armored by their speed, and Elementals clinging to the legs and perched on the shoulders of Falcon 'Mechs, Aleks' warriors engaged the militia with all assets simultaneously.

The battle lines came together with a crash that momentarily shamed the thunder. Falcon infantry dismounted and close-assaulted Summerite vehicles and 'Mechs with grenades and portable anti-armor weapons. Aleks in his Lily led his machines in slashes through the enemy line, back and forth, as his fast hover-mobile scouts raked the flanks of the gone-to-ground enemy infantry, keeping them out of the fray. With the two mechanized forces intertwined, the Summer heavy artillery was unable to fire effectively for fear of striking their own troops; they were hunted down and neutralized by Falcon VTOLs which, though outnumbered, had already gained local supremacy over the Spheroid air.

Slipping, sliding, throwing up great waves of mud and chopped vegetation, the foes savaged each other in a vicious dogfight. Aleks' *Gyrfalcon* was swarmed by a whole point of Nova Cats in Gnome power armor. They actually tore off the Ultra autocannon mounted on Lily's left arm before MechWarrior Mordechai in his *Spirit* and a cadet-crewed *Epona* hosed them off with lasers and Streak missiles.

The Ghost Bear abtakha Folke Jorgensson, jumping to his erstwhile master's aid, was knocked from the sky by a Gauss rifle hit and several long-range missile strikes from Legate Adler's *Centurion*. Although his right-arm quad Streak launcher was destroyed and the ammo stowage in his right torso blasted open, and his own left clavicle was broken by his fall, the dour Star Colonel with consummate skill snapped his own fifty-ton machine back upright, staggering the Legate, closing as he thought for the kill, with a Streak barrage from his left arm launcher. It shattered the long range launcher in the *Centurion*'s right torso and cracked the cockpit, momentarily dazing Adler.

Jorgensson jumped again, turning in air to light behind the Legate with weapons blazing. Adler tried to turn his 'Mech's torso to fire back. Jorgensson just orbited him, firing up the *Centurion* with large lasers and his remaining Streaks, until the Legate's 'Mech toppled with a shattered hip actuator.

In moments, a fuming Legate Adler was drawn from his cockpit, shaken but uninjured, by Solahma infantry. Ignoring the pain, the functional loss of one arm, and the diminished status of his firepower, Folke Jorgensson stalked off in search of further prey. Beyond even his thorny Clan-warrior pride, he would *never* show weakness in front of Falcons.

Soon Star Colonel Jorgensson took charge of mopping up the now-shattered Summerite combat team as Aleks, blissfully undeterred by the damage to his own machine, turned the Lily around and led a scratch Trinary to engage and defeat the thrust of vehicles and IndustrialMechs supported by infantry from the JumpShip-parts plant he had expected all along.

At the end of the day, Planetary Governor Minerva

Hayne was more than willing to accept Aleksandr Hazen's generous surrender terms, even though over half of the militia troops defending her capital had not so much as glimpsed the smoke of distant battle for the cloudburst which still raged long after the fighting in the hills was done.

In the streets of the surrendered city, Aleks celebrated with his warriors, encouraged them in their revelry, smiled, laughed, drank and sang with them. Yet his own triumph tasted of ashes in his mouth.

Almost a hundred of his Zetas had died, including Magnus Icaza's successor as commander of the Third Falcon Velites, Star Colonel Keith Buhallin, killed by laser infantry after he successfully toppled the Summerite *Legionnaire* by ramming it with his Skanda light tank in an apparent attempt to emulate Jorgensson's feat in seizing a BattleMech. Half again as many lay injured.

Summer had lost three thousand, killed and wounded. To anyone but a Clansman, the victory might have seemed one-sided.

Aleksandr mourned for all those dead and injured, Falcon and Spheroid. Because as always to his heart—that of a knight *sans peur and sans reproche* such as he had read about as an undersized, perpetually frightened child—a warrior's highest duty was protection, not destruction. To be sure, he still believed with his whole soul that even carnage such as today's was justified by its promise: to put an end to such suffering and evil forever. Because one day, tomorrow or in twenty years, Clan Jade Falcon would arrive in force to complete the work he and his fellow Galaxy Commanders had begun.

But it was *just* begun, he knew. That panged him too. For all the butchery and pain this conquest had caused, the greatest spasm of destruction yet awaited: the battle for Skye.

22

Outside New London
Skye
17 July 3134

"As I see it, lass," the handsome young officer with the collar of his Seventh Skye Militia dress tunic artfully undone said in a Skye-Irish brogue well-fueled by Skye-Irish whiskey, "our situation harks back to that confronting the empires of Terra herself, away back in the age of sail a century or two before spaceflight began. And thank you; you're a blessing to a man."

The last he said to a diminutive woman with glossy black hair bobbed to bangs across the front and long and unbound in the back, who had handed him a fresh glass. She wore a brief black dress fit to a trim but well-appointed figure and matching heels. Her features were pert and nicely chiseled, her eyes so blue as to be almost indigo. She smiled encouragingly.

He continued, duly encouraged. She was really quite lovely. Even if there was a haunting air of familiarity about her. "Back in those days, the major powers were separated by days and weeks of travel asea, their outposts and colonies by weeks, even months. Intercepting enemies or raiders or even learning of their activities was a matter as much of luck as skill. Rendezvousing or communicating with one's own far-flung forces was no easier."

Bodies and conversation ebbed and flowed about them in lazy currents between goosebumped white walls. The party was one of the more or less weekly affairs thrown by film mogul Hilario Gupta, owner of Islands in the Sky Productions, at his house that rambled like a random growth of giant white crystals on a forested hillside overlooking New London and Thames Bay from the north.

"Yet they managed to maintain world-girdling empires," the officer continued. He was lean and long-jawed and had curly chestnut hair curving down his cheeks as sideburns. A circle of admiring listeners, not exclusively feminine, surrounded him as he stood in one of the somewhat stark rooms of Gupta's polyhedron palace. "Indeed, they managed to have themselves a set of global wars from the sixteenth or seventeenth century onwards, although they didn't get 'round to calling them 'world' wars until the twentieth; still, only the unprecedented scale of the forces involved distinguished the acknowledged world wars from what had gone before, not their nature."

While he spread himself generously among his audience, he concentrated a little more on the little stunner in black with the flip bangs. For her part, she seemed to be listening with peculiar intensity. He smiled inwardly, and contemplated potentialities.

Another woman, a more than acceptable blonde, asked what was being done to protect Skye. "Well, we're training quite intensively with these newcomers from The Republic," he allowed, "helping them get up to speed on conditions on Skye, don'tcha know?"

"I'll bet it's a real pleasure training under that commander of theirs, if you know what I mean," commented a noted New Glasgow bon vivant and gossip columnist from the fringe.

The officer generously decided not to squash the plump, bearded poseur. He had written complimentary things about the Seventh. Which was none too common. "She's easy enough on the eyes, to be sure, now," he said casually. "But don't be fooled: under that glamorous exterior beats a heart as chill as that of any Kirk divine. They're as stiff-necked as our local Scots, now, this Northwind lot; only a trifle more rustic and rough about the edges. *Sassenach* at heart, they are."

A man had sidled up to the group. He wore a loose, color-swirled smock over white duck trousers and deck shoes. He was nondescript except for a head of slightly receding dark hair and Asian eyes. He leaned in and spoke to the black-haired woman, whose attentive smile had grown a trifle glassy.

"Pardon me, friend," the militia officer said, "but the lass is with me."

The interloper smiled. It was a friendly smile, disarming in its charm. Yet there was something behind it that chilled like liquid nitrogen. "Not anymore," he said lightly.

The woman nodded at the young raconteur, smiled radiantly, and rose to slip away with the newcomer.

Standing on the deck in the light of Luna, Skye's single moon, Tara ran her fingers through her long, luxuriant, spurious hair. It felt strange to have long hair again. She enjoyed the sensation, but was glad she could be done with it when this was over. It was about the way she felt about acquaintances' children: she loved to coo over them, and cuddle them and give way to rushes of maternal warmth. Then hand them back to their parents.

The young Limerick rake had a keen sense of history; her education had been comprehensive enough that she recognized the essential accuracy of his tales. Nor could she argue with his comparing Terra's age of sail to the post–HPG Inner Sphere. Although she wasn't as ready to endorse certain other of his observations. . . .

Another small contingent of troops had trickled in, of her own elite First Kearny, from facing down the Dracs—*and* the Dragon's Fury, led by Tara's own mentor, Duchess Katana Tormark—on Sadalbary on the frontier, where once upon a day young Tara had first won a name for herself as something other than a pretty little poster girl, and so well-mannered. Grim battle-hardened veterans they were, though they made it clear they felt it was they, not the less-seasoned troops who had fought with Tara against the Steel Wolves, had something to prove: for guilt chewed

them, that they had not been able to fight for their home
world themselves. They brought with them three BattleMechs, an *Arbalest*, a *Panther* and a powerful *Tundra
Wolf*.

If only we had had them on Northwind, she thought, *soldiers and machines. . . .*

She stopped the thought. She had dedicated her life to
fighting for the great experiment which was The Republic.
She could not allow herself to begrudge the sacrifices her
home world had made for the cause.

Or would.

They had come from the other end of The Republic, carried by a virtual command circuit: a chain of JumpShips
which, upon jumping into a system, could pass cargo and
passengers along to another vessel waiting with capacitors
fully charged, so that it could make the next hyperspatial
jump without delay. In this case it was as much happpenstance
as planning, hence the "virtual." Under Devlin Stone's re-
forms, The Republic had cut back on military starships as
well as BattleMechs, and the current Exarch was reluctant
to press civilian hulls into service, in which Tara concurred.
A combination of purpose-stationed Republican JumpShips
and cooperative civilian craft had, however, enabled recall
orders to reach this lot of Highlanders, and they themselves
to get here, in a blindingly short time, given the enormous
distance they had to traverse.

Yet their coming brought as much ill news as good, because it was only by unreasonable good fortune they
reached Skye in such good time—or at all. Such conditions
would seldom recur. Tara would be lucky to have half her
Highlanders here before the invaders, based on any kind of
reasonable projections as to when the Falcons might strike.

She sighed, drinking in a breeze tangy with the scent of
mountain conifers and crisp with coming autumn. Then she
shivered, although it was not chill.

*"The Falcons have loaded their expedition up with all the
'Mechs they can spare,"* Master Merchant Senna had told
them. *"We believe they carry about a fifth as many by proportion as their ancestors did a century ago. You do the math."*

Tara could. She had. She might match them in BattleMechs—in six months or more.

"Tara." It was Paul in his loud shirt, stepping out onto the deck behind her.

She turned. With the accountant came three men, each less likely than the next: a wiry man just taller than Tara, with intense dark eyes and a brown moustache, who seemed to vibrate with excess energy; a mobile wall of blond-bearded man; and an immensely tall and skeletally lean man with a shaven skull, gargoyle-sharp face and dark red goatee, who seemed to have short horns sprouting from his forehead.

"These are the lot I told you about," Paul Laveau said. "Countess Tara Campbell, I'd like you to meet the Firehouse Gang: Tom Cross, J. D. Rich, and Seymour Street."

"I'm charmed," Tara said, laughing. "Firehouse Gang?"

"We're wizards," said Tom Cross, the thin restless one.

"Wizards?" she echoed.

She cast a quick glance toward Paul. She had spent a lot of time with him both on and off duty the last few weeks, with a great deal of encouragement from her aide, who claimed she needed to get more recreation. TB gave the word peculiar emphasis.

Remembering a time not so long ago when a working relationship had turned into something more, and the catastrophic effects of that, Tara C. had held back. Despite that, she had found herself falling into fast friendship with Paul Laveau. His tireless work within the Palace showed he was as dedicated as she. He was also warm, wise and he made her laugh as no one she could remember had been able to do since her childhood—an ability she did not precisely look for in an accountant.

"Effects wizards," said the broad, blond Rich.

"As in movies," said the tall and lanky Street. His horns were clever prosthetics. She hoped. "Although I wouldn't exactly want to limit your conception of what's meant by *wizards*."

Tara turned to Paul, trying not to let her disappointment show. He had promised her more than mere diversion in bringing her here tonight. She had dared hope . . she wasn't sure what, really. But for something real, some tangible help for her increasing inward desperation.

"I'm delighted to meet you all," she said with practiced

brightness. "But I'm afraid it's soldiers I need now, and tanks and BattleMechs, more than wizards."

"Another way to think of us," Street said, "is as masters of illusion."

"Nice disguise, Countess," Cross said. "Of course, I made you the moment you walked in the door. Of course. But not bad. For an amateur."

"I'm afraid we can't do actual soldiers for you," J. D. Rich said, "or tanks or BattleMechs. But are you sure you can't make use of *appearing* to have a whole lot more than you do?"

She turned to look at him intently.

New London
Skye
17 July 3134

There was nothing unusual about Tara Campbell's face and voice blanketing the airwaves of Skye. Nor was it odd she should be appearing as part of a recruiting drive, especially under the present emergency. She'd begun starring on recruiting posters as a child.

What was peculiar was the particular *kind* of service to The Republic she was pushing.

"Are you willing to trade your life for freedom?" her vibrantly beautiful and charming, yet solemn, face asked from holovid tanks in living rooms and bedrooms and bars in New Glasgow and Donegal.

"Freedom for your loved ones, freedom for your fellow citizens of Skye, freedom for billions of citizens of The Republic of the Sphere whom you will never even know?" it asked, two stories tall, from cinema screens in New London and Limerick and Sgain Dubh.

"Will you leave your jobs, your families, the safety of your homes and everyday life," her voice asked from radio speakers on fishing trawlers in the North Sea and scientific stations on the southern polar ice cap, *"for nothing but a certainty of danger and an extremely high likelihood of death at the hands of a merciless alien invader?*

"If so," she told laborers at a sheep station in Otero County at the continent's far end, and in break rooms in

the mighty Shipil and Cyclops factories, *"then join me in fighting for Skye against Clan Jade Falcon.*

"Join me—join the Forlorn Hope!"

Duke Gregory practically self-destructed.

"Himmelsfahrtkommando?" he roared. It was the term Tara used in her German-language vidcasts. It meant, *trip to Heaven detachment.*

He upset the two-hundred-kilogram blood-oak desk in his office as if it were a toy and booted his personal desk-comp through a two-hundred-year-old leaded glass window into a cobbled courtyard two stories below. It narrowly missed the Minister of Health.

Yet when his howling rage had spent itself he laughed. "If the pretty little Countess is eager to throw away her life for Skye," he told his aides as they crept timidly out of the woodwork, "who am I to argue? At that, it might even shame some of our homegrown quibblers and carpers and special pleaders into piping down!"

Prefect Della Brown wanted to publicly censure Tara Campbell. She believed it all a publicity stunt. She also feared it sent a "negative message."

Planetary Legate Stanford Eckard resisted. If it was a "publicity stunt," it was one publicizing the threat to Skye—which, as rumors filtered into the system with JumpShips, of Jade Falcon attacks on Seginus, Glengarry and Izar, was becoming increasingly real to the people of Skye as well as its defenders. And after all, he observed, in any kind of honesty, the Countess had far greater experience than either of them at *either* publicity or war.

But in the end it was not Eckard's calm and reasoned arguments that caused Prefect Brown to swallow her resentment-born distrust of the glamorous offworld Countess, nor brought a smile to the scarred and pensive lips of Duke Gregory Kelswa-Steiner.

It was the response by the people of Skye, who turned out in unprecedented numbers in answer to Tara's call, and joined the Forlorn Hope.

23

Clayton (suburb of Gray Valley City)
  Zebebelgenubi
Prefecture IX
The Republic of the Sphere
24 July 3134

The redbrick steeple of St. Alban's church crumpled as it was pierced by the red lance of a large laser. It toppled onto the green below, the bells of its ancient mechanical clock jangling crazily. Watching it above the narrow pitched roofs and treetops of the houses on the next block, Captain Thomas Kaiser of the Republic Zebebelgenubi Militia felt as if it was his own heart slumping to ruin inside his rib cage.

He heard a rattle of heavy machine-gun fire as Clan infantry probed the infantry positions guarding his prize: a JESII strategic missile carrier, so fresh from the nearby Joint Equipment Systems factory in Gray Valley that it lacked a coat of paint. While the ninety-five-ton half-track self-propelled long-range missile launch vehicle lacked the extreme range of an Arrow IV or Sniper, its stupendous eighty-rocket volley gave it as great an offensive punch as any system on the modern battlefield. Using spotters, it was capable of delivering thunderous indirect fire on call. With its line-of-sight Artemis IV fire-control system it could maul a *Jupiter* with a single salvo.

In exchange, it was virtually without defenses, lacking armor, defensive weaponry, or speed. An enterprising infantryman could neutralize it with the pry bar needed to crack open the cockpit and hit the gunner in the head. So Captain Kaiser's mixed, understrength company of infantry and vehicles was solely devoted to shielding the giant belching beast.

"Blue Eye Four, Blue Eye Four," he said into his headset mike, "this is Blue Six, do you read?" A crackle of high-energy atmospherics was his only answer. *Another observation post gone.*

Zebebelgenubi was a brutally dry world, most of its water having been cracked into component hydrogen and oxygen by the high ultraviolet content of its Class A3 primary. Up here, in the lower reaches of the mountains of the northern-hemisphere continent of Gastagne, the watershed allowed Gray Valley City and suburbs such as this one, Clayton, enough irrigation to maintain a semblance of greenery, using tree and ground cover species selected or gene-engineered for low water usage. One thing even the residents of the Valley seldom saw was a completely clouded-over sky.

They had total overcast tonight: dark and ominous and flickering with lightning. Except it wasn't clouds.

It was smoke. The smell of burning stung the middle-aged captain's eyes and clawed the lining of his throat. Of burning wood, and plastics, and paper, and petroleum fractions. And the barbecue smell of human bodies. The whole sky to the west, where the JES factory lay, was the lurid red of an open wound.

The devils had entered the system, not through a conventional jump point forty days' space flight from the planet itself, but from a pirate point a mere six days out. Only the chance of a comet-hunting amateur astronomer on the southern continent of Valius spotting their DropShips in his photographs a mere three days out gave the planet's defenders any warning at all. Not that it had mattered much—since the invaders possessed the unassailable initiative granted by their ability to land anywhere on the planet they desired.

Even before eye-hurting blue drive flames appeared in the velvet early-evening sky right overhead, the local news had reported landings elsewhere on the planet: particularly at the primary spaceport at Nantucket, on the neighboring continent of Wurscht, which had apparently been seized after a brief, incredibly ferocious fight. Then all communications from Nantucket ceased—and the single DropShip appeared over the heads of the inhabitants of Gray Valley and the Joint Equipment Systems workers.

Communications had gone expeditiously to hell. First Kaiser got word the plant itself had mostly fallen. Then he started losing command layers overhead; not five minutes before Battalion had fallen off the air. He was on his own now.

Scanning the channels, his headset remotely controlling the powerful commo rig in his command vehicle, Kaiser had struck a Clan frequency. They broadcast in the clear, but not in words. Rather a series of shrill cries and whistles, emulating birds of prey on the hunt.

That sound frightened him more than anything in forty-five years of life. He quickly changed the freq.

His soldiers had punished the invaders, making them pay: his own launcher had already loosed a dozen salvos hissing into the night, toward targets called out by forward OPs. The smoke clouds above, low as they hung, seemed a domed ceiling supported by groined arches of crisscrossing missile trails. Even as Kaiser stood on the street with his HQ platoon around him, trying to get someone, *anyone*, to call new targets for his own captive monster to service, he heard another dragon roar, glanced up to see blazing blue-white comets passing overhead, trailing tentacles of white smoke that seemed faintly luminous against the dull, overarching gray.

Right to left they passed. Meaning: *they've already flanked us to the south.*

The captain had received countless reports of enemy vehicles ablaze, enemy 'Mechs exploding. Although his prior direct experience of war, against the CapCons, lay almost two decades in the past, Captain Kaiser knew to discount most of that as an adrenalized form of wishful thinking. Still: one thing the defenders could do was put a *lot* of metal downrange hot, and they had done so.

But the Clansmen shared one trait in common with their totem bird: terrifying *speed*. They charged hard and fast without apparent regard for their own losses. That meant it was hard to catch them with indirect arty fire, impossible to keep them in its beaten zone. Even their unpowered infantry, vulnerable to his own infantrymen's mostly chemical-projectile rifles, seemed to have one speed—a tireless flat-out run, screaming shrill bird cries as they charged and killed and died.

The crosswise LRM volley convinced him even as he sensed an increase in the battle-thunder from ahead, just over a round hill. "All units," he commanded on the general command freq, "fall back to B-1." Although Battalion had expressly forbidden it, he had chosen and disseminated fallback lines of resistance. He had never faced real Clanners hot from the by-god Occupation Zone, but he had been raised on books and trivids of the first invasion.

He heard cries of alarm from his own infantry in their hardpoints in homes and businesses and lying-up behind the walls of gardens lovingly tended in defiance of the dry and unforgiving climate—and now soon to wither under artificial flame: *"We're hitting them but they won't stop! Look out, look out*—satchel ch—"

Silence, quickly replaced by more warnings—and screams. A ball of yellow flame suddenly rolled into the sky from the hill's far side, right up the street. One of his tanks was gone, like *that*.

He turned and ran toward his own command vehicle, a wheeled eighty-ton DI Schmitt assault tank. His legs were transmuted to lead by the gut-shot realization: *it's already too late.*

He heard fresh outcries, in naked ears not headset this time: "Elementals!"

He glanced over his shoulder to see the squat armored figures with their horned-looking helmets, springing into view above the housetops up the block like malignant insects, backlit by the great burning they and their kinsmen had left in their wake.

And then something rose above the rooftops and chimneys like a moon. A great, metal-gleaming bird shape, complete with improbable outspread wings.

On all sides of him troops darted madly this way and that; and no direction offered more promise than any other. Before him his own Schmitt lit up as if its ammo stocks were exploding, blazing at the jumping enemy 'Mech with everything that could possibly reach it, medium lasers and 50mm rotary autocannon and long-range missiles from the launchers atop the turret. He heard the JESII's bearings whine as it tried to turn itself to bring its awesome firepower to bear on its monstrous enemy, hoped briefly that the microwave beam of its Artemis system, questing invisibly from within its bubble-mount, wouldn't inadvertently sweep across him and flash-cook him.

The 'Mech arcing toward him on pillars of white fire was a bizarre mix of man and bird, like a twisted metal statue of the ancient Egyptian god Horus. Its torso lit with flashes like a string of firecrackers as the Schmitt's autocannon, or someone's raked it. A laser fountained orange sparks from its heavy left leg.

It could take a lot of that, he feared. He had no idea what it was. But from its sheer size it must weigh eighty-five, ninety tons at least.

Trying to run while staring back over his shoulder at the monster, whose wings now seemed to fill the western sky, he put a boot in a pothole in the road, stumbled, went to hands and knees. Shouting aloud in frustration he scrambled to his feet, oblivious to the pain of sprained ankle and skinned palms and cracked knees, made a final dash for his tank.

Ruby glare dazzled him to left and right. Filled his eyes, his being. Heat enveloped him. He threw up his hands to shield his face. He heard a ripping roar like staccato thunder.

Two heavy autocannon from the descending BattleMech's arms bracketed him with fire, two medium lasers with sun-hot light lances. All converged on Kaiser's Schmitt tank.

Its multiton turret was thrust skyward on a piston of yellow-white flame. Much of the tank's frontal armor plate rushed to meet the captain, riding a wave of shock and fire.

* * *

Contemptuously, Malvina Hazen landed with the left foot of her 'Mech, the Black Rose, planted on the burning wreck that had been the heavy tank.

Near her right leg the bloated-bug shape of the strategic missile launcher stopped trying to pivot to kill her as its crew bailed out and ran back down the street. They feared the shrieking death promised by the Elementals, who sent red jets of flame licking forth as they leapt, still a block distant.

Even Malvina could scarcely blame them, for their mighty weapons could no longer help them. The Clanners called that feeling *powless*.

But their flight did them little good, except for the agony it spared them dying: Malvina's Solahma and Eyrie infantry had already secured several houses on this block. They began to harrow the street with their small arms. The fleeing Zeb missile man and woman did a brief neuronic dance as Gauss rifle needles sleeted through them like cosmic rays, then collapsed in shapeless bundles like discarded laundry.

Malvina laughed out loud.

She heard the Falcon calls in her own headset. They were code, a special Jade Falcon hunting language, which they could send in clear without fear of their enemies comprehending—while lighting flames of terror in listening enemies' hearts. It was a system—and tradition—invented by Malvina herself. It not only bound her Gyrs more closely to one another, a cohesion not even the toplofty Turkina Keshik shared, it bound her raptors more tightly to *her*.

That was important to Malvina Hazen. She had strategies and plans of a scope undreamed, not just by her sibkin but by Khan Jana Pryde herself.

"Forward, my Gyrfalcons!" she cried. "Slay all who oppose you. This world is ours!"

To her right a knot of Zeb troopers bolted from the porch of a narrow gray-brick house in loose-jointed panic, desperate to escape the flamer of an Elemental who had just walked her power suit through the wall into their sanctum. Lasers stabbed them and they fell, smoking and steaming. A Sekhmet assault vehicle rolled over the hill, crushing a private land car under its right tread.

To them she left the mopping up, and jumped.

*   *   *

They took her at her word, her Gyrfalcons. Too well.

She got what she wanted: one glorious battle against stiff opposition, which her troops nonetheless could overwhelm at speed with pure ferocious skill. And this was done.

She did not, for once, wish to win by indiscriminate terror. Zebebelgenubi's population was small, consisting disproportionately of extremely skilled workers, at the JES plant and other industries of prime strategic import. She recognized the indigenous laborers as assets valuable in themselves—and almost as difficult to replace as veteran warriors. She had no desire to risk slaughtering them. Indeed, once she taught the world a stiff lesson in the new reality by grinding its forces into bloody mud, she was tempted to follow her brother's weak-livered strategy of accommodating the local laborers, at least to an extent. Not abusing them overtly, say.

The matter was ripped from her hands.

Her Gyrs' blood ran boiling hot, flash-heated by their massacre of Militia troops and the not inconsiderable casualties the Zeb soldiers had dealt them. When they broke through the last defenses into Gray Valley City itself, they ran amok. They rampaged through the streets devastating at random, killing every living thing that crossed their sights. From the MechWarriors in their giant striding engines of destruction to the vehicle crews to Elementals to the fledglings and old warriors on foot, they gave themselves over to an ecstasy of annihilation.

Malvina ordered them to halt. She was ignored. They had already disregarded her very explicit orders issued before the landing. Now not even the secret language of shrieks and whistles she had taught them availed her. She raged and cursed and threatened, to no effect.

They stopped, in the end, when they got tired.

She halted her *Shrike* at the edge of a vast paved expanse and dismounted. She stripped off her sweat-sodden vest and trunks, and then the mesh coolsock they all wore like some priestly undergarment. The night air evaporated the sweat from her body, bringing blessed coolness, although it had a gritty quality, and each caress brought a hundred tiny impacts.

Naked, pale, tiny, unarmed and alone, she walked slowly

forward, the cement hard and warm with day's heat beneath bare soles, between the burned and brittle skeletons of trees, and the fallen statues, and the bodies. There were a great many bodies. Flies crawled on them, huge things with brilliant chrome yellow bellies that seemed to glow like sparks. The stench was not yet bad, nor had the bodies begun to bloat despite the heat; aridity made decomposition slow.

Besides, it was hard to smell anything over the reek of conflagration.

Returning to obedience, at least for the moment, her troops had followed her summons to assemble in a great central square. Around them the city burned like a pyre. No patrols roved the streets, because the streets were an impassable hell of heaped rubble and howling flame. No troops secured any perimeter, because even ten thousand corpses posed little threat to a Jade Falcon Cluster. Even the infantry were too weary now to raise their weapons, the MechWarriors wilted and dehydrated in oven-hot cockpits. Spent like fired cartridges.

Except their eyes, which smoldered still with bloodlust and defiance.

She looked into those eyes and saw mirrored—herself.

It was the crux.

She stopped before them and raised her hands above her head.

"Falcons!" she cried. Her words were thrown forward over her own shoulder, made huge by the loudspeakers mounted in the Black Rose, kneeling in vast metal supplication behind her.

Her Gyrfalcons stared sullenly at her. They did not know what to expect. Of her or of themselves.

"I salute you," she declared. "We are what humans were meant to be. We are humanity perfected by its own hand. We are the Future; we are Destiny.

"My brother Galaxy Commander has said we have no right to slaughter the Spheroids like beasts. And he is correct.

"It is not our right to hunt the lesser like the Falcons that we are. It is not our privilege.

"It is our duty."

And she had them, then, forever; and the night rang with their screams of salutation, and of worship.

24

Seventh Skye Militia
Cantonment
Outside New London
Skye
1 August 3134

Standing by the feet of her *Hatchetman* 'Mech, Tara Campbell gratefully accepted the two-liter plastic jug from a Seventh Skye Militia troopie and promptly upended it over her head.

She was quite unself-conscious about standing in front of several hundred near-strangers wearing only a khaki sports bra and brief trunks of the same color beneath her cooling vest, which stood open to allow the cool late-autumn breeze to lave her baked body. Not even on Northwind, a world far more prudish than cosmopolitan Skye, would such have attracted much attention: it was how MechWarriors dressed, unless they wanted to pass out from heat exhaustion in their machines. Since half a dozen BattleMechs had turned out for joint maneuvers this afternoon, plus a dozen Highlander and local Industrials, she wasn't the only one standing around scantily clad. Not all the female 'Mech jocks even wore halters—for Tara herself a matter of comfort and practicality rather than modesty anyway.

She shook her head, spluttered, bit off a mouthful from the jug, rinsed her mouth and spat into the churned-up gorse. She was going to be coated with greenish-gray mud directly: the autumn-dry ground cover on the practice field outside the Seventh cantonment had been well churned up by the afternoon's mechanized maneuvers, and the same breeze that brought blessed coolness also kicked up dust. It made no difference: she already knew she'd need a shower after this. Anybody did, who'd done more in a BattleMech than walk it sedately to a maintenance shop.

"Are we cut off from Terra, Countess?" the young private who'd brought her water asked anxiously.

She grimaced, covering the lapse with another splash of water on her forehead—which was still so hot she was surprised it didn't sizzle. The news had hit yesterday with the latest JumpShip emergence: the world of Zebebelgenubi had been seized by the fearful Malvina Hazen, with reportedly the greatest atrocity yet.

Zebebelgenubi was Skye's nearest neighbor in space, roughly two parsecs distant—and it lay with almost mathematical precision upon a line between Skye and Terra.

"Not at all, Heinrich," she said to the youth, whose hair had been shaved to a white-blond plush, which made his ears appear to stick out in a most unfortunate manner. She had heard his name called by a fellow Garryowen; she had been trained since earliest childhood never to forget a name: another facet of diplomatic upbringing. "JumpShips can still travel by way of Alphecca and Smyrna. It's not so easy to cut a system off from other stars without holding the jump points."

She smiled. "And thank you for the water."

He grinned back, shyly, and half-tripped walking away. Not realizing his clumsiness might have another cause she attributed it to wholly understandable fear: Zebebelgenubi's sun burned high in the early nighttime sky at this latitude and time of year on Skye. To know that the Jade Falcon's talons had closed invisibly about it could lead to sensations similar to a clawed foot clutching one's own heart.

Or at least hers.

With a clank of loose actuators and a blat of diesel engines, a ForestryMech sprayed with Skye autumn woodlands-pattern camouflage of dusty green and shades of medium green on a khaki base marched up to halt earth-shakingly nearby. It raised its giant chainsaw right arm in a salute and froze that way. The cockpit opened. A ladder of synthetic rope, white twined with blue and blue plastic rungs, snaked down. Lieutenant Colonel Hanratty descended with an alacrity startling for a middle-aged woman of her size. She grinned and sketched a salute at Tara, fully as unself-conscious of her state of undress, then accepted a water jug from another enlisted and went through the same routine as the Countess.

Seeing Tara speak to the mere enlisted man without biting his head off, other Garryowens of various rank began to drift toward her. She smiled and nodded encouragingly at them. She had noticed on earlier visits that they had an easy, democratic attitude among ranks: too relaxed, perhaps; the Seventh troopers occasionally treated their officers with something like contemptuous indulgence. It translated into general sloppiness, and could well, she knew—or anyway believed, since it was something taught in officer academies, although she had never experienced it—lead to a lethal tendency to debate orders in action instead of unhesitatingly following them.

Still, while the crispness of their formations did not make her hold her breath for the HPG net to come back up so she could comm the joyous word back to Northwind, they handled themselves and their machines competently enough. They hit their marks and maneuvered with immense panache, if seldom precision.

She suspected that they had been firmed up more than a bit by her own Senior Master Sergeant, Angus McCorkle, putting the fear of God into them despite lacking any identifiable "official" status. Early in his tenure with them he had stood without flinching against the wrath of an enraged Elemental—not poor Padraig, turning out to defend the farm despite his own unresolved post-traumatic stress disorder, but a Hell's Horse with a long black horsetail of hair hanging from the crown of his otherwise naked skull to the small of his immense, wedge-shaped back—and then, when the man's shoulder's bunched to crush him, brought him to his knees with an uppercut to the groin that observers swore lifted the monster several centimeters off the ground. Since that incident, they realized he was no phony parade-ground spit-and-polish hardass, but a *genuine* hardass, who wasn't going to go all runny when exposed to the heat of real combat—any more than a block of Endo steel exposed to a candle flame. And they respected him for it.

She hoped, now, to win their respect as well.

Which, it turned out, was going to entail facing their questions without flinching. "What about these Forlorn Hopes of yours, Countess," a female lieutenant asked defiantly. "Don't ye have faith in us?"

"O'Malley—" Hanratty commenced a warning growl.

Tara held up a finger to her. "I do," she said, meeting the young woman's scowling gaze square-on and nodding firmly. "I have faith in my Highlanders, faith in you, faith in the Ducal Guard and other planetary defense forces, and faith in God. But I would not be keeping my faith with you if I told you I was confident all those things would be enough.

"I have no wish to weaken your arms with worry. That's never done anyone a scrap of good. Yet I will not lead under false colors: the Jade Falcons are as potent a natural disaster as a hurricane. All the help that I—that *we*—can get in meeting them won't be too much. Fair enough, Lieutenant?"

The woman blushed and dropped her eyes. "Fair enough, Countess. I—I'm sorry."

Tara clapped the taller woman on the shoulder. "No need to apologize for asking a just question.

"Now." She turned to face the group as a whole, intermingled now with her own dismounted Northwinders, curious and perhaps a bit protective of their Countess among these not-altogether friendly outsiders. "When the sky lights up with the drive-flames of Falcon DropShips it will be too late for questions."

They nodded, as did their commander. Other questions came: more of technical particulars and less of challenge. Tara answered mechanically.

Inside she felt a twinge at the young subaltern characterizing the Forlorn Hopes as *hers*. She had intended initially to lead them in action herself. It seemed necessary, given her determination never to order troops to do anything she herself feared to do.

That intention blew up a storm as big as the Countess' new recruiting campaign itself, which still had the Herrmanns AG media group howling in chorus about how it was really concealed genocide against the German population. Legate Eckard had been primly disapproving. Prefect Brown tried, again, to forbid her—but lacked stature to make it stick: Brown might be senior in grade, but Tara was a Countess, and nobility told in The Republic as it did throughout the Inner Sphere. The Prefect urged Duke Gregory Kelswa-Steiner to intercede, but he refused; if the offworld glamour-girl wanted to throw her silly life away at the head of a lot of civilians armed with push brooms and popguns, he didn't mean to trouble himself over the fact.

Her own officers combusted, as intensely if not as flamboyantly as Prefect Brown. She was the most seasoned battle commander on Skye. Although the Duke had been no slouch in his time, she had fought more, for higher stakes, and much more recently. None had faith in career desk-pilot Della Brown, nor the dry-stick Eckard—not in their ability to handle forces in actual war. Nor was any Highlander commander eager to serve under the moody Duke.

As for lesser Skye leaders, the Northwinders who knew Hanratty liked her, and respected her well enough: but none was really sure she could manage her own scapegrace and scrap-built regiment in battle, much less a division-sized planetary defense against a first-division team like the Falcons. Major von Traub, commanding the Ducal Guard, they would not even consider taking orders from. While Duke Gregory, perhaps understandably, doted on the man for his loyalty—in contrast, say, to that of his son and heir—and was pressing the fractious Skye Chamber of Deputies to jump him up clear to his first star as Lieutenant-General, the Highlanders all suspected that, Elsie-connected as he was, he had been left behind by Jasek's defection because the younger Kelswa-Steiner didn't want him. Although the official face the Guard showed the Highlanders was a stainless-steel plating of military correctness that didn't quite mask frosty dislike, there was enough covert fraternization between the formations that the off-worlders knew they weren't the only ones to harbor those suspicions.

It had been Tara's own aide, Captain Tara Bishop, who changed her mind as the two shared a nightcap on a narrow balcony overlooking the Sanglamore quad, with enemy-held Zebebelgenubi gleaming like a self-luminous tumor in the sky.

"Do me a favor, TC," Tara Bishop said quietly. "Just take a step back and look at it from outside your skin."

"*There's* an attractive image." The two showed each other brief grins.

"What would *you* think of a supreme commander who chose to lead a self-professed suicide force? If you were a Militia grunt in the ranks—or a private soldier from the Regiment?"

Spoken by a Northwinder, in that tone of voice, *the Regiment* meant one thing only: in Tara Bishop's case the First Kearny Highlanders, in which she still technically served, on temporary duty assignment to the Countess' staff.

Tara's cheeks had tightened until her eyes almost vanished. "I'd think he—*she*—had despaired. Given up."

Eyes huge in Luna-light, Tara Bishop nodded.

Now came TB herself in her *Pack Hunter* with its Ripper extended-range particle projector jutting from its right shoulder. She had been making sure all stragglers from the just-completed exercise got rounded up. Tara waved at her aide and friend. The speedy thirty-ton 'Mech returned the gesture with its humanoid right hand.

The question session broke up. The Garryowens seemed satisfied with the answers she had given them. Tara happened to overhear one sergeant speaking to another: "Face it, Gerald my boy," the woman said, draping a comradely arm across the taller man's shoulders, "anybody who makes that Sassenach pig Herrmann squeal so loud as this one does *has* to be riding with the angels!"

In a few moments Tara Bishop sauntered up, wearing a midriff-baring olive drab T-shirt and exceptionally brief trunks beneath her bulky armored cooling vest. It was the taller woman's conviction, her superior knew, that she could walk around, in her words, "buck nekkid," and no one would so much as glance at her so long as Tara Campbell was in view. She was, as the Countess repeatedly tried to tell her, quite mistaken.

Tara B started to say something. Before the words came out of her mouth Tara's comm unit buzzed on her hip. She snatched it up, heart in throat: it had to be dire news indeed for anyone to comm her here.

"Countess," a voice said quietly, and tension rendered it momentarily unfamiliar.

Then: "Paul?" She turned away from as many bystanders as she could, shielding the unit with her hands. "Good heavens, I'm on maneuvers here—"

"Not a personal call. Emergency meeting going on in the Palace, room three-oh-five. You should be there."

"When?"

"Ten minutes ago, ideally. You didn't hear this from me. I'm out."

The line went dead.

Tara knew that Paul believed he was closing in on— whatever it was he was hunting. She really didn't need to know, and had more than enough things she *did* need to, frankly, so she never asked. She doubted this pertained to that in any way.

She had come to know him as a rock-solid man, who though intellectually as nimble as anyone she had encountered, was decidedly *not* prone to imagining things. It was the most accountant-like trait she'd seen in him. If he thought the matter vital—

Quickly, quietly, she explained the situation to her aide. "We need to get you back now," Tara Bishop said flatly. "Damn. Rush hour's about to get going. Traffic's going to bark."

She spoke briefly into her own hand communicator and turned a frown to the Countess.

"No VTOLs available to pick you up," she said. "Nothing inside half an hour."

"My *Hatchetman*—"

"Too lead-footed—with all respect."

"Your 'Mech, then." The captain's *Pack Hunter* had a top speed of 119 kph, almost twice as fast as Tara C's

Hatchetman. It could theoretically get her to the Lord Governor's palace in just over fifteen minutes.

"No time to rekey the neurohelmet to interface with your brain patterns, Countess."

As one the two women turned to stare up at the light BattleMech, standing with its cockpit ajar to let the breezes cool it and dry its pilot's sweat from the form-fitting command couch.

"Good thing you're small," Tara Bishop said, "and that we're really good friends."

25

Lord Governor's Palace
New London
Skye
1 August 3134

A Klaxon blared from the Lord Governor's Palace as a BattleMech descended from the light afternoon overcast to settle on the lawn right outside the porticoed white-marble entrance, light as a thirty-ton feather. A ready squad of Ducal Guards in full combat gear turned out to menace the *Pack Hunter* valiantly with their laser rifles.

"Hey!" their sergeant shouted. "You can't park that here!"

With a clunk of released catches and a hiss of air pressure equalizing, the domed cockpit cracked open. The apprehensive security troopies stared in apprehension—which turned to bafflement as not one but two figures emerged and rapidly descended to the painstakingly tended sod into which the 'Mech's feet sank inexorably.

Jaws dropped, female no less than male, when two scantily attired and remarkably attractive young women, bodies glistening with sweat, marched straight up to the squad.

"I am Tara Campbell," the short one in the lead said

haughtily, "Countess of Northwind and Prefect for Prefecture III."

"By God," the sergeant in charge said, forgetting himself, "you are."

The taller woman behind the haughty Countess, who carried a Rorynex submachine gun on a long sling around her neck and a captain's bars blazoned on her cooling vest, glared at the Guards. It was obvious she considered the security detachment hopelessly outnumbered.

The sergeant opened his mouth. He shut it. He felt irrationally as if *he* were standing bare-assed on the lawn with a whole traffic jam worth of gawkers all around and the sky abuzz with civvy VTOLs, and these confounded women were wearing Gnome battle armor.

He finally forced sound out: "The gun," he said, waving at the SMG. "You can't take a gun into the Palace. Security. *Regulations.*" His accent, not surprisingly, was *Steinerdeutsch*.

The two Taras exchanged glances. Tara B unshipped the subgun and tossed it unceremoniously to the sergeant. "I'll be back for that," she said.

The women swept on past. The patrol stood as if turned to statues. They made an interesting composition group with the parked BattleMech, pinging as it cooled from its high-speed jaunt into the heart of the prefectural government.

Helicopters swarmed overhead as the two women mounted the broad steps. They were mostly media: the civilian-cop traffic-control job that had been bird-dogging them the last couple klicks as the *Pack Hunter* jumped blithely into and through the gridlocked central-business district—coming close to but never *quite* squashing any land cars—had backed off as the 'Mech descended toward the palace lawn.

"*They're* getting an eyeful," TB commented. "Guess what's leading tonight's evening news?"

Tara produced an un-Countess-like grunt of annoyance. Then she rocked as an orange and white chopper with a *fenestron* antitorque shroud encircling its tail rotor descended so low its skids almost brushed the grass. The ferocious side blast threatened to slam her off her feet. Tara Bishop grabbed her biceps to steady her.

On the chopper's flank was painted the unmistakable winged-helmet logo of Herrmanns AG and the legend *Herrmanns HoloNews.*

The VTOL came down so near the security detachment that several of them had to duck and dart to evade the lethal flickering scythe-sweep of the main blade. The sergeant shook his fist and bellowed curses, red-faced and unheard for the aircraft's uproar.

Then his face paled with the adrenaline-dump of *real* anger. He cocked his head forward and spoke for the benefit of the microphone curving before his lips. His squaddies all turned toward the intruding news-helo and, standing or kneeling, aimed their lasers at the cockpit with what seemed unseemly eagerness.

The VTOL shot straight up as if yanked into the sky on a string.

Tara Campbell laughed aloud, then sobered. "Great," she said. "This is all we need."

Her aide shrugged. "They say there's no such thing as bad publicity. . . ."

An armed guard stood at the door, glorious in the full green-and-white plumage of the Palace Guard—a different outfit from the Duke's own squaddies on the lawn, building security in bald truth. She tried to bar Countess Tara from entering, holding her Imperator machine pistol crosswise before her.

Tara Bishop politely helped the Guardswoman back to her feet, picked up the gun off the floor, dropped the magazine with a clatter to the polished Skye marble, and handed the empty weapon back to its owner before following her boss through the heavy door of dark-stained local hardwood.

Duke Gregory looked up, salt and pepper brows ferociously abristle, as Countess Tara Campbell swept like a north wind through the door. His brows kept rising.

Prefect Della Brown jumped erect from her seat at the table across from him. "What is the meaning of this—oh, my God!"

"Prefect," Tara said, nodding crisply. "Legate Eckard. Your Grace."

"The disrespect—" Della Brown sputtered.

Tara cut her off with a gaze cool as liquid helium—and piercing as a laser beam. "Indeed," she said in a precisely metered tone. "However, given the emergency that confronts us all and the necessity of working together in the best interests of this planet and The Republic, I am willing to overlook the disrespect shown me by convening a meeting of this gravity without notifying me."

The Duke's brows had stopped short of displacing his scalp. He covered his momentary imbalance by bluster: "This is purely an internal matter—a matter of Skye politics. Nothing which is the rightful concern of The Republic."

"Prefect Brown is a Republican official," Tara said, "as is Legate Eckard. If they belong here, I belong here." She heard Tara Bishop slip in behind her and quietly shut the door, felt the reassuring warmth of her on her back.

"Please excuse the informal attire of myself and my aide, Duke Gregory," Tara C added crisply. "We were conducting vital field exercises with the Republic Skye Militia. Had we been given proper notice of this meeting we would have had time to change to something more appropriate."

"You've pushed it too far this time, Campbell," Prefect Brown began.

"Enough," Duke Gregory growled. He had clearly adjusted to the newcomers' state. A MechWarrior himself, he knew they didn't dress that way to be provocative. "The confounded woman is here, and I am in no mood to bandy words over sartorial details. However, I must insist that this is purely a local matter, and—"

The door opened behind Tara B. Chief Minister Augustus Solvaig entered wearing his umber and russet robes of state. He stopped dead and opened his mouth, his face going crimson.

Duke Gregory held up a big, scarred hand. "Peace, my friend. We've had the debate already."

The minister nodded with an emphasis that frankly surprised Tara Campbell. It set his jowls jiggling.

"I have made all necessary preparations, my lord," he said. "You have but to give the word, and a company of Ducal Guards will secure the Palace of Counsel and dissolve the Deputies."

"*What?*" Tara Campbell demanded.

"The Chamber of Deputies debates whether to send an offer of surrender to the invaders." To her surprise it was Legate Stanford Eckard who answered. "To Galaxy Commander Aleksandr Hazen, to be precise."

Tara drew in a deep breath. The scene seemed suddenly sharp, the colors bright, sounds piercing and painful to the ears.

The Duke had begun explaining the situation in his deep, sonorous voice. Tara heard the words with enormous clarity but without deriving sense from them.

But she didn't need to. She already knew.

Although it played no part in The Republican scheme as outlined by Stone, Duke Gregory's father had formed a Chamber of Deputies, popularly elected, to "advise" the planetary governor. The real point had been to bleed confrontational steam from a population possessed of two large minorities bitterly opposed both to The Republic and each other. The people of Skye would be granted a voice, precisely to keep the fractious talking instead of busting heads. But the Chamber possessed no actual legislative power.

So now the Deputies had got the bit in their collective teeth. Wishing to spare Skye and the rest of Prefecture IX the horror the whole world now knew had been visited upon Chaffee, Glengarry, Ryde and Zebebelgenubi, they were preparing to vote on a resolution calling upon the Duke to capitulate to the least fearful of the invaders.

"Which is treason," Duke Gregory concluded. "So, yes, Countess, I am preparing to dissolve the Deputies for the duration if that's what it takes."

"Your Grace, is that wise?" Tara demanded.

"Wise? To counter treason?" Solvaig made great show of shaking his head. "Why must we listen to this—this—"

"Add a noun to that," Tara Bishop said, deadly quiet, "and I call you out."

As he turned puce and sputtered, the Countess continued: "I grant there is no provision for such a body within the Republican Charter. Nonetheless, having consented to seat such a body, to suppress it by arms for fulfilling the function you tasked it with would, I submit, violate the spirit of that Charter. It would smack of plain tyranny. And cowardice."

Everybody else in the room talked at once, quite loudly.

Except for Captain Bishop, who contented herself with a brief, low whistle at Tara's back.

Tara stood her ground, head up, not bowing to the storm. The tiny hairs upon her arms seemed to tickle her individually, so keen had her senses become. When the tumult died down—the others needing more or less simultaneously to draw breath—she went on in a tone of reason backed with steel.

"Should we betray the principles they're fighting for," she said, "such as freedom of speech—which *is* in the Charter—we shall already *have* surrendered. We shall ultimately be no better than the Clans or the most oppressive Great Houses. We might as well be Dracs ourselves—or Wolves!"

Surprisingly Duke Gregory had subsided. "Grant me the wit at least to have thought of that, my lady," he said evenly. "But tell me—cowardice?"

"In retreating from that position your father took and you assumed," she said. "Giving your subjects a voice and then shutting it up when it speaks words you'd rather not hear. *Fearing* mere words—defending yourself against them with bayonets and bullets."

The Duke's face crumpled in a frown. But it was a pensive expression, not angry.

"Curious that this Countess should be so ready to take up the cause of traitors," Solvaig sneered. "And in the face of the Clans."

Eyes aflame, she rounded on him. "It is not those who preach surrender I champion—although I understand their feelings, as you who have never faced a foe in battle, seen friends die—*heard* them die—cannot. I *know* what it is like to see my home world devastated by Clan brutality.

"I have suffered at Clan hands. I ordered my ancestral castle—my *home,* in which I was raised from childhood—blown to rubble to prevent the Steel Wolves befouling it like the beasts they are. I saw my world's beautiful capital city, the city whose name I bear, destroyed out of nothing but spite. I saw Terra itself invaded—and my troops and I it was who threw the Clanners back.

"So do not *presume* to tar me with the brush of treason, Mister Minister, when I stand forth for the rights of Republican citizens to free expression."

Solvaig's face worked like a bagful of fists. He turned

pink and red and white by turns. Before he could find words, Legate Eckard spoke again, quietly yet with a firmness Tara had not heard from him before.

"I have sworn an oath to uphold The Republic and all its principles, intact. So have we all. I intend to honor that oath. And I do see the force in your arguments. But before we go further—Countess Campbell, have you seen any notice of weakened resolve on the part of the troops actually charged with fighting for this world?"

"I have not, Legate. They are ready to face the Falcons' worst." *Emotionally, at least,* she thought. *But one worry at a time, here. . . .*

"They don't pay any attention to debates in the Deputies," Tara Bishop said. "They don't give a rat's—don't care what anyone says there."

Without looking Tara raised a hand to forestall her aide saying more. She was right, and her words to the point; but they had entered a zone where it was risky for juniors to be seen *or* heard.

Eckard turned to the Duke, ignoring a glower from his nominal superior Brown, who had resumed her chair and sat with arms folded tightly across her rib cage. "Your Grace, in truth I see no sign of this debate in the Chamber weakening anyone's resolve in such a way as to justify shutting it down. Your Republic Skye Militia will fight, you have just heard. The Countess' Highlanders, veteran soldiers of unquestioned quality, will fight. And your people, the people of Skye, continue volunteering for Countess Campbell's . . . special initiative faster than our clerks can process their applications. Have you reason to believe the Assembly will actually *pass* a measure suing Galaxy Commander Aleksandr Hazen for terms?"

The Duke looked to his Chief Minister, who still hovered by the door like a pudgy pale thundercloud. "Augustus?"

"No, your Grace," he blurted. "But—but still, that such a question should even *be* debated, it demands decisive action, the *harshest* action—"

The Duke held up his hand again. Solvaig sputtered to a stop.

"I am no tyrant, Countess," Duke Gregory said. "Neither am I coward. And I understand that you imputed neither to me, only to actions which remain at this moment hypothetical. Which I think you will admit is just as well for all concerned."

Tara nodded. Child of career diplomats, she knew in her marrow when to yield as well as when to stand.

"Credit me, please, with understanding what I undertook in consenting to allow the Chamber of Deputies to continue to sit since my accession. I uphold my father's wisdom in creating it. My commitment to The Republic and its ideals has not wavered and never shall.

"Yet in the end I fight for the people of Skye. I will not sacrifice them to principles—not even Devlin Stone's. If that makes *me* a traitor I will answer for it—*after* we have whipped the Falcon scum back to their Occupation Zone!"

Tara snapped to attention. "Your Grace, I have said harsh words. I regret the necessity of saying them. Yet I would never presume to name you traitor for choosing your people's welfare over all other considerations. I only thank God I did not have to choose between Northwind and The Republic."

"Fair enough," the Duke said.

Then he sighed. "Very well. You have made your case, Countess, in a most eloquent and emphatic manner, if one as unorthodox as your fashion sense. I shall permit debate to continue unrestricted—so long as it remains no more than debate. Should the Deputies actually go so far as to pass a surrender resolution, then I shall feel compelled to take decisive action—to preserve the integrity of Prefecture IX and The Republic, as well as the welfare of Skye."

Her first day of training as a MechWarrior, her one-eyed, one-legged, one-armed instructor had said, "Whatever else you learn, learn to know what victory is." Tara Campbell had taken those words to heart—and suffered when she neglected to observe them. She nodded, and made herself do so briskly.

"On behalf of The Republic of the Sphere, I thank you, your Grace."

Prefect Della Brown frowned at her rival's presumption in speaking for The Republic. She said nothing, though. *She's not the house I'm playing to,* Tara Campbell thought grimly.

"Perhaps if your Grace spoke a few words in the Chamber yourself, it might help keep minds right," Legate Eckard said.

"The Duke is not allowed to make personal presentations to the Deputies!" Augustus Solvaig crowed as if it was a battle he had won. "It's in the old duke's Constitution."

"For which reason you yourself shall make the speech for me, Augustus," Duke Gregory said in a tone which did not invite demurral, "and do so eloquently and well. Have it on my desk in half an hour for my approval."

Solvaig looked to his master. Being so summarily dismissed did not sit well with him. He nodded and was gone.

Duke Gregory looked a long moment after him, brow furrowing. He turned to the Countess.

"You've won. Now I suggest you return to your preparations."

His beard split in a gigantic grin. "And if you show half the spirit defying the Falcons as you have defying me, those bottle-baby bastards don't stand a bloody chance."

26

DropShip **White Reaper**
Orbiting Zebebelgenubi
Prefecture VIII
The Republic of the Sphere
1 August 3134

Malvina awoke with a jar, like falling several centimeters.

She snapped upright. Around her the bedclothes were a swamp sodden with fearful sweat.

She was alone. Although not in the dark. She always slept with the lights on, alone or not.

She had been dreaming about the last time she slept with the lights out. The night of the sixth anniversary of her and Aleks' Decant.

The night they came for them.

There were eight of them, motivated by sound calculation in the scheme of Darwinian crèche economics: fewer mouths to feed equaled more food for all. So it was only fitting the runts, the two weakest, should sacrifice for the good of the sibko. It was the Clan way that had been dinned into them unceasingly since before their ears could make sense of speech.

Aleks fought back, furiously and in the grip of transfiguring fear, throat too tight to scream, his face white and twisted as the bedsheets now clutched in Malvina's woundwire fists. They concentrated on him as the boy, even though he was the smaller. Small and scared as he was, with his body wastes streaming down his skinny brown legs, he fought them: a merciless mortal battle, there in the dark of the studiedly cheerless dormitory room.

Aleks' hopeless frenzied valor had bought Malvina the freedom to act.

By the time two burly Proctors, mere laborers, had arrived to subdue the combatants with blows and stunstick, two nocturnal assailants lay dead. Yimm would survive, but hampered by having but a single eye died two years later in a training accident without help from Malvina. But only because it took her too long to get to him. The other five attackers who lived through that terrible night had predeceased him, not by accident, although several seemed so.

She shook herself, came back to herself. Her eyes refocused. She had been seeing it all as if the air between her eyes and the bulkhead of her cabin in *White Reaper* were a holovid stage.

They came back, she thought, riding a nebular ring of desolation. *They always come back.*

No matter how often she killed them. No matter how many she killed. They kept returning for her and her brother in her dreams.

She gripped her head in her hands and screamed. The bulkheads swallowed the sound.

She would hold to the lesson she had learned as a terrified child: keep killing until no one threatened her and her sibkin any more. She would kill as many as it took to make the attackers in her dreams stay dead, stay *away.*

And if what it took was for her to kill every living human being in the galaxy, then cast herself into the blazing heart of a star—

Her breathing had returned to normal. She lay down on her side, happily curled, resting her cheek on her folded hands.

Then at last we will all sleep in peace, she thought, and slept again, and dreamt no more.

27

Ceres Metals Fab 17
Warsaw Continent, Kimball II
Prefecture IX
The Republic of the Sphere
7 August 3134

Far away against a bank of slate-colored clouds whose tops
were night, an orange flame glared like a second sun at the
top of a flare tower burning off unused fractions of petroleum drawn from deep beneath the surface. The real sun
had just descended below the horizon of the industrial
waste-scape that surrounded the 305th Assault Cluster of
the Gyrfalcon Galaxy as far as the eye could see.

It seemed to have dissolved into a pool of burning blood.

In his command post in a reinforced concrete building
somewhere in the middle of Ceres Metals' Fab 17 on the
equatorial continent of Warsaw, on the world Kimball II,
Star Colonel Noritomo Helmer flinched as a barrage of
long-range missiles crunched in among his positions, even
though the impacts fell half a klick away at the least.

He was losing it, he knew. To respond that way to mere
artillery bombardment, and a distant one at that. The only

reason he was not fighting hourly Trials of Position was that none of his subordinates wanted to take over in the face of the Cluster's current situation.

Powless could do that to a warrior.

Snow began to fall again. It looked as if it would continue for a time, whitewashing earlier falls begrimed by industrial effluvia—where it hadn't gone to muck from the boots and blood of men and women destroying each other without mercy. Not just with 'Mechs and artillery and tanks and hovercraft, nor even rifles and grenades. But also with bayonets and rifle butts, knives and tools and lengths of metal bar stock; boots, fists, teeth. The still air tasted of petroleum and was stale with death.

He turned away from the doorway and ducked into the red-lit depths of the command center.

It was not that he lacked the tools of his warrior's trade, exactly, although his *Phoenix Hawk IIC* BattleMech had been rendered inoperable two days ago by Gauss-rifle hits from M1 Marksman tanks. It could probably be repaired— if they ever got out of the city-sized factory. But they lacked the appropriate parts.

A man with a sense of irony might have appreciated the poignancy of being caught in the middle of an immense complex devoted entirely to producing parts for engines of war, and being unable to repair one's own machines for lack of the proper replacements. Star Colonel Noritomo Helmer was not such a man.

What he did appreciate was that he had made a crucial mistake.

There were two habitable worlds in the Kimball system, Kimball II and Kimball IV. Kimball IV was a miserable world, dry, with an unbreathable atmosphere, on which domed colonies were maintained purely to work the hugely productive mines, especially extracting bauxite. It had barely any population to speak of, not a soul more than was necessary to work the mines and keep those who worked the mines supplied with necessities. Kimball II was a glittering prize: a hot, wet, lush world, fabulously rich, with abundant agriculture, mining and heavy industry, and a population just over two and a half billion.

The problem with Kimball II was that it was a rich world

with lots of heavy industry and a population of just over two and a half billion.

He should have gone for Kimball IV. It would have been an easy conquest and given him a shot at controlling traffic to and from Kimball II with his DropShips and fighters. At the very least, he would have had what his mission called for: a solid foothold in another Republican system. The Kimball II militia, geared toward defending its home world, would surely not have been able to dislodge him once he got good and dug in.

But it wasn't the nature of Turkina's brood to take an easy prize and then dig in. And Helmer was dazzled by the glitter of one of The Republic's richest worlds.

The blame was not all his: when Khan Jana Pryde insisted on including Kimball among the *desant's* objectives, she surely never had the miserable rock Kimball IV in mind.

The Star Colonel had decided to grab Kimball II's biggest prize first: Ceres Metals' colossal Fab 17. From here, certainly, he could compel the surrender of the rest of the world.

Except he had lost a third of his warriors and machines simply gouging out a foothold in the complex. And although Warsaw continent lay remote from population centers, the Kimballites had rapidly reinforced their forces at the Fab in the face of stiff opposition by his aerospace fighters. Who suffered losses in their turn.

Now he was stuck in a grinding fight. And not just any battle, but a battle of attrition, worst nightmare of any Clan commander. It was a battle that for all the might of his machines and prowess of his warriors he could not win— because no matter how many the Kimballites lost, they had made it abundantly clear that they were willing to lose more. As many as it took to eradicate the hated invaders.

He had options. He still had *White Fist,* the DropShip that had brought him to this cursed place. Indeed, it occupied almost the geometric center of his perimeter, like a gas giant ringed by moons—and like a giant planet seemed inexorably to be sucking his lines closer to it with each day that passed. He could have ordered his Cluster aboard and blasted away.

But that was not the Jade Falcon way. As he understood it, anyway.

He might, likewise, have followed his commander's lead: sent *White Fist* aloft to rain destruction upon the people of Kimball II, burn their cities until they broke. But, although he worshipped the White Virgin as blindly as all the other Gyrfalcons, he lacked the heart. Indiscriminate slaughter of noncombatants also was not the Clan way.

Besides, while he was not a particularly reflective man, a truth had nonetheless stamped itself upon his brain: if he outraged the populace sufficiently, the sheer mass of their two and a half billion could simply swamp his puny handful of warriors, 'Mechs, and Elementals as if they'd been dropped in the planet's abundant oceans.

He was not, needless to say, going to make the rendez-vous at Skye.

A warrior rushed in the door of the Tactical Operations Center. "Sir," she gasped, "we just had a runner from the Third Trinary. They are under heavy assault from the south. Enemies have infiltrated behind them through the sewers and cut their land lines, and are taking them under fire from the rear!" The Kimballites had power-jamming stations working from within the factory itself, making radio communications unreliable at best.

As she spoke, he heard a rise in the thump and crackle of distant battle. He stepped to the mouth of the bunker to see the flares of energy weapons underlighting the clouds, blue and green and scarlet.

The snow came down heavily now. A fat flake landed on his open left eyeball, stinging with cold until he blinked it away.

At least, he thought with grim satisfaction, *I did my duty and sent off my JumpShip to inform my Galaxy Commander that we cannot join her for the invasion of Skye.*

Even though it means we're trapped in this Founder-forsaken system.

Heaven's Gate
Ryde
7 August 3134

Anastasia Kerensky looked sharply out the window of the planetary police headquarters. "Is that Falcon still moving?" she demanded, staring narrow-eyed at a body hanging from one of the ornate cast-iron lampposts in the park outside. "It's hard to tell in the dark."

By the glow of the several surviving lights it was possible to tell that the trees were just budding out and the ground beneath was trodden bare. The mesh fence topped with razor-tape coils that had enclosed the makeshift holding pen for hostages, which the park had become under the military government Malvina Hazen had left behind, had been mostly trampled down.

Ian Murchison peered out the window. His expression was pinched, although whether with disapproval or something else Anastasia was hard-pressed to tell. *Disapproval's a part of it, certainly,* she decided.

"I believe another citizen just shot at the body," he said. "Or possibly struck it with a thrown brick. I can't see whether there's anyone close enough."

"Do you object to the way I dealt with the Falcon garrison?" she asked, taking a bite from a local fruit, making a face at its sourness, and then taking another. "Or the way I allowed local justice to take its course with the survivors?"

"Mob action is never pretty."

She shrugged. "I thought this particular mob action had its own esthetic. I found rolling Star Captain Simon in razor wire a particularly imaginative touch."

Her personal medico grimaced.

"Ah, well. Each to his own tastes." She cocked a brow at him. "Although I hardly think you'd have sympathy to waste on the Falcons, given what they did to this world."

"I must confess I scarcely know how to feel about all this," Murchison said. "*That's* hardly a new sensation for me, as you no doubt know."

She shrugged and daintily spat the pit of the fruit she had just consumed into a metal wastebasket, where it rang.

"I *am* disappointed we missed Galaxy Commander Malvina Hazen," she said. "I'm looking forward to making her acquaintance. But at least we know where she's headed."

She smiled, well, *wolfishly*. "And I have to admit it was damned thoughtful of the idiot subordinate she sent haring off to Kimball to provide us with a perfectly serviceable *Merchant*-class JumpShip. That by itself guarantees this little venture will prove a profitable one for the Steel Wolves."

"It's not what you came for."

She looked at him through the gloom of the office. A fluorescent light winked on and off overhead like a tic in an eyelid. "No," she said quietly, "it's not. What I want is blood."

PART THREE

Yarak

"*n. Falconry*. The eagerness of birds of prey to hunt."

—*New Avalon Institute of Science Unabridged Dictionary of the English Language,* Edition CCCV, New Avalon, Federated Suns, 3032

28

The Falcon fleet assembled: from Glengarry came Beckett Malthus in his *Nightlord*, from Summer came Aleksandr Hazen. His sibkin Malvina had been the first into Skye system from Zebebelgenubi. Her order had destroyed the unarmed Skye station.

She was viciously angry. She had lingered at the Zebebelgenubi jump point, waiting for Star Colonel Noritomo Helmer, due back sans a garrison left on conquered Kimball II. When the time came—and he did not—she had been compelled to jump to Skye. She would not miss the grand adventure, the culmination of their mighty and desperate enterprise.

The reassembled fleet waited another day at Skye's zenith point for Helmer's JumpShip. They had no element of surprise; Skye's defenders had known they were coming for weeks at least. A day could make small difference to the outcome, so Bec Malthus reasoned—although Aleks Hazen argued for immediate departure in-system.

Malthus took advantage of the twenty-four hour delay to convene a *kurultai* of all commanders and Bloodnamed warriors among the expeditionary force. At stake lay the final fate of Skye: how was the prize to be taken?

Although by the Founder's plan, literacy was universal among the Clans, they by the same design maintained an oral tradition as strong as any preliterate people's. Eloquence was esteemed, as much a part of taking and holding high place as prowess in battle—although there were no Trials employing it, if you left aside Bec Malthus. Whose preeminent gift was not *exactly* rhetoric.

The Hazen ristars had excelled in public speaking, as they did in all things. An epic contest was eagerly expected, even by Turkina Keshik warriors who under normal circumstances scarcely deigned to notice the doings of the lesser formations, the Delta and Zeta Galaxies.

Those expectations were not disappointed.

They stood upon the stage of the thronged and darkened auditorium inboard Malthus' battleship *Emerald Talon*. Bec Malthus stood upstage and at the center behind a podium. At his back rose a hologram of the Jade Falcon emblem, rippling slowly like a ten-meter-high flag in an imperceptible breeze. Beneath it hung the banners of Turkina Keshik, the Gyrfalcon Galaxy and Turkina's Beak. Flanking them were the flags of the worlds conquered by the expeditionary force: Chaffee, Alkaid, Glengarry, Ryde, Summer, Zebebelgenubi, even Porrima, and with them battle-stained regimental honors of units the Falcons had beaten down in having their way with their worlds. A gap showed where the Kimball II flag was meant to be displayed; with characteristic defiance, Malvina chose to flaunt even her failures—and whatever the cause, the failure of Noritomo Helmer to turn up on schedule with appropriate evidences of victory was Malvina's own failure, in her own mind no less than others'.

She stood downstage upon Malthus' left, clad in her mostly black dress uniform with its black cape about her shoulders. Her white-blonde hair fell like an avalanche down the back of her cape. On Malthus' right stood Aleks Hazen, imposing as a statue in his regulation green-and-midnight dress uniform. None wore a helmet.

"We have completed an epic journey," Malvina declared,

when a spotlight stabbed down white to grant her turn to speak, "and accomplished epic ends. We have carried the glory of Jade Falcon and the Clans almost to the heart of the Inner Sphere. And we have paid an epic price in blood."

The assembled warriors sat in silence as absolute as that outside the JumpShip's pressure hull. It was common knowledge that, including the absent 305th Assault Cluster, Malvina's Gyrfalcons had lost almost fifty percent of their fighting effectives to death or injury. She had taken a rich booty of *isorla*, especially in the form of Joint Equipment Systems tactical and strategic missile-launch vehicles. But it was warriors who were always the *desant's* rarest and most precious asset, and those she had spent like water.

"History will sing that the cost was worth it, for Turkina's glory and our own. Yet we must assure ourselves of victory, and more: on terms that do not leave us too spent to hold our gains until, as they someday must, the Jade Falcon *Touman* joins us to carry the banners of Crusade to the holy soil of Terra itself.

"In little more than one hundred hours, Falcons, Turkina will spread Her wings above our last objective. Skye will lie at the mercy of our beak and talons, helpless to do more than await our pleasure as to when and where we strike. And *how*.

"We carry with us the fires to burn their cities from orbit. I say, let New Glasgow burn!"

The audience reacted with a gasp. All knew that Malvina had made free use of terror in her conquests of Ryde and Zebebelgenubi. Yet what she was proposing struck at the root of centuries of taboo—and at the very heart of what it meant to be Clan. Only Aleks, it seemed, was unmoved—and no one in that bowl of darkness doubted that seeming was a lie.

"That we shall win decisive victory over Skye's defenders cannot be doubted," Malvina said. "Yet the planet's population exceeds three billion. We can afford no repetition of Chaffee on such a scale: we must assure that when they surrender, they *submit*, fully and forever, with no thought of further resistance. The way to ensure that is to let them taste in advance what defiance will bring."

The spotlight on her dimmed. No one applauded. Another spot pinned Aleks.

"I will not speak of Clan traditions," Aleks said in his rich, rolling baritone, only slightly strained. "You all are imbued with them in your genes, even as am I. I speak of results. On Alkaid and Summer I promised the populace in advance that I would honor the Laws of War. I employed the minimum force required to defeat defending forces on the ground, and afterwards kept my promise. By decent treatment of noncombatants and defeated foes alike I secured the willing cooperation of the planets' people. As a result Alkaid and Summer are fully secure with minimal garrisoning, already capable of resupplying us. All for minor loss to ourselves."

"When was it ever the Jade Falcon way to boast of *avoiding* casualties?" Malvina flared from the near-darkness. Passion made her break protocol.

"I speak of scant resources," he said, "of our own small *desant* amidst a vast ocean of Inner Sphere humanity."

"All the more reason to leverage such force as we can bring to bear," Malvina said with a shake of her head, "especially when it comes to securing the cooperation of those whom we subjugate."

Aleks' cheek twitched at her use of the word *subjugate*. "Does no one remember Turtle Bay?" he asked. Despite the ferro-fibrous strength of his will, his voice rose.

"Perhaps we remember it too well," his sibkin said, her own voice dangerously low, "for the wrong reasons."

"Clan Smoke Jaguar brought disgrace upon themselves and all the Clans by destroying the city of Turtle Bay from orbit," Aleks said. "All Clans denounced the act. And subsequently when the forces of the Inner Sphere—under their cynical and fraudulent evocation of the blessed name of the Star League—counterattacked, it was the Smoke Jaguars whom they chose to hunt down and subject to a Trial of Annihilation, destroying them utterly."

"The craven Wolves led the cry to turn away from the Smoke Jaguars and renounce the use of naval vessels. It was merely one in an unbroken chain of their betrayals of the Clan Way," Malvina replied.

"If we massacre civilians upon Skye," he said, turning from her, "we will not simply dishonor Clan Jade Falcon. We will also rouse, not just Skye, but the whole population of The Republic, if not all the Inner Sphere, against us."

"Give the barbarians a taste of the fate that awaits those whose who resist the Falcon's flight and they will collapse," she said.

Then she laughed, and her laugh was malice, glass and silver. "And what does it matter, anyway? They *are* barbarians. We held out the liberating hand of truth and rationality to them almost a century ago, and they spurned us. Even after decades of what they term peaceful coexistence, in which they have had ample time to apprehend our system's unquestionable superiority, still they refuse to accept it. I say, enough of coddling the weak, the inferior! If the masses of old humanity will not accept the future, let them make way for the New Humans: we, the Clans."

Her sibkin had turned to stare at her. "The Founder was explicit, that it was our duty to protect the weak, the lesser, to uplift them, *protect* them—"

"And if that be so, I say: the Founder was wrong."

Her brother's cheeks went pale. Unnoticed in the dark at the rear of the stage, Beckett Malthus' bearded jaw gaped open. Here was his foremost string upon her, the deep secret that he alone had discerned, which if revealed would mean her certain death. Her unspeakable heresy— which she had just blurted out before every subcommander in the *desant's* ground forces.

"The Founder did well when he designed us: our life, our traditions, the Canister," she said in a voice that rang so loud she scarcely needed amplification. "But not even his vision could encompass all the future. In his greatness, Nicholas Kerensky simply could not conceive how unworthy the mass of humanity would prove.

"Wise as he was, the Founder failed to grasp an essential truth: in creating us, he created a superior order of human being. He honored the relentless forces of evolution, as he taught us to honor them. And what is the way of evolution, if not that the superior shall drive the inferior into extinction?

"Yes, I speak heresy. But my heresy is to honor truth above the words of one long dead, even one we rightfully honor above all. We are the force of evolution, and it is our right. Whether or not the fact comforts us, it is a scientific inevitability that we shall displace the Spheroids utterly, soon or late. I say, let us spread our wings to the winds of destiny, and speed to seize the future in arrow flight, as befits true sons and daughters of the Falcon!''

In the fury of the warriors' applause and hawk-cries, Aleksandr knew she had won the day. Unseen behind him, a look of wonderment and calculation transfigured Beckett Malthus' bearded face.

29

Jade Falcon Naval Reserve Battleship **Emerald Talon**
Zenith Jump Point
Skye
10 August 3134

When it came to the decision by the *kurultai*, almost all of Aleksandr Hazen's Zeta officers voted for his proposed forbearance from terror. The officers of Turkina Keshik and the Gyrfalcon Galaxy were surprised: such near unanimity was rare among the Clans, especially a *dezgra* unit supporting a new commander.

They were perhaps more surprised when some Keshik officers and even a few Gyrs voted with Aleksandr's warriors.

Yet in the end, Malvina's proposal of calculated savagery won by a margin of almost two to one—her heretical pronouncements notwithstanding.

"I challenge," Aleksandr said simply, when the results were formally announced by Star Colonel Rianna Buhallin, Bec Malthus' aide de camp.

"Such is your right," Beckett Malthus intoned solemnly.

"In accordance with tradition you shall be opposed in your Trial of Refusal by two warriors, reflecting that your will has been rejected by that proportion."

"I will fight him, augmented, alone." All heads turned to stare at Malvina. She was literally half his size—her body mass half his—but in the cockpit of a 'Mech, that mattered not at all. "My *Shrike* carries twice the firepower of his *Gyrfalcon*. And he has never beaten me in BattleMech combat."

Aleksandr Hazen raised his head. His smile was nova bright.

Bec Malthus did not bother to ask if Malvina meant what she said. As well ask a bullet if it meant to hit you.

It was a huge breach of tradition. He doubted he was the only one unsurprised that Malvina should propose such a thing. *At the least,* he thought, *this should prove amusing.*

"What venue?" he asked her in a voice subdued even for him. "Our choices are somewhat circumscribed."

"I care not. Let Aleksandr choose."

And that was unorthodox as well. *Where* will *she lead the Falcon,* Malthus wondered, *if allowed her head?*

Aleks' smile widened. "I shall, sister," he said. "I shall."

Sanglamore Military Academy
New London
Skye
14 August 3134

"I fail to understand, Countess," Legate Eckard said, not unkindly. "Is it not poor tactics to announce our dispositions in advance to the Falcons—not to mention make them before we even know where they will land?"

Once half-abandoned, Sanglamore Academy now bustled as de facto planetary-defense headquarters. The two Taras occupied a former classroom with the Duke, Eckard, Prefect Della Brown, and several cadets serving as ducal aides. With the Countess were Colonels Ballantrae and Scott, commanders of the First Kearny Highlanders and the Fusiliers respectively, and Republican Guard commander Major Linda Hirschbeck.

"It's all the same," muttered Duke Gregory. He stood

with his hands clasped behind his back, staring out a tall narrow window with a pointed arch and leaded glass at the overcast day. Fallen leaves blew across the imported terrestrial grass of the old quad three stories below, gone yellow as winter impended. "They'll spot our major concentrations from orbit, wherever located."

The Legate made a circular gesture of his hand. "As I say."

Making herself stay seated, since she feared she would look uncertain if she gave in to the desire to hop up and pace, Tara nodded. Tracked by powerful telescopes since its emergence was reported, the Jade Falcon fleet was now within hours of shaping Skye orbit. The tension had grown almost unbearable.

"You're right, Legate. The thing is to understand the Clan mentality. Their predisposition is to fight—and they believe they can defeat any number of Spheroid fighters."

Duke Gregory half-turned. "They've always been attracted to the idea of One Big Battle, haven't they?" It seemed that in the extremity of the current situation, he had come to completely accept Tara Campbell. Concern for his planet had overcome his desire to find things to sulk about.

"Precisely so, your Grace. And actually it's in their strategic interests: it's much easier on them if we'll agree to all clump up and get beaten by them at once, rather than making them engage in a long grind to conquer the planet."

"Wouldn't it be in our interests to act counter to theirs?" Della Brown asked. The Prefect's voice lacked challenge: the question seemed sincere, rather than another attempt to undermine the Countess.

"That's an excellent military principle, Prefect," Tara said. "Yet in this case I believe our interests coincide with theirs. More particularly, the interests of the people of Skye whom we're defending. The longer we draw this thing out, the more they suffer."

"Then too," Eckard said, "there's this lot's demonstrated propensity for atrocity."

With supreme effort Tara kept her face and voice under control. "Precisely."

"Your Grace," said one of Gregory's aides wearing a commo headset. "We are receiving a transmission from the commander of the Jade Falcon fleet. He wishes to speak to our chief battle leader."

Duke Gregory pursed his bearded lips. "Countess Campbell, I believe this call is yours." To her utter surprise, the Duke had chosen to defer to her recent—and greater—experience in leading troops into battle, particularly against Clan forces. He would command Skye's indigenous forces under Tara's operational command.

She drew a deep breath and turned to face the holovid tank at one end of the room. The Duke nodded.

A heavy, handsome face, bronze-bearded and large-pored, appeared in the tank. "I am Galaxy Commander Beckett Malthus," it announced, "commanding the Jade Falcon expeditionary force."

"I am Countess Tara Campbell, commanding for Skye," she said crisply.

"Countess Campbell, I wish to issue a batchall: a formal challenge—"

"I know what it means," Tara said with calculated rudeness. "Here are our terms: we will fight you in the hills west of New London; there are plenty of surfaces hard and flat enough to land your DropShips. You bring what you have, we bring what we have, winner take all."

The expression of placid superiority never wavered. That was in itself highly unusual for a nitroglycerin-touchy Clansman. *That bears out Master Merchant Senna's assessment of the man,* Tara thought. *Doesn't it?*

"Lady Campbell, you are hardly in position to dictate—"

Here's where it gets tricky. "This is not any of your Clan bidding. There is no negotiation. The alternative is to fight an endless guerrilla war—and no matter how many of us you murder, there will still be more of us left to slaughter you in your beds. Or are you afraid, Galaxy Commander Beckett Malthus, to meet us force against force? Perhaps you doubt your Falcons' invincibility."

The man's brows had fisted as she spoke and his face darkened, slightly but perceptibly. "You speak rashly, Countess. Your words are far larger than you. And you will soon learn their folly.

"A Clan warrior fears nothing. We shall meet you in the country west of your prefectural capital."

He raised his right hand, palm up, squeezed his fingers into a fist. "And crush you! Beckett Malthus out."

The image vanished.

Tara looked to her aide. A breath she was unaware of holding gusted from her in a sigh that shook her whole thin frame.

"Countess!"

"Huh?" She sat up on her cot. Sunlight streamed in the window of her office, afternoon by its buttery hue.

A female cadet stood in the doorway. "Apologies for disturbing you, milady. But you asked to be informed when the Falcon fleet entered Skye orbit."

Tara rubbed her face briefly. "Quite right." She struggled to recall the woman's name. She was even shorter than Tara and dark-haired. "And thank you, Kathy."

"There's more, Countess. The Falcons communicated with us to confirm that they will land to fight us tomorrow morning. But one of their DropShips has entered atmosphere ahead of schedule, on course for the North Pole."

North Continent
Inside the Arctic Circle
Skye
14 August 3134

A great armored ovoid descended through a sky of perfect arctic blue. Five hundred meters above a frozen lake two kilometers wide by seven long, it slowed to a hover on its blue drive pencils. Bays opened in its flanks. Six BattleMechs emerged and descended toward the ice surface.

Contrails drew white traceries in the dome of the sky overhead as Falcon aerospace fighters contended with Skye craft sent to intercept the DropShip. Because this landing played no part in the agreed-upon combat terms, the locals were treating it as open season.

Four 'Mechs came down at the points of a square two kilometers on a side: Malvina Hazen's aide-de-camp Star Captain Matthias Pryde in his *Uller*, Star Colonel Folke Jorgensson in his *Black Hawk*, Star Colonel Rianna Buhallin in her *Mad Cat*, and Galaxy Commander Beckett Malthus in his black and silver *Vulture*: the Circle of Equals for Aleks' Trial of Refusal. The three BattleMechs without jump jets temporarily repaired that lack with strap-on booster kits.

Malvina's ninety-five-ton *Shrike* and Aleks' fifty-five-ton *Gyrfalcon* touched down facing each other across a thousand yards of blue-white ice, drifted with gritty decayed snow that eddied in a wind that knew no rest.

Being seasoned battle commanders, the principals realized that if the intercepting fighters should take down the DropShip, they would at a stroke decapitate the *desant*. Being Clan, they accepted that risk. Some things were just important. Besides, the site was remote; the defenders were unlikely to commit too much of their aerospace strength defending a howling waste. The Falcons' fighter coverage was excellent, and the DropShip itself a formidable opponent.

It hovered, now, overhead, like a great dull-gleaming cloud.

"Galaxy Commander."

"Speak, Star Colonel Rianna Buhallin."

"I am troubled."

"Why so?"

"Why do you permit this? There should be two MechWarriors vindicating the Will of the Falcon. The senior Clan champion should have chosen the field. Yet here is one who has claimed Refusal, and was adjudged wrong by a margin of two to one, facing but a single champion—and on ground of his choosing."

"So the Clan champion willed it, Rianna."

"But it is wrong! The ritual—"

"Galaxy Commander Malvina Hazen has seen fit to alter ritual to suit her. She claims to represent the forces of evolution. I propose to see if she is right."

"Can we so disrupt our ways, with our greatest battle impending?"

"If your honor will not permit you to serve in the Circle of Equals, Star Colonel, I will replace you. Only speak quickly. Battle, as you say, impends."

"Beckett Malthus, I will serve."

"I knew you would, Rianna, child."

* * *

Standing on the snow-clad shore, Bec Malthus' *Vulture,* Turkina's Crow, raised its right arm. Its two extended-range medium lasers pierced the sky with cyan lances. It was the order to begin.

Ornamental wings folded, the two 'Mechs sprinted toward each other. At long range, Aleks fired a burst from Lily's right-hand autocannon that kicked up a string of white explosions right in front of Malvina, then cut into a clockwise run around Black Rose.

Malvina slowed. Her sibkin's tactics perplexed her. The *Gyrfalcon*'s weapons outranged hers. It was much faster than her *Shrike,* especially if Aleks triggered his myomer accelerator signal circuitry. He could, in theory, use his speed advantage to stay out of her reach forever and pick the Rose to pieces. Naturally, it was not so easy: Aleks must stay within the one-kilometer Circle or forfeit, limiting his scope of motion. His lasers and autocannon did not shoot *that* much farther than hers, nor her missiles. Solid hits from her battery would quickly disable his lightly armored Lily, especially if she could lock her targeting computer onto a limb.

And then, Aleks had never beaten her 'Mech to 'Mech. No one had.

Yet here he was throwing away his sole advantage, spiraling toward her. Malvina was not so caught up by her own Mongol rhetoric to believe her brother's head had grown soft, no matter the state of his heart.

She triggered her medium lasers. The cyan beams, just visible in the sun-glare from sky and ice, missed just behind the *Gyrfalcon.* One tip of the middle "feather" of its right wing sparked white and gave off pale-gray smoke; no more.

Malvina stared in startled frustration. Then the battle computer in her mind told her: her diabolic brother, concentrating on moving without even trying to shoot since his opening barrage, was already so close that he orbited her faster than she could track the *Shrike*'s massive torso on its waist-swivel.

She would have to move her feet to keep him in front of her weapons. She could still move her arms faster than she could traverse the torso; she aimed the big double autocannon across her body and fired an Ultra burst.

Leading the running 'Mech was a trivial solution—she thought. Yet even as she fired Aleks stamped a sharp-edged claw hard into the ice for traction and changed direction. Malvina's 10-centimeter shells missed, to raise sequential geysers of pulverized ice several hundred meters beyond.

Aleks pivoted the Lily's upper body and returned fire with the 5-centimeter guns mounted in either arm. Malvina jumped. Inexplicably, the spray of projectiles fell just short, smashing holes in the ice and throwing up ice shrapnel that clattered harmlessly off her rising BattleMech. He followed with a short ruby flare of his large lasers that melted an infinity-sign hole right beneath Black Rose's taloned feet.

Does he think I'll fall through into the lake? she wondered. That would be folly: both 'Mechs were airtight and proof against the pressure of water far deeper than the DropShip's millimeter-wave radar probing of the bottom showed the lake to be. Dumping her into the icy depths would simply cool her cockpit to a level of actual comfort, at most.

She jetted her 'Mech backward before descending on still-solid ice. She turned in flight, swinging past Aleksandr, then let go with her lasers once more.

As if reading her intention, Aleks, still at a dead run, cut a different way again. He ran now with full MASC boost, risking actuator lock for speed over a hundred klicks an hour. Malvina could not lock him up with her targeting computer. She fired her autocannon. A hit blasted a shard of ferro-fibrous armor off the side of his right thigh. The running *Gyrfalcon* wobbled at the impact, then steadied itself and juked again.

She scowled fiercely. "Am I that predictable?" she raged.

"Only to me," came back promptly through her neurohelmet.

"*Damn* you!" A bone-piercing wind buffeted the BattleMech; it was merely hot inside her cockpit, not baking.

Judging on the fly that he would cut away from her she fired another autocannon burst—and at the same time launched a missile volley from her torso 10-rack aimed to beat the zone he would run through if he did.

Instead he turned *toward* her. Charging, he blasted on Ultra with both autocannon. Explosions smashed across

Black Rose's chest armor, rocking the huge *Shrike* back on its rear toes.

The ferro-fibrous plate was where she was hit; Malvina knew in a flash that her sibkin had done no serious damage. Nonetheless she uttered a shrill nasal scream, of outrage rather than alarm.

She triggered her whole battery: missiles, autocannon at double rate, both medium lasers. *Let him dodge faster than light.*

He couldn't, of course. Far less his fifty-five-ton 'Mech. Instead, he anticipated her again, jagging to her right. The root of Lily's left right wing arced and sparked. The wing fell off.

With both wings retracted, the mass of the remaining left one did not even unbalance the *Gyrfalcon* significantly. Not for a pilot of Aleks' consummate skill.

"How are you *doing* this?" she gritted, turning the Rose's feet to keep tracking him. "You have never beaten me!"

"Times change, sibkin," he said. *"We change, quiaff?"*

"Neg! You shall not win." She blazed with the paired autocannon, tracking with the muzzles pointed exactly at him so that the bursts would overtake him if he cut tightly toward or away from her. Then she led him with an LRM volley.

The ice before his racing BattleMech erupted in a white cloud of ice splinters, snow and steam. Instead of shying away—and being smashed by her powerful weapons—he plunged straight ahead into the cloud.

He did not emerge from the other side.

Malvina poised, tense, waiting. An aerospace fighter fell smoking from the sky, to burst in yellow glaring billows against the hip of a conifer-clad peak several kilometers away. Malvina noted it in the compressed three-sixty display beneath her windscreen and never glanced its way.

"What do you play at, Aleksandr?" she demanded.

"It has been years since we played this way," his voice said, *"but all I learned I learned from you, my sister. Ten thousand times I lost to you; and now perhaps I shall lose—"*

Right in front of the *Shrike*'s talons a crimson beam

stabbed up through the ice. Its crack nearly deafened her within her cockpit.

"—*no* —"

Ultra autocannon fire chopped ice behind her right hip, drawing a curving curtain of glittering particles whose facets diffracted the pale sunlight and broke it into rainbow fragments.

"—*more!*"

Driven by the power of its MASC-augmented legs, the *Gyrfalcon* pushed upward from the lake bed, fifteen meters beneath the surface, and slammed its fifty-five metric tons upward against the ice between the Black Rose and the jagged gape left by Aleks' opening salvo. Ice squealed, groaned—and gave. As if the cuts Aleks had made with his large lasers were hinges, a great plate of ice beneath the *Shrike*'s feet was driven up and over.

As was the ninety-five-ton BattleMech itself.

Malvina cried out, and then the monstrous machine crashed down on its side with an impact that pounded her into the side of her cockpit. She blacked out.

The *Gyrfalcon*'s jump jets would not function under water. Instead, Aleksandr ran submerged to where the bed began sloping up toward the shore, blasted the ice clear to let his head and shoulders emerge as he slowed to a walk. Slowly, shedding a great rippling skin of water, the Lily rose from the lake. When his jets were clear he jumped to stand beside the fallen Rose.

"I fear I have done you no kindness, sister dear," he said softly. "But I could never hurt you."

He raised the White Lily's right foot and planted it on the Black Rose's torso.

"*I declare Galaxy Commander Aleksandr Hazen the winner of this Trial of Refusal,*" Bec Malthus said ponderously. "*We shall conduct the invasion of Skye as he desires.*"

=== 30 ===

Galaxy Commander Beckett Malthus' Cabin
Jade Falcon Naval Reserve DropShip Bec de
  Corbin
Orbiting Skye
15 August 3134

"What do you mean?" Galaxy Commander Aleksandr Hazen demanded. He was not smiling now.

Bec Malthus turned away to look at a white-swirled blue arc of Skye, rotating beneath them. It was an image on a screen inset in the bulkhead of his cabin; as a ship of war, the *Bec de Corbin* needed its hull integrity too badly to allow actual viewports in the living quarters. "I mean precisely what I said. Savor the occasion, boy."

He glanced back at the taller, younger man from beneath bushy brows. "I will not relieve Galaxy Commander Malvina Hazen of command of the Delta Galaxy. Did you seriously anticipate that I would?"

Aleks breathed heavily and his cheeks were flushed. "Yes. She fought to vindicate the Mongol position. She lost."

Neither Malvina nor her BattleMech had been seriously

injured. Her right shoulder had been dislocated, and she had sat in furious, white-lipped silence as a couple of Turkina Keshik warriors yanked it back into place—as the *Bec de Corbin* rose back up through a still-contested sky, and a twisting dogfight that eventually claimed seven Falcon aerospace fighters and a dozen Skye craft. Only three aerospace warriors had successfully ejected from their stricken machines, and they had been left behind for the Republicans to recover. The Falcon would be back to reclaim them, soon enough.

"She fought to vindicate the decision of the *kurultai*," Malthus corrected. "She fought as Clan champion, not as herself. Come, you know this: you learned it in the crèche, everybody does. You beat her in a Trial of Refusal, in which you were the refuser, not she. You did not best her in a Trial of Position for command of the Gyrfalcons— which Khan Jana Pryde has forbidden, and so do I." He did not bother to state what, in Clan terms, was obvious: that if Aleks did not want his sister in command of the Gyrfalcons, he should have killed her when he had the chance.

"Malvina has become obsessed with her Mongol cult. You have seen what it has done to her—heard her profane the Founder himself! She lost to me. The Mongols are discredited. And she, by allowing fanaticism to overcome her, has unfit herself to command a Galaxy of the Jade Falcon *Touman*!"

Eyes curving slits, head tipped to the side, Bec Malthus asked, "Are you sure your true motivation is not vengeance upon your sister? That you have not allowed this matter to become personal?"

Aleks Hazen's eyes flared. His big handsome face went gray. He seemed at once to grow taller—and Beckett Malthus wondered, for one of very, very few times in a lifetime spent playing others, if this one he had not *overplayed*.

"All that I am, all that I do, is in the service of the Jade Falcon and humanity—true to the Founder's vision," Aleks said in a low, clotted voice. "Beyond Clan Jade Falcon I *have* nothing 'personal'."

Malthus made himself smile a false smile, nod and gesture approvingly. It was an easy thing for him to do: he had done it so many times. He would've patted Aleks' great, boulder-hard shoulder, except that to lay a hand on a Clan warrior without invitation, even one such as Aleksandr Hazen, was necessarily to die on the spot.

"Just so, lad: so you do," Malthus said in tones like warmed syrup. "And now service to the Falcon means subsuming your own desires—let us call them judgments, shall we?—to the greater good of Turkina. The coming battle is the climax: all rides upon it. Galaxy Commander Malvina Hazen is far too valuable an asset to withhold from this fight."

Aleks paced to the curved outer bulkhead and slammed his fist against it. Then he pressed it to the metal and laid his forehead against it. "She will never honor the Trial's outcome."

Malthus came up behind him. Lightly. "Do not be so melodramatic, lad. Rejoice: you are about to reap the victory you have done more than any *except* your sibkin to win! It is a deed which will resound through the Remembrance as long as our people have tongues and ears."

"*She* will throw victory away with a terrible crime, which will raise all humanity's hands against us."

"Then defeat her again! Subdue Skye quickly, using your humane techniques. Allow her no scope by succeeding. If not—"

He shrugged expressively.

"Are you so eager, then, to try Malvina's Mongol ways here on Skye?" Aleks asked.

"I am eager to win. If you suspect I may hang back so that the fighting goes poorly, to create a pretext to remove Malvina's hood and fly her free to slay to her bloodthirsty little heart's content, you suspect quite wrongly, boy. It is *my* head which failure will forfeit."

Aleks pushed off from the bulkhead. He started to say something, but a cursor blinking alive on the viewscreen and an almost-simultaneous buzz from Malthus' intercom stilled him.

"*Galaxy Commander, bridge,*" a voice said from the bulkhead. "*Galaxy Commander Malvina Hazen's DropShip White Reaper has departed orbit on a landing trajectory.*"

Aleks and Malthus stared at one another. Launching was not scheduled to begin for two more hours. "If that confounded woman proves me *wrong* for having kept her in command," Malthus said in a voice like pebbles in a crusher, "rest assured that I will do what you would not!"

Hemphill Mine
West of New London
Skye
15 August 3134

White Reaper fell through thin high overcast toward Skye, to a point ten kilometers west-northwest of New London. Strapped into the crash harness of her *Shrike*—more tightly than she had been for yesterday's duel with her accursed sibling—Malvina watched the planet hurtle at them through vision blocks slaved to the DropShip's hull-mounted video pickups.

Well, she was showing Aleks and that *surat* Malthus that, defeated in Trial or not, she had *not* bowed the neck. And she was about to show her Gyrfalcons and indeed the whole *desant* that she was still fit to be ristar and Galaxy Commander.

While Malthus' ship had descended over the North Pole for the duel, the other DropShips began orbiting Skye. They duly swept the surface with their potent sensor arrays: telescopes, infrared, side-looking and oblique radar, magnetic and gravitic anomaly detectors. Naturally, they devoted especial attention to the next day's chosen battleground.

And they had struck pure palladium: a shallow kilometer-wide bowl gouged from the Holyrood Hills twenty kilometers northwest of New London and almost due north of the *desant* DropShips' agreed-upon landing zone. It was an open-pit copper mine, permitted by Skye's stringent environmental laws on a guarantee that once the ore played out, the land would be returned to its previous formation and reseeded, a technique used with success across human space. Unfortunately, it had been idled not by the playing-out of the vein, but by the Blakist Jihad. Since then—analyst-techs drew the information from a commercially available database of Republic worlds purchased from a Lyran trader in the Falcon OZ during invasion planning—schemes had alternately been mounted to reopen or reclaim the mine. Despite both The Republic's economic boom and its emphasis on environmental protection, neither had quite come to pass.

Now, it seemed, Duke Gregory had found use for it at last: pulling a fast one.

A gypsy camp had sprung up in the big bowl, now itself grown green with years. It featured the usual array of "caravans"—the interstellar nomads' colorfully painted transport, wheeled and ground-effect—and pavilions, as well as evidence of long-term settlement in the form of shacks and larger structures of plywood and plastic sheeting, with corrugated metal roofs.

The encampment had, according to intel analysis, probably sprung up in the last few days—weeks at most. The crafty Spheroids plainly hoped the combination of metal roofs, ludicrous variegated vehicles—probably hulks towed over from a nearby scrapyard—and the metal ore yet in the ground would baffle orbiting Clan detectors. In their haste, they forgot one thing: the neutron emissions of idling fusion bottles for what appeared to be the equivalent of a pre-Republican company of at least twelve BattleMechs. Malvina's techs believed the 'Mechs were augmented by a lance of armored vehicles and, from analysis of several freestanding figures draped in brightly patterned cloth, perhaps a lance of IndustrialMechs as well.

Had they sallied forth to take the Falcons in flank as they advanced from their specified landing zone, a force that size might have dealt a staggering blow. Had it bided its time, waited until the attack had rolled away out of range, and charged for the landed DropShips, it might have caused pure catastrophe, albeit at the cost of its own near-certain destruction under the spacecrafts' powerful defensive batteries. A company, even of rare BattleMechs, was no large price to pay for even one DropShip, and they might well take out more.

But if *they* were the ones surprised. . . .

Not six hundred meters away, a sixty-ton Falcon *Visigoth* swept by, bleeding smoke, its armored sides sparking with hits from a barracuda-shoal of three Skye aerospace fighters. A PPC bolt took out its starboard engine. It pitched forward and exploded in a yellow fireball.

A moment later a pursuing Republican *Sholagar* came

apart as two medium pulse lasers and a large laser from the *Overlord*-class DropShip made it the apex of a deadly tetrahedron of light.

Malvina emitted a triumphant cry as the other two enemy fighters sheared off and streaked away. It was echoed by her MechWarriors, waiting like her in their steel and synthetic cocoons for battle. A thirty-five-ton *Sholagar* was a poor exchange for a heavy Clan fighter in all truth: but she wanted to keep their passions focused on *victory*.

The green hills and autumn yellow fields of Skye rushed up to embrace her like a lover's arms.

A derelict blacktop parking lot, frost-heaved and weed-grown, provided a superb surface for DropShip landing jacks. Even before the bulge-belted egg of a vessel settled and its drive-flames died away, its bay doors opened and a trio of BattleMechs of the Fifth Battle Cluster sprang into the milky dawn leaking out of the hills to the east, led by young Star Colonel Cedric in a *Night Gyr*. Cedric had won in barehanded combat both promotion and the twice-vacated command of the Golden Talons, whose emblem, now painted on the BattleMech's chest armor, was a black shield sporting a pair of golden claws gripping a dead wolf beneath a gold "V." He had bid low for the honor of neutralizing the imperfectly hidden Skye 'Mech force: his Alpha Trinary with himself in command.

Two more 'Mechs, non-jump-capable, clumped out of the DropShip after him, followed by vehicles and infantry. Isorla had been kind to the Trinary, thanks to Cedric's zeal.

A JESII strategic missile carrier loosed its full breath-robbing volley of eighty long-range missiles into the open pit, turning it into an instant *faux*-volcanic crater of smoke and leaping flame. With captured Shandra and Fox light vehicles racing them, the Golden Talon BattleMechs charged into the decommissioned mine with all weapons flaming.

MechWarrior Silas plunged his *Uller* into the pit at its full ninety-seven-kph speed, running the machine with big, clanking, jarring steps. The roof blew off a long shed as he pounded past, rust orange, chrome yellow, and gaudy blue panels fluttering like leaves away from a roaring column of orange fire.

Before him through shifting smoke curtains he saw looming a figure like the statue of a man draped in a parachute:
a suspected IndustrialMech. He charged it at speed—then
braked with a curse as a medium laser cracked right past
him. It ate a plate-sized hole in the canopy, brown edged
and self-expanding like a cancer as it burned with almost
invisibly pallid flame.

Silas reached out with the *Uller*'s left hand, grabbed the
canopy and tore it away. He triggered a pointblank blast
from his right-arm LB 5-X autocannon into the middle of
a *MiningMech* modified to carry a quad SRM launcher and
two .50-caliber machine guns to support the house-high
rock cutter on its right arm.

Shattered armor splashed from the 'Mech like water from
a thrown stone. The 'Mech was already afire from the
laser strike.

Silas frowned. The right shoulder and torso were burning
lustily, producing clouds of white smoke. Runnels of liquid
flame streamed from it, eroding deep canyons in what was
supposedly metal plate and mechanism. The central torso
region gaped open, bleeding—

Junk. A short cylindrical object slipped out and fell to
the ground, and it took Silas' astonished eyes and brain a
full second to recognize it as an electric motor, such as
might be used to operate a small water pump. Less identifiable pieces of metallic scrap, rust-smeared and now
scorched, dropped thudding to the grass-covered ground.

"These are no 'Mechs!" Silas called on the Trinary frequency, his young voice breaking. "They are p-plywood
and foam, filled with scrap metal!"

A new horrific certainty hit him like a rogue asteroid.
He opened his mouth to add, *It's a trap!*

But just then, two hundred kilograms of liquid-poured
pentaglycerine gel filling the QuakerMech's lower legs detonated in obedience to a distant command.

Standing in a copse of saplings crowning a hilltop sixteen
hundred meters south of the mine pit, skinny, intense,
brown-moustached Tom Cross lowered the command deto-
nator whose red button he had just thumbed as yellow
flame shot a thousand meters in the air. As the mad genius
behind most of the actual nuts-and-bolts design of the giant

death trap, he had won the right to open the fireworks show. He wore a two-liter cooking pot overturned on his head by way of a helmet, with the handle turned around like the bill of a ballcap.

"Bingo," said the gangly Seymour Street, stroking his red goatee. He wore his devil horns again. He had been in charge of fabricating the decoy QuakerMechs.

J. D. Rich stroked his blond handlebar mostache with a thumb and nodded judiciously as secondary explosions sent bright flashes through what was now an immense pillar of black smoke rising from a guttering red pedestal. "Nice shot," he admitted. "Clean."

He was the pyro man, the Master Blaster, who designed and supervised the placing of the charges, augmented by tons of gasoline with some gelling agents mixed in to lend it what Walt Whitman—his favorite ancient poet—termed the quality of *adhesiveness*. He had wired the hundreds of charges for remote detonation himself—a demanding, dangerous task.

The drivers of the three Shandra advanced scout vehicles that had carried them here, a corporal and two privates from the First Kearny Highlanders, all young and female, were jumping up and down with their coal-scuttle helmets slipping all over their heads, dancing and weeping and laughing and hugging each other. Cross turned a quizzically cocked eyebrow at them.

"What?" he demanded.

"It *worked!*" Corporal Shannon Hayes exclaimed. "You just wiped out a whole Jade Falcon Trinary all by yourselves!"

Tom Cross frowned in authentic puzzlement. "Of course it worked. It's a very fine day."

"You know," Street said ruminatively, "the environmental-protection people are going to have cats about those vials of radioactive emitters we borrowed from the university to spoof BattleMech fusion-engine signatures."

"They would," said wide, blond J. D.

"We should, like, go now, probably, probably," said Tom Cross, his skinny body seeming to vibrate as he shifted his weight from foot to sneakered foot. He was one of the highest-paid professionals on Skye; his kicks were the cheapest known, imported fruits of Kurita slave labor. "Those Falcons are gonna be pissed."

"No doubt," Seymour Street said. "Your occasional flashes of contact with reality never cease to amaze me, Thomas, me boy."

He turned to the three Northwind troopies, who were starting to giddy down as the truth of the mad SFX genius' words penetrated their euphoria. Twirling his moustache, which wasn't really built for it, he said, "Well, ladies? Shall we?"

In the Black Rose's cockpit, a quarter-kilometer from the mine pit—any closer and her heat-gauge started climbing—Malvina stared into the glaring furnace that was cremating her Golden Talons. Despite the heat her face felt frozen.

The trap, fiendish as it was, had not devoured Trinary Alpha whole: several heavier vehicles and almost all the foot-sloggers, lagging behind the 'Mechs and scout cars, had survived. But all of its 'Mechs, and every vehicle and warrior who had descended into the mine, were a total write-off.

She was only glad Cedric had bid right down to cut-down: the hell pit would easily have swallowed a Cluster whole, conceivably all her Galaxy. Sadly, the youthful MechWarrior was as far beyond her gratitude as her retribution for losing his command in the blink of an eye.

"Galaxy Commander Malvina Hazen," said a voice in her neurohelmet, relayed from White Reaper, now grounded in a draw seven hundred meters behind her to keep it safe from debris cast out by unceasing secondary explosions. "This is Galaxy Commander Beckett Malthus, Supreme Commander of this expedition. You are to hold in place until the rest of our ships touch down. You are permitted to fire on any enemies detected within range, but I order you neither to advance nor withdraw until I give the order for the planned general advance."

"Yes," she said.

She refused to acknowledge the deliberate provocation of Malthus' suggesting she might withdraw. He was nothing to her, no more than a bellycrawler now.

All that mattered to her was the ambition, burning in her belly like her lovely 'Mechs and warriors in the smok-

ing crater glowing like a wound in the placid green countryside. That and her desire to avenge herself upon the
slithering Spheroids.

She would fight now as she had agreed, obedient to Malthus' commands.

But once battle and world were won and the bellycrawlers beaten, no force in the universe would stop her taking
her revenge. Not Malthus' orders. Not the words of the
Founder, centuries in the grave.

Not even, indeed, her loved and hated brother.

31

Weston Heights
Suburb West of New London
Skye
15 August 3134

As Tara Campbell walked out of the dawn toward the joint operational command post, set up on the green lawn in front of the red brick main building of a Tharkad Synod Lutheran seminary on a long bluff in the western New London suburb of Weston, the Seventh Skye Militia pipers set up a festive, earsplitting skirl.

" 'Garryowen,' " she said, forcing a smile. Still, the catchy melody and the lively enthusiasm with which it was emitted helped nudge her mind out of brooding over the orders she had just given—sending hundreds of men and women to die.

"By the way, Master Sergeant—you wouldn't happen to've learned who Garry Owen was, have you?"

She had spent comparatively little time with Seventh people herself, and what she had had been too full for peripheral questions. None of the Duke's military staff knew. Not even Paul Laveau knew; he was unfamiliar with the song, he said. Which vaguely and quite irrationally disappointed her: while there was no good reason he *should* know, the knowledge of human history and culture he had unobtrusively shown her was so wide-ranging and deep that she had come to expect him to know at least *something* about any given subject.

To her surprise Master Sergeant McCorkle nodded. "Aye, I have. But it's not a *who,* Countess. 'Garryowen' means Owen's Garden. A district, so I'm told by these Skye heathen, of Dublin back on Old Terra."

The bluff around the seminary building, which was trimmed in white with a white portico, was alive with quietly purposeful activity. Particularly around the somewhat bulbous Mobile Command vehicle, beyond which her *Hatchetman* awaited her, parked on the immaculately tended grass fifty meters away. Heads kept turning to the west where a pillar of smoke rose high into the gray-blue sky. It thrilled Tara's heart with both triumph and trepidation.

" 'And the Lord went before them by day in a pillar of smoke, to lead them the way,' " the Master Sergeant quoted softly.

" 'The Lord is a man of war,' " she quoted back to him. "Amen."

She smiled. It was not a gentle expression. "At least we've drawn first blood, haven't we, Top?"

His answering smile was startlingly bright in the gloom. "Aye, Countess, that we have."

They heard the thuttering of a helicopter rotor, and then a Skye attack VTOL swept in a low half-circle overhead. As it drifted away and up into the sky to hover protectively, the chop of its blade gave way to the clank and thud of a big BattleMech walking the street below. In a moment an *Atlas* lumbered up the hill.

"Skye Alpha comes to grace us with his presence, it appears," McCorkle said.

Tara made a face. As he had conceded her operational command of the Skye defense forces, so Duke Gregory Kelswa-Steiner had granted Tara the call sign *Skye Six,* Six being a traditional designation for *leader.* She would not believe he had chosen his own appellation without conscious irony.

In keeping with his taste for the unexpected, instead o
the skull almost invariably painted on the front of an *Atla*
round head, Duke Gregory's machine sported the snarlin
face of a grizzly bear, a species long since imported to Sky
where it thrived. The image suggested nothing so much a
the forbidding, hirsute visage of the Duke himself: a not
of self-deprecating humor that illuminated an unlooked-fo
aspect of the Duke's personality.

A complex man, Tara thought. *I'm glad he's finally de
cided we're on the same side.*

But she frowned slightly, and shook her head.

"I wish he wouldn't," she said. "A Falcon aerospace joc
or two might just get lucky, and then we'd be without ove
all command." She did not mention that Prefect Del
Brown and Legate Stanford Eckard were well out of harm
way in the Lord Governor's palace in downtown New Lo
don; she meant what she said.

"But he's here anyway," she said with a shrug, as Tar
Bishop's *Pack Hunter* came striding around the corner o
the seminary building. "We might as well go make nice s
he'll go back to his own command post where he belongs.

Sutton Road
Approaching the Gyrfalcon Landing Zone
Hemphill Mine
15 August 3134

The Forlorn Hope was on the march.

That Malvina Hazen had jumped the gun on the planne
landing was a bonus for Skye's defenders. Tara ordered h
Hope to engage the Gyrfalcons in hopes of catching the
on the advance. That was the fight Tara and her belove
Republic faced this day.

They came from varied life paths, for various reason
And in all flavors: English-speakers, German-speakers, R
settlement Program babies, all the mix that made up th
populace of a cosmopolitan modern world. Duke Grego
had insisted on a minimum age of twenty, the age of majo
ity on Skye, which Tara agreed with. The oldest know
recruit was a female retired teacher and marathon runne
who admitted to eighty-seven.

Each had his or her reason for volunteering to march into the Falcon guns. All shared a single purpose: throw the invaders into disorder, disrupt and weaken them, give the following Militia and Highlander units a chance to crush murderous Malvina in detail before the Turkina Keshik and Zeta Galaxy could come up to support. It was a slim and desperate chance—a forlorn hope.

It was a beautiful day. Beautiful opportunity awaited the Forlorn Hope: Malvina's Gyrs were *already* in chaos, reeling from the catastrophic trap and isolated from the rest of the *desant,* even now in view, burning its way down the sky to the designated landing zone to the column's southwest.

But everything had already gone wrong.

Weston Heights
15 August 3134

"Pull back," Tara Campbell said fervently into the microphone in her hand. She was patched to the Forlorn Hope's leader through the mobile command center. "Colonel ter Horst, this is a direct order."

"Regrettably," ter Horst's voice returned, "I cannot comply, Countess." He had been a baker yesterday.

Tara's lips skinned back from her teeth. Captain Tara Bishop stood by, practically vibrating from her frustrated inability to do anything to help her superior and friend. "You *have* to, Joop! This is supposed to be a spoiling attack, dammit. It's intended to break up a Falcon advance. But Malvina's *not advancing.* And you can't do anything to dug-in Falcons but die in windrows."

True to form, Malvina had dived into the Firehouse Gang's pit trap headfirst. Now, unexpectedly, she showed prudence. Aerial observation revealed she had emplaced her surviving forces southeast of the still-smoking pit in a semicircle bowed toward New London. Behind the line lurked half a dozen JESII launch vehicles.

"You're already out of our Long Tom coverage," Tara radioed. "Turn around and come back. Or just ditch the vehicles where they are and make your way out of the Falcon axis of advance on foot—head your people northeast, toward Cowpens."

"We have come too far already—"

"Don't you *see?* I can't send troops to support you. *Make your people stop!*"

"I have so ordered, Countess. But they do not obey. They drive by me when I try to block their road." She could see his shrug: "What can I do, then, but stay at their head, having brought them so far?"

Tara Campbell squeezed her eyes shut against a hot torrent of tears. She wanted to fall to her knees and cry till she died. *I cannot break down,* she knew. *I'm still in command.*

"Then may God have mercy on all our souls," she whispered.

As he desired, Joop ter Horst was first to die. The blue kiss of a particle-projector beam exploded his command vehicle: his own delivery hovertruck in makeshift armor.

With courage that would have done credit to Knights of the Sphere, the rest of the column turned as one off the hardtop and into the fields to charge the Falcon battle line. They were intent on getting close enough to deliver one good blow with the support weapon—machine gun, laser, or rocket launcher—bolted to every vulnerable vehicle.

Some succeeded. Some even drew Gyr blood.

In the horizontal storm of fire with which Malvina Hazen answered them, death came quickly to all, whether their final efforts told or not.

Twenty klicks to the east Tara Campbell stood on the peaceful green seminar lawn and listened to them die.

Countryside West of New London
15 August 3134

Between hills covered in trees to whose branches a few defiant brown and orange leaves clung, and fields of Terran sunflowers tall as Elementals nodding plate-sized autumn-yellow heads in sunlight, Aleksandr Hazen's Zeta Galaxy advanced at speed.

Time and again lead vehicles, usually speedy Nacon or Fox hovercraft, were blown into brief yellow fireballs by roadside ambushes. These were quickly smashed by heavy fire from BattleMechs and tanks. Surviving ambushers were rooted out by infantry and burned down by Elementals. The columns streaming toward New London slowed but did not stop.

The attack columns only halted when confronted by roadblocks held in force. If these could be expeditiously reduced by tank and 'Mech weapons, indirect bombardment with long-range missiles and VTOL strikes, they were. Otherwise, the Falcons simply veered around them. Their BattleMechs and tracked and hover vehicles moved readily cross-country. So did most of their wheeled AFVs; the ones that broke down were abandoned without thought and left burning.

Behind Aleks, Malvina's shattered Gyrs followed painfully to his left. Galaxy Commander Beckett Malthus, Supreme Commander, seemed preoccupied with securing the drop zone, and was releasing his Keshik warriors to follow the advance as planned with the stinginess of a Lyran merchant.

The defenders had one thing the Falcons had no ready answer for: long-range artillery—Snipers, Thumpers, Long Toms—which could dump devastating barrages upon the charging ground forces from ranges far beyond their ability to retaliate. Although a fierce air battle raged, of aerospace fighters and VTOLs, occasionally a Falcon pilot would spot one of the giant, not-very-mobile launchers, stoop on it and destroy it—usually at cost of his or her machine, if not life. Clan aerospace jocks were not Decanted to die in bed, any more than their Elemental or MechWarrior comrades.

All hardly registered on Aleks. For the first time in his life he strode to battle without the fierce, anticipating joy of a Falcon born.

All he cared for was *advance*. He drove his Galaxy not harshly, but relentlessly. So long as Turkina's Beak Galaxy kept moving forward, he had his best defense against the brutal punishment of Skye artillery. He could outrun the massive barrages with their long flight times, kill such enemy spotters as he could with infantry and fast hovercraft scouts to blind the distant launchers, and change speed and route periodically to keep the highly skilled Republican artillerists from correcting their fire by simply calculating where his troops would be at a given moment and arranging for a few tons of high explosive to meet them.

It did not work perfectly. Aleksandr Hazen had not been raised to expect perfection. It worked *enough*.

He fought his command and his BattleMech with mechanical precision. His Galaxy now functioned as smoothly as a veteran formation: subcommanders and individual warriors used their own initiative, so that he need rarely issue orders. When enemies came within reach of Black Rose's weapons he killed them with little more thought than he would have given to swatting mosquitoes.

If he could not take pleasure in battle, Aleks would at least take comfort in sheer practice of his craft, the trade to which his entire life was bent.

And then his onslaught ran slam into its first big check: Northwind Fusiliers and Garryowens, dug-in in strength along a system of ridges rising like a wall between the Falcon LZ and New London. With weapons bore-sited in advance to turn every passage through, from road-cut to gully, into a killing ground.

The Zeta charge screamed to a halt—as Long Tom rockets screamed down the sky upon them.

= 32 =

Weston Heights
Skye
15 August 3134

"**W**e haven't got a chance!" Panic shrilled from the radio at Tara Campbell, standing in the artificial gloom within her command crawler. *"They're swarming right up and over us! Third Platoon is overrun, and we've lost contact with First. Even their infantry runs up hills like bloody mountain goats!"*

"Easy, Sergeant Masamoto," Lieutenant Colonel Hanratty said soothingly. "Don't let them get behind you. Pull back, lad—you've done your job."

Another voice screamed, *"'Mech!"* from the speaker.

"Jumpin' right for us," Masamoto called. *"Run for it, boys—dear Lord, those* wings! *For the love of —"*

A scream. A rising squeal of overheating electronics. Silence.

After a moment in which she died a thousand times, Tara turned away from the faint dust of atmospherics popping from the speaker. "Comments?"

Colonels Ballantrae and Wilson, commanders of the First

Kearny and the Fusiliers, stood behind her in the compartment. Tara Bishop hung to the side. Major Hirschbeck was forward at her Republican Guards command post, in woods just west of Weston Heights.

"They bypass us when they're not outflanking and overrunning us," Bishop said. "We're hurting them—hammering them, even if you let the air out of damage reports. But we're not slowing them *down*."

Tara's two regimental commanders might have taken umbrage at a junior officer speaking up so forthrightly, especially with such a grim assessment. But both were seasoned combat veterans. All they did was nod.

Rather than try to hold an unbroken line, Tara had chosen to defend in depth in the forested hills to the west. Her forward forces were spread out, not bunched, positioned so as to support each other, either by immediate fire or rapid maneuver. The concept was analogous to using foam spacers between armor plates to defend against a shaped-charge warhead: the incandescent jet would lose energy and burn out before it could pierce the inner defenses.

To an extent it's working, she knew. *Just not so well as we expected.*

Not as well as we needed *it to.*

Western Outskirts of Weston Heights
15 August 3134

The combat-modified ForestryMech, sprayed with gray and tan and green in camouflage blotches, staggered as Aleks' *Gyrfalcon*, approaching at a run, raked 5-centimeter shells across its lightly armored chest. The thirty-five-ton machine seemed to stagger. Then Aleks triggered his large lasers. Metal plate ran like lava in glowing pink streams. Billowing black smoke, the machine toppled backward into the wreckage of the two-story motel. It had literally walked through the flimsy frame and pasteboard structure moments before, blasting a lightly armored Nacon scout car in its vulnerable rear and exploding it to flames with its 20mm autocannon, then raking a mixed Solahma-Eyrie infantry Point moving cautiously on foot down the blacktopped road.

Chunks of light debris flew away from the motel's façade, some flaming, as Aleks' troops opened up on it with small arms and heavy weapons. He suspected it was a pointless expenditure of ammo and energy. Had there been any other enemies lurking in the long structure, they undoubtedly had already faded back into the broken, forested country and the buildings that had begun to encroach upon the right-of-way as the Falcons neared the western edge of the New London suburbs.

The ForestryMech jock had been braver than wise. The Republican defenders had already taught their foes that even 'Mechs and heavy tanks could hide in the cover of the strip-urbs, strike and then fade back before even cat-quick Jade Falcon reflexes could strike back effectively.

And the more ferociously the Zetas lashed back at their ambushers, the more rubble they dropped in their own path. Even ground-effects vehicles could be blocked, and BattleMechs slowed. Nor was rubble or even enemy action all that was slowing the once-irresistible Falcon advance to a mere creep.

Above the strip malls and service stations Aleks could see the pristine pitched roofs of hilly Weston a scant few kilometers to the east. There, he knew, the real battle would begin. He radioed Galaxy Commander Bec Malthus.

"We must halt," he said simply. *"Quiaff?"*

For a moment there came only silence back. The Supreme Commander followed Aleksandr along the country roads at a deliberate pace. His Keshik scoured out the pockets of resistance left behind by the Zeta's lightning strike.

It was highly necessary. So Malthus' official report to his Khan would read.

"Very well," Malthus said in a neutral voice. *"Aff."*

Weston Heights
15 August 3134

"We're not holding them, your Grace."

Standing outside watching what seemed a forest of smoke pillars growing off away in the west, it was harder for Tara Campbell to speak those words than to face enemy fire.

Will he come back and confirm my deepest fears: that I am perpetually out of my depth, just a pretty actress playing at war?

Instead his voice came rolling back, deep and calm as surf on a pleasant day: *"I never expected we actually could keep them from the suburbs, much as I hoped we might. What then, Countess Campbell?"*

"We're getting a bit of a respite. Our units claim Aleks Hazen has bogged down in the built-up fringes west of here. Hit-and-run tactics are hurting them, slowing them down. But I think it's their own speed that's really slowed them. All that running up hills and smashing down trees has taken a toll. Our boy badly needs a break to rest his troops, throw some hasty repairs into his 'Mechs and vehicles, stock up on ammo from the transports they've got following them."

A sudden scream of rocket engines made her duck and look rapidly around. An aerospace fighter curved around the seminary, no farther than half a klick away and about the same height above the hilltop, and vanished into the lowering overcast that had taken charge of the sky. *One of ours,* she realized with relief. The aerial forces had neutralized each other so far: the Jade Falcons had the clear edge in skill, but the defenders had numbers and motivation.

She was painfully aware a single lucky aerospace pilot or even VTOL jock could end her battle before she had a chance to strike a blow on her own account. But then, as a wise old great-aunt had told her once back on Northwind, nobody could promise you'd get through a given day alive in peacetime, much less war. As it was she was already feeling the old agonies that she *was* alive, when so many had died already, and so hard.

"Beckett Malthus is coming up the road after Aleks," she radioed the Duke at his command post two kilometers north. "He seems not to be in any hurry. I suspect he's holding his Keshik out as a reserve, looking to get in on the kill."

"What about that damned Hazen woman?"

"I'm afraid I've told you all the good news I've got, Duke Gregory. We did hurt her Gyrfalcons at the mine"—*And they massacred my poor Forlorn Hope volunteers!*—"but the survivors have snapped back and are on the move.

We're hearing it from our forward units—and one report is all we're getting from most of them. The Delta Galaxy is coming up on Aleks' left. And coming *fast*."

Among those with whom contact had been lost after a single desperate warning was Lieutenant Colonel Linda Hirschbeck, CO of the Republican Guard.

"They won't race through built-up areas so easily."

Tara hesitated. *They can't*, she assured herself. *It's not physically possible.*

She remembered reading of the superstitious dread the Clans had inspired in her forebears, after the first horrid shock of contact almost a century ago. She felt more than a touch of it now.

"No, your Grace," she said.

"Then we shall stop them in the suburbs. Skye Alpha, out."

"God willing," she said softly, to the empty air.

She looked around at her officers, waiting on her at a discreet distance. "Saddle up, everybody. The Falcons are on the way."

She forced her mouth to grin. "You didn't really think we'd get the afternoon off, did you?"

Malvina Hazen drew in a deep breath, redolent of the sweat that bathed her body, the smell of diesel fuel and scorched lubricant seeping in through the 'Mech's seals, the smell of the autumn forest that could not quite be dispelled by the others.

"Gyrfalcons—*forward!*" she screamed.

Black Rose stood up to its full height, strode from the trees, spread its wings and set off down the brushy fore-slope at a spine-jarring run. Vehicles and 'Mechs erupted from the woods to either side of her. Even over the thunder of the massed charge she heard the whistle as her three remaining JESII launchers, parked in a valley clearing behind her, loosed their overwhelming salvos toward the front rank of buildings.

Charging, the Gyrs withheld their fire. No point expending ergs without good marks to aim at. But neither did any fire greet them.

Two hundred forty long-range missiles crashed down among the buildings. Roofs were holed, walls collapsed in cascades of bricks and dust and smoke. Flames reared up, roaring like awakened beasts.

A long line of vehicles interspersed with BattleMechs and Industrials swept forward across the open space, infantry riding the tanks, Elementals on the 'Mechs. A softball field backstop was crushed by a hundred-ton Mars assault vehicle. The gaily painted bleachers splintered beneath the feet of machines that walked like men.

A rumbling-rushing noise commenced, grew, rolled across the sky above Malvina's head like a giant cannonball in a wooden chute. She screamed in impotent fury as a heavy artillery barrage smashed down behind the ridge. Huge orange fireballs rolled up the sky, trailing black smoke, as her strategic missile carriers blew up beneath the expert Republican counterbattery fire.

Then from the gutted apartment blocs—and where they had fallen, from the buildings behind—a hellstorm of fire gushed out and over the charging Gyrs.

A Bellona that had surged disrespectfully out in advance of Malvina leapt into the air on a column of flame as if its forty-five tons were no more than a stone. Secondary explosions plucked it apart in midair as its stored LRMs and flamer fuel blew.

Cursing, Malvina darted aside to avoid the flaming liquid: the last thing she needed now was excess heat.

She caught some anyway as an autocannon blast opened up the battle armor of the Elemental riding on her left shoulder and spilled fluid fire down the *Shrike*'s back armor. She slowed to keep her temperature levels under control. She restricted herself to firing measured bursts from her dual 10-centimeter autocannon until the fuel burned itself off.

Fifty meters to her left, MechWarrior Tyrus' *Cougar* staggered as a hypersonic nickel-ferrous slug from a BattleMech Gauss rifle took it just to the left and below its protruding cockpit. It fired back with its LRM launchers and the large pulse lasers in its arms. A PPC bolt struck. The right arm fell away in a shower of sparks.

The Falcon 'Mech seemed to erode in sprays of heavy autocannon fire. Laser flashes sublimated armor from it in puffs of vapor. Its left-shoulder LRM storage exploded. Its upper structure wrapped in yellow flames and streaming smoke from every joint, the *Cougar* fell forward. Tyrus did not eject.

And then the Northwinders charged Malvina.

Out of the rubble, Highlander 'Mechs and vehicles appeared as if materializing and rushed to meet the oncoming Gyrs. From the cover of the ruins, unpowered infantry raked Falcon infantry off the backs of vehicles and shot down their dismounts caught in the open. Elementals sprang to burn them and blast them from their hiding places. VTOLs appeared from the east, skimming the red clay chimney pots of Weston Heights, and clawed the Elementals from the sky with lasers and autocannon.

Falcon helicopters swept in to engage. A furious VTOL dogfight twisted in the sky, slashed across by missile trails and punctuated with gouts of yellow flame.

As above, so below. The lines came together, passed and turned to rend. Falcon and Northwinder 'Mechs blasted smoking chunks from each other at touch range. Armored fighting vehicles circled and shot, engines snarling like rabid wolves. Big Gnome power-armor suits rushed out to strike the smaller Elementals with lasers and short-range missiles—or grapple them. Malvina's aide-de-camp Star Captain Matthias Pryde crushed the driver's cage of a Fusilier Shandra scout car in his *Uller*'s right fist.

The *Uller* reeled as a huge shell from an SM1 tank destroyer shattered its right hip actuator. Another tore away its right-arm LB 5-X autocannon and ammunition box. Then the light BattleMech was knocked to pieces by a long-range missile salvo from both racks of a First Kearny *Ryoken II*.

"*Stravag!*" Malvina screamed. As the *Uller* collapsed like a broken toy, she turned to attack her ADC's killer. A shadow crossed her cockpit on the left.

Malvina stepped forward with her right foot to turn her ninety-five-ton 'Mech toward it, then flung up the Black Rose's left arm as something flashed down at her from above.

Impact rocked the *Shrike* and clacked Malvina's teeth together hard. An enemy *Hatchetman* had sunk the depleted-uranium blade of its handheld weapon deep into the barrel of her outer autocannon.

With the *Shrike*'s three-fingered right claw, Malvina seized the hatchet haft just above where the enemy 'Mech gripped it, yanked it out of her autocannon, and flung both weapon and *Hatchetman* away together.

Tara Campbell braced as best she could as her *Hatchetman* hurtled backward. It landed on its posterior on bare ground with a thudding crash. It slid several meters before stopping.

A few flakes of snow had begun to drift lazily from the sky.

A few red flickers on her display indicated minor damage from the impact. Nothing that would affect performance. Likewise her own status: she guessed some bruises on rump and ribs.

That would change quickly if the monstrous winged BattleMech turning ponderously toward her actually brought its weapons to bear. With all her superb skill, Tara scrambled the *Hatchetman* to its feet.

She did not know what the monster was. Not even the master merchant's voluminous info-dump had contained much data on newer Jade Falcon BattleMech types. She knew—could *see*—it was an assault 'Mech, and at the high end of that weight range. More importantly, she knew from reports from prior worlds on the Falcon hit list that this was the machine of none other than Galaxy Commander Malvina Hazen. The stylized black rose insignia confirmed it.

Brutal, confused swirl though it was, the battle was clearly going the way of Tara's mixed force of Highlanders and Garryowens. The defending troops had employed an ancient trick of waiting for the assault they knew was coming from the woods in buildings just *behind* the outermost ones. The apartment blocs shattered by the last salvos of Malvina's looted JESIIs had been utterly empty.

Then Tara's troops had rushed forward to catch the Gyrfalcons in the open with all the fury of their fire. Tara had not ordered the countercharge; she presumed her soldiers were overcome with impatience to avenge their brothers and sisters who had been so systematically stamped out by the advancing Falcons, and eagerness to show that Clanners were no more mettlesome than Northwinders and Skye-folk. She felt some of that as well—which was why she had not tried to halt it.

And it seemed the chance for the killing stroke against the Gyrfalcons, to whom Tara's people had dealt the second bone-breaking blow of the day. Then the Countess spotted the tall, winged BattleMech striding through the smoke and dust and decided to stake all on a kill shot of her own.

Unfortunately, Malvina had sensed the hatchet descending and blocked it from crushing her in her cockpit. Now it was she who would put an end to Tara Campbell, if Tara did not take quick, decisive action.

Raising the hatchet, Tara charged.

Wide-eyed, Malvina Hazen watched the enemy machine attack a BattleMech more than twice its mass with its ridiculous, primitive hand weapon cocked. It was an act of mad courage she would expect from a Falcon, not a bellycrawler.

But based on ice-cold calculation: the Spheroid's sole chance of survival was getting too close for Malvina to use Black Rose's weapons—and the hatchet could disable even her far larger 'Mech with a single shrewd or lucky stroke.

The attack's sheer unexpectedness gave Malvina no scope for maneuver, skilled as she was. All she could do was grab the hatchet-haft again as that blade expanded toward her viewscreen. She cocked the Shrike's left elbow back and swung the arm toward the Hatchetman, intending to press the muzzle of her remaining autocannon to the lesser 'Mech's chest and blast it into smoking chunks with hundred-millimeter shells.

But the Hatchetman wrapped its manipulator-tipped left arm over and around the Shrike's right upper arm, hugging itself against the Shrike's right side. It was outside the arc of Malvina's long-range missiles, not that she could use them at touch range, below and to the side of where her shoulder-mounted lasers could reach. And to Malvina's sudden, tooth-grinding fury, the machine was also too close to bring her autocannon into play: the muzzles just clanked impotently against the Hatchetman's side armor.

Then her mood broke like a glass rod. She laughed. "Very well, Countess Tara Campbell," she said aloud. For she also had recognized her opponent: by the signature machine with its Highlander emblem of armored fist upholding a sword by its bare blade, and the odd swatches of blue-green plaid painted on its armor. And also by the enemy MechWarrior's un-Spheroid-like prowess and bravery.

She put her 'Mech's right arm over the other's back. *Squeezed.* "If you will not let me shoot you, I will crush you!"

The cockpit filled with blue glare.

Listening to the creak of crumpling armor plate and watching the red lights blinking in her display that warned of the *Hatchetman*'s structure beginning to fail under the awful, inexorable pressure, even as her mind clicked through a list of possible options of *what to do next*—nothing promising, here—Tara Campbell had a flash in which to wonder if she'd done the right thing by opting to tackle a BattleMech that had to be nearly a hundred tons with her forty-five-ton *Hatchetman.*

The answer still seemed *yes.* Reports indicated Malvina's hawk-headed monstrosity was unusually fast for a 'Mech its size. Unfortunately, the *Hatchetman* was slow for a 'Mech of *its* size. And while the Falcon's arsenal was nothing special for an assault 'Mech—what one might expect from a heavy, or even a really burly medium—it was more than sufficient to shred Tara and her ride in seconds if given the chance. Even though Tara was sure she'd taken out at least one of those big Ultra autocannon with her first chop. Mostly.

With an almost musical but nonetheless alarming sound, the armor housing over her left-shoulder actuator began to buckle. *Getting tight, here*, she told herself. She considered punching out, but wasn't sure the ejector would do anything more than blast her right into Malvina's BattleMech. She realized she was humming the Seventh theme, "Garryowen," tunelessly through clenched teeth. . . .

Blue light surrounded her. She raised her close-cropped head to see the Falcon 'Mech's head haloed in blue radiance.

"Is this a private dance, TC," Tara Bishop's voice said over her radio, *"or can I cut in?"*

* * *

Malvina uttered a wordless falcon-shriek of pure rage. She had been so engrossed in the not-unpleasurable task of crushing Tara Campbell to death that she had neglected to watch her three-sixty vision strip. Now an enemy *Pack Hunter* stood but meters behind her.

The Spheroid machine was two-thirds the man of the inconsiderable *Hatchetman*, a bug, to be swatted with little thought. But it was a bug with a deadly sting: a Ripper Series A1 extended-range particle projector cannon. Which it was currently blasting into the back of the *Shrike's* head.

A fast hunter-killer, the Spheroid lightweight was more built around the PPC than mounted with it. It still could not sustain continuous firing without its internal heat soaring until emergency overrides shut down its fusion plant. The MechWarrior evidently didn't care, but was gambling all on this single throw.

Where do the bellycrawlers get such warriors? Malvina wondered. She *did* care. The heat in her cockpit was rapidly becoming more than even she could tolerate.

Still clutching the *Hatchetman* in a literal death grip, she pivoted Black Rose's torso counterclockwise, dragging the forty-five-ton machine as a man might a clinging child. At the same time, she opened out with her right arm. She could shoot this puny interloper with her remaining 10-centimeter gun, and if that—or thermal buildup—did not knock it out of action she could quickly follow with lasers and LRMs.

The hideous blue glare inside the cockpit winked out as the tip of her left wing momentarily cut the particle beam.

She smiled. To kill two such redoubtable warriors, one the renowned Tara Campbell, within seconds of each other should merit several stanzas in the Jade Falcon Remembrance. Not to mention securing the conquest of Skye at a stroke. . . .

At once Tara Campbell knew what her aide and friend was doing: *Alpha Strike*. She had the PPC locked on and would fire it until shutdown. And she was in trouble even before Malvina brought her autocannon to bear. Tara saw at least two Gyrfalcon 'Mechs making for the little machine, firing as they ran.

"TB," she called, "behind you! Break off now!"

Silence answered. Tara quit holding onto the enemy Bat-tleMech's arm. Instead she put her hand on the jump-jet housing beneath its right wing and pushed. The odd *Parasaurolophus*-like crest sweeping back from her *Hatchetman's* head bent upwards in the middle. But she writhed free.

Tara Bishop's beam went out. Her *Pack Hunter* blazed like a torch on Tara Campbell's infrared display from the terrible heat that had closed down its systems.

"Tara, punch out!" The Countess ordered desperately as streams of 'Mech weapons fire converged on the inert machine.

Malvina fired her autocannon. The *Pack Hunter* was knocked backward by explosions.

Tara turned to bring her own 10-centimeter cannon to bear. Her *Hatchetman* rocked back to the recoil of an ultrafast burst.

The Black Rose's beaked cockpit exploded into black smoke and red sparks. The winged great 'Mech crashed to earth like a building collapsing.

As the *Pack Hunter* fell the top of its head blew off. Tara Bishop ejected.

Tara Campbell turned to strike the enemies who had savaged her friend. They were already back-walking, shooting this way and that at Republican mobile forces beginning to converge on them.

Tara's neurohelmet crackled with a sudden cloudburst of reports. Already being driven back, the Gyrfalcons now retreated as word of their invincible commander's fall spread like fire. They went firing, in good order, as befit Clanners. But they went.

Away over the shattered apartment roof-line, a parachute blossomed. Tara Bishop's zero-altitude ejection system had functioned as designed, and by lucky accident launched her like a mortar round in the direction of safety.

If, of course, she was still alive to *be* safe. Tara's heart twinged. So many had died today. But TB was her friend.

"*Countess!*" a voice cried on the First Kearny net. To her surprise she recognized the voice of Lieutenant Gelb, recently promoted to command of a heavy armor lance. "*More devils! They're coming out of the woods!*"

It was not approved radio discipline, but it worked. Tara

looked around to see the muzzle flashes and brilliant colored beams of many heavy weapons, clearly vehicle- and 'Mech-borne, stab out from among the trees. She gave the order to withdraw.

It tasted like the ashes cast up from beneath the feet of the advancing enemy 'Mechs.

33

New London
Skye
15 August 3134

"Excuse me."

At the softly spoken, almost diffident words the short, round-bellied man with the red muttonchops whirled. He still had a pair of black formal socks, gel-soled for comfort, clutched in a cheese-white hand. He had been on the verge of stuffing them into his valise on top of a hastily packed jumble of clothing and effects.

"Who the blazes are you?" Chief Minister Augustus Solvaig demanded. The fighting to the west was audible as a constant mutter of distant thunder, punctuated by distinct *crumps*.

"No one," said the man who had invaded the bedroom of the chief minister's surprisingly modest bungalow on New London's northwest side. "Just a fool. A knave, if you like."

Eyes bugging from his pale, pitted cheeks, Solvaig sized him up. He didn't look like much, only slightly taller than the chief minister himself, within a centimeter or so of average height for an adult Inner Sphere male. His hair was dark, not long but not particularly short, receding from a widow's peak. Yet his manner was confident beyond arrogance—beyond even the arrogance of a man who had strolled uninvited into the bedroom of the second most powerful man on Skye. And the black motorcycle leathers he wore were trimmed close to a figure that might have belonged to a professional gymnast, wide across the hips but flat of belly, carrying no slack.

"How did you get in?" Solvaig asked.

"Picked the lock." He smiled and tipped the shades with the upward-angled half-oval lenses down his nose. His eyes were dark and Asian-shaped.

"And you, Mr. Chief Minister. What might you be doing?"

He waved around at the bedroom. Drawers hung open as if ransacked. Various possessions lay jumbled on the bed.

"Deserting a ship you think might be sinking?" He chuckled and shook his head. "Your pardon, Excellency; I malign you, I know. I should say, rather, that you're taking advantage of the confusion to depart because your work here is done."

His smile widened to expose his eyeteeth. "Your real work, that is."

"Whatever you want," the minister said, "I can make it worth your while to do nothing more than stand aside and allow me to walk out of here. Very worth your while indeed."

Then his left hand snapped up from behind him holding a laser pistol. His right still held his socks. He presented the deadly energy gun for a pointblank hip shot as if he knew how to do it.

But the intruder, smiling blandly, was already sliding toward him like oil over water.

Close: too close.

Weston Heights
15 August 3134

Malvina Hazen still clung to life, if barely, when her sibkin, ignoring the shrill warnings of the radiation counter in his cooling vest, tenderly extracted her from the wreckage of her cockpit.

The enemy had already vanished back among the shat-
̶d apartment buildings. Aleks' Zetas had secured the
ground. Lead elements of Turkina Keshik had come

up as well; their Solahma and Eyrie infantry had begun probing into the built-up area.

A Turkina's Beak VTOL touched down to dust the badly injured Galaxy Commander off to the Turkina Keshik landing zone. Aleks stooped to lay his sister gently on the stretcher. The blood that wrapped her body like a net came mostly, he had ascertained, from superficial cuts by flying fragments. But blood ran from her mouth, a bad sign, and her *Shrike's* cockpit had been full of toxic gases, products of burning or heat-induced outgassing from internal components.

He knelt beside her, gazing down at her lovely and curiously peaceful face—as if this were the first true ease she had known in years, if not her life. Her pink, fever-flushed forehead already bloomed with bruise-like petechiae, produced by radiation-sundered capillaries. In themselves, he knew, they signified little: they were temporary, and could be produced by minor exposure not otherwise harmful.

He brushed a stray lock of hair, its near-white pallor sullied by oil and char, from her forehead. Then he stood and signed for the medical techs to take her aboard the helo. It lifted in a swirl of dust.

"Let us go," Aleks radioed his companions, once back in White Lily's cockpit. "Time to finish this."

New London
15 August 3134

"*—fighting moved into the western suburbs of New London,*" the impersonal news-voice said from the speakers of the burly Harley-Indian-Messerschmitt motorcycle. "*Duke Gregory Kelswa-Steiner has vowed to turn the invaders back before they reach the city proper. . . .*"

Ten blocks away from the chief minister's house the average-sized man put down a booted leather-clad leg as he swung the 1800-cc bike to a stop. The streets here were deserted. People were staying home, trusting to their Duke.

More fools they.

The man sat upright in the saddle and pushed his shades down his nose. A chill breeze blew snow in his face, and a choking stink of smoke. To the west a column of brownish-white smoke rose from a base that seemed as wide as a small city in itself. Its lower portion was lit from within by an unhealthy pallid-orange light, with flares like parti-colored lightning adding their hues at random intervals. The battle sounds had grown to a sussurating growl.

"It's no concern of yours," he said to himself. "Your job here's done."

As if in reply, a column of orange sparks shot into the air like an immense Roman candle. It was clearly closer than the smoke column. The crump and crackle of the serial blasts reached him far sooner than he wanted to hear them.

The news said the roads to the spaceport northeast of town, on the north shore of Thames Bay, were jammed up tight: it was why he had the radio on. So he told himself. If there was transport available off-world it could lift without concern: the JFs had left no ships in space near Skye to intercept them.

Nor were Falcon aerospace fighters a concern, although interlaced contrails and the occasional black smudge where one rocket jock had gotten lucky and another's luck had all run out scored the sky high to the southwest. The New London spaceport was guarded so densely by heavy weapons and air-defense batteries that not even Falcon fighters cared to test it. Clanners abhorred waste, after all.

Of course, if any bottoms were lifting offworld, passage inboard them would be at a mad premium. But getting onto or off planets despite all obstacles was a specialty of the man on the big Elsie bike, which grumbled on idle as if eager to be off again.

It was far easier than, say, impersonating an *accountant*. Even a forensic one. He suspected his superiors were delib-erately tormenting him with his latest cover.

Then again, they'd have long since liquidated him, if he weren't one of their top field operators.

"And much too professional," he said aloud, "to let per-sonal attachments get in the way.

"And then again," he said as the raps of more explosions reached his ears, louder and sharper and from close enough by that he got a little after-ring of high-frequency harmon-ics in his ears, and even thought he felt a puff of dynamic overpressure on his face, "then again, the Falcon invasion threatens the whole Inner Sphere. Let them get their toe-hold here and their whole *Touman* will follow—and how long will it take every holdout Crusader crazy and young glory hound from all the damned Clans to join the march toward the center, after that?

"And then again—" he sighed—"I've always been a romantic fool at heart."

He turned his fat front tire to the west and all the fuss, and kicked the bike to roaring life.

Weston Heights
15 August 3134

Taking control of the advance, Bec Malthus showed no mean skill as a battle commander. He threw his fresh Turkina Keshik against the Highlanders and militia, driving them briskly back through the houses and schools and shops of Weston. Aleks' troops followed in echelon left, supporting the Keshik and sending out Elemental patrols to mop up bypassed pockets of resistance.

Shocked by their charismatic leader-goddess' fall, the Gyrfalcons had cracked right across. If there was one thing Malthus knew, it was Jade Falcon character; if he sent Delta Galaxy into battle again it would snap. Its men and women would hurl themselves shrieking on the nearest foe without thought of defense, not stopping until all were slain. Having at the moment no need for suicide attacks he sent the Gyrs off to the north to guard his flank—mainly to lurk in the woods, where they could assuage their raptor egos sniping at Duke Gregory and serve the authentic function of keeping him from aiding Countess Tara Campbell.

Tara Campbell, for her part, fought as good a withdrawal, maybe, as could be fought. She would have credited her troops, the steely skill of her Highlanders and the Seventh Skye Militia's fury at the violation of their homes. The Garryowens hungered especially for revenge: their comrades had borne the brunt of the Falcon advance. Both the formerly careless and disreputable locals, now in their glory and fighting like tigers, and certain backwoodsmen from Northwind's northern continent displayed a startling facility for rapidly improvised and savagely lethal booby traps.

Still, a fighting retreat, no matter how brilliant, is nothing more than *losing slow*. Turkina Keshik was proud, fresh and fearless. The defenders gave them as much as human flesh and Clan could stand, and more. When at last the Republicans broke contact and fell back upon their seminary hill, the Keshik warriors stopped to rest and tend their wounds.

So in the end it fell to Aleks' once-despised Turkina's Beak, tired but triumphant, to mount the last advance and seize the prize: the planet Skye.

* * *

Let Bacchus' sons be not dismayed,
But join with me, each jovial blade—
Come, booze and sing and lend your aid
To help me with the chorus.

The man whose name was not, any longer, Paul Laveau was well and truly *in the wind,* riding flat out, leaning over the bars of the HIM cruiser and shouting a song into its teeth:

Instead of spa, we'll drink brown ale
And we'll pay the reckoning on the nail;
For debt no man shall go to jail
From Garryowen in glory!"

Okay, he admitted to himself. *I lied to Tara when I said I didn't know "Garryowen." It was one of only two I told her. Of course, the other was a* little *more substantial. . . .*

He was so near the fighting now that a misaimed volley of LRMs brought down the facades of two trim brick houses, one yellow, one red, in the center of a cross-street block to his left as he passed. The racket of explosions and collapse could barely be distinguished for the general din.

Ahead of him, just half a kilometer away, he could see the hill with the seminary building on top of it and the Highland command post on the near slope. Just to his right stood Tara's distinctive *Hatchetman,* with a bend in the weird tailfin assembly on its head crest. Five other BattleMechs stood or clanked around, getting set to meet the Falcon onslaught.

Much nearer to his left he saw a big Clan 'Mech striding among houses. His face split in a wide grin as he recognized an old friend among hostile strangers: "A *Phoenix Hawk IIC,* by God!" Though the Falcons had it tarted up with that ridiculous hawk head—the wings it had already—they seemed to be sticking on all their new models and upgrades these days.

He stopped the bike, kicked down the stand, dismounted and opened the big panniers beside the rear tire. He removed certain items which he tucked into zippered pockets of his leather jacket and pants. One particular item he tucked, gingerly and not without a silent unbeliever's prayer, inside the front of his waistband.

Then he remounted, retracted the kickstand, ripped the engine back to life, and sang:

We are the boys that take delight
In smashing the Limerick lamps when lighting,
And through the streets like scorchers fighting
Tearing all before us.

He rode full-throttle toward the *Phoenix Hawk*, just as if he knew what he was doing.

Or not.

"Countess," Duke Gregory's gruff voice said, *"we're sorely pressed up here. Can you send us help?"*

Tara straightened her *Hatchetman*'s legs to shoot its shoulder-mounted medium laser over the brow of the hill at a Bellona tank that had nosed forward between two houses to her right to try to get a shot at the seminary defenders. The shot gouged armor from the turret's front. The hovertank fired its own large laser back, burning another track across the abused sod a few meters down-slope from where Tara's machine lurked and sniped. It ducked back amid a blast of debris kicked up by its fans.

"Negative, your Grace," Tara said, crouching again so that she could just peer over the blades of grass on the hilltop. "I'm sorry. But we're about to get all we can handle here: looks as if they're massing for a big push. If something breaks I'll send you all I can as soon as I can, but beyond that I can't make any promises."

"Understood," the Duke said promptly and without rancor. Under the stress of combat he behaved far more reasonably than most times Tara had dealt with him before, at least up until the very last few days.

Not that it was likely to mean much for long. *"Here they come!"* she heard somebody shout as the Duke signed off, from her external audio pickups, not over the radio net.

And 'Mechs and vehicles and Elementals and infantry swarmed out of the battered houses as Galaxy Commander Aleksandr Hazen mounted his attack on the planet Skye's last line of defense.

"Give 'em hell, Highlanders!" she shouted. Republican 'Mechs and vehicles rushed forward to the crest to pour desperate fire upon the attackers.

Not Paul Laveau sang as he scaled the *Phoenix Hawk*:
We'll break windows, we'll break doors,
The watch knocked down by threes and fours,
Tonight the doctors work their cures.
And tinker up our bruises.

The light 'Mech stood at the rear of what looked like a supermarket, shooting its torso-mounted autocannon over the loading dock at a pair of Demon wheeled tanks. Its pilot, distracted, had not noticed Paul's approach. Nor was the MechWarrior likely to even dream anyone would be rash enough to climb the machine's back with a pair of gripper gloves. Paul wondered, briefly, what the Demon drivers made of the sight.

We'll beat the bailiffs out of fun,
We'll make the mayor and sheriffs run
We are the boys no man dares dun
If he regards a whole skin.

It made him smile: that always was his favorite verse. Even if he couldn't hear himself over the cannon yammer.

He had his rationalizations well in a row by then. It was not in his employers' interests for the Falcons to get a grip anywhere in the Inner Sphere, Republic or otherwise. So he was permitted to do his chaotic part to spike their nefarious schemes.

When he reached the *Hawk*'s shoulder he was slightly breathless from the exertion of swarming up the enemy machine. Weeks of sedentary detective work had told on him. It certainly wasn't trepidation: his illustrious great-grandmother, Cassie Southern, had taught him the fine points of taking on 'Mechs bare-handed as well as *pentjak*. Even if, unlike her, he was glad to keep his damned trousers on.

One of the Demons exploded. The other reversed hastily out of sight around a corner. Paul didn't mind; he had been concerned they'd blast him shooting at the *Phoenix Hawk*. He sang to himself, scarcely voicing:

Our hearts so stout have got us fame,
For soon 'tis known from whence we came—

He planted his feet on the *Phoenix Hawk*'s shoulder, hoping it wouldn't decide to run anywhere, slapping his left hand against the cockpit armor to anchor himself. He bit the non-adhesive back of the right-hand gauntlet to loosen it from his hand, shook it free, let it drop. His freed hand reached for that which he carried in his waistband.

Where'er we go, they dread the name—

Yanking his left hand free, he used it to punch the rescue bar. The cockpit popped open with a hiss of equalizing air pressure.

The MechWarrior turned with a look of utter astonishment—

Of Garryowen in glory.

Into the ruby flash of a laser pistol.

Tucking the pistol away again—because you just never knew when one of those might come in handy—Paul swung himself into the cockpit with his butt on the instrument panel. He punched the harness release and tumbled the decapitated body out into the now-cold winter air. A woman. It gave him a qualm, but no more than killing a man. He felt no guilt at taking the life of a Clan warrior, any more than he would a trachazoi pouncing with the intent of eating his brain. But he had resolved never to take killing a human being lightly.

He retrieved the neurohelmet set. Inside the cockpit was a mess. But the squeamishness had been trained out of him long ago, by harsher teachers than his great-grandmother.

At eighty tons the *IIC* mark of *Phoenix Hawk* was the classic *Hawk* on steroids. He was familiar with the basic modularized Clan control systems, and he had trained on simulators of just this model. He could drive it, except—

Like all BattleMechs, the *Phoenix Hawk* was secured by having its neurohelmet keyed solely to its assigned pilot's brainwave patterns. It would respond to those patterns and only those unless reprogrammed. Overriding that protective system was an exceedingly difficult, tedious prospect.

From a pants pocket he took a device molded of off-white plastic, just smaller than his hand with fingers pressed together. He slid into the pilot's couch and pressed the device against the inside of the neurohelmet. He pressed a contact pad on the white plastic object. A red light appeared.

'Jacking a BattleMech was highly tedious *unless* one's employer provided one an exceedingly specialized, rare and classified piece of equipment. Then it wasn't much challenge at all.

But it did take time. He forced himself to refamiliarize hands and feet with the analogue controls. It was not the return of the Demon or its friends that troubled him.

It was whether he'd get control of the purloined assault 'Mech in time to do any good. Because he could see from his vantage point that the final assault had begun in earnest. And things did *not* look good for the home team.

"Skye Six, this is Skye Prime," said the command post operator in Tara Campbell's headset. Despite being crouched down fighting for her life, the Countess felt a stab of pride: the commo tech managed to maintain professional steadiness in her voice, despite the fact that her own existence was now measured by how long it took one of Aleks Hazen's furiously attacking Zetas to cross the crest of the hill and take a shot at the fat, flimsily armored command crawler. The way things were on the hill, it would not be long. *"Message incoming for you."*

For a moment Tara's eyes were dazzled as some kind of warhead flashed nova right above her cockpit. The windscreen pitted but did not crack.

"I'm a little busy for chat, Skye Prime," she radioed back, trying to blink away maroon dirigibles of afterimage. Had it been Duke Gregory on the horn he would have come in directly on the exclusive high-command push.

"Sender identifies herself as Galaxy Commander Anastasia Kerensky, commanding the Steel Wolves," the voice said. It seemed to waver slightly.

34

Weston Heights
Skye
15 August 3134

The whole *world* seemed to waver around Countess Tara Campbell. "What?" she shouted.

"New London spaceport traffic control reports a force of unidentified DropShips approaching Skye on a trajectory that will bring them into atmosphere moving west above Thames Bay, Six."

Just when I thought things couldn't possibly *get worse,* Tara thought. "Put her on, Skye Prime."

A moment; the white noise background subtly shifted value. Then a low, silken voice: *"—Kerensky calling. Have you decided to pull your thumb out of your—"*

"This is Countess Tara Campbell," Tara broke in crisply. "So you've come to join in feasting on Skye's corpse, have you? Are you the Steel Jackals, now, to feast on Falcon leavings? You've been skulking long enou—"

"Softly, softly." The insufferable bitch actually *chuckled.* *"Is that any way to talk to your prospective savior, Countess, dear?"*

"What the hell are you talking about, Kerensky? I don't have much time—"

"No. You don't. So listen fast and decide faster. We're here for one thing: to drink Jade Falcon blood. My terms: amnesty—"

"Never!"

"Shut up and hear me, little Countess! Amnesty for me and my people while we remain in Skye system. Also what isorla *we can grab from the Falcons. And afterwards—any generosity The Republic might care to extend will be appreciated."*

The Falcons had surged halfway up the slope in a maelstrom of noise and dust and flame: a dozen BattleMechs, untold vehicles riding turf-tearing treads or blasts of driven air, endangering the unpowered Clan infantry running flat out among them, as Elementals bounded in and out of the scrum. In its midst waded Aleks Hazen's 'Mech, outrun by Zeta warriors who had lunged impatiently in front of him at his command to charge. He withheld his own fire, clearly saving himself for Tara Campbell.

Tara's own forces were being pushed back. *Slaughtered* might be the word. She felt craven for cowering still in safety, yet her sole motive was to live long enough to die with her BattleMech's hatchet buried in the head of Aleksandr Hazen's 'Mech.

Yet now, the bloodstained claw of the costar of her deepest, darkest nightmares—Paladin Crow was the other—was extended toward her holding. . . .

. . . Hope?

"What do we get in return for that generosity?"

"Salvation. Decide, Countess. Take your time: five seconds."

Clearly she must consult Duke Gregory before making any decision so momentous. "Yes," she said.

"Your word on the amnesty, Countess. Swear."

"I swear on my honor as Countess Northwind—amnesty, damn you!"

"Bid well and done, sweet enemy."

A brain-searing crack split the sky as a lone *Jagatai* aerospace fighter streaked overhead, supersonic out of the east—blasting windows out of a quarter of New London—low enough that Tara's eyes could actually make out the snarling metal wolf's head painted on its airfoil undersurfaces. All action stopped on the battlefield as heads raised to stare.

Drive thunder drowned even the din of mechanized carnage. Blazing comets passed overhead, headed west and somewhat south: DropShips, descending rapidly to land. Not even Anastasia Kerensky was reckless enough to risk her ships in a direct duel with the Falcon landing craft. She did seem intent upon landing close enough to threaten them with a quick march of her forces.

The Falcons had to respond. Tara saw battle machines bearing the Turkina Keshik insignia turn away to race back to defend their landing zone. Beckett Malthus would not care to risk his ships.

But Aleksandr Hazen's Turkina's Beak warriors turned their faces forward and grimly pressed their advance. Aleks was just the sort of action-trivid hero to consider even his means of escape fair price to pay for victory and a world— or even glory, curse him. Tara did.

"I just sold my soul," she said to herself, microphone squelched, "to the ravagers of my home world. And they'll never get here in time."

A shadow swept over her from behind, upheld by lightning, so huge Tara cringed within her cockpit, fearing irrationally it was about to crush her. The squashed, vaguely aerodynamic oblong of a *Broadsword* BattleMech-carrier DropShip, an armored ovoid, overflew the battlefield at less than five hundred meters. It flayed the Falcons with missiles, lasers and particle projectors, as its own antimissile batteries exploded Falcon salvos and its massive armor shrugged off the lashings of energy beams. A single hatch opened in its flat belly. A squat black figure fell from it.

Blue-white jets flamed from the plummeting BattleMech's sides. It slowed, but was still moving fast when it hit—right through the pitched roof of the seminary structure that had miraculously survived until now.

The *Broadsword* swept on, black smoke streaming from smashed hardpoints but not sorely hurt, to pass out of view along the trail its comrades had blazed. Other BattleMechs fell from it, into the houses behind Turkina's Beak. The near wall of the seminary building bulged, and then a *Ryoken II* BattleMech strode forth in a cascade of bricks. Flashes rippled 'round it as its pilot blasted loose the explosive bolts which had clamped the short-burn-time rocket booster packs to the machine.

"Sorry," Anastasia Kerensky radioed. *"Had to break my fall. Put it on my tab."*

The BattleMech strode straight toward Tara's *Hatchetman*. Her belly clenched: her body awaited treachery. Instead the *Ryoken II* halted a few meters away.

For a moment the two women warriors stood, confronting one another directly for the first time.

As if to mark the occasion the fighting ceased in the general area of the seminary structure. As intact Republican vehicles and BattleMechs came up to form a line on the hilltop flanking the two women, the Falcons formed a similar line facing them from below.

A hawk-head 'Mech stepped to the fore. Its whole body seemed to lean forward to thrust the autocannon and large lasers which were its arms toward its foe. A scarred and blistered insignia of a steel fist gripping a white lily was recognizable on its chest. The enemies appraised each other.

"Galaxy Commander Aleksandr Hazen," Tara said, voice booming fiercely through her *Hatchetman*'s external speakers. "You and yours have fought superbly. Now spare your Clan further waste of brave warriors. You cannot win now, even if I fall. Agree to end this now, and to depart Skye system at once, and the Falcons may withdraw safely, with all your weapons and gear. My word of honor as field commander of The Republic's armed forces on Skye."

An amplified chuckle greeted her. *"Your honor I trust as my own, Countess Tara Campbell. But what of the Wolf who stands at your side?"*

Reflexively, Tara glanced at the image of the modified *Ryoken II*. Her reflex was to say, *I will answer for her as well*—although her desire was to say, *take care of her*. Either might provoke her volatile enemy to turn on her, sparking a three-way battle that could see the Steel Wolves in possession of Skye.

Aleks saved her. *"In any event, I must decline your offer with thanks, Tara Campbell. When have you known a Clan warrior to count the odds? Let us play out this game."*

"On your head be it," Tara said. She added in a quick hiss over the radio, "He's mine."

"I'd as soon pluck one Falcon as another." The Countess could almost *hear* her archrival shrug. *"Knock yourself out. I've got your back."*

Undeterred by having just received possibly the least-reassuring reassurance in the history of human speech, Tara Campbell keyed her command channel, and cried, "In the name of Devlin Stone—*charge.*"

She obeyed her own command, throttling her *Hatchetman* into a full-speed run right at Aleks Hazen's unfamiliar 'Mech. A beat, and both battle lines followed. Nasty Kerensky had her speakers on. She was laughing.

Aleks Hazen's armament was powerful: if he simply stood his ground and fired he could take Tara's BattleMech apart with his weapons before she could reach him. Instead, he ran to meet Tara, unwilling to stand while his warriors charged. Or that was how intel analysts explained it later, backed by reams of sociocultural analysis by all the best experts.

The *Hatchetman* shook convulsively to autocannon impacts. Tara's cockpit filled with red glare as if her foe's large lasers were shining their hell light right inside, from all the telltales warning her of danger and failures. She kept the 'Mech moving forward first with consummate skill and then pure *will* as it stumbled, slowed.

But Aleks was not shy about closing with her. Her whole ferro-glass viewscreen seemed to fill with the image of that hawk head, almost lost in the glare of laser beams and muzzle flame. She cocked her huge hatchet back another few degrees and brought it down, falling into the rushing 'Mech as much as striking with it.

She saw blue lightning arc as it sank home in the cockpit's center. Felt a terrific jar of impact transmitted up the *Hatchetman*'s arm. Then another fearsome clangorous impact as the running 'Mechs collided.

Her vision blanked. She was falling—

Approaching up the slope behind the rushing Falcons like a latecomer to the dance, Paul Laveau saw what Tara, her 'Mech lying with its limbs all tangled with its erstwhile foe's, could not.

At their beloved leader's fall the Zetas went berserk. But rather than trying to generally engage the Republican battle line, they converged on their beloved commander's fallen

'Mech. Their only desire now, Paul guessed, was to recover Aleksandr's body and ward off the disgrace of having it fall into enemy hands—or, infinitely worse, Steel Wolf claws.

But vengeance did not fail to occur to them. A camouflage-painted Zeta *Shadow Hawk IIC* closed quickly upon Tara's prone 'Mech, preparing to destroy her with its powerful laser battery and advanced tactical missiles. Determination not to defile Aleksandr Hazen's corpse was likely all that was keeping the Zeta MechWarrior from pummeling her already.

What the Wolf Bitch—*There's a woman who knows how to make an entrance!*—might do or not do to save her enemy and ally was moot: she was dueling coolly with a pair of tanks and a light 'Mech of a design unfamiliar to Paul. Though his stolen *Phoenix Hawk* was an assault 'Mech, Paul did not trust its armament—a pair of 10-centimeter autocannon and a machine gun, useless here—to neutralize the *Shadow Hawk* before it killed Tara.

He jumped.

"Tara!" he called over his loudspeakers. "*Move!*"

Tara Campbell felt as if she had been beaten with bats, but her breathing was normal if hurried and no blood seemed to be coming out anywhere but her left nostril. Her vision blocks blinked once and came back on as her external audio pickups relayed a warning in a familiar—if impossible—voice.

"Paul?" she said. She was already responding. Using arm and hip actuators, she rolled her *Hatchetman* right off Aleks' fallen machine. Unfortunately, the depleted-uranium blade of her hatchet was stuck in the 'Mech's head. Nor could her 'Mech readily let go. She found herself on her back, stuck tight as a *Vulture* stopped to take aim. Worse, a big Falcon *Phoenix Hawk IIC* was jumping in its eagerness to be in on the kill. She rolled the *Hatchetman* wildly, trying to bring its torso-mounted weaponry to bear on an attacker. It was hopeless.

The *Phoenix Hawk* smashed the long slender "toes" of its feet through the top of the *Vulture*'s fuselage, peeling open the cockpit in a death-from-above attack. The *Vulture* toppled to its right.

The *Hawk,* knocked off its jump-jet thrust-columns, somersaulted over an astonished Tara in her *Hatchetman.*

"Watch that last step, Countess!" the inverted 'Mech said to her in Paul Laveau's voice. Its eighty tons landed on its winged back with a crash that lifted Tara's fallen 'Mech half a meter off the ground.

The movement worked her hatchet free of the cockpit that served as Aleks Hazen's tomb. She scrambled her machine to its feet.

Without concern for their own survival, every Turkina's Beak BattleMech, vehicle, Elemental and foot soldier in view seemed to be converging on their lost leader—and Tara. For the moment, though, the avenging fury of their fire was focused exclusively on the 'Mech that had committed such an inexplicable act of treachery.

The *Phoenix Hawk IIC* lay supine, arms outspread, immobile. Then it vanished amid a storm of dirt and sod thrown up by volleys of rockets, short range as well as long. Dazzling beams of colored light stabbed and crackled into the maelstrom.

Rippling flashes illuminated the cloud of dirt and smoke as ammo stored in the fallen BattleMech's torso lit off. It had a CASE system to vent ammo explosions out the back—but the armored hatches covering the vents were jammed, pinned closed against the soil of Skye by the 'Mech's eighty tons.

"Paul!" Tara screamed. But he was beyond her help now—and she needed help herself just now, as a Star of enemy 'Mechs, led by a *Black Hawk* bearing what looked like Ghost Bear emblems as well as Falcon ones, switched fire to her. Her *Hatchetman* rocked as an Elemental battle suit landed on her right shoulder and clung like a giant stinging insect. It began ripping open her cockpit armor with its manipulator.

A blue beam touched it from behind the *Hatchetman.* The battle armor came apart in a ball of black smoke and red flame, surrounded by a buzzing blue corona. Tara felt her short hair stand on end from her sweat-wet scalp as side current from the particle beam fluxed through her cockpit.

The squat shape of a seventy-five-ton *Ryoken II* materialized at the Countess' shoulder. A metallic wolf's-head emblem laughed on its side armor. "That should ensure you keep your end of the bargain," Anastasia Kerensky's voice said in Tara's headset. "Not that I trust your naïve honor any less than that gallant, dead nitwit did."

Shoulder by shoulder the two women, mortal enemies until mere moments before—and no doubt again, in not much more time—fought the fanatically onrushing Zetas. Step by step they gave ground. Not even Anastasia Kerensky's Wolf pride mandated she throw her life away for the dead husk of a Falcon hero.

Firing died away on the scarred and smoldering hillside as the Zetas swarmed around Aleksandr Hazen's 'Mech. The *Phoenix Hawk* lay ignored by his side, a smoking, shattered wreck. Looking at it, Tara felt a stinging in her eyes.

Elementals tore open the smashed cockpit with their hand-like manipulators. Gently, they extracted the body of their commander. They gave it into the open right palm of the *Black Hawk* with the Ghost Bear insignia, which knelt to receive it. Then they retreated among the houses of Weston Heights, where smoke and explosions indicated their comrades were skirmishing with the Steel Wolves BattleMechs hot-dropped in their rear.

Ever the cagey battle leader, Anastasia Kerensky had ordered only a handful of her troops dropped: just enough to threaten Aleks' rear and make clear even to stiff-necked Jade Falcons that the battle here was lost. But not enough to weaken her attempt to pirate a few of the valuable Falcon DropShips. She was content to leave the fighting for the moment to the Steel Wolves, and agree with Tara Campbell's command to her exhausted Highlanders and Garryowens to cease fire.

When Aleksandr Hazen's honor guard vanished, she turned her 'Mech to face Tara's and popped the hatch. The *Ryoken II* was savagely scarred by beam and blast; its right hand, which Anastasia lifted in mock of the Highlander salute, had been half melted by particle beams.

Tara likewise turned her *Hatchetman* and opened her canopy. For the first time the two long-time antagonists looked at each other in the flesh.

"And so we meet, little Countess," Anastasia Kerensky

called. "You're every bit as appealing as the trivids make you out to be, in an underfed, gamine way."

"And you're as striking as witnesses report, Anastasia Kerensky," Tara said, "although one wonders if you can really fight unaugmented."

The other scowled, then laughed. "I cede the last word to you," Anastasia said. "It's little enough."

"In the name of The Republic of the Sphere," Tara said in her most neutrally formal voice, "I thank you for your assistance. And—thank you for saving my life."

Anastasia's laughter was silver and malice. "Ahh, little Countess—but what if I missed my real target? It will long amuse me to imagine you tormenting yourself with wondering."

The cockpit of the *Ryoken II* closed and the 'Mech clanked into motion, turning away from Tara's *Hatchetman*. "Well, I'm off for a spot of bird hunting." Kerensky's words came over Tara's headset. "Remember that my word's good if yours is."

"My word is good," Tara replied. "But once you're out of the system—if our paths cross ever again, I'll kill you."

"But first you must catch me," the Wolf Bitch shot back. "And then—we'll see who kills whom."

Her BattleMech strode away, leaving Tara standing alone.

Three hours later, the Falcon DropShips lifted from their primary landing zone, trading shots with Steel Wolf 'Mechs and armor as they rose up on pillars of flame through the black bellies of the clouds, which now poured down rain as if to cleanse the burned and blood-soaked soil of Skye. At the same time, Gyrfalcon landing craft took off from their LZ near the still-smoking pit of the Hemphill mine.

The Battle for Skye was over. The great Jade Falcon *desant* had fallen just short of its last objective.

35

New London
Skye
16 August 3134

"So she's really gone?" Captain Tara Bishop sat half-upright in her hospital bed, which was folded up into a sort of recliner. Outside, the yellow morning-after sun of Skye shone on the season's first fall of snow.

Tara Campbell nodded as she placed the giant bouquet she'd brought in a vase on a shelf across from the bed. "She's really gone, along with all her little Steel Wolves. They broke orbit twelve hours after the Falcons lifted, headed for the pirate point they used to jump into the system to avoid tipping the Falcons they were here. Not to mention running afoul of the Falcon *Nightlord*."

Tara Bishop shook her head. Her cheeks were gray and sunken and her hair hung lank—the latter an artifact of anesthetic from the surgery to pin together her broken right femur. All told, she had come out surprisingly well from being blasted by a half dozen Falcons: a few broken bones, scorched a bit around the edges. She was alive, unparalyzed and still had all her parts—which made her wounds minor in MechWarrior terms.

Nonetheless, Tara could see there was something wrong. She sensed a sadness in her friend.

"What is it, TB?" she asked gently. "What's bothering you?"

The captain blinked three times rapidly and turned her face to the wall. "Nothing. Really, Countess."

"Don't even try to run that past me," Tara C said.

Tara Bishop shook her head on her pillow. "It's nothing compared to the victory we won—you won—"

"We won."

"—not to mention the losses we took. Hell, I'm embarrassed to be malingering here when there are beds going begging for people who are really hurt."

"A broken thighbone isn't exactly goldbricking, Captain. And everybody's accommodated: it took some improvisation, but New London's a big city. And the overflow crit cases we airlifted up the coast to New Glasgow last night. Now: give."

Tara Bishop sighed. "I can't make myself stop thinking I'm Dispossessed now." She spoke a MechWarrior's greatest nightmare, right behind being burned alive trapped in the cockpit. A BattleMech had always been brutally hard to come by—and after Devlin Stone's Redemption Program it had become a hundred times harder. "Like I say, I know it's not much compared to what's happened to so many people. And I always knew it was a risk, every time I strapped on my poor *Hunter*." She shrugged, unable to continue.

Tara C restrained a smile. "That's *it?* You aren't Dispossessed."

Her friend looked at her sharply. "Don't try to blow smoke up my—don't try to sweet-talk me, Countess. I've spent enough hours in my *Pack Hunter* to know she was dying when I punched out."

The Countess nodded. "I'm sad to say we couldn't salvage your BattleMech—"

"Then what—"

"—but we won, remember? There's plenty of salvage, and nobody'd deny you earned a high spot on the list. You'll have your pick of a variety of rides, courtesy of Clan Jade Falcon."

Tara Bishop stared at her. Her eyes were huge; and hardened veteran that she was, she could not speak as they filled with tears. She looked at Tara as if the Countess had given her life itself.

To a MechWarrior, she had.

Tara Bishop gripped her friend and Countess by the hand, and held it tight.

Duke Gregory Kelswa-Steiner sat in his darkened office, smiling broadly.

It was not because of the great peril from which his planet and people had been delivered, nor yet because of the smashing victory he had taken part in winning against fearful odds—granted, with help from a most unlooked-for quarter. Or rather, they were not the immediate cause of the gleeful expression illuminated on his bearded visage by the light bleeding from the holovid stage.

Rather, it was the scene there reenacted: furious mobs smashing the windows and doors and trashing the ground floor of the New London planetary headquarters of Herrmanns AG Media.

While the rest of Skye's mass media sang delirious praises of the world's defenders, especially the ever-so-photogenic young noblewoman who had led them to victory (granted, alongside the equally photogenic young woman who until recently had been her bane and Galactic Enemy Number One), Herrmanns had raised the roof with shrill accusations that Countess Campbell deliberately let the Skye volunteers of the Forlorn Hope be slaughtered to preserve the lives and BattleMechs of her precious Highlanders.

The accusation particularly annoyed the Duke, and had no doubt deeply wounded the Countess, because it was *true*. As far as it went. What that fat simpering fool Arminius was not saying was that she had announced that as her intent from her very first appeals for recruits to the *Himmelsfahrtkommando*. The plan *was* to preserve her veterans—in sufficient strength to deliver a decisive blow to the invaders.

Skye's other media organizations had turned Arminius von Herrmann's own vitriol back on him, at redoubled pressure and scalding hot. Whether inspired by their denun-

ciations or something else, the people of New London—
and New Glasgow as well, 300 kilometers north—had taken
matters into their own hands and rioted, attacking Herrmann's facilities.

Certainly, the Duke's own intelligence service had nothing to do with the riots. They had their hands full sorting
through the aftermath of the invasion. Especially the Solvaig mess. . . .

Sirens and whistles sounded from the holovid track.
Down the street a Seventh Skye Militia Demon crept, its
loudspeakers calling for order. Files of Garryowen and
Ducal Guard infantry trotted alongside it, unarmed but still
wearing their stained battle dress. The crowd gave reluctant
way. It responded more quickly when a captured *Eyrie* appeared on the scene to back up the peacekeepers, wings
spread to fill the street, barbaric Clan badges painted out
and the flags of Skye and The Republic, and the Duke's
personal coat of arms, hastily but not unskillfully daubed
onto its front armor.

The Duke was pleased at the several-layered stroke of
propaganda, and also by the way his Guard and the Garryowens, who in former times had got along as well as
Wolves and Jade Falcons, acted together in perfect unison
and apparent comradeship. Still, it was too damned bad
they had to intervene, especially before one or another mob
caught Arminius and tossed his fat ass in a blanket for a
while. But order must be preserved, even at such cost.

Duke Gregory sat back in his chair, massaged his temples
with the tips of his blunt, powerful fingers. The chair itself,
sensing his muscular tension, began a motorized massage
of his shoulders and upper back.

The riot coverage faded, replaced by a bust of Skye's
late chief minister. Apparently, the stress of readying Skye
to defend itself against horrible odds had caused the great
man to break down, the female newsreader said in a plum-
mily regretful voiceover: he had been found dead in his
apartment after the battle, an apparent suicide.

The Duke muted the sound. *Ah, Augustus*, he thought,
*at least you were considerate enough to spare the world you
betrayed the agony of a public trial.* Although it was a
damned shame, Duke Gregory felt, to be cheated of the
subsequent public execution. The Duke would have *paid*

for ringside tickets when his former chief minister—and friend—went to the wall.

But Augustus Solvaig had stolen a march on the firing party, vaporizing the upper half of his balding head with a laser pistol.

He had left behind abundant evidence, at his flat and in his palace office, that he was a mole planted in the Duke's cabinet by the Marik-Stewart Commonwealth branch of SAFE, the former FWL intel service. A dispatch not yet encrypted for sending off-world told how he had done what he could to weaken Skye's defenses against the Jade Falcons. He believed that a successful Clan invasion of The Republic through Steiner space could greatly aid both resistance against the aggression SAFE knew the Lyrans planned against Marik-Stewart domains, and future Marik-Stewart efforts to reclaim territory from The Republic itself.

Nothing he left gave a clue, however, as to why he'd blown his head off at the very moment his schemes were being consummated. Forensic pathologists judged that he had died sometime around the battle's height, when a Falcon victory seemed all but certain.

Duke Gregory lowered his hands to his lap. He wore a heavy burgundy robe over a pair of light blue silk pajamas. It was late in the day for him to be lounging about watching videos, and duty would soon enough draw him out of his warm, dark office into the cool light of day. But for now—this was what he paid his staff for, dammit.

Jasek, he thought unbidden. *The boy never liked Augustus a damn.* The lad had just been entering adolescence, head swimming with lurid tales of the glories of House Steiner, when Augustus Solvaig had appeared from the obscurity of the planetary government's bureaucracy and begun his rise to prominence—and increasing access to the innermost councils of the Governor of Skye and ruler of Prefecture IX. Jasek thought Solvaig was a rodent, and said so, in that forthright way of his.

He was in many ways a reflection of his old man, Jasek was—and the reflection was not to the father's discredit. The boy had passion, after all, and the courage of his convictions, and the wherewithal to act upon them. That counted for something, even if he had turned his back on his own father and The Republic which both had sworn to serve.

His defection had left the planet cruelly exposed. No denying it. Yet Skye had pulled through.

Much as the Duke resented Tara Campbell and her Highlanders as interlopers when they first arrived, they saved Skye. In post-battle interviews, Countess Northwind had lavished most of the credit upon The Republic Skye Militia, and the Duke himself.

Well, if I'm going to admit I was wrong, I might as well make a habit of it, Duke Gregory thought. *Within reasonable limits, of course.*

He rubbed thoughtfully at his bearded chin. Sometime after the battle, the Countess had mentioned to him in passing that she doubted House Steiner had designs upon either Prefecture IX or Skye. That seemed confirmed by Solvaig's report to his secret masters: they planned to jump the Mariks. No skin off of any portion of Duke Gregory's anatomy, withal.

The Stormhammers, the army Jasek had . . . extracted from Skye's armed forces, based themselves upon Nusakan, Terra-wards from Skye—not far from Falcon-held Zebebelgenubi, in fact. Perhaps, the Duke thought, he could get discreet word to the boy, make overtures toward reopening communications.

Falcon captives, holding themselves bondsmen and women, had explained the scheme to grab a foothold in The Republic, in hope of a follow-up by the whole Falcon *Touman. They may not have Skye,* the Duke thought, *but they have themselves a foothold, and no mistake.* The Falcons still held worlds in Prefectures VIII and IX, and even Chaffee in the Commonwealth.

The Republic had not heard the last of Clan Jade Falcon. When they heard more, it would be well to have Jasek Kelswa-Steiner standing at his father's shoulder against them.

The Duke made mental note to order that planning for certain contingencies cease at once—and that all evidence of that planning be destroyed.

For some reason his mind went back to the police, and later intelligence, reports from the scene of Augustus Solvaig's demise. It seemed that, on the bureau in his bedroom, near where the body lay, a single playing card had been discovered. No one had any idea what it meant. No decks of cards were found among the chief minister's effects. So far as the Duke knew, Solvaig didn't *own* a pack of cards. He was not given to games of chance. Except, perhaps, the ultimate one.

It was a false note, a loose end, and Duke Gregory vigorously detested both. Still, the universe was full of questions he was never going to learn the answer to, no matter how that vexed him. The card was doubtless of no significance whatever; perhaps it had been left there by some fool of a patrol policeman early on the scene.

He picked up the remote control. Surely, there was time to watch the crowds busting Arminius von Herrmann's windows once more before duty dragged him back to the weary business of helping his world recover from the invasion.

"Countess Campbell?"

In an airy hospital corridor, well lighted by tall windows along one wall, Tara Campbell, walking with her head down in thought, paused and turned to see Legate Stanford Eckard overtaking her.

"Legate," she said with a smile. "Good day to you."

"And to you, Countess. I am pleased to find you here."

She made an agreeable noise. She was still distracted: thinking about Paul. How he happened to materialize on the battlefield just in time to save her was as big and apparently unsolveable a mystery as how he happened to know how to pilot a Clan BattleMech—or how he'd got hold of one in the first place.

They had grown close, these last few weeks, very close. He was the first man the Countess had let anywhere near, emotionally since . . . since Northwind. Now he was dead, in saving her, and she mourned for him.

And for what might have been.

She shook off her grief. "How may I help you, Legate?" she asked.

He smiled. "You have helped more than words can possibly express already. I have thanked you before for saving Skye; I do so now, and intend to do yet again."

His manner grew grave. "I have received a report from

Republican intelligence. With matters as up-in-the-air as they are, I am not sure it would reach you through normal channels, although doubtless it is intended to."

He handed her a flimsy piece of paper, pale yellow. With a quizzical glance at him she held it up and read.

Her eyes skipped quickly over EYES ONLY and TOP SECRET and various routing codes and time/rate stamps, and got right to the meat: a warning that an operative of Loki, the terrorist branch of House Steiner's intelligence service, might be en route to or have arrived on Skye. His mission was unknown. Threat-assessment was low: House Steiner maintained a neutral-to-friendly stance toward The Republic, blah, blah. But alertness was in order, since Loki had been known to have its own agenda.

Although his actual identity was unknown, this operator was familiar to counterintelligence agencies throughout the Inner Sphere as the Knave of Hearts. Some Republican security experts, the report indicated, doubted his very existence, believing him to be pure Lyran Intelligence Corps disinformation, a bogeyman to frighten the Liao, the Mariks and of course the Davies. But several sightings deemed moderately reliable indicated his appearance was that of an ethnic-Asian male in his thirties, medium height and athletic build, no other distinguishing characteristics. . . .

"Countess?" The Legate's own Asian face mirrored the perplexity in his voice. "Are you quite all right?"

She raised her face to his. She blinked her eyes at sudden moisture. But her mouth smiled.

"It's nothing, Legate Eckard," she said. "Just emotional aftershocks from yesterday."

Legate Eckard nodded. "I see," he said. Plainly he didn't.

She remembered, of a sudden, forensic reports from Solvaig's residence, and the unexplained presence of a playing card: a jack of hearts.

Paul, she was thinking, *you bastard.* Yet the thought lacked heat.

You lied to me.

Still, she knew that—unlike a certain other—he had never betrayed her.

Any more than he had died yesterday on Seminary Hill when his stolen *Phoenix Hawk IIC* exploded. She felt certain of that now, irrationally perhaps. No body had been found. It had seemed neither surprising nor mysterious at the time: another stone added to the crushing weight of post-battle depression that followed victory as surely as defeat, once adrenaline subsided.

Smiling, she thanked the Legate and handed him back his scrap of paper, now crumpled from her brief fierce grip. Then, head held high, she strode off down the sunlit corridor, leaving the Legate looking curiously after her.

"There you go, Rabbi Martínez," the travel agent said, handing a chip encased in clear protective plastic to the red-bearded man in the heavy winter coat trimmed with lustrous black direbeast fur from the northern forests of Skye. "Your passage aboard the DropShip *Grimalkin* day after tomorrow, continuing to Syrma aboard the Gold Star Lines JumpShip *Illuminatus Prime*."

He smiled. "Have a safe and pleasant journey home." It had been centuries since anyone would have found anything remarkable about a rabbi being named Martínez, any more than that he should have red hair. Or eyes of distinctively Asian shape, albeit a piercing jade green in color.

"Thank you kindly, young man," the rabbi said, with an accent indicating his origin was in the northwest quadrant of Syrma's northerly continent Amygdala. "I must admit I am eager to return home. I fear I found my sojourn here far more adventurous than I anticipated."

The agent bobbed his sleek head and laughed. "It's been that way for all of us, Rabbi."

Saying a last farewell, the man turned and pushed his way into the bright, cold morning. He walked down the street in the direction of New London's most discreetly luxurious hotel.

The man who had just displayed credentials establishing his identity beyond question as Rabbi Yitzhak Martínez, of Talwin, Syrma, Prefecture VIII of The Republic of the Sphere was indeed headed home. His home just wasn't Syrma.

He should, no doubt, have checked a certain cavity behind a certain loose stone in a certain retaining wall beside Thames Bay, to see if a new assignment awaited him. But to Hell with that: he had a vacation coming. What could his superiors do, send him on a suicide mission?

They'd long since tired of trying *that*.

He intended to live as high and handsomely as possible for a month or three. Nor would the comptrollers have a gripe about that: it wasn't coming out of *their* tight fists, clutched like a drowner's upon the Archon's black budget.

He didn't know precisely where the late and thoroughly unlamented Augustus Solvaig had come by his pile of fine rubies and emeralds from Skye's mines, worth far more than their mass in gold. He did know the minister wouldn't be having any further use for them.

He paused to gaze into a display window. A trivid set inside showed a petite, pretty woman with short, platinum-blond hair being interviewed by reporters. He stood a moment, hands in his pockets, watching.

Then he touched the brim of his fedora, turned, and stepped right out with his cane tucked underneath his arm. It was a good day to be alive. He had long ago learned to appreciate each new day he got; "good" was just a bonus.

No passersby thought it strange he was whistling "Garry-owen." It was on everyone's lips, these days.

Jade Falcon Naval Reserve Battleship Emerald
    Talon
Zenith Jump Point Orbit
Skye
21 August 3134

"Welcome back to the ranks of the living, Galaxy Commander Malvina Hazen," Galaxy Commander Beckett Malthus said warmly, coming into the stateroom in his flagship, which had been converted to a convalescence chamber. "I came as soon as our medical technicians announced you had resumed consciousness."

The room was dark, lit only by discreet butter-colored lights near the floor. Malvina sat upright in the bed, with a white smock hanging loosely on her shoulders, as if she had shrunk. The eyes she turned to him were like ports open to the endless night outside the hull.

"We ride a spaceship," she said. "By that very fact I know we failed."

"Not so," Malthus said. "First, though, I regret I must inform you that your sibkin, Galaxy Commander Aleksandr Hazen, died a death worthy of Clan Jade Falcon and the Bloodname you both shared on Skye."

She closed her eyes briefly. "I know," she said. "I saw him die. In a dream."

He nodded. If he doubted, he was not one to say so. Especially not to this woman at this time.

"How can you say that we have not failed?" she demanded. "Has all life been burned from the face of Skye?"

"Oh, no. We left scarcely a mark. Yet the battle for Skye was an epic one," he said in honeyed tones, "which will long be sung in the Falcon's nests. And while our *desant* fell short of conquering Skye, it succeeded in its most significant objectives: Chaffee, Ryde, Zebebelgenubi, Alkaid Summer, Glengarry: we hold all these worlds yet, with the Kimball II system doubtless soon to fall if it has not done so already. We hold a beachhead in Republic space. Khan Jana Pryde will deem the initiative a success."

He smiled broadly. "Once she receives the report I am drafting.

"In all candor, Aleks' death was his last great service, to the Falcon and to us personally. He has given himself to be accountable for our setback upon Skye, as well as a martyr of the first magnitude. Not only was his death, facing two famed enemy MechWarriors, so immaculate as to erase all taint that might accrue to his reputation through defeat, but one of his killers was none other than the Steel Wolf Anastasia Kerensky—than whom no more perfect Jade Falcon hate-object could possibly be devised."

He started to say more—how glory, acclaim and historical immortality would be the outcome of the Falcon's Flight, not infamy at all. And how all should accrue to the ristar Malvina Hazen, the Falcon's remaining Eye, whose very survival would be deemed miraculous in Clan Jade Falcon's Remembrance. . . .

But when she looked at him with pale fire in her eyes,

the words died in his throat. He held himself lucky indeed they were all that died then.

"Do you not see how little that means to me?" she demanded. "I would see them destroyed."

"Whom?" Bec Malthus asked.

"Skye. You. *Us*. Clan Jade Falcon. I would see us exterminated and our genetic material poured into the foulest cesspool in existence. I would see the Clans destroyed. I would see the crawling maggots of the Inner Sphere destroyed. I would destroy them all. All!"

She ran her hands up over her face, her fingers back through her hair. "And most of all I would destroy myself."

He stared in horror. "It is the sickness speaking, Galaxy Commander. You cannot mean—"

"I do! I mean it all and more! I would cleanse the universe of the blight of humanity with purifying fire—the fire of suns, if I could. There is only one in all the universe I would have spared. And he died. Trying to save me!

"Is that not a delicious irony?"

She put her face in her hands and wept as if to turn herself inside out.

He stood by, bearded broad face immobile. A normal Clansman would have been shocked, disdainful at such a display of weakness by a heroine so acclaimed.

Bec Malthus sought to hide, not contempt, but exultation. He did not misread her passion for weakness, as his fool Clansfolk would. In this small woman he saw *power*— power beyond imagining, could he but channel it.

And he was just the man to do it.

When Malvina's rage and grief subsided enough to let her hear, he said, "You shall have what you desire," very softly.

She lowered her hands slowly and looked up at him. "What do you mean?"

"All," he said. "I perceive in you the certainty of infinite clarity. In the purity of your hate, I find redemption. The worlds of Man lie at your feet. You shall trample them."

She rose, her face too proud to show the pain her body betrayed by its stiffness and slowness. "Have you heard nothing of what I said? I reject Clan customs and titles. I reject all!"

"But you hold within you the key to infinite power, Malvina Hazen. Its light burns within you with a terrible beauty. It has transformed me.

"You have already bound your Gyrfalcons to your will—bound the whole Expeditionary Force, when you spoke heresy against even the Founder and none called for your downfall. You hold the ability in your hand to devastate, and destroy, and master all. Your anger and your hate give you that power. And when you have conquered you may do as you will."

"And you will serve me, to gain what I desire?"

"With all my heart. You are, I now see, the destiny of Jade Falcon—of all humanity. Humankind shall be united, once and forever, beneath the banner of the *Chingis Khan*: Emperor of All."

"I shall master them," she said in a voice that rang from the bulkheads, "but only to destroy them."

He folded hands over his breast and bowed his head. "It shall be as you command," he said.

Inside, his heart sang triumph.

About the Author

First, last, and always, Victor Milán thanks his friends and fans who have loyally supported him for so long.

As a child, Victor fixated on the idea that it was possible to write thrilling action-adventure stories that people didn't have to turn off their brains to enjoy. He's spent the last three decades doing his best to prove it by writing novels and stories to excite—not insult—intelligent readers.

Born in Tulsa, Oklahoma, Victor spent most of his first couple of years of life in Puerto Rico. As a child he moved to Santa Fe, New Mexico. Shortly thereafter his family relocated to Albuquerque, where he's lived, with a few interruptions, happily since.

In 2004, Victor will celebrate thirty years as a professional writer. Other gigs along the road have included cowboy, semipro actor, artist, bouncer, computer techie, and Albuquerque's most popular all-night progressive rock deejay. He's also trained as a machinist.

Mostly he writes: more than eighty novels published so far, from pseudonymous adventure series, such as *The Guardians*, and installments in the current *Deathlands* and *Outlanders* series (most recently *Sun Lord* [May 2004]) to the award-winning SF novel *The Cybernetic Samurai* and its sequel, *The Cybernetic Shogun*. Victor has also written historical novels, westerns, *Star Trek* and D&D novels, the cult-favorite Black Dragon trilogy of BattleTech novels, and the technothriller *Red Sands*. He's a charter member of the Wild Cards mafia.

Victor Milán has a public side as well. For more than twenty years, he has served as master of ceremonies for St. Louis science-fiction convention Archon's Masquerade, proud to play a part in making it the world-class show it is. His inventive interpretive readings of his tales have begun attracting audiences, as has his "You Can Be a Writer" lecture tour.

When he's not entertaining his growing and much-appreciated cadre of fans, Victor enjoys playing *taijiquan*,

birding, ferrets, guns, and riding his recumbent tadpole tri-
cycle through Albuquerque's scenic North Valley. And, of
course, his lifelong passion, *reading*.

"The Great Broadway Corpse Drive," the first story of
Victor Milán's darkly humorous contemporary-fantasy
cycle *Ghost Hunters,* can be read in splendidly illustrated
form on his Web site, www.victormilan.com. Currently he's
hard at play writing his high fantasy novel *The Dinosaur
Lords.*

He's a nice guy. Let him entertain you.
Thanks for reading.

Victor Milán